RUDE AWAKENINGS

By Keith M. Donaldson

Rude Awakenings
© 2009 Keith M. Donaldson. All Rights Reserved.

No part of this book may be reproduced in any form or by any means, electronic, mechanical, digital, photocopying, or recording, except for the inclusion in a review, without permission in writing from the publisher.

First edition printed in 2009 by Trafford Publishing Company.
This second edition was published in 2012 by Boutique of Quality Books Publishing.

This is a work of fiction. All of the characters, names, incidents, organizations, and dialogue in this novel are either the products of the author's imagination or are used fictitiously.

Published in the United States by BQB Publishing (Boutique of Quality Books Publishing Company)
www.bqbpublishing.com

Printed in the United States of America

ISBN 978-1-937084-60-8 (p)
ISBN 978-1-937084-61-5 (e)

Library of Congress Control Number: 2012933625

Book interior by Robin Krauss, Linden Design, www.lindendesign.biz

Previous Books by Keith M. Donaldson

From the Laura Wolfe Series
Death of an Intern

The Hill People

Dedicated to Rich DeLuca

FOREWORD

Rude Awakenings is a work of fiction, developed and written over a two-year period beginning in late 2007. Recently, I have refined the work with editorial and design enhancements, and that is when the irony really struck all of us who came to participate in the new look: how much the fiction story has become more factual than creative. Although one review does claim Rude Awakenings to be prescient and clairvoyant, I claim no supernatural talents. It just seemed to make sense, and intrigued, I let the story lead me.

The premise for this story is a country facing third-world status. That was not a fantasy in '07 and is not today. Our country has been heading down a dangerous financial road for many years, regardless of the political party in power. As our two financially myopic major political parties seemed intent on driving themselves further to the right and left extremes, for this novel, I created an independent party that actually gains a foothold in the White House, embraced by the fed-up American voter.

This book is considerably more than a battle over our national finances, however, as you will quickly learn when you turn the page. For example, on the new president's first day in office, a nuclear explosion devastates Detroit, Michigan, and Windsor, Canada—something I most assuredly do not want to have replicated in real life. This is, after all, a work of fiction.

Rude Awakenings is not without humor and engaging characters, including good guys, and bad guys, and even a rekindled romance "against all odds." The book's dynamics are two-fold: one, speaking of political possibilities and hope; and two, storytelling straight from the heart of this ol' scriptwriter and novelist. There is much to ponder within these pages. I hope this speaks to you on many levels and whets your appetite for courage, in life and in love.

— Keith

"I was no party man myself,
and the first wish of my heart was, if parties did exist,
to reconcile them."

~ George Washington ~

"Just as Lincoln got contradictory advice from the extremists of both sides
. . . so now I have to guard myself against the extremists of both sides."

~ Theodore Roosevelt ~

"I predict future happiness for Americans
if they can prevent the government from wasting the labors of the people
under the pretense of taking care of them."

~ Thomas Jefferson ~

1

The White House
Tuesday, January 22, 2013
0524 hours

The door to the president's bedroom opened, and lights from two side lamps came on as two men entered. One headed for the bed where the nation's newly elected chief executive slept; the other remained at the door.

"Mr. President," the man called out above a conversational level. "Sir?"

A slight groan came from the sleeping figure, his back to the visitor.

"Sir, I'm Agent Moore."

The groggy president rolled onto his back and rubbed his eyes, squinting, as he waited for his eyes to adjust to the lights. "Good morning," the reclining figure groggily uttered. "My alarm not go off?"

"No sir. We have a serious emergency."

"What? Oh, is this a drill for the new guy?" he asked, propping up on his elbows.

"I wish it were, sir. There's been a nuclear explosion."

2

Michael Paul Macdonald had barely been president of the United States for seventeen and a half hours and was less than four hours from climbing into bed after a night of delirious celebrations.

"When?" he asked, pulling on his sweatpants, laid out for his morning workout.

"At 0522:21, which was two minutes ago, sir."

Macdonald pulled on his sweat shirt. "Where?" he asked, beginning to tie a shoe lace.

"Detroit, sir,"

He lurched up. "In our country? I thought . . . where are we going?" he asked bending to tie the other shoe.

"Situation Room first, sir."

"One bomb?"

"So far," Moore said, as he and the president rushed to the private elevator that would take them to the basement.

"Good God," Macdonald exclaimed. "Who's been—?"

"Everybody, sir." The elevator doors opened, and they jogged, with Moore leading, through halls Macdonald had not yet seen, under the White House and the West Wing, and into the Situation Room. Army NCOs were busily hooking into NORAD's Distant Early Warning system control center in Colorado.

The system was designed and built during the Cold War as the primary air defense warning line in case of an over-the-pole invasion of North America. It covered the tundra of northern Greenland, Canada, and Alaska. There had been no reports of an intrusion into NORAD's umbrella surveillance, yet a nuclear explosion had flattened an American city.

An Army major appeared, handing the president a sheet of paper containing the latest report. "We're ready for you in the Com room sir. You'll record your message there."

The written information was skimpy, but enough. The major escorted him to a chair and small table, upon which sat a microphone. Macdonald studied the brief message prepared by his military aide, and then said, "I'm ready."

On cue, he ad-libbed a less-than-one-minute announcement about the attack, concluding with his assurance that he would be back to them shortly with more detailed information.

It was not the message he'd envisioned he would make to the American people on his first day in office. When finished, he announced, "I want to go to the Oval Office."

Agent Moore was at his shoulder. "This way, sir."

The new employees arriving at the White House had received mixed messages on their smartphones about "explosions in Detroit." Once in the White House, they quickly learned exactly what had happened, and that the nation's defense system had gone to DEFCON 1 and orders were automatically issued for all military personnel to report to their bases and prepare to defend the United States against attack. All commercial and private aircraft were being ordered out of the air, and all pending commercial flights were grounded.

Hundreds of new White House and Executive Office employees, most recovering from the exciting events of the night before, continued to straggle in. They had been celebrating the inauguration of the first-ever Centrist party president and vice president. All were suffering from some gradation of sleep deprivation.

Instead of searching for their assigned offices, they were, by position or rank, ushered to the Oval Office, Situation Room, Cabinet Room, Roosevelt Room, or some other hastily arranged space. Secret Service agents ordered all electronic communication devices be turned off or confiscated. Security wanted no calls in or out.

Questions flew through the air: "Where is President Macdonald? Who did it? What's happened? Are we being invaded?"

These rookies had believed their first day on the job would consist of finding their desks, the restrooms, and the coffee machine—not facing a national emergency.

The presence of generals and military aides entering the West Wing added to the ominous desperation pervading throughout. Unassigned people milled around, waiting. Conversations were questions that received no answers.

The Situation Room, with its wall-embedded television monitors, was beginning to fill rapidly as cabinet designees, senior White House staffers, generals, and admirals came in from a meeting with the president in the Oval Office. The low murmurs were interrupted by a uniformed guard.

"The President."

President Mike Macdonald then strode in, looking like he had just come from the gym. Six foot five, solidly built, and grim-faced, the newly elected president entered the tension-filled room.

"Good morning," said Darlene Sweetwater, the president's Chief of Staff. "This is not how we hoped to start our first day in office. All cabinet designees and senior staff please sit along this side of the table."

Once the civilian leadership was in place, President Macdonald sat so that others would follow. The few empty seats at the table's ends were quickly filled. Others stood or sat in folding chairs along the wall.

While everyone was arranging themselves, President Macdonald had a brief, whispered conversation with Darlene. When he turned to the assemblage, he spoke in a calm, firm tone, belying the bitter rage he felt.

"About a half hour ago, I broadcast a short announcement to the American people. I explained what has happened and assured them that their government was fully engaged, responding to this despicable act, which has brought death and devastation to millions in America and Canada."

That sudden reality brought forth groans.

"The investigation into this attack is already underway. We will find out who did this, and we're going to find out fast. I have been apprised that the device set off in Detroit was not flown in. NORAD reports no sightings of any unknown or unauthorized planes or missiles. We have no understanding of the type or class of the device."

He looked across the table. "General Gibbons?"

General Carla Gibbons was the first female chair of the Joint Chiefs of Staff, and she responded in a steady, strong voice, "Thank you, Mr. President. Nuclear bomb experts are being flown as close to Detroit as we can get them. We are viewing hundreds of satellite photos and security surveillance tapes from prior to the blast. Although the bomb took out all local video recordings, some feeds went to sites twenty to fifty miles out from the central city area—a plan developed soon after 9/11.

"Our satellite readings have identified the device as creating roughly a two-mile primary radius with radiation rings reaching four to eight miles out, depending on the terrain. Initial radiation readings are low. There appears to be up to a mile-wide crater formed by the explosion that transcends the Detroit River into Windsor, Canada. The bomb's position is estimated to have been four to six hundred yards into the city from where the river bank once was.

"Satellite photos do not show a poisonous mushroom cloud. I am confident our senior staff and scientists at the Pentagon will quickly come to a more definitive understanding of the type of ordnance used, especially once our team is able to reach ground zero. It is an hour from daylight there, but satellite readings indicate heavy smoke clouds blanketing a very large area."

The president suddenly stood, and others began to do the same. He waved everyone back to their seats. "No, please. I feel the need to be on my feet. Thank you, General. We all appreciate your efforts and quick reaction."

Macdonald stopped behind his SecState designee, Nadine Rankin.

"We new folks are all shell-shocked. The only combat I expected to have this morning was with the US Senate regarding my cabinet designees," he said offhandedly, lightly patting her on the shoulders. "SecState designee being one of them."

"I assure you, Mr. President, we are fully engaged and totally focused," Gibbons said. The other generals sat poised, ready to move on orders from their commander-in-chief.

"I know you are, General." He swept his long arms out indicating the entire room. "Heck, most of us don't know each other very well. As for me, I have a wry sense of humor, which gets me into trouble from time to time. It has a mind of its own and pops out at the most inopportune times." He smiled and continued to circumnavigate the large table, occasionally nodding or whispering hello to those from his campaign.

Macdonald, forty-four, was born October 3, 1968, to Edna and Paul and raised in Ft. Collins, Colorado. Extremely bright, he started kindergarten at four and, after a month in first grade, was skipped up to second grade. He was a rawboned, 170-pound six-footer at the end of his freshman year and played basketball and football.

In June 1985, at sixteen, he graduated number two in his high school class and enrolled at the University of Colorado on a partial academic scholarship. He grew in size and physical talent and became a starting linebacker his sophomore year. He was touted as a potential All-American.

He never dreamt, in his wildest imagination, that he would enter politics. A former Marine, he became a Rhodes Scholar and later earned a PhD in finance from the Wharton School of Business. He had once shown great potential for pro football. However, he never got that far, breaking his leg in two places near the end of his junior season.

His leg healed well, and he had planned to rejoin the team at spring practice. He was all about football, hoping for that elusive professional career. But fate played a more dramatic and tragic hand: his father was killed in a late-winter car accident. Although his mom taught high school and his dad had provided for them in case of his death, Macdonald felt it might not be adequate enough to see his younger sister and brother through college.

Also, he had no way of knowing how well he would heal. His future wasn't as clear as it had once seemed, even though he was on a full scholarship. His responsibility was to his family, and he needed to lessen the load on his mom. He had always wanted to be a Marine and had considered joining after college, if he didn't earn a pro contract.

He enlisted and went to Parris Island in July 1987. Macdonald was immediately singled out as a leader, both physically and mentally. Following basic, he was chosen for Force Recon training. The Marine leadership saw him as officer material, but he needed to complete his college degree requirements to go to Officer Candidate School.

He was whisked off to Penn State in January 1988 to earn a degree in political science, while also studying military history and global economics. He worked three consecutive semesters, earned over fifty credit hours, and graduated that December. He spent the Christmas holidays with his mother, sister, and brother, and right after New Years, he entered the Officer Candidate School.

He graduated in April 1989, with his mother present. Second Lieutenant Macdonald was assigned to Force Recon for command training. Shortly after his team was formed, they went through more intensive training, and late that summer they deployed to the Middle East. Macdonald was second in command.

After Desert Storm, the team's leader was reassigned and First Lieutenant Macdonald was given command. Macdonald was fast-tracked to captain. He had planned to make the Marines his career.

Now, over twenty years later, he still exuded an athletic prowess. Away from the football playing field, his size was more pronounced. He had a hearty, broad-jawed look, his rugged features appealing. But more importantly, underneath all of that, there was a brilliant and creative mind.

Eighteen hours after he had become president on the promise of fiscal reform, he was now a new president at war, a commander-in-chief facing an invisible foe.

"Mr. President," said the Secretary of Defense designee, Senator Ogden Garrett, cradling a phone, "National Geospatial satellite photos confirmed NORAD's report; no unauthorized air traffic was over Detroit or Windsor prior to detonation. Geospatial believes the blast was at ground level."

Uneasiness flooded the room. Gibbons made a phone call. Rankin said incredulously, "What happened to ground security? How could somebody just drive a bomb—?"

"Right!" President Macdonald interrupted. "That is precisely what we need to find out." He had now circumnavigated the room and stopped behind his Chief of Staff's chair. He surveyed the room. He missed not having Gus Vaughn, fellow Marine and his Homeland Security Secretary designee, with him. Vaughn had flown back to Arizona immediately after the inauguration to finish transitioning in the new director of Southwest Border Operations, his old position.

Macdonald whispered to Darlene. "Have someone reach Gus and get him hooked into here."

"Sir," Gibbons called out, holding a phone. "General Kirkpatrick reports that Air Force Two is now airborne with the vice president and has cleared Washington air space, accompanied by six fighter-jet escorts. They will take up a high-altitude position over southern Indiana."

"Thank you, General," Macdonald said, sitting.

He turned to the woman on his left, Cynthia Bolden, his personal secretary and special assistant. "Cynthia, get me the Michigan governor. General Gibbons, fill up our military bases around Detroit with Military Police and every medical unit you can spare."

He discussed logistics with Darlene until Cynthia interrupted.

"Mr. President, I have Governor Carlton."

"Put him on speaker. Governor?"

"Mr. President."

"Henry, what can you tell us and what do you need?"

"I have a report one of our National Guard planes made from thirty-eight thousand feet. The center city area looks like a scorched parking lot. We helicoptered down from Lansing, but were kept twelve miles out from downtown, even though we were upwind and wearing biohazard suits. There are reports of hundreds of fires dotting the landscape; mounds of debris are now where buildings once stood."

Macdonald shook his head. "Okay, we're augmenting your National Guard, mobilizing US troops from New England to Illinois and from Kentucky and the Carolinas north. They'll be in the air, on trains, trucks, whatever. Vice President Dudley is in the air and on the phone. You know what she can do."

"We're grateful, sir," Carlton replied. "We're conscripting every closed-in arena, church, school—whatever we can safely use. The governors of Ohio, Indiana, Pennsylvania, and Illinois have called up their Guard units in full civil-defense mode. Windsor, Canada, is reported to be leveled. The first victims coming out of the blast area are all from the outlying Detroit suburbs. The folks downtown never had a chance."

"We will get you numbers and e-mail addresses to assist you in reaching me. We'll supply enforcement units as fast as we can. General Gibbons, or her surrogate, will call you. I'm available day or night. Good luck. Our prayers are with you." The line went dead.

"I have a feeling I'm going to be saying that a lot these coming days," Macdonald said, looking at the determined faces of his people "Okay, I'd like all cabinet designees to go to their new offices and get together with senior staff. They're in a vacuum, waiting for everyone to get situated. Your presence will be reassuring. I may pull you back at a moment's notice, but get started.

"One thing. Be careful about drawing hasty conclusions based on assumptions. We want to know who did this, but we have to deal with facts before making deductions. We will try our level best to keep you up-to-date.

"Darlene, call the former secretaries of Defense, State, and Homeland and the directors . . . get everyone you can find in here."

Macdonald's eyes swept the room. "Don't get caught up in the enormity of this disaster. There will be plenty of time for that later. We're all rookies today, but we'll be hardened veterans by the end of the week.

"A.J.," he said, addressing his press secretary, A.J. Delarosa. "I'll meet the press within the hour, but not to take their questions. I want to get our message out, not theirs."

3

Following Desert Storm, Marine Captain Mike Macdonald's Force Recon team was assigned to the American Embassy in Kuwait. There were suspected secret activities in Iraq, Iran, and Afghanistan to learn about. The US ambassador to Kuwait, William R. Hendrickson, took a special interest in the young captain, whom he found exceptionally bright and receptive to learning.

Macdonald would remain based there until August 1992—a time that reshaped his life in an unexpected manner. The ambassador was in need of a chess opponent and taught Mike the game. The two spent many evenings matching wits and tactics, while the ambassador also taught the young Marine about global economics, politics, and international trade. Some of those teachings came back to Macdonald now.

"Countries have discovered our Achilles heel, Mike," Hendrickson had told him. "Economics—trade, currency, and oil—are all intertwined. After we rebuilt Germany and Japan following WWII, they began manufacturing small cars in the late 1950s, which American auto manufacturers and their unions pooh-poohed as posing no threat to them, saying Americans thirsted for big cars loaded with chrome, fins, and frills. At that time, the dollar was worth three hundred sixty Japanese yen. Today, it's more like one hundred twenty yen.

"Unfortunately, you will encounter obstinacy and arrogance all through life, Mike. Mark my words, our adversaries are constantly looking for ways to defeat the US of A—and will, if we don't take care of business at home."

4

President Macdonald entered the Oval Office from his private study, where he had just concluded a call to his mother. She was staying in the Willard Hotel for two more nights with his brother and sister. The women had been terribly shaken by the bombing, while his brother, who was an Air Force pilot, was ready to bomb someone in retaliation.

A.J. and two of his staff were awaiting the president, but Cynthia came up on the intercom before they could get started: "Mr. President, British Prime Minister Howard is on line three."

Reginald Howard had been a wannabe Member of Parliament when Mike Macdonald was at Oxford on his Rhodes Scholarship in 1992 to 1994. Howard and Macdonald first met in a pub and became fast friends along with Mike's fellow classmates, Russian twins Vasiliy and Alexandra Mednorov. That was during the time the USSR was dissolving, and Russia and eastern bloc countries were adjusting to an open society, supposedly independent from each other. Macdonald, Howard, and the twins had serious sessions dissecting democracy and capitalism. Reggie would have been at Mike's inauguration, but local "nastiness," as Reggie described it, needed his personal attention.

He asked Cynthia to round up Darlene and join the meeting, then hit the speakerphone.

"Mr. Prime Minister," Macdonald said with a smile in his voice, and then referring to Howard's adeptness at darts, asked, "How's your right wrist?"

"Mr. President, how good to hear your voice. I'm afraid my wrist has lost its flexibility, old boy, but I'll still take you on. Sorry about your trouble. An uncivilized thing at best, and on your first day. Seems you're caught in a tough scrum."

"We're in a hell of a mess."

"Any ideas? No, of course not. No time, eh?"

"Our speculations are that it was on the ground, possibly assembled where it went off. Our chair of the Joint Chiefs of Staff has stepped up to fill the void of no sitting Secretary of Defense. Fortunately, I retained some solid holdovers from my predecessor, and we're calling others who a day ago held some key intelligence and armed services slots. That why you called?"

"Ha. Never could pass up a good challenge, you know," the prime minister chortled. "I'll be over in February, as planned, unless your nasty friends pay us a visit. We've doubled up with your Intel chaps and started digging. NATO has checked in. They're chasing down their assets," Howard said in his Oxfordian accent, which included his own mixture of culture and cockney.

"You know the players better than I. Fortunately, DCIA Eubanks is on board."

"Good choice, yes. He and I have already had some 'scrambled tea.' It is midday over here, you know. We had the news of the rotten egg in your breakfast before you did, I suspect. Well, I'll let you get on with it. You know where I am."

The line went dead. Macdonald smiled ruefully at A.J. "Well, at least we're not alone."

5

"Okay, A.J., I'll talk to the press. Darlene, call General Gibbons and have her join us for the press briefing. I would like you two flanking me on the platform. I don't like the image of my being up there alone. A.J., instruct the feed camera to include all three of us."

"Consider it done." A.J. made the call, and the president continued his instructions.

"Okay. Before I start telling people when they can go to the bathroom, I better get to work. Remember, this doesn't have to be perfect the first time out. The important thing is to get out in front and show the world our game face."

A.J. excused himself and his team, and they hurried off to the briefing room.

"Okay, Professor Sweetwater, class is in session."

"Well," Darlene began, as they sat on the facing sofas in front of the Oval Room's fireplace, "this wasn't a spur of the moment thing. They've attacked our armpit—a new administration without a sitting cabinet and a legislature faced with a three-party system and no official Speaker of the House.

"To people outside our country, a change of leadership could appear the perfect time, especially since we've been lacking decisive leadership. With our economy in the tank, the attackers could have seen this as an opportunity to create massive chaos."

Macdonald looked with admiration at his Chief of Staff, who was also his former poli-sci professor. He marveled at how, once again, he was the student. Darlene Sweetwater was half Native American, with a distinctly logical mind; she found politics a combination of promises and fraud.

When he had been in her classes, the save-the-world college activists had a hard time assimilating her approach to politics. He, on the other hand, had been intrigued. Despite her tough views on American politics, she considered her country truly to be the land of the free, and that, regardless of its flaws, it was worth saving and improving. To this day, he was in awe of her frankness and sagacity.

"Mr. President," Darlene said softly, as Macdonald puzzled over the situation, much as he would do in her class years ago. "Sir?"

"I know. I have to focus. We've lost millions of people, and we surely knew a lot of them—shook their hands, shared a meal, talked about how we would really make a difference." His voice, barely audible, cracked.

"Mr. President," Cynthia said in a soft version of her commanding tones, "the first question may be who the real target was. You? An attempt to destroy your presidency before it began? Or might it extend to something more global, like the destruction of our economy—currency and oil markets?"

"I go for the 'you' premise, Cynthia," Darlene offered. "A weak president wouldn't need to be targeted. They saw you, sir, as everyone did: as being decisive and as a take-charge guy. It could be a pure act of terrorism. Maybe a foreign power that saw your presidency as a threat to some plan of world domination. Or maybe it could be some group who simply fears your presidency."

"You shouldn't speak so harshly of the United States Congress, Darlene," Cynthia quipped sarcastically.

They broke up with laughter. A witticism always seemed funnier when it came from the team's usually stern taskmaster.

"The Hill's old way of life is certainly threatened now, with three established parties. I wonder how they'll divvy up the two cloakrooms," Darlene mused, snickering.

Cynthia, composing herself, agreed. "We brought in seventeen new Centrist senators. They, plus four independent senators already there, who have promised to join our caucus, give us a solid impact."

"And," Darlene added, "our eighty-seven new Centrist representatives in the House will be joined by four of the six independents who have committed to the Centrist caucus."

"It's better than what we expected," Macdonald said, "especially upsetting two four-term senators, a Rep and a Dem. Now with no single party having a clear majority, the act of compromise may become an accepted way of governing."

He scratched his head thoughtfully. "Enough wishful thinking; let's focus on who we need in here to assist us. Rankin and Ogden have their hands full," he said of his secretaries of State and Defense designees, respectively.

"Particularly after the rude and uncooperative way their predecessors treated them during the transition," Cynthia said sharply.

Macdonald nodded. "Maybe Kap can help Rankin," he said, referring to Millard B. Kaplan, his Secretary of the Treasury designee. "He and she developed a great rapport during the campaign. There's a case of a liberal and a conservative working together."

"Yes sir. I'll make the calls," Cynthia said, standing. Darlene sat back. After the door closed behind the president's secretary, she said, "What a treasure."

"She took a quarter-of-a-million-dollar pay cut to take this job. You can't repay that."

"Anything else on your mind?" Darlene asked, knowing his mind moved at the speed of light.

"I'd like a meeting upstairs, away from prying eyes, with General Bingham, Sergeant Major Egan, and Ambassador Hendrickson. I want to know my options. Let's get them in here this afternoon."

He sat back, stroking his jaw thoughtfully. "Who's escorting my family around the Capitol?"

"Jeri, our Miss Congeniality. They will be here for dinner tonight. She has already reassured them that those plans are still in place. You do have to eat, you know."

Macdonald smiled. "Okay, and keep reminding me I don't have to do all the thinking, but don't get upset with me if I forget that."

"We know where your heart is."

Cynthia entered hurriedly. "Excuse me, sir, the Majority Leader, or whatever he's called these days, wants a meeting. As a result, a whole bunch of the rest—"

"Batchelder?"

"Yes sir."

"Okay. How about we meet with all the leaders from the Democrats and the Republicans. See if we can use the East Room. Oh, and call our entire caucus."

Cynthia departed, barking out instructions before the door closed behind her.

"It will be interesting to see who shows up," Darlene said.

"Make sure our party members know that it is extremely important they be here."

6

Macdonald wondered if his lessons in international relations and diplomacy from over twenty years ago would hold him in good stead today. After a shower and change of clothes, he stood in the anteroom to the White House Briefing Room, waiting for his cue from A.J. His first message earlier that morning, as shocking as it was, had received positive comments in messages flooding White House sites.

"Ladies and gentlemen, the President," A.J. announced.

Darlene led the way, followed by President Macdonald, then General Gibbons.

A.J. knew that most of the White House press corps had met and interacted with the president-elect, but when he stood between the women—tall by their own rights at five-eight and five-nine—he towered over them, projecting power. The visual was certainly superb on TV.

Macdonald spoke deliberately and told them of his conversation with Britain's prime minister and what the Brits had been doing from the moment they heard of the bombing. He explained that the United States was receiving overwhelming cooperation from the world's intelligence agencies and that humanitarian support was on its way to the United States and Canada.

"In the Detroit theater of operations, now referred to as the DTO, survivors are everyone's number-one priority. Thousands are now streaming out of the affected areas and relating their gut-wrenching experiences. The early arrivals at aid stations appear uninjured, but as time passes, those who lived closer to the explosion are showing signs of injuries and burns.

"At this moment, the radiation fallout appears to be minimal. Nuclear scientists, hazmat teams, scientific and human forensic specialists, and other disaster support personnel are arriving by the minute and are carefully moving into the affected areas, constantly testing the air quality as they go.

"Radiation will linger, even though our satellites show smoke and dust clouds drifting east over southern Canada and Lake Erie. People east of Detroit along Lake Erie and immediately south of it should wear facemasks and cover bare skin, or better, stay indoors. That goes for those in northern Ohio and New York. Precautions are on a new web page that A.J. will provide to you shortly."

Macdonald went on to praise the quick work of many governors and their National Guard units in rapidly establishing shelters. He thanked General Gibbons for mobilizing Army MPs and MASH units to evacuation centers in support of the Guard. All of that would be under the command of Air Force Major General Austin Kilpatrick. Navy, Marine, and Air Force police had also been deployed to assist the National Guard.

"State Police augmented by the arriving National Guard have their hands full aiding the survivors. Military attack helicopters are flying in a ring around the city, maintaining a ten-mile no-fly radius. We will soon have satellite photos on the Internet. I am not going to take questions, because I've told you everything I know.

"The Senate and the House were demonstratively altered by the election, and there is no Majority Leader or Speaker of the House. I hope to have a sitting cabinet very soon. My retention of CIA Director Jim Eubanks means we have excellent continuity in the intelligence arena. He is also acting as director of National Intelligence. He knows the players and has been in frequent contact with the international intelligence community.

"We have asked leaders from the former administration to please join us this morning and remain available to us until we get our people in place. We will ask the senators for a speedy advise-and-consent of our cabinet designees to better fulfill our sworn obligation to protect and defend the country. "

Throughout the press briefing, Macdonald's eyes mostly swept the room. He used no notes. When he wanted to apply extra emphasis, he'd focus directly on the lens of the TV feed camera, as he did now.

"I promise you, we will find and prosecute the people behind this horrific attack. I cannot keep you from speculating, but I can ask that you not act against any persons or places because *you think* you know who is behind this. We don't know, so we doubt you know either.

"The assassins' only calling card is the bomb. As I have told you, we have people risking their health, maybe even their lives, to ascertain the model and class of the nuclear device. Believe me when I say your best guess may be your worst. Thank you, and may God bless America. "

7

When Darlene closed the Oval Office door, she smiled at Macdonald and said, "I thought that went very well."

"I guess, for what it was," he said as he sat in his large, black-leather swivel chair. Leaning back, he rubbed his face with both hands.

"My point," Darlene said, standing on the nation's seal in the middle of the Oval Office, "is that your physical and verbal message should have a long, positive life, since they'll write about your demeanor in their articles and broadcasts as much as the content of your words."

He pushed forward in his chair and sat upright. "Okay, we've got the Capitol Hill gang to deal with in seven minutes. Since we're minus secretaries of Defense and Homeland Security, I've asked General Gibbons to lead off with the latest on the rescue effort. She has General Kirkpatrick in place, and he is receiving continuous updates from Governor Carlton."

"Right, sir, and A.J. will run a courier service to us in the East Room with updates. There will be a podium, and your 'cheat sheets' in fourteen-point type on top of it."

"I may need them this time, Professor. I've aged five years in the last four hours." He stood. "How did I ever let you and Bryanna talk me into doing this?" he asked, holding his arms out, palms up.

The new communications center on his desk let off a buzz, which startled both of them. Cynthia's voice: "Mr. President, you are due in the East Room in five minutes, and I am told it may take you that long to get there."

Darlene responded. "Thanks, Cynthia. Do you have some things for us?"

"I do."

"Let's go," Macdonald said. They moved into Cynthia's hub of activity. "Do

I get a half hour for lunch, after this?" he asked, winking at her, as she handed a thick folder to Darlene.

She responded in her most aloof tone. "I'll have a Reuben on rye for you when you get back."

The walk took almost all of five minutes, due to his greeting certain staff members along the way. Most had been with him throughout the campaign. He was "Mike" to all of them, and though they now addressed him as Mr. President, he hoped they would still think of him in the former.

The presidential entourage, which included General Gibbons and three other high-ranking military officers, walked past the grand staircase that Macdonald had descended, with his mother on his arm, the prior evening at the inaugural dinner. Then, he had entered the State Dining Room to the majestic strains of Hail to the Chief; today, he entered the East Room without fanfare, only a voice that intoned, "Ladies and gentlemen, the President of the United States."

Everyone rose and observed the presidential entrance, which moved to waiting chairs on the front row. Darlene and Gibbons continued to the podium, President Macdonald stood off to the side looking over the jam-packed room, solemnly acknowledging several associates. There were no media in attendance.

Large portraits framed the small platform, as well as the Stars and Stripes and the presidential flag. Darlene stepped to the podium. "Please be seated."

Macdonald always marveled at Darlene's confident and cool manner. *Her years of having to get the attention of restless teenagers has prepared her well,* he mused.

"The chair of the Joint Chiefs of Staff, General Carla Gibbons, will give you an update from the Detroit theater of operations, and then President Macdonald will speak." She moved aside for the general and stood next to the president.

The medal-bedecked general stepped up and began her progress report.

"Military cargo planes are flying into airfields as close to ground zero as possible, dropping off supplies and removing the most severely injured to hospitals out of the area. You will have updates on that growing number as we receive them. US military forces will be sending in all available MPs, SPs, and MASH units from bases around the country.

"Specially trained FBI and nuclear forensics teams are staging as close to ground zero as possible. They will go in, backed up by Special Forces units trained for this type of work.

"Our satellites have not located any survivors inside two miles. Beyond that, we are picking up stragglers and getting helicopters to them." She paused, shuffling some papers to give everyone a moment to absorb the horrifying truth.

"The National Geospatial-Intelligence Agency is concentrating its resources in a fifty-mile radius around Detroit, including well into Canada. The British government is sending troops, humanitarian aid, and supplies to the Canadians. NATO countries are amassing humanitarian aid to both our countries.

"The device went off at 5:22:21 Eastern Standard Time. We judge it to be a so-called suitcase bomb. President Macdonald will speak more about this. Most suburbanites had not begun their commute into the central city, which hopefully will lower the projected losses. Still, based on census figures, we expect up to three million dead and at least that many injured. The future cost in lives from radiation is incalculable."

The general stepped back. "Mr. President."

"Thank you, General." He moved to the side of the podium as Darlene placed a sheaf of papers, the cheat sheets, on the podium. She and the general took front row seats.

"I'd like to make a wisecrack to relieve the tension, but I won't, even without the media here to misinterpret it." That got a laugh. He had a reputation for his wit—with differing opinions, depending on whose ox was being gored. He cleared his throat.

"Many of us, if not all, have lost a friend or relative this morning. We won't know for months the total effect of this reprehensive act, but we do know we have people to rescue and we need to do it quickly.

"We are at DEFCON 1. This is not like 9/11, where we could take all of the planes out of the sky and say, 'okay, we're safe.' We will resume commercial flights at 2:00 this afternoon, and we will widen our no-fly zone around the DTO to a fifty-mile radius, which is to keep thrill-seekers from clogging up the sky and keep that airspace clear for airlifting supplies in and survivors out.

"Why now? Everybody's guess is as good as the next." He shrugged. "We don't know."

That created a murmur.

"Okay, back to business. There are two questions before this governing body. The first is how we manage the federal government with a three-party system in Congress. For the good of the nation, we need to get that set now. The congressional bickering and in-fighting we have been exposed to the past three weeks has got to stop. We must have a Speaker of the House—now—to establish some order in the House and for constitutional succession. We do have a new senator pro tempore in the Senate, but that needs to be made official by the Senate.

"We are at our most vulnerable with the changing of the guard. Before the end of this day, if not sooner, we must demonstrate we are in full control of this government and fully able to assist our citizens.

"Britain's prime minister, Reginald Howard, told me earlier this morning that their Intel, our CIA, Interpol, and NATO's intelligence teams have been hard at work from the moment after the bombing. We are not alone, but we must show our famous resilience: when we're knocked down, we bounce back stronger. And that must begin today."

Members of his Centrist party cheered and applauded, accompanied by his staff. The Republicans and Democrats were unenthusiastic, *especially*, Macdonald thought, *the ones who know I am addressing them.*

"Second, we are weak economically, and this attack has made our slim resources even thinner. To forestall any panic or rampant speculations, I earlier instructed my Treasury Secretary designee to order all exchanges and major banks not to open, on my authority, but to allow our local banks to stay open and permit up to three hundred dollars in personal withdrawals per day. Don't quibble over this; it is only a temporary stopgap. I don't want a run on the banks.

"All of you must ask your constituents to stay calm; monetarily their deposits are safe. All US markets and exchanges will be closed today and will remain closed through tomorrow, Wednesday, effectively giving us forty-eight hours to get our finances stabilized. We took a small hit in the European markets, before their exchanges stopped trading for the day."

A murmur flooded the room. He held up a hand in a "stop" gesture.

"Please. We in this room have hard decisions to make immediately, before anyone leaves this room. Nothing can be tabled or sent off to committee."

Macdonald walked behind the podium for the bottle containing his favorite lemon-flavored water and took two big swallows. He flicked through Darlene's papers, then walked to the opposite side of the podium and continued.

"My nominees for secretaries of Treasury, Defense, State, Health and Human Services, Transportation, and Homeland Security, the Attorney General, and the director of National Intelligence need to be sworn in today."

An uneasy mumbling spread through two sections of the room.

"I know this is stepping on toes and circumventing the advise-and-consent prerogatives of the Senate, but we are in extreme conditions.

"Some, like Secretary of Commerce Royce and CIA Director Eubanks, are carryovers from the previous administration. We will pass out a single sheet listing my designees."

Staff members quickly spread out across the room.

"We are at DEFCON 1 and Code Red. I have the power to declare martial law under these dire circumstances, which I would prefer not to do. Southern

Michigan, northern Illinois and Indiana, and parts of northwestern Ohio have already done so for security purposes.

"Forensic specialists, scientists from the National Nuclear Security Administration, and an FBI antiterrorism team will enter downtown Detroit as quickly as possible. You will be kept current as appropriate. Okay, now, please break into your caucuses. I will stay in the room and be available for any questions or debate. I plead with you to get this done painlessly."

8

The room exploded into a plethora of conversations. Macdonald met with the Centrist caucus members and White House senior staff to be sure there was complete unanimity on the designees. There were two questions about one designee, but nothing serious enough to derail the nomination.

"Excuse me, sir," a press aide said to the president.

"Yes, Jamal."

"Senator Batchelder asked if you could join them."

He nodded his reply and beckoned to his Chief of Staff, "Darlene."

Senator Edward Batchelder (D) from Washington State had been the previous Majority Leader. His caucus had rearranged their chairs into a three-tiered semicircle in a far corner, positioning their backs to the room. Macdonald and Darlene made their way along a wall to get into a small open area.

"Okay," he said, "my back is against the wall. What can I do for you?"

There were a few snickers, but this improvised caucus of Democratic senators and representatives got right to the point. First on their list was Secretary of Defense designee, Senator Ogden Garrett (R) from Oklahoma, who had been a vociferous supporter of the previous Republican administration's Pentagon.

Macdonald explained Garrett's stance on that war and quickly pointed out Garrett had also supported a slow withdrawal from Iraq long before it happened and an orderly reduction of our forces after the troop surge in Afghanistan. He was for the streamlining of DOD overall, cutting expenses.

"I want Ogden because he knows the intricacies of the Pentagon. He has been the ranking member or chairman of the Armed Services Committee, and he's a damn fine administrator who has extensively studied the needs of the military and where early cuts can be made. Regardless of his carrying out the previous administration's doctrine, he did not misuse his committee position. In fact, he and your current chair, whom I see is absent, have a very solid respect for one another."

The next question about Garrett was tainted with partisanship.

"Look," Macdonald complained, "I don't expect us to agree politically very often, but this is not the time for partisanship. If you don't like him because he played with the Republicans, look at it this way: he's not a Republican now, and I am not a Republican president. He's a good man with the background and experience we need."

An aide squeezed up to Darlene and whispered a message, which the president overheard.

"Guess what?" he said with a smug grin to the Democrats in front of him. "The Republicans must want to ask me about Nadine. I'll say the same thing to them: 'no partisanship.'" He knew the Dems liked Nadine Rankin, his SecState designee, and he could see they were frustrated. However, some did nod halfheartedly, apparently in consent of the process. He and Darlene moved to the Republicans. Two Centrist senators were amongst them, but Macdonald chose to ignore that. Their first question was indeed about Rankin.

"She and I spent many hours discussing world subjects which, by the way, I originally learned from a very good Republican Secretary of State and ambassador to Kuwait. Nadine is an extremely able diplomat. She will focus on healing the wounds caused by the extreme conservative and harsh liberal policies that have confounded our world image. Internationally, we have lost considerable respect from policy flip-flopping."

They mumbled and made some comments, mostly antiliberal rhetoric.

Macdonald shook his head impatiently and laughed lightly. "Look, the Dems want to dump Ogden, the same as you want me to dump Nadine. I don't want to give up either; I want to keep them. Let's compromise; we'll nominate both." He and Darlene briskly moved away. He was enjoying the political conundrum caused by the new three-party system.

The president stopped to chat informally with the generals about troop movements and the possibility of another attack. Although they were at the ready, each considered an attack to be a nonissue. The invisible enemy, though, was what had them all stymied.

"Code Red, DEFCON 1 helps us catch our breath," Macdonald said. "Maybe it's my Force Recon training, but this bomb doesn't smell like an all-out attack is imminent."

"Mr. President."

It was Democratic Senator Batchelder with Republican Senator George Meredith, the previous Majority and Minority Leaders of the Senate.

"Where's Senator Woodward, gentlemen?" Macdonald asked, referencing Centrist Senate Leader Margaret Woodward. He knew they probably had overlooked her, as she was neither Republican nor Democrat. Working within this three-party system had its challenges.

"We thought . . ." Batchelder stammered. "Well, she . . . she's a rookie . . . they're all rookies."

"Excuse me, Senators. Darlene, would you please ask Margaret to join us."

"Really, Mr. President . . . that wasn't . . . we are trying to work with you, sir," Meredith said flustered.

"And I you, Senator. But eliminating Margaret . . . well, I'll take responsibility for that . . . the Centrists had no questions for me, and I didn't think of adding her to the discussion either. So, let's just say I'm making up for my goof. Good enough?"

His candor flummoxed the two senators, who nodded unenthusiastically, as Darlene and Senator Woodward arrived.

"I explained to the Senator what was going on, sir."

The three senators politely greeted each other.

Batchelder spoke first. "Mr. President, you have us, shall we say, over a barrel."

"Not pork, I hope," Macdonald quipped.

They smiled cordially, but he suspected the two men were burning inside.

"We have our differences," Meredith added, "but we agree you are quite evenhanded with your selections, even if the Dems have those carryovers. However, we both question Frank Bender for director of National Intelligence, from different points of view, mind you."

Batchelder weighed in. "Frank's past positions from his days with National Security have been, shall we say, polarizing. We both have concerns that need to be discussed."

"So, we're okay with Treasury, HHS, State, Defense, Transportation, AG, and Homeland Security?

"We also agreed on Interior and Agriculture," Batchelder added.

"Excellent. So, except for Bender, there are no major hurdles?"

"We don't know much about the rest. I mean, they are new to Washington, for the most part," Meredith said

"They're solid middle-of-the-road," Macdonald said, feeling much better.

"Please take your cover sheet and apply your initials alongside the ones you are approving today, then trade sheets and repeat the initialing, and then each sign the bottom of both. We'll make copies."

"Sounds like you know contract law, Mr. President," Batchelder said with a smirk.

"My father was a banker."

9

At nearly thirty-eight in June 2007, multimillionaire Mike Macdonald lost his wife Sandi to acute leukemia. Married six years, they had no children—she had been unable to conceive.

They'd considered adoption, but decided instead to look into working with youth, investigating various social programs and neighborhood community organizations in New York's inner city. The couple came across an organization seeking volunteer tutors to work after school one day a week and signed up. Their involvement quickly escalated to two and then three afternoons a week.

They learned while they taught and listened to what the young people didn't have and didn't know. Mike and Sandi quickly learned that money was part of that equation and expanded on what they had donated by setting up a tax-deductible trust fund, which they started off with a one-million-dollar donation.

That caught the eye of their high-society friends, and the word spread about what Mike and Sandi Macdonald were doing. Two couples asked if they could donate money, but the Macdonald's wanted their time and talents too.

Sandi and Mike's 501[c]3 tax-deductible corporation was named CAPABLE: Children and Parents—A Better Life Experience. This eventually caught the eye of the five borough presidents, as well as the mayor and City Council.

The Macdonalds established a learning center for eighteen-month-olds through kindergarten, along with a skills learning center for the youths' parents, who were requested to enroll in special free-education programs where they could learn about child-rearing, handling a bank account, and social and health needs.

CAPABLE took no government money.

Security was needed to encourage volunteer tutors to sign up. Sandi worked with community and local church leaders to establish Neighborhood Watch programs. The mayor, in turn, added foot patrols to secure the locations where classes were held. Sandi also arranged special transportation for the volunteers.

CAPABLE grew into a viable, life-enriching experience for hundreds and hundreds of families. The nonprofit raised over eleven million dollars in its first six months.

Sandi was the president of the Board; a close friend, Nancy Armstrong, became the paid chief operating officer; and Jane Whitely, Mike and Sandi's gal Friday, became the executive director. A year later, the Board established a hundred-million-dollar goal for an endowment fund. It was a bold move, but the wealthy volunteers were too vested in CAPABLE to let it fail.

That major fundraising for the endowment began a month before Sandi's routine annual medical exam in January 2007. It revealed her acute leukemia. CAPABLE had brought considerable notoriety to Mike and Sandi Macdonald, and several articles had been written about the high-society, power couple and their volunteer work.

Sandi's fatal illness devastated Mike as well as their friends. It created a huge public outpouring of affection, not only in cards and e-mails, but in donations for CAPABLE.

Mike renamed the foundation the Sandra Rollins Macdonald Endowment for Children, which quickly became known as the Sandi Fund. Upon her death six months later, the endowment had received over a half billion dollars from all over the world.

In the fall of 2007, Mike decided to begin work on his oft put-off book, *The Theoretical Framework for the Collapse of the US Dollar.* The book would highlight the lack of financial management by the US political establishment, beginning in the early 1990s.

Mike knew economics and politics went together and called his former mentor, Ambassador William Hendrickson, who had been the guiding force behind him gaining a Rhodes scholarship. Hendrickson didn't feel qualified to mentor Mike's book writing, but did suggest he call his former political science professor at Penn State.

When Mike contacted Professor Darlene Sweetwater, he found that she was now Dean Sweetwater. To his surprise, he also learned she was familiar with his wife's passing and the establishment of the Sandi Fund, to which she had made a contribution.

He explained his idea for the book, and they met for breakfast on a Saturday morning in State College, Pennsylvania, when the Nittany Lions were in Evanston,

Illinois, playing Northwestern, making things relatively quiet in the small town that weekend.

The book took a year to write, rewrite, and edit. It came out April 2009.

Throughout the writing and editing process, he'd made time to stay involved with CAPABLE, especially with the children. He ran fundraisers for the Sandi Fund, which surpassed a billion dollars a year after her death.

Because Mike had not been close to the currency and stock markets, he had kept CAPABLE's funds in municipal bonds, CDs, or cash. This was fortuitous for the fund during the financial collapse in the fall of 2008.

He had personally invested seventy-five million dollars in the euro, realizing a sizable gain when the dollar dropped to $1.45 against the euro in late 2008. He also had twenty-eight million dollars in tax deductible US T-Notes. Back when he and Sandi had become heavily involved in their philanthropic work, he'd sold his hedge fund and deposited his profits, after taxes, into his Swiss account—all legal and later fully disclosed when he began his run for the White House.

He didn't get out as clean as he would have liked in the fall of 2008, when he lost nearly thirteen million in wealth in his equity portfolio. The CAPABLE trust fund owned over five hundred fifty million dollars in T-Notes and had about sixty million in secured bonds. The balance was in insured accounts.

10

President Macdonald finished up in the Situation Room and headed back to his private study to take a call from Vice President Bryanna Dudley. He and Dudley had become friends during his fundraising efforts and would later become political allies. Now the former governor of Indiana was cruising at forty thousand feet over the heartland of America, which included her home state.

Back in 2010, in the vacuum of disaster support created by the US Congress, she had activated DOER, the Disaster Organization for Emergency Relief. It now had over two hundred fifty thousand registered volunteers in the Midwest following the 2010 hurricanes, tornadoes, fires, and floods that had ravaged the eastern and central sections of the United States for over half a year.

When then-independent Governor Dudley had proposed DOER, Mike had been a private citizen. He heartily endorsed its concept and began arranging fundraisers to establish a nonprofit disaster contingency fund, which could provide instant financial resources for people and supplies. People aiding people, in an organized and preplanned way, had proved highly successful in late 2010.

It was then that his philanthropy became entangled with politics.

In early 2011, DOER was backed by the multibillion-dollar private trust fund Mike Macdonald had created with a personal ten-million-dollar donation in Sandi's name. Neither the president nor the Congress could get their hands on that money. The Federal Management Agency (FEMA) was billed by DOER. There was a lot of shameless posturing and wrangling by the legislators, but eventually around eighty percent of the money was replaced by federal funds.

That was when the winds of discontent began to howl, virtually and literally.

The story of how that repayment transpired was long in development, but basically involved the creation of the Centrist party. The independents had always been a disparate group of disgruntled Democrats and Republicans. Dudley, a registered independent, had felt no cohesiveness with other independents or moderate-thinking people. She'd begun to think nationally and felt "independent" didn't quite fill the bill. So, in February 2011 after a year of meetings and marketing awareness sessions, an official third party emerged, turning an adjective to a noun.

The Centrist Party of America was formed and its first chair was Governor Dudley. Their first official act was to insist that Congress face up to its responsibilities and pay the DOER bill. The increased number of independents in Congress trumpeted the Centrist's cause. The ruling Democrats quietly resolved the issue to Dudley's and Macdonald's satisfaction.

Michael Macdonald had become a prominent name on the national political scene by early 2011. Dudley welcomed the likeable and wealthy financial guru to the Centrist's cause with open arms. That was when several influential people began looking at supporting the viable but fledgling third-party Centrists.

Bryanna Lorraine Dudley was born March 29, 1966, in Terra Haute, Indiana. Her white father had a degree in electrical engineering and worked his way up to vice president of the developmental division for a major wireless company. Her mother had been born to an Asian mother and an African-American father. Bryanna was five-five, had short, jet-black hair, a deep-tanned complexion, and grey-green eyes. Her look was exotic, and her temperament was charismatic.

When she became governor, she announced that some areas of the state had woefully fallen behind, because some legislators had not gotten their piece of pork. The politically correct crowd used the term "earmarks"— it sounded more respectable. She didn't care, and the public adored her for it.

She called it a language coverup that went along with so many other depravities in government. She suggested there should be an open season on pork. She'd establish a budgeted figure for the pork-ears and then say, *"The pork is on the grill; come place your orders; there's only just so much pork to go around, but everyone will get chance."*

Dudley called for a state summit of engineering companies to develop a coordinated plan to replace what she had been doing piecemeal. In less than three years, her early set-asides, which she had begun as a lieutenant governor, had blossomed to over four hundred fifty million dollars.

She wanted to give people every opportunity possible to survive a disaster. Two years before the Centrists' first national election, Indiana was the envy of the country, and she received requests from neighboring states to meet with them.

She'd asked her task force personnel to handle that job—she had a state and a party to run.

11

Macdonald was warmed by his thoughts of Bryanna and was happy he would have these few minutes of quiet conversation with her in the sanctity of his private study.

His intercom buzzed. "Mr. President, the vice president is on line four."

"Thank you, Cynthia." He picked up the designated receiver. "Madam Vice President."

"Mr. President."

"You getting used to your new office?" he asked, referring to her being aboard Air Force Two.

She laughed. "Not exactly what I had in mind for my first day."

"I hear you. You must be extremely pleased with how quickly DOER has become the nucleus of the recovery."

"I am."

"I'm told those thousands of volunteers you registered over the past two years are responding to text messages, tweets, and e-mails. I understand they are showing up at their prearranged posts in droves."

"My former lieutenant governor may be a Republican, but he's thinking like a Centrist. I heard he's mobilized thousands more."

"You taught him well. How do you like the airborne luxury of AF2?"

"My only answer is awesome. The communication systems are phenomenal. We have a constant flow of satellite pictures. How are Darlene and Cynthia taking to their first day as government employees?"

"By 0730 this morning, they were veterans and struggling to keep me on point."

"You'll do fine, sir. You were made for this job."

"Okay, but don't ever assume I can do it alone. I need all the help I can get."

"Just like I did when you came along."

They laughed warmly. "We put together a good team. They're doing great in this berserk world we woke up to."

"Just keep being the Mike Macdonald we all know, Mr. President. It's easy to lose your perspective in all this turbulence."

"I hear you Madam Vice President. Gotta go. I've got a military briefing coming up."

"Thank you, Mr. President."

As soon as he hung up, Cynthia buzzed him. "Commerce Secretary Royce is holding for you, sir."

"Right, I put a call into her. Where's Darlene?"

"She and Mr. Kaplan are talking with our party's senators and representatives, making sure there is no let-down in getting our Cabinet designees seated. I'll let you know when they are ready for your next meeting."

"Okay. I'm moving over to the Oval Office. I'll take Royce's call there."

He quickly made the transition and picked up the phone. "Frances."

"Mr. President," she said flatly.

"Sorry to keep you holding. This is a crazy day. I'm concerned about the free flow of commerce. Trucking is disrupted. What's our plan?"

"Per your earlier request, I talked with the former Secretary of Transportation and your designee, J.T. Russell. Both are on their way to my office. General Gibbons is sending Lieutenant General Dominic to aid us regarding the National Guard's involvement and what you've ordered the US military to do. We are also linking the close-in states into our conference room."

"Okay. How about adding Vice President Dudley up in Air Force Two?"

"Yes sir. How—?"

"I'll have Cynthia pick up when we finish. She has all the details about how that works."

"Thank you, sir." The Commerce Secretary then gave him a rundown of where things stood and added, "I am amazed at the coordinated effort. All of our regional offices are receiving FEMA e-mails, as well as those from the governors. Right now, no bad weather has been forecasted for the next twenty-four hours."

"We're owed a couple of good breaks. I'll let you go. Good luck."

A second after the light went off, Cynthia entered the room. "It's time, sir."

"Damn. I forgot to put Secretary Royce on hold for you. Royce has a link-up with midwest governors on transportation and flow of commerce issues. I want the vice president hooked into that."

"I'll call Secretary Royce right back."

Macdonald's phone rang, and Cynthia picked it up. "This is Cynthia . . . yes.

Sir, it's Darlene. She and Secretary Kaplan have finished with the staff meeting and are ready when you are to meet in the residence."

"I'm on my way."

Cynthia relayed the message and hung up. "Sir, you are still having supper with your mother, brother, and sister. The Robbins family asked to be excused due to the present situation."

Mike was sorry his in-laws wouldn't be there, but it would make things easier with it being just his family.

12

Darlene and "Kap" met the president in the hall outside the Cabinet Room, and they walked together.

"I thought your meeting with Congress went amazingly well, sir," Darlene commented.

"You wowed them, Mike," said the portly Kaplan, giving the president a pat on the back.

"Mr. Secretary," Darlene said pointedly, "we have all agreed that regardless of prior relations with the president, we will address our former student, colleague, etc., by the title he has earned, even in private."

Kaplan said, "I know, Darlene, but—"

"It's important, so that we don't slip up in public. I've known him since he was nineteen, but our roles have reversed."

Kap looked pleadingly at his former student, who only shrugged in response.

"Please, sir. We who worked long and hard with you to win the presidency want to address you formally. It is as much our reward as it is yours," said Darlene

They reached the waiting elevator and its military attendant, who snapped to attention.

After the door closed, Macdonald said, "I'm okay with that, but remember . . . we were friends first, and we will be forever."

"Agreed," Darlene said relieved.

"Same goes here, *Mr. President,*" Kaplan said, emphasizing the title good-naturedly.

That pleased Darlene. The elevator door opened, and they walked out into the Great Hall.

Macdonald and Kaplan had become kindred spirits after Mike's time at Wharton, e-mailing often. When Macdonald geared up for his presidential campaign, he asked Darlene to visit Kaplan to sound him out about being their key financial advisor/strategist.

Back when Macdonald had chosen to enhance his education, he left behind a lucrative currency trading business. When he went to Philadelphia, he kept his posh two-bedroom condo in New York's Soho District for his sister Jeanne Marie to continue using as she advanced her career as a concert pianist.

Macdonald hired a financial advisor to watch over his holdings, pay his taxes and the condo bills, and see to Jeanne Marie's financial needs. In those early years, he had made money far too easily and spent it the same way. He was spoiled by the fact that he could always rectify a short indebtedness by making trades.

Overspend and make more was a mantra he had to understand better, if he was to build a successful financial company. That was why he'd chosen the Wharton School of Business at the University of Pennsylvania in Philadelphia. He wanted to gain that knowledge and add a PhD to his name. The school had a strong emphasis on quantitative analysis. His goal was to see if he could develop a series of mathematical models that he could utilize in his own currency trading.

He would soon learn that his personal spending habits compared too favorably to those of the federal government. If the Feds overspent, they printed more money. In Macdonald's case, if he overspent, he would make more commissions. It seemed a simple formula: big spenders needed to make more. However, that was not possible for the majority of American workers.

"I don't know how many days or hours we have to instill a nationwide confidence in our finances," Macdonald said, bringing his mind back to the present. "We've lost the luxury of rolling out our plan in stages, as we had originally strategized."

"Disasters have a way of paving their own roads to recovery," Kaplan said, as they stood just outside the elevator. "We are in a maelstrom of monumental consequences—a bomb that none of us could have predicted, nor could have prevented."

Darlene agreed. "Yet, no matter the depravity, it has put us in a unique position politically. We now have a larger platform from which to launch our financial recovery program and maybe in a more effective and lasting manner. I believe America will listen to and follow you, sir."

Macdonald smiled, standing between his two trusted advisors, an arm around their shoulders, as they formed a semi-huddle. "We're where we want to be, because we believed we were the ones who could turn this country around. You're right; this is the time to ask a few hundred million people to help out."

Kaplan grunted, "But, ah, which is going to come first, the war or the economy?"

Mike squeezed Darlene's shoulder and winked. On his nod, they responded together: "The economy!" That elicited a laugh from all three.

"Although," the commander-in-chief added, "we've got to talk about a little retribution before we get back to the finances. Two of these men we are meeting with are experts on search-and-destroy. I know their language—I have taken their orders. I need their style of leadership. Now I am in a position to provide them the resources they will need. Come on, let's get at it."

The three walked into the president's living room, where four men rose to meet them, as Darlene went to a phone. Macdonald had added the FBI director to the mix. The president and Secretary of Treasury shook their hands and each had their own personal greeting for the other.

"Let's get relaxed. We have more refreshments coming up," Macdonald said. He then removed his jacket and loosened his tie. He was the only one who would.

Darlene rejoined the group and greeted the four: Maj. Gen. Barry Bingham; Sgt. Maj. Jack "Kick" Egan; Ambassador Hendrickson, a tireless worker in his presidential campaign; and FBI Director Andrew Mark Thornton.

"Mr. Director," President Macdonald said. "I'm sorry Attorney General Jamison can't join us; however, I'm pleased you could."

"I'm honored to be included, sir. Whatever I can do—"

"Okay. I want your frank, I-don't-care-whose-toes-are-stepped-on opinion."

The director lightly cleared his throat. "Yes sir."

Darlene cleared her throat, just as she must have done so many times when standing before a class of students at Penn State. She was always the one who brought focus to the campaign meetings, which could be extremely frantic.

"Excuse me, gentlemen. Yesterday, our number-one priority had been to turn around catastrophic financial foibles from the past decade. The circumstance of this morning's bombing has not dampened that desire, just delayed us. We are going to move ahead with our economic plans, but first we must deal with a monstrous act.

"General Bingham, we will need to know from you how we can create a Force Recon type of operation, which we will then take to General Gibbons and the Joint Chiefs for their approval."

"Ma'am, Mr. President. I've been out of Special Ops for eight, nine years. I've—"

"Sir," Macdonald interrupted.

Bingham blanched at being addressed sir by the president.

"You are one of the smartest tacticians and strategists I have ever met. Also, I was gung ho and you made a listener out of me. Our roles have changed since then, but my unwavering respect for you and Sergeant Major Egan has not. I realize I am presuming a lot, asking you to be here, but my comfort will only increase when I know that you two and Ambassador Hendrickson will be leading the way for me."

"Gentlemen," Darlene said softly. "There could be another bomb out there."

"Sir," said Egan. "Are we at liberty to seek out some other tunnel rats?"

"Yeah, something like that, Kick. We had some super good contacts in the areas where the bomb may have come from and where we spent some time eating sand," the president said. "Whaddaya think?"

"I think, sir, that some old friends need to be revisited," the retired sergeant major said.

"Sir," General Bingham said. "May I have a word with you, privately? My apologies to everyone, but this is a very sensitive matter, and the president has not been briefed."

Macdonald studied the general and saw he was sternly serious. "Mr. Director, please update everyone on the DTO investigation. Chief Sweetwater can catch me up later. General, we'll go into my office."

13

"You seem concerned or maybe perturbed," Macdonald said worriedly, as the two men sat in facing armed chairs. Macdonald had only known this career Marine officer during his three years in the Middle East, and then not very well. They had reconnected during the campaign in 2012, when he spoke to military groups. The general couldn't actively campaign, but instead showed his support in other ways.

"May we go off the record? I need to be frank, direct with you, sir."

The general's request surprised the president, who smiled. "I'm having a tough time adjusting to our new roles, General. I left the Marines to go to Oxford and never dreamt that we would ever again have a professional relationship. Sure, let's go off the record. If something's eating at you, I want to hear about it."

"Thank you, sir. When you were running Force Recon missions, you knew your job as well as anyone I'd ever had under my command. You also had the respect of Ambassador Hendrickson and Sergeant Major Egan. I am sure you know a nod from Kick was the toughest plaudit to come by."

Mike smiled, but sat quietly. This officer was taking a big chance speaking openly to his president; such an act was probably rare if not unheard of.

"You mentioned earlier, sir, about wanting to form up a group with me and Sergeant Major Egan taking the lead. That's not the way things work at DOD. Since I have been teaching men who have gone on to become members of Black Ops, I can tell you that we have the finest and most dedicated group of people you could find any place in the world. They are prepared to go any place and do anything they are so ordered to do.

"As I am sure you will remember from Force Recon, these are fiercely loyal and extremely skilled fighting contingents, a tight fraternity that does not accept outsiders, not even the most well-meaning. You had a unit like that.

"You are no longer a Force Recon captain, you are the commander-in-chief—the person they serve—whose orders they take and fulfill to the best of their ability. When you say, 'go,' their involvement with you ends; they are on their own to carry out your orders. The same goes for the generals of the JCS and on down their chain of command.

"This goes for me too, sir. I was in that chain when I delivered you your orders. However, I am not in that chain now, and I am sure I would be resented if I intruded into it, no matter how much respect they held for me, even if I were doing so on the orders of the president."

Bingham shifted in his chair and cleared his throat.

"I thank you, Mr. President, for the respect you hold for me. I doubt I could properly express the pride I feel. Under our current circumstances, there may be ways I can be of help to you, and I would be honored to serve, but this is not one. I cheer your passion and support your urgency, your desire to find the enemy and destroy them. From where I sit, which admittedly is on the sidelines, I see a president who people will follow and a military that will stand a little taller because you are their commander-in-chief."

The general relaxed ever so slightly in his chair. Macdonald was moved, especially hearing this from a man he deeply respected. It was also a little unnerving.

"General Bingham, I am in awe of the honor you have bestowed upon me. Thank you for your wisdom and saving me from disrespecting the very people I hold in high regard."

Bingham cleared his throat. "Thank you, sir. I would like to add one more thing."

"Certainly."

"You don't need me to be a go-between with the chair of the Joint Chiefs. She is a solid soldier and an outstanding leader. She knows the capabilities of the people under her command and will advise you well and make happen what you want to have happen."

"Does this mean," Macdonald interjected, "that I can't ask for your advice?"

"It is not my place to tell you that, sir. But I would suggest, officially, I am not in that conduit; it is you and the Chief, no in-betweeners. However, acting unofficially, I would be honored to answer your questions, with no authority attached to that dialogue."

Macdonald smiled. "If today is any example, I'm going to need a guardian angel."

"I am sure you will do extremely well, Mr. President."

As he was about to rise, Macdonald paused. "What about Sergeant Major Egan, General? He's raring to get into this thing."

General Bingham smiled and shook his head. "The same would go for him in the Black Ops, sir; however, you may want to discuss that with DCIA Eubanks. He and Egan must have crossed paths in the 1990s or maybe even have been on some missions together."

"Thank you, General, you have given me excellent *unofficial* advice."

They chuckled as they stood and shook hands heartily.

14

When Macdonald and Bingham returned to the group, Macdonald pulled Darlene aside to privately brief her on his discussion with the general. Bingham would explain the details to Hendrickson and Egan, and they departed the room.

Macdonald sat with Kap and FBI Director Thornton, who began explaining a very specific plan regarding the DTO and antiterrorism.

Upon the director's conclusion, Macdonald nodded agreeably. "I like your idea of a special task force within your antiterrorism group to chase down the ruthless, bloodthirsty pillagers who prey on victims of disasters. Attorney General Jamison and I are in full support of your thinking. We need to vigorously prosecute them. The haters are as despicable as those who bombed us and should be treated accordingly."

"Thank you, sir. That was a difficult concept to get across in the previous Republican administration when we were ferreting out the corporate and financial scum."

"I'm with you on this—and I've read your positions," the president said cordially. "In fact, Judge Jamison, Chief Sweetwater, and I spent considerable time studying how you ran the Bureau, and we read your recent speeches on immigration and national security. We are very comfortable with your positions. I would like you to become joined at the hip with the Attorney General; he will also need a little time to get up to speed."

"I understand, Mr. President."

"I hold him in the highest regard, both as a person and a jurist. We want a clean operation. I know previous administrations have gotten into trouble by not being cognitive of the law. I can't emphasize enough that everything we do has to be legal. I don't want any blips."

Darlene returned to the room.

Macdonald continued. "If you see that we are going down the wrong road, I want you to tell us that immediately. I can be a little overexuberant at times. The Judge is a patient man, a good balance for me, but there may be times I slip up."

"I appreciate your candor, sir. I hope you won't mind mine. I have studied up on you, but still don't know you well, except that you are held in high regard by people I respect. Having said that, I have assigned my senior assistant director to communicate directly with Chief Sweetwater, concentrating solely on the forensics investigation in the DTO. Have you talked with DCIA Eubanks on the DTO? I ask because he and I have worked very closely together in the last couple of years. You held him over, so—"

"Yes, but I didn't know of your close relationship," the president said. "Darlene, let's widen our DTO oversight group to include Director Eubanks.

"I look forward to meeting your assistant director," Darlene said.

They shook hands all around and Darlene escorted the director to the elevator, where a protective service agent took over. She returned to the president and Kap.

"Mike . . . eh, Mr. President," Kap said sheepishly.

"Hold up a minute, Kap. Darlene, I think it's time I get back downstairs. Kap and I will be in my study. Let Cynthia know where I am, but have her hold messages for ten minutes or so."

"Remember, you have a 5:30 p.m. session in the Situation Room."

He nodded. "Okay. Kap?"

The three took the elevator to the lower level. The temperature was mild, so they took the outside route along the colonnade, past the Rose Garden and through the empty Oval Office to the study. Darlene split off from them, going into Cynthia's office.

Once situated and the study door closed, the two men sat facing each other in stout, leather chairs on the visitor's side of his modest desk. "The debt and the collapsing dollar can capsize us, Kap, before we have a chance to get up a head of steam."

"It could. We need to establish strict curbs, in the event folks get overly dicey. The currency market will go berserk no matter what, so let it. We need to ratchet up our economic program, fast. We could also use a backfire."

Macdonald let out an involuntary burst of laughter. "Ha. Exactly Kap, and I've got one that should be shocking enough to maybe freeze the shorting of the dollar."

Kaplan looked stunned.

"It'll only be a holding action, at best," Macdonald said to his SecTres, "but I think it will get people's minds on something else."

"All right, don't keep me in suspense."

"I'm going to announce a faded-in, ten-percent reduction in the purchase of overseas crude oil over the next ninety days. We'll eliminate imports immediately from Venezuela.

"Also, I talked with the Iraqi president in late November. I had planned to reduce our oil import from Iraq by fifty percent while receiving the remaining half at no cost as war reparations. I thought we'd sell the free crude at auction and assign those revenues to alternative fuel research and production. I'm going to still reduce the import, but we'll have to keep any money we make for other things right now.

"We were going to phase this in beginning March, over a six-month span, but I had the ambassador inform Iraq's ambassador here in Washington a couple of hours ago that we would have to begin this new plan February 1 and complete the transition in three months."

Kaplan was still stunned. "How . . . how can you do that?"

"Before the bomb, I'd received a commitment from our largest supplier, Canada, for a twenty-percent increase in our import of gasoline. Their new refinery went online three months ago. Our US refineries aren't capable of producing that much of an increase in crude refining right now. Our purchases will help the Canadians financially too."

"When did you do all this?" Kaplan asked, amazed.

"I had a quiet meeting with the Canadian prime minister in Buffalo three days before Christmas."

"You're a crafty so-and-so," Kaplan said, shaking his head.

"We also started talking to the top petroleum execs the day after I was elected. Before the bombing, I'd called for an oil summit for January 23, tomorrow, at the Reagan Conference Center a couple of blocks from here. We've told them to come as planned, but we've also requested a joint session of Congress for 2100 hours tomorrow night.

"We're inviting them to be my guests in the gallery. J.T. Russell was in on some talks with me when I was selling my plan to them. He'll be my point man. He'll have Secretaries Royce from Commerce, Gilbert from Agriculture, and Hawkman from Interior with our Senate Leader Margaret Woodward assisting him.

"J.T. will meet them tonight in the East Room. I'll put in a quick appearance. Being from Texas, J.T. knows a lot of the oil people. All of the attendees will be our guests in the House gallery, along with the top execs from alternative energy corporations and energy nonprofits. Secretary of Interior Hawkman is arranging all of that—probably four hundred people in all."

Kap nodded.

The president went on. "We have to increase America's crude oil production before we can get rid of our Middle Eastern oil imports. We will not, however, run from our friends who need our business.

"In those meetings with oil execs back in November, two CEOs tried giving me a runaround, but after I laid some financial facts out on the table . . . well, let's just say they were shocked I knew what I knew."

"I know you well and *I'm* shocked," Kaplan said admiringly.

"Somehow, an order has existed for maybe five decades that we are to rely on foreign oil and hold back on the development of our own resources. The past administration continued that policy by deftly hiding behind the environmentalists when pushed for additional drilling sites. It was a perfect ploy.

"I want to change that policy—get to the bottom of this moratorium and find out where those nebulous orders come from and who's enforcing them."

"You're saying we were purposely not producing American oil?" asked Kaplan.

"Exactly. What I don't know is the origination of this conspiracy. I was told this by a former oil man, but need to corroborate it. I'm telling you because it ties in with our attempt to reduce the debt. Our current problem will put this project on the back burner, but I want you to chew on it.

"We have to overcome an archaic way of doing business. You would have thought the financial crisis in late '08 and '09 would have . . ." He exhaled a sigh of disgust. "A debtor country sets a bad example for its people."

"You get no argument from me on that," Kaplan said. "In the last fiscal year, credit card debt, which had dropped over twenty-five percent by the end of '09, is now within twelve percent of the deadly 2008 figures. I blame most of that on the residents of that Castle on the Hill at the end of Pennsylvania Avenue, where the wicked witches of the east ply their evil brews, boiling constituents' ears in their pork stew."

"Thanks, professor."

"Yes. I also speak in tongues."

They laughed as good friends would over an old bromide.

Macdonald smirked. "I used to laugh at those wet-behind-the-ears kids struggling to translate your metaphors. Our problem, now, is that a lot of them are working up on the Hill and they still don't have a clue."

"Yeah, but you've got the hammer. An undesirable hammer, for sure. Nevertheless, it's there."

"I think the Dems and the GOP invented political gridlock just so they could avoid doing the people's business."

Kaplan snorted. "And we can't let them use that political tool. We have to sledge it to death."

Macdonald leaned back in his chair. He admired how Kap felt, always had. He was a free thinker, with solid technicals to back up his pronouncements. *Kap will be a good alter-ego for me when he goes up on Capitol Hill to push the administration's budget,* he thought.

"Kap, we're in a tough struggle to hold the minds of the American people that we won over in the election, but in a different way. We got a lot of those voters because of their dissatisfaction with the two major political parties in power. We want to hold onto them by performing as we promised and winning them over by our actions. We want them to think positively about us and forget those Dems or Reps, whoever they had previously voted for."

"Mike, it's what you believe in—and your consistency in those beliefs—that counts. I'm from academia, about to face the biggest challenge of my life, and scared shitless. If I didn't believe in you, I wouldn't be here. I could write my books and throw darts at the 'stupid' politicians. Now I'm on the hot seat."

"Kap, you'll do great. You only have to change the attitudes of two hundred twenty million people and educate a hundred million young ones coming up. That should be a snap for a man of your largess."

"Are you attacking my feckless approach to diet?"

"No, that's lard-ness, a different subject altogether. A physical checkup can't hurt."

"You ex-Marines are too gung ho."

Mike laughed. "Former Marine, please," he corrected, as he stretched out his legs. "Okay, let's gear up the financial presentation. You want to go to Detroit with us tomorrow? Early."

"I'll pass. My largess might become something less socially acceptable."

"I'm anxious to bring Bryanna down out of the skies."

Kap looked curiously at his former student. "You don't think there's another bomb out there, do you? Is there something you're not telling me?"

"No, not really. I have no way of knowing if there is a second or a third bomb.

We're a weakened nation, Kap. We've eroded a little every year for a long time. Our eight-trillion-dollar war machine is, to use your word, feckless. True, we can knock anyone out of the sky, bomb cities and caves—and only produce a lot of devastation and resentment. This is almost Vietnam all over again.

"Our so-called strength has become our weakness. The machismo of *'we won't be beaten head-to-head'* is the wrong focus nowadays. Unfortunately, regarding whatever private deals somebody made forty or fifty years ago, I seriously doubt any of them are around today."

Kaplan nodded. "I've read and heard reports that accuse prominent people of making spurious arrangements with the Saudis and other Arab sheikdoms as far back as the Nixon administration. They may have been good at that time, but . . ."

"Maybe now we can find out. Somebody has protected those records like the Knights Templar did the Holy Grail," Macdonald said, yawning, trying to clear his head.

"Yeah, but they were all beheaded in the thirteenth century, although it is said some survivors ended up in Scotland and buried everything there."

"I've got to stretch," Macdonald said, standing and doing so, trying to bring some life into his body. "Tell you what; I'll get some picks and shovels. You and I can spend a couple of nights a week digging under the White House."

Kaplan rose awkwardly. "I keep telling you, young man, I am not favorable to physical exercise. Thanks for the respite, but I must be off to my office and become introduced to my motor pool secretary."

15

President Macdonald stood behind his chair addressing a packed Situation Room. "The supply logistics are working beautifully. Thank you. But how are we coming with the people who lived on the fringe and upwind of the blast? What's their power and energy status?"

A woman across and down from him at the long conference table stood as she spoke.

"Margo Clay, deputy administrator of FEMA, Mr. President. The power grids have been re-conformed to meet the demands for those living approximately twelve miles from ground zero. We've caught a break on the weather. Temperatures west and north of the DTO will get down into the upper thirties, but mostly it will be in the forties over the greater area. Tomorrow, most temperatures will range into the mid fifties. A cold front will move in late Thursday, though, dropping temperatures into the low twenties."

Macdonald shook his head. "Thank you, Ms. Clay. Seventy-two hours. What can we accomplish for the evacuees in the next forty-eight hours?" He didn't wait for an answer. "Countless people are without the homes in which they went to bed last night. Tomorrow morning I'm taking a group of House and Senate leaders on a flyover of ground zero at sunrise plus thirty minutes, and then we'll put down as near to ground zero as is possible."

"Mr. President." It was Commerce Secretary Frances Royce. "General Kilpatrick believes Detroit's airport is still unusable and suggests Toledo is the closest safe airport."

"I realize my being on the ground isn't going to help recovery efforts, but I want to see it and let everyone know this government is fully engaged. How are we coming with the hotel and motel chains?"

Clay from FEMA answered. "Acceptance was slow to catch on, but at the last count I saw within the last hour, there were nearly seventy-five thousand rooms in Indiana, Illinois, and western and northern Michigan. Most chains appear to be offering from fifty to seventy-five percent off their rooms. Chief Sweetwater will continue receiving updates. The DOER volunteer network has been spectacular, overwhelming FEMA's phone-calling efforts, but they are stirring up altruism and getting better-than-average results."

"Okay. I'll be addressing the nation tonight at 9 p.m. Eastern time. It's going to be much more than just me this time. We'll have video. The air corridors within fifty miles of the DTO are closed to all except us. The military has been videoing in a precise grid-by-grid pattern. Plus, we are continuing our satellite surveillance in the DTO for survivors."

Macdonald looked around the packed Situation Room. "I can't thank you enough for your unselfish efforts on a horrendously difficult day. It may take us awhile to sort out where we all belong in here. I only found the Oval Office with some assistance," he said wryly.

There was a smattering of laughter.

"As you may know, some former White House staff members have been offering their assistance, sharing their history in this building, which has been of great help to us. Their knowledge and outside contacts are helping to reduce the stress heaped upon our rookie team. If any former staff is in here, I thank you. Make sure we have your names and IDs to properly compensate you."

He stood back from his chair.

Darlene stepped up. "Thank you, Mr. President." With that, the room burst into spontaneous applause. Darlene whispered that he should go. He nodded, waved his thanks, and left the room. Darlene stayed behind to coordinate the next phase of assignments.

He stopped outside the entrance, the applause still strong, and spoke to a Secret Service officer, who nodded he understood and went into the Situation Room.

Macdonald waved again, and then he, Ambassador Hendrickson, General Bingham, and the military aide carrying the black briefcase with all the codes needed to launch missiles headed for the Oval Office.

Since General Bingham had set him straight on how DOD worked, Macdonald had puzzled over how to utilize his old friends, if at all. Today's events suggested to him that Hendrickson's post might best be as an executive assistant to Alisa Padget, his incoming National Security advisor. He'd talk to General Gibbons about General Bingham.

"Have a seat, gentlemen," Macdonald said, as he stripped off his jacket, while going behind his desk. He pressed a button on his communications center. "Cynthia, I'mmmm baaaack," he said in a universally familiar lilt, "with guests."

Cynthia entered the room. "Sir, you are scheduled to eat with your family at 6:30 p.m., which is approximately forty-five minutes from now. You meet with the Cabinet and Joint Chiefs, next door in the Cabinet Room at 7:30 p.m. When are you going to work on your speech?"

"I haven't written one yet," he lightly scoffed. "Darlene's working on my cheat sheets, as always."

She looked disapprovingly at him. "If you say so, sir." She left, closing the door after her.

"Okay. How long has it been since we ran ops in the Middle East?" Macdonald addressed the question to General Bingham, but Ambassador Hendrickson indicated he would answer.

"We continued for a while, after you left for Oxford, but things became fairly benign until 9/11. We quickly geared up for Afghanistan incursions and continued them until the invasion in October. Then we moved to more overt missions."

"Our type of activity was considerably cut back over the past few years," General Bingham said. "I would imagine, though, that some of our *friends* might still be around. Also, sir, Director Eubanks returned my call about Sergeant Major Egan. The DCIA remembered two incursions they made together. He'll try to meet Egan tomorrow morning and ascertain whether he can be of help to the agency.

"I've also passed that on to the Sergeant Major. He asked me to relay his appreciation to you for including him. He also understood very clearly about DOD. He's looking forward to talking with the DCIA."

"Our dollar may not talk as loudly as it once did," Macdonald interjected. "We'll have to use euros now. Our contacts were shrewd dealers then, and I am sure they are today. They were somehow always up on the currency exchange rates."

"Yes sir," Bingham said. "They may have been Bedouins or mountain Kurds, but they traded in their beads a long time ago for satellite and wireless communications. There are no longer any *corners* left in the world. Some of these folks may still live in caves, which are not all bad if you have ever been in the better ones. However, they're technically and financially astute and greatly underestimated."

"Exactly," said the ambassador. "That was something we could never get across to the previous president—his administration thought too colloquially."

"Gentlemen, I appreciate your candor . . . it brings back fond memories."

His guests chuckled. "General, with your permission I would like to talk with General Gibbons about keeping you here or loaning you to CIA. There may be a need for something more clandestine than military, say, where you might be of assistance to Director Eubanks, as you suggested Jack would be."

"That is up to you and the Chief, sir, but I would welcome the opportunity, if it comes to that."

"Okay. It's probably best you not be here when General Gibbons arrives, which should be at any moment. Please go to Darlene's office. She may not be there, so seek out one of her deputies. Tell them I want you to talk with Darlene. We'll see where things go from there."

"Thank you, Mr. President. Mr. Ambassador."

"We'll catch up later, Barry," Hendrickson said.

General Bingham went out the left hand door.

"He's a good man, Mr. President."

"Absolutely," Macdonald averred. "He is a straight-up guy. He saved me from looking like a boob to the DOD."

The ambassador smiled. "I think DCIA Eubanks may very much want to have him as a consultant. Barry told me he was receptive to his recommendation of Jack."

"Ambassador, today's tragedy is going to force me to make some adjustments to my staff. I know you were looking forward to sliding back into retirement, but I'd like to hire you as an executive assistant to Alisa. I don't want you weighted down with any administrative duties, but rather as a councilor to me. I'd like to make your status official. What do you say?"

"I say thank you. Being a widower, I won't be taking those trips Ginger and I had planned before she became ill."

"This is not gratuitous or because I'm looking for a chess player. You have a lot to offer and you know me well. I wasn't expecting a war . . . well, you know what I mean."

"It is my pleasure to serve you, Mr. President."

The intercom buzzed. "General Gibbons is here, sir."

"Show the General in." He turned to his old friend. "I'd like you to sit in, in your new capacity."

"I'd be honored, sir."

16

President Macdonald had been pleased when General Gibbons accepted the inclusion of the ambassador to their meeting. Concerning the assignment for General Bingham, she wanted to discuss that with the superintendant of the War College. But she'd acknowledged that a short-term loan was probably doable.

The meeting had been enlightening for Macdonald. Gibbons posed interesting scenarios of how to respond militarily. They had no target, but she confided that the special operations people were fully engaged, waiting to be called on.

Macdonald now moved along the colonnade alone, going to the residence where he would have twenty minutes to shower and dress for dinner with his family, whom he needed more than anyone else right now.

Arriving in the private quarters, he conferred with his valet about what to wear for the Joint Session later that evening. After the valet left, he headed to the bathroom, and for some reason, his mind flashed back twenty years to Oxford.

Attending Oxford had unknowingly begun his road to the White House. It was where he'd met Reggie Howard. They had become occasional pub buddies, and it was Howard who taught him the fine art of dart-throwing. Now each was the leader of a great country. How weird was that?

Oxford was in the district that Howard would eventually represent as a member of Parliament. Along with Howard, Macdonald had also formed friendships with students from around the world, but mostly fell in with the Russian twins, Vasiliy and Alexandra Mednorov, and their strong-minded and pragmatic fellow Russian, Raisa Illyanavich. The twins were twenty-two and inquisitive. Stoic Raisa, like him, had turned twenty-three in early October.

The twins had studied English in high school and college. Raisa had too, but she rarely spoke it. The twins were interested in western culture, but Raisa was not. Vasiliy later confided privately to him that he should be careful around her, as she came from a strong communist background. Her father had been KGB.

Reggie liked putting together Saturday soirées to wherever. It started with a couple of day trips to London, which everyone, including Raisa, seemed to enjoy.

Then the first weekend in November, Reggie and his current girlfriend Lori wanted to take an entire weekend and treat them all to a fair. Raisa turned his invitation down, as did Vasiliy. Alexandra had also said no, but Lori prodded the reticent Alex to join in. Vasiliy also encouraged her to go, since it was the type of thing she enjoyed.

She acquiesced. Away from Vasiliy and Raisa, Alex became more carefree. She became a frolicsome, gay-spirited, somewhat madcap, green-eyed beauty. Mike had confided to Reggie he was extremely attracted to her, but was concerned about becoming involved. His British friend pooh-poohed his concern, saying he could use some female companionship—*all work and no play*, that sort of thing.

Although nothing sexual happened that night with Alex, Reggie later in the week told him he and Lori had caught Alex observing him. Reggie took that as a cue to plan another weekend in a fortnight, to show them the city of Bath and its Roman baths.

However, on the Saturday morning when all four were planning to go to Bath, Reggie was called away—a last minute thing, he said. With Vasiliy and Raisa gone off to London for the day, Reggie insisted that Mike and Alex take his car and go it alone; he'd call ahead and change the reservations to just two people. Reggie then waved them off in a big flurry, with maps in hand. They were both excited about the adventure and stopped often to explore. Alex had expressed her joy: "I am free like the bird."

They sometimes walked hand in hand, as Reggie and Lori always did. It was friendly and fun. The group usually stayed at youth hostels on trips, and Reggie had made arrangements for them at one about a kilometer from the center of Bath. Mike and Alex had checked in, and then followed Reggie's advice of an inn known for its ambiance and good food. They located it and were immediately charmed by its quaint décor, robust fireplace, and soothing candlelight.

Macdonald warmly remembered the sensualness of the inn in Bath. Sitting across from Alex, he had reached out and taken her hand. In acceptance, she softly caressed the back of his hand with her thumb. Her green eyes sparkled with girlish teasing, inviting him.

He had been with women over the years, particularly when he was a football star and there were raucous fraternity parties and sleepovers. He had seen one woman fairly steadily during his year at Penn State. She'd wanted sex and had no interest in a permanent relationship, which suited him.

But that evening with Alexandra in the cozy pub, illumination coming only from candles and the fireplace, he fell in love. He had never known such desires and wanted to take her right then and there. When the food came he could barely eat, she only dawdled.

With her head tilted down, she searched his eyes through her long lashes. They pushed through the meal, dispensed with dessert, and left the pub's coziness for a cold, wind-whipped street, racing to their car two blocks away. The drive to the hostel had been frantic. Once inside, their first kiss was intense and ravishing.

He remembered: coming up for air, she had giggled. She could feel him against her. They frantically pulled off their clothes. He loosened his belt, and she reached for him. He thought he was going to explode. He bared her breasts, and she kissed him hard while pushing down his pants. They sank down onto a clothing-strewn bed, consumed with disrobing, until they finally lay fully naked, exploring. She was so beautiful. She expressed her desires to him. Both were the aggressor.

That night was a sprint that turned into a marathon. They made love all night, barely dozing in between. When it came time to shower and dress, neither wanted to let the other out of touching distance.

It was noon when they left the hostel. Their voracious thirst for the other was barely quenched, but the ache in their stomachs took precedence, and they found a café near the Avon River and later walked along the Kennet and Avon Canal. They visited the Bath Abbey and bought a variety of picture postcards for show-and-tell.

His and Alex's madness for each other did not stay a secret long. Everyone quickly knew they were lovers. When Vasiliy expressed his happiness for them, Alex was elated. It also meant they could be a couple in public, which made everything much easier on them. They went on to enjoy dozens of pleasant weekends traipsing with Reggie and his girlfriend Lori.

On their last night in Oxford, they had made love and cried. They'd planned to write every week, and he'd fly to Moscow as soon as he made some money. They wrote for a while, but with him back in the States and beginning a new life as a civilian and a currency trader, all his good intentions waned, and the writing fell off.

Eventually, weekly letters became monthly; within a year, he realized that she had stop writing. The path they had followed—with her writing and him responding—then changed as her correspondence ceased.

Macdonald's valet informed him that his family was in the dining room. He put on his tie and jacket and went to join his mother, sister, and brother.

17

The Oval Office
Same Day
2215 hours

The president and his team, a tired group consisting of Darlene, Cynthia, Kap, and Ogden Garrett, were wrapping up a horrific, intense day.

"I'm afraid my adrenaline is oozing away, folks."

Kap laughed at Macdonald's comment. "I lost all mine some place between the antipasto and the asparagus."

"It's been a long, tough day, sir," Garrett said. "You have accomplished wonders. I had two years left in my third term when you asked me to run DOD. I thought I'd seen some whoppers of negotiations in those years, but Ed Batchelder giving in to you on the designees, especially with me as SecDef, tops them all."

"Strange times breed strange bedfellows, Ogden. Okay. Go home everybody, unless you're sleeping over. My wakeup call is 0430 hours."

Kaplan and Garrett took the cue, stood and said their good nights, congratulating Macdonald again on his nationally televised speech and the way he had handled the Congress.

After the two men departed, Macdonald asked, "You ladies need anything from me?"

"We're still in the Blair House. Can we extend that to the weekend?" Darlene asked. The Blair House was the guest quarters across the street from the White House and available to presidential guests.

"Your wish is my command."

Darlene turned to Cynthia. "You ready to walk across the street with me?"

"Good night, Mr. President," Cynthia said.

"Good night, Mr. President," Darlene said.

"My. I guess that makes it official."

The three laughed. He gave each a hug. "You two are the greatest teammates."

They shared parting words and left. He plopped into his desk chair, swiveled back and forth looking at nothing in particular. He mused, *did all this happen in just one day?* He then launched out of it and headed for the French doors, which opened when he was just a stride short of them.

He was greeted by Agent Jackson, a sandy-haired former Lacrosse player from the University of Maryland. He was one of several agents Macdonald had gotten to know on some level over the past year. They had been chatty during down time on the campaign.

"Mr. Jackson?" he asked.

"Mr. President," the agent said formally.

"Get a couple of sticks, we'll play out on the lawn."

"Sir?"

"What does a guy do for fun, when all the kiddies have gone home?"

"Ah, the kitchen is still open, sir."

"This late?"

"A small staff until the president retires. Your house, sir, is a 24/7 operation."

"Of course. I should have realized that. But . . . back to fun."

"There's the bowling alley Mr. Nixon put in or the jungle gym behind your office."

"That'd be a sight. No tackling dummies where I can take out my angst?"

"Sir? I mean . . . I mean, there's the workout room."

"Ah, yes. I'm hoping to get there one of these days. Do others use it?"

"Many, sir. Staff, agents. It has its regulars."

"When I use it, I don't want to displace anybody. Just want to take my turn, get my reps."

"Yes sir."

"Thank you, Jackson. I think I'll retire now." The nearly sub-freezing cold was getting to him. He set off briskly along the colonnade, Jackson a few steps behind him. He neared the inside corner of the West Wing and the Gallery and stopped. "Could I get some ice cream now, if I wanted?"

"What flavor, sir? I can call it in, and they'll bring it up to you."

"No. Take me to the kitchen; I'll have it down there. Call them. I want two huge scoops, no, three huge scoops of the best vanilla they've got, smothered with chocolate sauce. Nothing else. Get some for yourself."

"Follow me, sir."

Many evenings, he and Sandi had indulged in a bowl of ice cream, snuggled up close on the sofa, looking at the New York City lights.

Once I get the hang of this place, I might enjoy it, he thought. *Maybe they'll let me raid the ice box.*

18

Macdonald had enjoyed his soiree into the White House kitchen and the delicious ice cream. Now in his bedroom, he was seated in his favorite lounge chair alongside a window that looked out over the south lawn and the Washington Monument.

The chair, and a four drawer file cabinet placed against the interior wall near it, had been shipped in from his New York condo.

As he sat ruminating about his day, his mind left the present and slid back to when Sandi had died. He wished she could share in this view as they had in their condo: large windows overlooked Central Park to the northwest toward the George Washington Bridge. He reminisced about the many times they had crossed the Hudson River on their way north to New Paltz in New York State's Catskill Mountains, a favorite place for skiing or hiking.

His longing for her prompted him to get up and take a file folder from the cabinet. It held several letters he had received after her death. His interest was on one in particular. Sandi had passed over six and a half years earlier, and he had not had any other woman in his life since. Until now, that was.

He opened the folder and removed the letter from his former Oxford classmate Vasiliy Mednorov, Alexandra's brother. His "Lexi" now lived only a few city blocks from where he now sat. They were to make contact over the coming weekend, but that, unfortunately, would have to be put off until . . . he didn't really know.

The letter was dated August 2, 2007.

> *Michael, my dear friend:*
> *I looked you up on the Internet after I read terrible news about your wife, Sandra. I am so sorry we had no time to meet her face to face. Good*

intentions, eh? I print carefully for you to better read. I use Internet and e-mail, but this feels more personal. That is why it is late arriving to you.

You are in our thoughts.

I read you have doctorate in economics and finance. Always you want to learn more. I too learn, but just courses, no more degrees.

I took a wife 11 years ago; we have two boys and one girl, no twins like me. Life is comfortable. Like Americans, we have TVs, car, dishwasher . . . many things better here now . . . than before. It's good. I move up, now head of Financial Monitoring and Foreign Exchange Control, Central Bank of Russia. We go to Black Sea for vacation with big shots, hmm.

Alexandra . . .

A spike of adrenaline shot though him now as it had years earlier, at the sight of her name, even though he had seen her three weeks earlier.

. . . does well. She, too, like you, widowed. Four years now. Boat accident on Black Sea. She broke bones, fractured skull, in hospital six weeks, recovery three months. Sergey killed.

Mike put down the letter. The bridge of his nose tingled. His thoughts were back on Sandi and her constant battle with pain. The two women he had loved so deeply, suffering, even though he knew now Alex had fully recovered.

She and Sergey love challenge of sports: ski, motorcycle, race boats. They marry 1996. Good man. No children. I told her I would write this from both of us. After she recovered, she took leave to go to Bonn University. She, like you, now a PhD.

She has important job, no more crazy sports. Michael, she was sad for you. You both have lost someone you love. Maybe more than one time, eh?

Raisa not in financial work. She is with the FSB. You know, the new KGB. She is in finances, but for government. She still has strong feelings for the old Russia. Never married.

What is it you like to say? Ah, yes. Don't be a stranger.

Your friend, Vasiliy

19

Air Force One
Nearing Detroit
Wednesday, January 23
Dawn

"Mr. President," AF1's pilot announced, "we will be over Detroit in ten minutes. We will pass over Lake St. Clair, Grosse Point, and then will begin banking left in a three-mile radius of downtown Detroit and Windsor, Canada."

"Damn," Homeland Secretary Gus Vaughn said to Macdonald. "I'd forgotten all about the Canadians. I mean, do we know how many casualties?"

"It's a big number, Gus. Ground zero is south of what was once the Hodge Freeway, near the river. The investigative team now believes the bomb was elevated on top of a building, but that's only conjecture."

"General Gibbons has been doing okay?"

"She has been in complete command, while having to deal with me. How do you think the JCS felt having to deal with a president who came from Wall Street?"

"Yeah, but you were a Marine first. She had to know about your Force Recon duty."

"That was probably the only thing that gave her any hope."

Gus laughed. "I hear you, boss. We all have a steep learning curve."

"I held it together pretty good in those first minutes in the Situation Room; she saw I wasn't in a panic mode. She never flinched when I told her how I wanted the US military used. Within two hours, MPs and medical units were moving into the DTO. Now, when we get on the ground—"

"Mr. President," the pilot interrupted, "We are in sight of ground zero out the left side. Traffic control informs us that the radiation floating east is dispersing over southern Canada and the northern portion of Lake Erie. We are going down to ten thousand feet. Any planes we see are military or scientific prop planes and choppers testing the air and taking pictures."

The two former Marines moved forward to the window on the left side. The president's office looked out the right side; the plane's arc was counterclockwise. The day was clear except for a light haze rising up and drifting eastward—a myriad of smoky tints in a light breeze.

Through the haze could be seen a gradation of damage to the skyline. Some skyscrapers revealed partial damage to the sides facing ground zero, while others were totally destroyed. "That crater is huge, Mike. Son of a bitch, what sick fuckers."

"The inhumanity," Macdonald said chokingly.

"This is the Captain. We have been cleared down to five thousand feet, and we will now close in to a one-mile radius."

The plane descended as announced, riveting the two colleagues to the window, as the scorched ground and mounds of gray and black debris became more detailed. The size of the immense crater reminded Macdonald of the meteor crater east of Flagstaff, Arizona, which he had visited with his parents some thirty years earlier, except this one was filled with murky water.

He remembered his last visit to Detroit, nine days before Election Day, where he had stood in a jammed Ford Stadium. Now he couldn't even locate the stadium, even using binoculars. The impoverished downtown that had been so beautifully revitalized was no more. The renaissance that had been spreading outward was no more. The fires dotting the terrain were the only movement and color against the bleak grays and blacks—a sad contrast to the azure sky.

Macdonald groaned, sat back and wiped his eyes. "If I had a tackling dummy in here, I'd beat it to shreds. Let's go back to my office." There, he tapped the intercom button. "Captain, once we've completed a full circle, I'd like you to reverse direction and do a full orbit clockwise."

"Yes sir. We will also be dropping to twenty-five hundred feet. Sir, on this pass, I'd like to give those on the ground a wing dip, show them the colors."

"I like this guy's thinking," Gus said.

"Great idea," the president replied. "Please notify everyone about the wing dips. I'm sure some are a little edgy."

"Will do, sir."

The 747 descended and banked east, crossing the river a mile from the bomb-made lake. The first wing dip occurred soon after. During all this, Macdonald called and talked with Darlene. When he finished that call, he said to Gus, "I need you to call Bryanna and fill her in on what we've seen. Let her know I'm scheduling a conference call that will include her at 1700 hours Washington time. The subject will be politics and what I'll be telling Congress tonight." He then pressed the intercom. "A.J."

He came on in seconds. "Yes, Mr. President."

"I'm coming down to your area to fill everyone in on what's going to be happening."

"Yes sir. My contacts on the ground in Toledo say there will be a welcoming committee: local brass and newly arrived survivors."

"Okay." Macdonald punched off. "A.J. appears to be back on course, Gus. In fact, I believe we all are."

"I'm with you, boss . . . like I was in the Middle East twenty years ago. I like you going with the economic plan; it got you elected. The opposition parties were rocking on one foot, while you were solidly on both."

"Like we did in Force Recon, keep them guessing. Okay, we need to show the world our administration is running on all cylinders, Gus. Our 2013 Economic Recovery Plan that tens of millions of voters gambled on us for is still our vision for this country. Even with this atrocity we see below us, we are on mission; totally focused."

"Right, sir . . . be solid as a rock. You have the economics; Bryanna and I have the recovery; and CIA and DOD has the investigation. I agree with you that nobody's coming after us with another bomb. You can bet they are just waiting for us to collapse like a tissue in a rain storm. Well that ain't gonna happen."

Macdonald smiled. "Not on my watch, it won't."

20

Despondency shrouded the tarmac at Toledo Airport, despite the gallant efforts of a local college band playing celebratory tunes. The people who crowded the rope line showed happy faces while greeting the new president, but fell somber after he passed. Most were local to Toledo and hadn't lost their homes.

A National Guard detachment had brought about seventy-five Detroit survivors to the field to meet President Macdonald, who did not put on his campaign face. He saw and felt their emotions, and worked diligently to stay positive.

He grimly received the applause as he faced the crowd, as well as a battery of TV and film cameras and a hastily put-together microphone tree.

The president began by praising Michigan Governor Carlton for his quick response in assembling the Michigan's National Guard, thousands of police, fire and rescue teams, and forensic specialists—and for his coordination with General Gibbons, who in turn had mobilized the United States military police and military medical units from across the country.

He lauded Vice President Dudley's DOER program and the mobilization of over a quarter of a million citizens who had formed "the largest bucket brigade this nation has ever witnessed." He then introduced Gus Vaughn.

His secretary of Homeland Security explained the massive effort underway to learn the origin of the nuclear device, assuring the audience that scientists, technicians, and nuclear experts would be sifting through debris as soon as possible.

Macdonald and the folks traveling with him were taken into a hangar to talk with the seventy-five survivors. Their stories were beyond belief.

The shock wave and huge storm of debris had crashed through their homes with tornado-like force. Most people were asleep and suddenly without a house or clothing. Some had been thrown about like rag dolls. Many were crushed and killed, others badly injured, and some miraculously walked away with only bumps and bruises. The sky was dark as pitch—no sun, no electricity. The air was heavy with pummeled debris. People roamed about barely clothed in the nighttime, bitter cold.

They had scrounged for any kind of covering. Slowly, the ambulatory collected what they needed themselves, collected surpluses for others, and headed toward the sounds of crying and screams.

There were no first-responders. Electronic devices found in the debris did not work. The survivors were alone in the blackness. They all agreed it had been the most frightening experience in their lifetimes. In a technological world where instant communication was a given, nothing had worked—except their own fortitude.

As dawn's bleak glow spread over them, they were able to gain their bearings. Some had been still in their own neighborhoods; others weren't so sure. Nothing looked familiar. No one knew what had caused the damage; most guessed tornadoes.

Not knowing the origin of the storm or from which way help might come, they'd continued to scavenge for clothes, food, bottled beverages, and other such necessities. Slowly there had been realization and concern as to why there were no sirens.

The National Guard had been the first to reach them. Then they'd learned the grizzly truth.

President Macdonald and his party mingled with the victims for over an hour. The victims' stories would be repeated in print, on radio and TV, and in social media many times—spreading the message of horror and desperation.

A.J. had arranged a mini news conference for just the local media, who, as he told Macdonald, were in awe of the number of rescue and support people who had been pouring through Toledo heading for the disaster zone.

When it came to Q&A, they were curious about Gus Vaughn. Macdonald told them, "Augustus Vaughn will become a household name in a very short time. He and I were Marines together twenty years ago. He retired a full colonel and most recently ran the southwest border patrol operation before I appointed him secretary of Homeland Security. He's a do-er and will work well with the vice president."

On the flight back, following a fifteen-minute briefing with the traveling press corps, A.J. reported to Macdonald that the scuttlebutt seemed very positive. The president was getting high grades on being caring, knowledgeable, and decisive. There were no longer any concerns about who was in charge, which was a complete turnaround of the media's initial concerns twenty-four hours earlier.

21

Macdonald's arrival at the White House on the Marine One chopper was his first time landing there. He looked out on the South Lawn as the helicopter settled down between the huge trees and thick underbrush along the periphery of the grounds.

A small group watched from the Rose Garden. He saw Darlene approach as he descended from the chopper and exchanged salutes with the Marine Guard. Darlene walked with him across the expanse of lawn as she brought him up to date on a myriad of issues.

As he listened, he also acknowledged the assemblage with a wave. Most were the ones who had earned a White House job after the grueling months on the campaign trail.

Upon entering the Oval Office, he was greeted by Cynthia who reported, "One congressman questioned the use of US military personnel on US soil. I sent back a note stating that we were operating under DEFCON 1 and that their duties were limited to assisting the National Guard, because thousands of Guard members were away from their homes and scrambling to join up with their outfit."

Darlene went on to her office, while Cynthia continued to brief him about correspondence and callers, most of which would be answered by staff. Macdonald plopped down on the sofa. He was still wearing his Air Force One windbreaker.

Cynthia moved down her list, "Jane is back in your New York condo. She had the companionship of a female Secret Service agent. There was a message from Alexandra Mednorov asking that you call her."

That surprised him. Back on January 5, they had agreed to wait at least to the weekend after the inauguration before talking.

"Apparently Ms. Mednorov sounded anxious and emphasized it was important. Do you want me to get her on the line?"

"No, I want to talk with Darlene first. I need to go up and change. I'll have lunch in the residence. Ask Darlene to join me in a half hour, for lunch, if she wants. Just let me know."

"Will do," Cynthia answered officiously.

He went out the French doors and headed for the mansion.

Alexandra's call concerned him. They had seen each other for the first time in eighteen years on the day after Thanksgiving and again that Saturday afterward, two and a half weeks after his election.

At their Friday luncheon, he'd been impressed with her poise and demeanor, exuding a confidence that embellished her natural beauty.

She'd left for a scheduled afternoon meeting downtown at the World Bank and returned for supper. Unfortunately, at her meeting with the president of the International Finance Corporation in London, he had asked that she change her morning flight on Sunday to an evening one on Saturday because he needed her to be at a meeting in London Sunday afternoon.

Macdonald had put her up at the Plaza Hotel, only a few blocks from his condo. He had some business to attend to Saturday morning, so she used that time to walk down Fifth Avenue and look in the windows of the posh stores. She went in St. Patrick's Cathedral, toured around the Rockefeller Center ice skating rink, walked the nine blocks back to her hotel, and then joined him at his condo.

Their intended afternoon together and Saturday supper had become a late lunch and a much shorter visit. As president-elect, he couldn't just go out for a casual walk on the streets of New York, but he could take her up to the roof of his thirty-six-story apartment building for a pleasant interlude on that clear and mild day.

In the week before Christmas, they had talked twice by phone—the second being on the twenty-fourth, when she was at Vasiliy's home in Moscow. The Christmas Eve call was especially enjoyable and lasted well over an hour, including a long chat with Vasiliy.

Although he had been continually busy after the holidays, he had looked forward to Alex's return to the States on Saturday, January 5, two days before, she was to start working at the World Bank in Washington. He had asked her to fly into New York, where he would be for meetings that Friday, and as before he put her up at the Plaza. He had asked Darlene to keep that Saturday open. Alex had shipped her luggage directly to her Washington office, allowing her to travel lightly. The Secret Service in New York discreetly handled her arrival and departure using a taxi of its own.

Macdonald's mind reverted to the present as he entered his White House bedroom, where he shed his travel clothes, showered, and put on a dark-blue suit, white shirt, and yellow tie, the outfit his valet had laid out for him. He paced the residence's sitting room before finally stopping at a small desk, upon which was a phone and a computer.

His thoughts were broken by the ringing of his phone. "Yes," he answered softly.

"It's Jane, sir."

"Hey. How are you?" Her voice brightened him. "I was just about to call you. Have a good trip home?"

"Oh, it was fine. Agent Hines was a pleasant companion."

He smiled at the precise way she said that.

"I'm calling about Ms. Mednorov; she called again a few minutes ago, actually. She is very anxious to talk with you. There was an edge to her voice, not her usual lovely low tones."

"Where is she?"

"At work." Jane gave him the number. "She will be there until six."

"Okay, I'll take it from here. Thanks, friend."

"You are always welcome. I hope she's all right."

"Me too." He called Darlene's private line.

"Ms. Sweetwater's line."

"Darlene there?"

"She's on her way up to see you, sir."

"Okay." He hung up.

If Alex is in trouble, how can I help her?

When he last saw Alex in early January, she had been escorted into his New York condo by an agent. She was dressed in a knee-length winter coat over a business suit. She had come directly to him, kissed both his cheeks, and hugged him. The embrace had felt good.

The agent had waited politely for the greetings, and then reminded Macdonald of the required search. She took Alexandra's coat, and the two women disappeared into the office. He had gone into the kitchen for the wine and two glasses.

When he returned to the living room, Alex was already sitting on the sofa, smiling. Her suit jacket was folded over a chair's back. He smiled to himself when remembering her teasing words. "It was very quick; I have so little on."

She was wearing her favorite light-blue, collared blouse and a single string of pearls with matching earrings. Holding up the wine bottle, he had said, "I understand Jane discovered your preferred wine." He poured the wine and sat beside her on the couch. They clinked their glasses in a toast.

"To a renewed friendship," he had said.

"To more," she'd replied softly.

22

"I really want *you* to call her, please Darlene. This isn't about romance; something's wrong, maybe seriously wrong. Alex wouldn't be calling me about something trivial because we had agreed, as I promised you, to wait until this coming weekend to allow me time to get settled in. She knows who you are and what you do—she will respect your position."

"All right." Darlene looked at her watch. "It's nearly 12:30 p.m. Let's eat lunch and go over the 'five points.' We'll break in one hour, leaving me time to see to things downstairs and take five minutes to call her from the privacy of my office—a corner office, by the way, which I am going to love once I have the opportunity to get it organized."

"Did Mom get off okay?"

"Your brother took charge. He's flying to Denver with her and should be there within the hour. Jeanne Marie is staying two more nights to see some friends who are working here. Cynthia and I, along with a few staff will transition out of Blair House over the coming weekend, barring another catastrophe."

He smiled and gave her a knowing nod. They then settled into reviewing the five points in his campaign platform. The fixing of the national debt was a daunting task, made only worse by the bombing. The government had set the terrible example of living on credit, and a hundred million or more citizens had followed suit.

"Our country's financial status has lost the confidence of the rest of the world, Darlene. Americans and their government have shown no frugality. Living on credit is at the root of our debacle—and bomb or no bomb, it's time to suck it up."

He got up and began his usual pacing. "It's going to take an extreme amount of effort on everyone's part or the whole country will collapse on top of Detroit."

His gruff tone concerned her. "Are you all right?" Darlene asked.

"What?" He saw her questioning look. "Oh, sorry. I guess I'm letting the enormity of the bombing affect my concentration. And I'm upset because Congress has perpetuated our growing financial fiasco, which has been right in front of everybody for years. It's all public data," he said intensely.

"You remember how the media took us to task thinking we were making up the numbers?" he said with disgust.

"To me, that says the congressional leadership has other agendas, Mr. President. We need a true public debate and not pontificating partisanship. Their puffery, to the contrary, is designed to hide the obvious and dissuade real debate."

"They don't know Kap, chum. He's a terror when it comes to Medicaid fraud and Medicare mishandling. He's champing at the bit to tear into them with a pack of mad CPAs. And then there are all those government guarantees—the nasty little leeches not found in any budget or line item, but they consume more and more of our country's capital every year."

Darlene smiled, seeing his tension drain; he relaxed as he got into finance.

He was on a roll. "Americans like to invest in our tax-free treasury notes, as do foreign governments, who unfortunately buy hundreds of billions of them and are accumulating a bigger and bigger chunk of us every day.

"Another of our big, yet rarely talked about concerns is the American corporations that foreign companies are buying up, along with their heavy investments in our banks and financial institutions. We may soon no longer be the rulers of our own destiny. Left unchecked, that sort of unabridged power will create a deleterious effect on our economy, from which we might never recover."

He sat and leaned back. "We'll survive this bomb. But if we don't reduce our debt, the next bomb will be a mega-headed economic one, reducing us to a third-world country."

"Proving," she said, "that what no nation has ever been able to do to us militarily, they may easily achieve economically."

Macdonald nodded. "I remember my father worrying after the Japanese auto and electronics industries began flooding the American market . . . that they could take us over economically and financially without bloodshed by using their newfound wealth—which they got from us—to suck up our Hawaiian and West Coast real estate."

"Well, typically, if Americans are not feeling any pain, they'll ignore things," she added. "Now we have all the pain we can handle. Let's hope they listen tonight."

"I wish we could magically lower prices and credit card interest rates, Darlene, but I don't believe that would resonate the right way. It would be like the bailouts in 2008 and 2009 and the other economic job-making scams paid for by the taxpayers up through 2012.

"The poor stayed poor. The dependent stayed dependent. Borrowing cost less and the many said *thank you, now I can spend more and charge more because it won't cost me as much*. That's been the culture since the mid-1900s. We borrowed to move up socially and now the bubble has burst."

"I don't believe talking about financial instruments and derivatives will help right now, sir. I suggest we highlight them, indicating that the details are addressed in the printed version of the Recovery Act, and move on."

"I'm for that," he said, checking his watch. "Where does the time go?"

23

Throughout the afternoon, the coterie moved through the outline of the president's speech and the details of the Recovery Act of 2013. A capsulated version of the act would be delivered to the House and Senate membership following the president's speech. The full-blown report would be sent to them by noon the next day.

In the final analysis, the content of his speech would be a joint effort with Darlene, Bryanna, and Kap. They had been the silver cord of campaign policy with him and would remain so during his presidency. His and Kap's financial wisdom along with Bryanna's and Darlene's political aplomb was what drove their unified ship.

"Since Vice President Dudley won't be here tonight, who will take her chair?" Darlene asked.

Macdonald puzzled on that as he visualized the podium and the two large chairs behind it that normally held the vice president and the speaker of the House. "How about nobody? It would create a dynamic visual honoring the dead and injured, and those made homeless."

"A constant reminder of where the vice president is and what she is doing," Darlene added. "I like that."

There was a knock, and Nancy Armstrong entered the Oval Office. "Got some news from Capitol Hill."

"Come in," Darlene said to her deputy.

"The House, with our ninety-three Centrist members, unanimously joined the Democrats to elect the Speaker of the House."

"That is good news," Macdonald said. This was the first in what he hoped would be how the Centrists would collaborate with the Republicans and Democrats.

"I'm finished here," Darlene said. "Mr. President?"

"No, that's fine. Go on . . . and thanks to both of you."

Darlene and Nancy left to direct the herculean task of preparing the Recovery Act.

Macdonald joined Kap and his team on developing the content of his speech. He stayed with them until 1700 hours, when he excused himself and passed through Cynthia's hub of activity. "I'll be in my study," he announced to her.

"Yes sir," Cynthia acknowledged.

He hadn't been in there two minutes when Cynthia buzzed him.

"Sir, you have a phone call on the scramble phone. You only have nine minutes."

"Thanks." He picked up that receiver and said, "Hey, tar heel."

He heard a light giggle. "Hey, linebacker."

He paused after using their eighteen-year-old nicknames they had for each other in Oxford. Alex filled the gap.

"I am so sorry for your nation's troubles, Michael. I have seen you on TV. You have been magnificent, but I would not have expected less."

"I only have eight minutes," he said softly, wishing she were with him so he could feel her against him.

"I need to see you. It may have a bearing on your disaster, *mon cher.*"

The disaster? "The bombing?"

"It is something I must see you about. No phone."

"This is high security, what we call scrambled." *How could she know something about the bombing?*

"No, please! I have called you from a phone in an outside box."

"Right."

Darlene, always thinking, had her use a public phone. His mind turned to tomorrow's schedule. After the Presidential Daily Briefing (PDB) with CIA Director Eubanks, he had a phone conference with Bryanna and Gus, and then a meeting at 1000 hours with Kap and his financial experts that would run to noon.

"Linebacker?"

"Sorry. Running through my schedule. How about lunch here at half past twelve?" he asked, eschewing military time for her sake.

"I am open for that."

"Okay, hold on. Be right back." He phoned Darlene.

"Yes sir?"

"I'd like a private lunch tomorrow, including you."

"What's going on? It's not like you to—"

"It's about the bombing." There was a two-beat pause.

"What? She works for the World Bank, how—?"

"I don't know," he admitted.

"She can't just waltz in here."

"She already has clearance. New York, remember?"

"Oh, of course. What do you need from me?"

He told her and returned to Alex. "Okay, you're on. You'll get a call, same as in New York, okay?"

"Yes, Michael. You will see that what I believe happened did happen."

24

House Chamber
Joint Session of Congress
Wednesday, January 23, 2013
2100 hours

There was a numbing silence after the video report on Detroit, narrated by Vice President Bryanna Dudley, faded out on large screens. Dudley had done a superb job of outlining the recovery program using stark video taken by Signal Corps photographers.

They had interspersed startling pictures from satellites showing the before and after views of a great American city. It ran twenty-five mesmerizing minutes.

Macdonald had made his ceremonial entrance, but sat in a folding chair alongside Darlene on the chamber floor. The Speaker respectfully waited and then lightly gaveled the House to order, stating, "Ladies and gentlemen, the President of the United States."

Somberness was instantly replaced by a deafening roar of cheers and applause. Pent up emotions erupted, spilling forth as President Michael Macdonald mounted the platform and shook the Speaker's hand. The vice president's chair was empty. Macdonald took his position behind the podium and checked out Darlene's cheat sheets placed there earlier. No one had seen his speech, because it had not been written out.

Slowly, the historic chamber came to order, and he went through the sobriquets and profusely congratulated Vice President Dudley and Secretary of Homeland Security Augustus Vaughn.

"Our enemy wants us emotionally immersed in this catastrophe so that we, as the governing body of the United States of America, will ignore what lies beneath the surface of this scurrilous attack. Yes, the nuclear device has our full attention. It has the world's attention. Investigations have been going on here and abroad since the moment after it occurred.

"As you have just witnessed, we are progressing with humanitarian search and recovery. Millions of our citizens, tens of thousands National Guardsmen, and thirty-two thousand United States troops have joined forces to find survivors and treat the injured.

"We are also involved with the prodigious problems in our economy. Both Detroit and our economy must be given speedy and effective attention. Neither will overshadow the other."

Macdonald took a drink of water while observing the minor rumblings below him, the exact reaction he was hoping for.

He raised his voice.

"You heard me correctly. Yes, we want to capture the criminals and string them up by their toes on the Monument grounds."

His tone was fierce, his eyes hard.

"Yes, we all want retribution, as do our dedicated friends around the world working 24/7 to track down those murderous, heartless fiends and bring them to justice."

The august body stood as one applauding and cheering, venting their emotions. He paused until everyone resumed his or her seat.

"We elected officials have sworn an oath to protect and defend, but not just with our military. You and I have also sworn to keep this country free from economic takeovers. That is why I and my centrist colleagues were elected, and we will not shirk from that responsibility.

"Shortly, the entire world's financial, commodity, and equity exchanges will reopen. Our dollar could lose more value tomorrow than it has collectively lost since 9/11."

That prompted considerable shifting and negative moans.

"We cannot—we must not—sit passively by like trees caught in a hurricane and become uprooted. No! We must protect our entire population. That is our number one job!"

The mild, short applause showed a lack of enthusiasm for the budgetary battles they knew were coming. *Maybe they are beginning to see where I'm going*, he thought.

"We, here tonight, from government and business, must be the bastions who deliver a strong and unyielding force against economic failure. We must take hard measures to reestablish our financial independence and rebuild our financial credibility and muscle.

"As horrible as it is to conceive, much less to say, there are contributing poisonous conditions that have existed for nearly half a century, which were considered at first to be a correction for existing conditions, but when continued, have proven disastrous in today's world. They need to be diminished and, in some cases, eliminated!"

He observed frowns, legislators looking from one to the other, not sure about what they had just heard. He took a drink of water, observing the ones who sat silently because they knew of what he spoke.

"I have been in office less than two and a half days. Some of you have been here two and a half decades. The old days are gone. The actions over the past years have been called into account by this bombing. Our nation has been failed fiscally by the very people elected to protect it."

Groans mixed in with applause demonstrated the division that would confront him.

"We and Canada have millions dead, millions injured, and maybe millions over the years sickened or murdered from the bomb's aftereffects. We have tens of millions working *until they drop*, helping evacuees with housing, clothing, and food. There are figuratively dozens of 'bucket brigades,' extending hundreds of miles from all areas of our great country, conveying materials and goods to the recovery centers across northern Illinois, Indiana, Ohio, and northern Michigan."

The body stood en masse cheering and wildly applauding.

"We also strive to protect the flow of commerce across the entire country to those not directly affected by the bomb. Life must and will go on everywhere. If we don't act to save our monetary system and restore our fiscal integrity, if we fail in that restoration, you can forget about rebuilding Detroit . . . because we will be the financial equivalent of a third-world nation, and others will own more of us than we do.

"We can't let the American people down. We can't give in. We won't give up!"

Standing ovation.

"Ladies and gentlemen of the United States Congress, you and I can dig our country out of the ashes of Detroit *and* our financial morass. We have been challenged to think far beyond our comfort zones. Metaphorically, we are confronted with five ticking financial time bombs, which must be defused in order to stabilize our financial and economic houses.

"First, our debt, both as a nation and as individuals, is out of control. We ignore balancing budgets. In the previous four years, our dependency on foreign products propelled our 2008 debt from ten to nearly seventeen trillion dollars today. This is unacceptable!"

Centrists jumped to their feet applauding and cheering, accompanied by many in the gallery. The Democrats and Republicans looked glum.

"One government statistic, which has been dropping precipitously for decades, is the Current Account Balance. It is the sum of the value of our Exported Goods and Services minus the value of the Goods and Services we import. Simply put, we are in a long-term deficit position.

"We have funded this debt by selling US Treasuries, which mortgages our future. Well, the *future is now*, and we cannot pay up. China, Japan, the UK, and the Mideast oil-producing nations now buy over fifty percent of our T-Notes each year. They know this attack places us in a financial stranglehold—and those of you who do not agree are, at best, naïve.

"*'Debt is okay'* has been everyone's mantra. Financial responsibility was an anathema. Then 2007 and 2008 happened, and that world turned upside down. In 2009 alone, a third of suburban Americans fell deeply into debt. Buyouts of major banks and mortgage companies increased our national debt by the hundreds of billions."

Mumbles from the crowd.

"In effect, the American expansiveness trapped tens of millions in rapidly devalued housing. Nobody wanted their gas-guzzlers. Nobody wanted energy-sucking homes now that they owed more than they paid. The only buyer was the government." He took a drink of water.

"The federal government became the biggest commercial corporation in the world with no one qualified to run it. It is like giving your child their weekly allowance on Sunday, and on Monday, they say, 'I spent it all. I need more,' and you give it to them and repeat that every day.

"Complicit with this onerous debt, one unassailable statistic says it all: the US savings rate is the lowest of all the top industrial nations. The US savings rate hit a high of approximately three and a half percent in 2003. At the 2008 election, it had declined to less than one half of one percent, and today, that rate has dropped into the negative. It's sad, it's sickening, but it is solvable.

"The second ticking financial time bomb is government guarantees, which have profound budget consequences. These guarantees are made up of *explicit contingent liabilities:* government insurance schemes, which include FDIC deposits, pensions, war risk, crop and flood insurance. And there are *implicit contingent liabilities,* like those extraordinary bailouts and the costs of uninsured natural disasters, war reparations, and tax cut extensions.

"The third ticking time bomb relates to financial instruments. Rather than have everyone's eyes glaze over, I will discuss just one class of the instruments: *derivatives*. These are grouped into two classes: Exchange Trades comprised of stocks, commodities, and currency; and Over-the-Counter Traded Derivatives, like mortgage derivatives.

"Why do I want to talk about this? Because of the sheer dollar volumes involved. Just remember, in 2008 and 2009, we bailed out the mortgage markets with trillions of dollars we had to borrow. We are still paying for that mess."

He paused and looked up to the gallery, then resumed.

"The fourth ticking bomb is our continued reliance on foreign oil purchases that is sucking over seven hundred billion dollars per year from the life blood of our people.

"You conspiracy advocates will love this one: there are people in this country who dictate the foreign oil policy. That's right, OPEC does not dictate the price of oil; a secret cabal in this country does."

He stepped back from the podium, raising his arms, palms up.

"Look up to the gallery; if you haven't all ready, you may recognize almost every chairman, CEO, president, or CFO of America's oil, natural gas, coal, shale, wind, solar, water, and nuclear companies and organizations."

Members on the floor craned their collective necks to see the hundreds of men and women looking down on them.

"The oil executives all know about this. Effective one half hour ago, after I entered this chamber, an order was executed to immediately reduce our purchase of foreign oil overall by ten percent."

Shocked cries filled the House.

"Before the nuclear attack on Detroit, gas was selling at an average of $3.88 a gallon for regular. Instead of exploding to over five dollars a gallon, as some pundits have predicted, this administration with unselfish cooperation from these men and women . . ." and again he gestured to the gallery. "Tomorrow, our American oil wholesalers will reduce the price of gasoline in all octane grades twenty cents per gallon.

A commotion began to grow, and Macdonald raised his powerful voice.

"With the oil companies' help, local authorities will be able to enforce this at the pump. All price gougers will lose their licenses to do business and be prosecuted to the fullest extent of the law. We couldn't do this without these folks."

Many members looked up to the gallery, maybe seeking out an oil executive they knew. Macdonald rearranged his cheat sheets.

"Oil reserves will be used to cover any shortages, which, by the way, we don't expect. We will begin drilling where licenses have been unused. We will produce twelve percent more crude oil within six months. They," making a smaller gesture at the gallery, "said this can be done."

"When we attain our needed production figure, we will repeat the procedure. Within the year one very large, new refinery will be opened in southern Alaska. We will also buy gasoline from Canada, utilizing their new refinery. Plans for refineries in this country have languished in desk drawers. We are going to fast-track the approval process."

There were groans and cheers. Congress wasn't expecting this.

"We will increase the use of natural gas. We will install incentives to convert all urban bus fleets to natural gas, as was done here in Washington years ago. We will spread that out to whatever else is practicable and give tax credits for doing it."

Applause.

"Along the way some environmental areas will be disturbed; however, our environment is resilient, and we will consult with environmentalists on how to restore or improve all lands affected.

"We will begin building new nuclear energy facilities. We have millions of low-income, poverty-ridden citizens who cannot absorb the added energy costs. With no positive action from us, these costs could double or triple and people will needlessly die. We must act now!"

Loud cheers burst forth.

"Ticking time bomb five, exploding before your very eyes, is entitlements: Medicare, Medicaid, and Social Security. Your own Congressional Budget Office estimates that by the year 2025, over fifty cents of every dollar collected in taxes will go to supporting these areas. Combined with the interest on the debt, which is estimated at about sixteen cents on the dollar, the total payout reaches over sixty-five cents of every dollar collected before we get to the rest of what this country needs.

"Thomas Jefferson wrote, *'Democracy will cease to exist when you take away from those who are willing to work and give to those who would not.'*" Applause began to roll again, but he held up his hands and said loudly, "*'Therefore,'* Jefferson went on, *'it is incumbent on every generation to pay its own debts as it goes. A principle which if acted on would save one-half the wars of the world.'*"

This received a mixed reaction.

"Federal programs, no matter how well-intended, eventually become boondoggles. The way to recovery is for every one of us to pitch in, as is being done this very minute in the Midwest. We cannot stifle economic growth and expect financial handouts to cover up our sins!"

There was an explosion of applause. He took a long drink.

"To get the alternative fuel program off the ground, we will have the US Treasury loan the fund one hundred billion dollars, which will be equally matched by the oil companies. That two hundred billion dollars will be repaid beginning the sixth year of operations at no interest, over the ensuing five-year period.

"I put a lot on the table tonight, but I am sure not unexpectedly. As you may remember from the Centrists' campaign, we ran on this five-point program. You will receive an encapsulated version tonight and the more detailed one tomorrow.

"We call this," and he held up a stapled eighteen-page manuscript, "the Fiscal Recovery Act of 2013. Members of my staff are at the press gallery door with copies. One to a customer." He paused and looked from one side of the great chamber to the other. "We need an up or down vote on this by noon on Friday."

Gasps and protests were shouted, but the louder applause drowned them out.

He raised his voice. "With three viable political parties in the House and Senate, you will have to fashion a new way of getting things done. So let's work together. We have precious little time.

"Some ideologues, members of the media, and bloggers will try their best to upset things and pick apart this program. Just remember, if we do not set these programs in motion, we won't survive. Faced with a mammoth physical recovery, the ensuing rebuilding, and our national indebtedness, runaway inflation is a reality, setting us in an irreversible tailspin into oblivion.

"I ask all members, if you don't think this country is teetering on the brink of an economic catastrophe, to bring that to the White House tomorrow morning, and we will hear you out. And please, only one person representing one argument. Do not bring anything that is not supportable and corroborated with names and dates. Spin and anecdotal posturing will get the boot."

The Recovery Act of 2013 was a slap to many of their faces. It would now be up to the Centrist senators and representatives to push for action.

"I thank you all for your time. Please pray for the salvation of our country. God bless America."

Prodigious clapping ensued.

Macdonald turned to the Speaker and shook his hand. Smiles were exchanged. Macdonald had always liked the Speaker, which was why the Centrists supported him. Right now, though, Macdonald wasn't so sure the feeling was mutual.

25

White House
Thursday, January 24
0500 hours

The alarm clock in the executive mansion's master bedroom went off at 0500. Macdonald rolled over and hit the *off* button, but did not pause his motion and swung his feet onto the floor. He quickly slipped into workout attire and half jogged to the elevator, exchanging "good mornings" with protective service agents along the way.

He and an agent descended to the lower level and jogged lightly to the workout room in the basement of the Eisenhower Executive Office Building adjacent to the West Wing of the White House.

When he arrived, there were three men, surprisingly no one he knew, working out. They greeted each other cordially, and Macdonald went straight to work, starting with a series of stretches. He then did twenty minutes on the treadmill at a comfortable eight-minute-mile pace. He followed that with some work on the free weights, concluding his session with ten minutes on a Stairmaster.

He toweled off and headed to the residence for a quick shower. He donned slacks and a favorite pullover and entered the Oval Office at 0628, just ahead of his scheduled intelligence briefing from DCIA Eubanks. He hoped for a quiet morning leading up to his lunch date with Alexandra. He poked his head into Cynthia's office. "Good morning."

"Good morning, sir. Your speech is receiving high grades and so are you. Director Eubanks cleared the gate a minute ago."

"Okay. I'm going to try out my new breakfast routine."

The card table he had requested was set up on the east side of his office, near the French doors that led out onto the colonnade. Two straight-back chairs were arranged so he and Eubanks could sit and discuss the state of the world, while enjoying a little nosh.

His standing order was for coffee in a pot on a heat pad; orange juice; a sliced cinnamon raisin bagel, heated, but not toasted; and light cream cheese. He poured his coffee to half full—he liked it steadily hot—and picked up the morning bulletin with excerpts from major East Coast newspapers and hard-copied Internet headline stories. He scanned two articles on his speech and one on the DTO recovery.

The Internet was reporting no decline in the dollar against the euro, after a six-percent drop the day before, which was considerably less than pundits had predicted. It appeared to him that the European markets were hedging, waiting for the American exchanges to open in three hours, the first time since the bombing.

Asian markets had been slightly down earlier, but losses appeared minimal. *Hopefully, a positive reaction to my speech,* he thought. Some articles said his emphasis on economic changes and his charge to Congress to make these changes happen was a surprise. That was the kind of reaction he wanted and why he had emphasized his intention to protect America's financial well-being and global economy.

One article opined that he seemed more troubled by Congress than who the bombers were. Macdonald liked the comparison. The bomb was history, the economy was the future. *We'll get the bombers.*

Cynthia's door opened, and DCIA Eubanks entered.

"Good morning, Mr. President."

"Good morning, Jim. Have some breakfast?"

Macdonald poured him some coffee.

"I take it black," Eubanks said.

"Good man."

Macdonald waited for the director to retrieve two folders and place his closed case on the floor before handing the DCIA his mug. Eubanks placed the famous "Presidential Daily Brief" (PDB) on the table and took the mug. "Thank you, sir."

Macdonald had been thanking his lucky stars since the bombing that he'd retained Eubanks. Following his election, he'd had several heart-to-heart discussions on the state of the world with Eubanks, and he'd liked Eubanks's answers. The director was highly thought of inside Langley and around the world. Reggie Howard thought him to be a consummate professional.

"Hope you don't mind my informality."

"No sir. I'll just minimize my dog-and-pony show."

Macdonald laughed. "An added benefit I hadn't considered."

Eubanks handed him his PDB folder, and then sat quietly, his demeanor suddenly dour, which Macdonald picked up on immediately.

"A problem?" he asked. "Something I said?"

"Oh no, sir. It's in what you are about to read."

Macdonald scanned the first page and got the gist of the director's concern. When he looked up, Eubanks spoke.

"They are a rarely-heard-from Sunni terrorist splinter group, which had been active in the late stages of the Iraq war, 2009 to 2011."

"Is this the group that wanted to dismantle the Iraqi constitutional government that we helped set up?"

Eubanks showed surprised that he knew that. "The same. They wanted an independent Iraqi state based on Sharia law."

"Why would they take responsibility for the bombing? Hadn't we given up on self-confessions after the first day?"

"Yes sir, we had, and we question the legitimacy of this claim, but we can't ignore it."

"I agree."

"At best, there are two hundred members, a tiny percent of their size two years ago. We first picked this up in Baghdad yesterday—gossip on the street type of thing. We had not heard any static about the bombing from anyone."

"This is ridiculous," Macdonald said, slapping the paper he was reading. "They want one trillion dollars? What do they smoke over there?"

Eubanks snorted a laugh and took a swig of coffee. "This is good."

Macdonald sat back, eying the DCIA. "You're not taking this seriously, are you?"

"Oh, I'm taking it seriously, sir; I just don't happen to believe it. We give it no credibility. I do worry they may make a big noise, say they have another bomb, get the media interested."

"Ouch!" Macdonald stood, but waved Eubanks to stay put. "You'll find I do a lot of thinking on my feet, but that doesn't mean everybody else has to." He walked around, ran a hand through his short-cropped hair, obviously perturbed.

"I was told this would be a tough job, Jim, because of the unexpected. We're getting an overabundance of that. Last night, we thought we had a grasp on what tack to take, show our country and the rest of the world what we're prepared to fix.

"A collapse now would make 2008 look like a hiccup. According to the papers, Internet, and social media, we have the people's attention, because we are showing we can handle a major physical recovery while working feverishly to head off a financial disaster. We have pleaded with our own radicals in this country to not act against anybody they think bombed us. I'm sure you've seen the e-mails and the rest."

"I have, sir. They could get us into things that—"

"Darlene," Macdonald said into his intercom.

"Good morning, Mr. President."

"I need you."

"I'm on my way."

He joined Eubanks at the card table. "We've got to blunt this thing before it gets legs, Jim."

Darlene entered and saw the DCIA. "Good morning, Mr. Director."

Eubanks stood as she walked to him and shook his hand.

Macdonald handed her his folder. "We have trouble in River City. An Islamic splinter group." He paused to let her scan it. "We're concerned this could elevate into a Bin Laden–type claim."

"Oh," she exclaimed, lowering the paper. "This doesn't make sense."

"Right, but they may claim they have a second bomb."

"Planted in our country?" She looked at the CIA director.

Macdonald said, "That's the dilemma. I'd like to make light of this. Warn people off rumors of this type. But if I'm wrong and another bomb goes *boom*, I'm out of a job."

"So?"

"How 'bout we go public with what we know. Go into Iraq covertly, grab these creeps, and question them. Call Ambassador Hendrickson and read this to him, get his reaction. Then call Alisa and see what she has on this. Jim, share this with Lowell Kuhn at NSA. I'll hold off saying anything, if I'm given that luxury. But we have to act fast."

"I'll get to A.J.," Darlene said, "so he won't be blindsided if a reporter asks about 'a rumor.' He can say we are asking around, need a short moratorium."

"Jim, tell Darlene what you know about these folks."

The DCIA did so, while Macdonald called Cynthia.

"So, what's the plan?" Darlene asked when Eubanks finished.

"Search them out," Eubanks said.

Cynthia entered. "I have some phone messages." She handed them to the president.

Darlene went to the phone.

Macdonald flipped through them.

"Sir," Cynthia said, "we need to increase our phone- and mail-screening efforts. We're stretched thin, and our people are still learning their way around here."

Eubanks interjected. "Maybe we could get some people over here whose business it is to screen."

Cynthia brightened. "That would be a big help, sir."

"I'll make a call," said Eubanks

Darlene and Cynthia moved away from the president and conferred quietly.

"Cynthia," Eubanks called out. "How many?"

She thought a moment. "Four," she replied.

Eubanks went back to his phone, and Macdonald gestured the women to join him.

"I'm not sold on this group being the bad guys," he said. "However, the threat of them blabbing about a second bomb planted somewhere in our country creates a disastrous scenario. Darlene, get the Attorney General and FBI director here ASAP. Cynthia, get Gus Vaughn."

"Yes sir."

"Jim," he called out, gesturing that he had a question. Eubanks put his phone on hold. "Let's get all the intelligence folks on a conference call in fifteen, twenty minutes. I'm going up to change."

"You don't need to, sir," Darlene said. "I called your valet. He'll be here momentarily."

26

The seats around the White House Situation Room conference table were filled and aides sat in chairs along one wall.

"My gut tells me there's something missing," Macdonald said, looking at the summary points displayed on two large computer screens. "I'm not faulting anyone's efforts; it's just that I don't see anything definitive."

"Mr. President." Gus Vaughn's voice came from the speaker. "I agree. We don't have one damn fact . . . because these Iraqi SOBs are lying through their teeth."

There was some squirming from the intelligence and security professionals, who had been pulled in from CIA, DIA, and NSA, along with National Security Advisor Alisa Padget, senior staff, and assorted military officers.

Macdonald didn't react, but smiled inwardly. The retired marine colonel will take a little getting used to for some. He answered his former "tunnel rat": "Jim and I thought that, earlier, Gus; however, in my current position of running the security of this country, I felt we needed to be a little more circumspect."

"I hear you and agree," Vaughn said in his regular tone. "But this is just between us guys and gals, right?"

"Absolutely," Macdonald replied.

"Secretary Vaughn?" Eubanks asked. "You worked over there. Do you still have any contacts in Iraq?"

"Some."

"So then, you're familiar with Islamic fanaticism. Why would this run-of-the-mill sect want to take on this burden?"

"That's a good question with only one answer."

"Exactly," Eubanks replied.

"Face!" Vaughn spat out. "Nobody's been paying the poor little boys any attention, and I mean in their own neighborhood. They want to show everybody that they're still the real deal."

"And they most likely have lost conscripts to groups showing more promise," NSA Deputy Director Nolan Stroud said.

"Right," Vaughn shot back. "They're losing influence. Their ego is bruised, like you inferred, Director. How do we prove that?"

"If this is what we're dealing with, Jim, how can we lock it down?" asked Macdonald.

"Find out where the bomb came from; see if there are two missing," Vaughn said flatly.

Macdonald said, "Ambassador Hendrickson and General Bingham are making some headway in that regard, but we need to put more boots on the ground, intelligence-wise."

Someone cleared his throat, getting Macdonald's attention. It was Director Eubanks, his eyebrows raised.

"Hold on, maybe we already have?" Macdonald acknowledged Eubanks.

"As you requested, Mr. President, CIA added General Bingham and retired Sergeant Major Egan to a special task force. They and three of my officers flew out of Andrews 0330 hours for Baghdad, right after we knew of this problem. I have two operatives currently there who will join up with them later today. We can't predict a timeline; however, even without the forensics from DTO, the scent is getting stronger."

Macdonald beamed. "Great, Jim. But in the meantime, how do I handle this if these bozos go public? Will our press people respect our moratorium?"

Darlene shook her head. "The scoop will be too tantalizing not to break it. I've left instructions with the press staff to call me the minute anyone hears anything about this coming from the media, sir. A.J.'s hanging with the media, just in case something breaks. We're monitoring Twitter and Facebook. NSA is concentrating on cell phone activity coming out of Iraq."

Macdonald was pacing. "Other than self-aggrandizement, what can anyone gain from admitting to something that they didn't do?"

"Cause trouble, ride the coattails of the real killers," the NSA's Stroud said. "Show their Middle East cohorts they're still around."

"Maybe they're checking you out, sir," said Eubanks.

Some people in the room were startled, but Darlene gently laughed. "Well, they're in for a surprise if they think we're anything like our predecessors, who usually fried their own butts when it wasn't even necessary for them to turn on the burners. However, even if it's repugnant, we should look at it from the opposite side and see what if anything is agreeable from that perspective."

"I've been saved by that philosophy more than once, Jim," Macdonald said. "Earlier, I had thoughts of going public to hopefully dilute the news when it hit. However, it was pointed out to me there was more to lose than gain by that maneuver. There was no point in putting out a fire before it had been started." Chuckles and words of agreement rolled through the room at the president's self-deprecating humor.

"Okay, folks, enough. Let's find the perps who have not perked. And let's hope the next shoe that drops is our lucky one."

27

FBI Director Andy Thornton and Attorney General Martin Jamison were on one of the twin sofas in the Oval Office when Macdonald and Darlene walked in. Both stood and greeted the president and Chief of Staff. Darlene then went to a phone and buzzed Cynthia, who quickly entered the room.

"Pull a couple of those chairs over there up to the desk," Macdonald instructed, as he went behind it and sat. "Secretary Vaughn will be coming up on the scramble phone."

Cynthia whispered something to the president, who nodded, and she pressed a phone button.

"Mr. Secretary, do you know who's in here with me?"

"I sure do, Mr. President."

"Okay. It's all yours Director Thornton."

The FBI director cleared his throat. "Good day, Mr. Secretary. The coordination has been seamless, sir. We now know the type of ordnance used; it was confirmed onsite by NNSA's nuclear bomb specialists. They work with over a hundred countries to fight nuclear proliferation and terrorism, and have amassed considerable knowledge of all known bomb material.

"They helped to eliminate Libya's nuclear weapons program and closed down the Russian's Novniknova reactor in 2010, permanently shutting down the last remaining plutonium production reactors in Russia. It is NNSA's opinion that the nuclear warhead came from Gravastock in southwestern Russia, a few miles from the Ukrainian border, near Voroniak. It is very close to the Russian border, making it a short distance for extraction, sir."

"Man," chortled Vaughn, "ain't that something."

"I understand CIA's Advance Squad is being briefed as we speak," Thornton said.

Macdonald said, "Okay, what's happening with the criminal investigation in the DTO?"

"If I may, sir?" Attorney General Jamison asked, "Mr. Secretary, I'd like to say everyone is in awe of what you have accomplished in such a short period of time and with so many different organizations involved."

Vaughn laughed. "The vice president, Governor Carlton, and General Kirkpatrick get the kudos for all of that, Judge, but thank you. I'll pass along your props. The combined NNSA and the FBI forensic teams are doing a tremendous job. You must have some pretty weary folks out there, Director."

"Okaaay," Macdonald clapped and rubbed his hands together. "Now that we know where the bomb most likely came from, we could soon have an idea of how many devices are missing. What's next, Mr. Director?"

"The counterterrorism division is cross-checking all computers. After 9/11, we moved into a cooperative mode. I invite you to come see our operation after things cool down."

"I'll take you up on that. Gus, are there any Detroit City Hall personnel who have identified themselves to you? I'm thinking about the ground zero area being underwater and getting land records they might have stored outside the city. I know that's not my job, gentlemen, I'm asking to know if that approach might be relevant."

"You're right to ask," Vaughn said. "On the question of City Hall personnel, the answer is no, but the FBI has teams specially trained to recreate the infrastructure, right, Director?"

"Close, but yes. However, local knowledge would be of significant help. As to the devastation, our people say this exercise had to take more than rudimentary technical knowledge. A regular bomb guy couldn't have handled the assembly. They needed highly-trained technicians and scientists to dismantle, properly ship, and assemble the device."

"So," Vaughn jumped in, "how do nomadic Arabs go a thousand miles or more across a few borders and into a highly secure, guarded bunker, much less bring out one or two warheads and whatever else they needed, and then get them back over that same terrain?"

"That's the sixty-four-billion-dollar question, Gus," the AG said.

Macdonald leaned to his left. "Darlene, call Nadine. We'll need some diplomatic guidance on how to deal with the Iraqi government. And call Director Eubanks. We need him here ASAP. We need to put those two together and find a way to get these *Iraqi Banditos*."

"Mr. President?" Thornton said. "I'd like to assign one of my antiterrorism

ADs to that group to help with our coordination. It's obvious whoever did this had stateside help. We may be looking at some homespun traitors."

"You've got it," Macdonald said, enthused.

Darlene said, "I'll take care of Secretary of State Rankin and SecDef Garrett—who can talk to General Gibbons, if that hasn't happened already. You never know when we might need military manpower and technical support to assist in the DTO."

She collected her things. "I'll also ask Ambassador Hendrickson, in his new capacity, to audit the Eubanks-Rankin task force." She left the office.

Director Thornton watched her leave. "If you don't mind my saying, sir, and I barely know Ms. Sweetwater, but she acts like a veteran COS. Better. She is very impressive."

"She was the glue who held us together throughout the campaign, Director," the AG said.

"Okay, let's get back to the Islamic cells here," Macdonald urged. "Our incoming mail and calls are accusing them fifteen-to-one to be the bombers, and that's a dangerous ratio."

"Yes sir," Thornton replied. "Fortunately, only half a dozen Mosques have sustained minor damage. Your requests for calm and asking folks to put their focus on recovery efforts must be having an effect. It has helped us and local police from having to divert valuable assets from the investigation to criminal activities."

AG Jamison jumped in. "We've received useful tips about groups proposing to take unilateral action, and the Bureau has been able to intercept or ward off several actions. We've arrested thirty-seven suspects around the country. We're flooding social media outlets with our public relations campaign against vigilantes."

Macdonald nodded. "Use everything we've got, water down the hatred. Even some in the White House press corps are developing weird scenarios. Any diversion of manpower to protect innocent Muslims will drag down the recovery—"

Darlene rushed in. "CBN just went public. The Iraqi group we were talking about are taking credit for the bombing."

A.J. rushed into the room through the same door behind Darlene. "The shit's hit the fan, sir. The press room is going ballistic. CBN—"

"I know," the president said, standing.

"What are you going to do, boss?" Vaughn asked over the speaker.

"The first thing is for us to stay calm. A.J., tell the press I'm on my way. Alert the electronic media. This is a Code Red directive—we'll use the emergency broadcast intercept on all radio, cable, and broadcast stations."

A.J. flew out of the office as a phone rang. Darlene answered and quickly said, "Sir, it's General Gibbons."

Macdonald took the phone. "General? . . . Fine, as many as you can." He hung up. "We're sending US troops to protect mosques. The National Guard will stay with the recovery. Martin," he turned to the AG, "how can I legally declare Martial Law?"

28

Oval Office
Prepping for Press Briefing
Thursday, January 24
1125 hours

President Macdonald paced, waiting for his staff to corroborate information, readying him to talk again to the country and the world. Cynthia was concerned that staff hadn't fully prepared him for a Q&A.

He reassured her. "I have to do this. I will just admit to not knowing something if I don't know. I won't spin it. This is the first time we've been faced with a real enemy, even though I will emphatically say their claim is bogus."

The number of people in the Oval Office had swelled considerably, but did not include Darlene who chose the quiet of her office to carefully prepare his cheat sheets.

A.J. entered. "TV's requested we go on the half hour, seven minutes from now."

"I'll be in my study," Macdonald said abruptly. He went in, stripped off his shirt and soaked a rolled up hand towel with cold water and placed it on the back of his neck. He repeated the compress two times before toweling off and redressing. He straightened his tie, looked himself up and down.

Mom would approve.

Darlene greeted him with a stack of her cheat sheets. She had a one-page bulleted cover page, like an agenda, which he would place alongside the more detailed sheets. She had armed him as much as possible.

An anxious A.J. called to him. "Mr. President."

They went through Cynthia's area and the agents opened a path through staff, who called out *atta boy, good luck, you'll be great*. He was hustled down the stairs and into the small anteroom off the Press Briefing Room. This was the fourth time in three days he'd waited there.

A TV stage manager cued A.J., who entered the briefing room and said, "Ladies and gentlemen, the President."

They all rose as Mike Macdonald walked purposefully up onto the small platform, waved to everyone to be seated, and placed Darlene's material on the podium as prescribed. His eyes then met the feed camera straight on.

"This is not a good morning. We are here again because we are faced with a lie."

There was an instant rustle of moving bodies on chairs.

This was not a time for platitudes. "We have been dealing with this lie since early this morning, when it was only a street rumor in Baghdad. We and some of you sitting before me know a lot about this motley group, which at one time was the largest Sunni terrorist organization in Iraq.

"They fought al-Qaeda; they fought us; they fought the Shia; they fought the Iraqi military and the Iraqi government that we helped establish; and then in 2009, they faded away. Their numbers reduced to a couple hundred. They became yesterday's news. The few who are left are no longer the big bad boys, not even in their own neighborhood. They are frauds."

He felt a little dry and took a drink. *At least my hand isn't shaking.* He replaced the glass. He had on his linebacker eyes.

"The people who have made this barbaric claim defame all Muslims. They are shameful and disrespectful of all Islam. Their only explanation so far is that they want a trillion dollars, or they would do it again."

There was an explosion of noise from the press corps.

He put his hand up, but the noise was slow to subside. "Please, calm down. They cannot—I repeat, they cannot—do something *again*, when they never did that something *in the first place*. Get that straight. They did . . . not . . . bomb us," he said slowly and emphatically. "They do not have a second bomb or a third bomb. They never had the first bomb." He shook his head. "Believe me. What I say is true.

"We are painfully aware there was a bomb. When nobody laid claim to this horrific act against us in the first few hours, it was because the real bombers didn't want us to know their identity. I want to know and you want to know—we will know! I want retribution. I want the murderers. They took millions of our friends, family, and countrymen. I want them real bad! Believe me, we are working on it. We are working on *recovery and retribution.*"

He broke his gaze to look down at Darlene's table of contents. He took another drink, replaced the glass, and looked around the room. His heart was pounding.

"You here in the White House briefing room," he said his voice now calmer, "want to ask me questions. Well, I've just answered the biggest one you could have posed. You won't find the *'who dunit'* answer in this room, because today we don't have one. We may know in an hour, a day, a week . . . we don't know now. However, I can share a piece of positive news: we have fully identified the bomb. This has happened because of the most outstanding effort of skill and determination I have ever witnessed, and believe me, I've seen some miraculous bravery and heroism in my time."

No one was coughing or squirming now.

"The FBI, amidst all the chaos surrounding this bogus claim, called me a half hour ago from ground zero. The specialists—nuclear bomb scientists, bomb investigators, forensic experts, and counterterrorist agents—put the final piece of the puzzle together and now know the make, class, and model of the bomb."

He thought a couple of news people were going to jump out of their seats.

He put his hands up. "No, I am prohibited from telling you more. I'm sure some of you have been doing your homework and putting your years of journalism to good work.

"Now, the question becomes one of character. Those of you who may have already uncovered the *where* are faced with a delicate problem. What is the value of a scoop? Will you rush to judgment, as the news organization that scooped all of you erroneously did? Now they have well-deserved egg on their face. We could have saved them that embarrassment, if they'd just called us. But no, they had to be first.

"They caused unnecessary grief and unrest in our country. What is the cost of the people's right to know? I think I've satisfied that question. One of you may uncover where the bomb came from, but that in no way will positively translate into who used it. We will know exactly where it came from, but we won't know who brought it here."

He took out a handkerchief and wiped the perspiration from his face.

"I am sorry, but my bile is up. A ragtag group makes a claim, and you begin jumping all over the place, screaming at us. Where is your famous corroboration? Do you trust that source? Have you verified their claim? No, you just started screaming. You took an unsubstantiated, flimsy claim that bears not one iota of proof and turned it into scandalous headline news.

"Unless my words reach every segment of our society, which has shown remarkable restraint, this irresponsible journalistic act, this misplaced fervor, could very well get more innocent Americans killed."

He saw that last blast had not gone over very well. Good.

"When the embers of hate are fanned into flames, terrible things can happen. We, unfortunately, have hate groups in this country. That's what they are all about, just like the miserable Iraqis who laid claim to killing millions of us. I don't want anyone girding up their venomous hatred and . . ." He half shrugged at his audience.

"Moving on. I want everyone to understand that we do not have one iota of proof against anyone. We have no hint of who the perpetrators are, and we will not make assumptions. Listen to me: we do not know who blew up Detroit and Windsor, Canada. But we do know it wasn't the ones who have claimed the act. Even so, we sure would like to talk to them."

He glanced at Darlene's papers in front of him. "Okay, that's another question answered. We have many other matters going on 24/7, including the recovery work, where millions of hard-working Americans are giving of themselves to ease other's burdens. We also have the Recovery Act of 2013, which I proposed to Congress last night."

He smiled and raised his eyebrows. The audience before him seemed uninterested in this; still, he continued.

"The Senate and House will have to forgive me; we won't be able to deliver the detailed report to them at noon today as promised. We were working on it, but became sidetracked with this. But our economic recovery is as important as ever to the life of this country, as is our national security.

"I can understand your mistrust of your government, seeing how many times you have been let down, but I hope you can see that we, your new government, do not vacillate. We are not wafflers. We will act, and are acting, on what needs to be done for you.

"Okay, out there in our great country: listen up. I don't want the list of bad guys to include misguided Americans because of some vengeance they perpetrate on innocent fellow citizens.

"Lastly, I am saddened to say that Attorney General Jamison and FBI Director Thornton are prepared to enact Martial Law under my authority in areas where trouble does break out. Attacks on the innocent people will end in arrests.

Vigilantism will diminish our recovery work, meaning that supplies and assistance for the needy will be encumbered. That would be traitorous. So any such act of hatred will be considered an act of treason and be treated accordingly."

The president emptied his glass. He needed to pause and give his pulse rate a chance to slow down. He took a long, slow, deep breath.

He lowered his voice, but not his intensity. "Please be a good neighbor and take care of each other. Do not take the law into your own hands. We all need a lot of love right now. We must keep our focus on helping our casualties and pray for miracles of survival. I ask every American to put his or her efforts into support at all levels.

"I hope I have helped you understand the truth. I assure you that the people in my administration are working tirelessly on your behalf. We will not let you down. God bless you and God bless America."

He took a step back, then turned and started off the platform.

This time the maligned press corps was not about to let him leave quietly. On his turn to go, they began yelling questions and closing in on the podium. The Secret Service moved swiftly, blocking off the enraged journalists. Macdonald was whisked out of the briefing room and taken to the Oval Office.

"I'm not sure whether I should cheer or cry," Darlene said.

Kap was one of the first to reach the president, whom he gave a spirited handshake. "I haven't seen that good a whipping since I broke my mother's favorite vase. That hurt for weeks."

"You showed you were in charge," SecState Rankin said.

"We have a lot of irons in the fire," said Darlene.

One of which, Macdonald hoped, was his appointment with Alexandra.

29

Once the Oval Office had been cleared out of well-wishers, Macdonald looked at his press secretary. "Well?"

"I would say the mood was vituperative, sir," A.J. said.

"Any foaming at the mouth?"

"It was messy. They didn't get their 'air' time."

"Unfortunately, that's probably the most important thing to them. Look, I answered the questions before they were asked, didn't I?"

"Yes, but you preempted their follow-ups. You know, those little 'I want to get my position clearly stated' questions."

Macdonald laughed, "Are they really all prima donnas?"

"Actually, most are pretty good eggs."

"They've got to know I'm angry with them."

A.J. looked at his boss like a little puppy, begging.

"Okay, what do I need to do to soothe the savage—"

"Give them some time?"

Macdonald looked at his watch: 1208 hours. "Right now, for about twenty minutes, or until Darlene comes and gets me for my next appointment. No TV, audio, or recording devices."

A.J. had grabbed the phone even before his boss stopped talking. "Joyce, announce that the president is on his way to the briefing room and that there are to be no cameras or audio of any kind." He hung up.

"Let's go through Cynthia's office. I need to alert her where to send the medics," slapping the six-foot-two press secretary on the back.

The press corps members who had stayed in the building were mostly on their smartphones or standing in small groups when A.J. entered and called out, "the

President," and stepped onto the podium. The president held at the door. A.J. spotted two manned cameras.

"Ground rules," A.J. said, pointing at the cameras. "No cameras, no live feeds or taping. No film. President Macdonald has an appointment in eighteen minutes or whenever Chief Sweetwater comes to get him. Okay? TV, film, cells, wireless, cameras off, inactive. We're using up your time."

The lights on the two TV cameras went off. "If any audio or video piece surfaces from this session, you will all lose your White House credentials. Police yourselves." He saw two still photographers put their cameras down. A.J. stared at them. "In the camera case. Police yourselves; we're serious." He scanned the room. Once satisfied, he said, "Thank you," and stood aside. "Mr. President."

Macdonald stepped up and went to the left side of the podium. He did not use a microphone. He assumed a casual stance, hoping to project a friendly appearance.

"First," he said, in an apologetic manner, "I meant no offense earlier. I was mad as hell about the phony claim. Look, we have a lot of stuff going on here and 'you know what' is piling up. Plus, I had things I wanted to say, and TV had asked if we could keep it under a half hour. Let's start on the first row and go from my left to right."

There was a comical scramble for the two open chairs on the front row, losers spilling into the second row or standing. He nodded to a middle-aged woman in seat number one.

"Sasha Carmelo, *Cleveland Plain-Dealer.* How can you be so certain the Iraqi group didn't do it?"

"Intelligence. People on the ground in Iraq. Because of where the bomb came from and because it was early-morning gossip on the streets."

"A follow. What time did you learn of it?"

"About 0635 hours. It was the first item on the PDB. Yes," he said, nodding to the next reporter on the first row.

"Shouldn't you have known sooner?" an MSNBC reporter known to him asked.

"Why? I mean, it was gossip and reported to me as such. I didn't like the news, but waking me at 0330, for that?" He cocked his head, as if to say *come on.*

"Look, folks, if this is all you have, A.J. can answer all this for you." He nodded to the next in line.

"You mentioned you know the ID of the bomb and where it came from. Could you elaborate on that?"

"Could, but won't. It would serve no purpose. Why tip our hand? If you don't believe me, you don't believe me. Maybe the bombers will think we're bluffing, which is not all bad. We'll play our cards as we see them. Besides, if we said where, we'd put some valuable assets at risk. Yes," he said, to the next in line.

"Angela Rodrigo, *Philadelphia Inquirer.* Last night, you laid out an extremely vigorous agenda to Congress. Have you heard back from them? Are they adhering to your schedule?"

"No and that's okay. We have backed our request off until Tuesday afternoon of next week, barring any more surprises. Look, we want our agenda to begin as quickly as possible. Until the bogus *'We did it!'* this morning, the e-mails . . . we've gone from two to six veteran screeners answering the public's calls and categorizing their e-mails. The incoming was running better than eighty percent in favor of one or more of the items I put forth. The public wants action."

Rodrigo followed. "Will you be producing the more detailed outline for your recovery plan later today?"

Mike grinned. "Man, you're tough." There were some chuckles. "You remind me of a former college coach."

No chuckles, just a stirring.

"If you can promise us no more time-consuming interruptions, Chief Sweetwater and her staff could have it whipped into shape and on its way to the Hill tomorrow. And . . ." he paused for effect, looking them over, ". . . have copies for you all as well."

The questioning continued along the same line. He relaxed. It seemed that the DTO search-and-recovery was being given high grades, for which he gave credit to Vice President Dudley for her excellent organizing abilities.

Darlene came in a little after the half hour.

"Okay, I've got to go," Macdonald said. "I'm sorry if I didn't get to all of you. If you still have questions, write them out and give them to A.J. We'll get back to you." He left a less disgruntled group than the one he had started out with. In retrospect, he realized that he needed to be more cooperative.

"Ms. Mednorov is in the residence. You understand that there will be an agent in the room, don't you?"

"I didn't, but I can understand it."

"They'll be in eyesight, but far enough away to give you speaking privacy."

"Fair enough." He felt his anxiety level rising as he split off from Darlene and walked to the mansion and into the waiting elevator. The two agents trailing him stopped there, as one spoke a quiet message. The door closed. It was just shy of three weeks since he'd seen Alex, but it felt like a year, similar to how the past three days had felt.

The elevator door opened, and he was greeted by Agent Hines, who had been on duty in New York during Alex's first visit.

That was smart planning; a friendly face must be reassuring to her.

They walked together into the sitting room, which sat between the master bedroom and the private dining room. Alexandra was sitting at the end of a sofa facing him, her legs crossed, looking at a magazine. She looked up.

"Hey, tar heel," he said, extending his arms.

"Mr. President," she said formally, walking to him in her strong stride and accepting his embrace and the exchange of a kiss on each cheek. They backed off and looked at each other. "Michael," she said lovingly. "It was nice to see Agent Hines, a person I had met before."

"We have a light lunch coming up," he said, feeling his throat muscles slightly tighten.

"Yes. Your Chief of Staff gave me some choices. I will try your clam chowder and a Caesar salad."

"Good choices. Let's sit."

He dragged over an armchair to sit opposite her as she sat back down on the sofa. "I guess you are well situated in your apartment."

"Oh, yes, I am near here, next to the George Washington University. It is nice to be among students."

He knew where her mind was. "I'm sorry I've been so hard to reach."

"No . . . your responsibilities; it is so terrible," she said soothingly.

Through her tone, he felt her empathy.

"Yeah, it's been a little hectic this morning. You may have heard."

"Yes. At the World Bank, they all want to watch you, hear what you say. Your words have such impact."

"I hope. What's going on?"

"It is something terrible," she blurted loud enough that Agent Hines took notice. "It is Raisa."

That startled him. "Before I left Moscow, Vasiliy received a directive from Raisa telling him to be prepared to transfer one trillion euros from the Central Bank into twelve mostly foreign corporations. Vasiliy said it was a most unusual investment tactic by a government."

"Do you know if he followed through?"

"No. I went to London and then came here. Vasiliy would not call. I know he was fearful to not do as she said."

"What do you think prompted something like that?" he asked, keeping his voice soft, as his pulse raced.

Her expression darkened. "Vasiliy did say he had researched the companies. They were registered corporations only, no employees or product."

Shells! Shell companies? "The monies that Vasiliy controlled, were they government money, not accounts of private investors?"

"He controls only the Central Bank government accounts."

"Oh my god," he said, standing and pacing.

She watched him apprehensively. "What?" she asked.

"Does anybody at World Bank know? Have you . . . ?"

"No. I tell only you."

"And they don't know you're here?"

"No. I am free to move about. I have no supervisor."

He called Darlene. "What's on my schedule later in the day?" He listened. "Okay. Let's round up the team for a six o'clock here. We'll feed them . . . right. It's a mind blower. Call Eubanks, the Ambassador, Kap, and Nadine. I may want Gus and Bryanna on a conference call too. We'll need Alexandra back here this evening . . . I realize that . . . no. . . I'll cover all that with you later . . . right."

He hung up. *Oh, man,* he thought, *what are we getting into?*

"Lexi," he said softly, addressing her as he had years earlier. "I'll need you back here around five, okay?"

"Yes," she said demurely. "I can be here."

30

Following his lunch with Alexandra, Macdonald met with Kap in the Oval Office. He finished telling the SecTres about the Russians, then watched as Kap's expression turned to one of abject amazement.

He said, "How could a country that fifteen, twenty years ago was decaying, fighting the black market, and bleeding economically get off the deck and deliver us a deadly blow?"

"Trillions of euros of oil, Kap."

"They drilled while we swilled."

Macdonald laughed wryly. "They've been laughing at our country's stupidity since the mid-'90s. While we were tied down in Iraq and their old nemesis Afghanistan, they were pumping oil and natural gas and building thousands of miles of pipelines throughout Asia."

"Shit, the fucking Congress, Mike—regardless of who was in charge—has run this country into the ground."

"Fortunately, we have now made that delinquency well known to the American people. I'm with you on the two major parties sharing equal blame. I vividly remember a conversation on that exact subject with you and Darlene when we began setting up our campaign and gathering hundreds of Centrists to run."

Kap grunted. "I don't know why you two ever wanted an old academic fart like me to join you. Don't get me wrong, I'm glad you did. Damn, Mike, our country's weaker than a sick kitten, and now you're saying somebody may have a valid economic scheme to tear our guts out?"

"Darlene and I have been on the phone from the moment Alex left until you got here. We've called all the movers and shakers we know. If another financial earthquake hits us, it could open a hole into which all of lower Manhattan could sink."

Kap ran a hand through his already unruly, white hair. "You paint a rosy picture," he said cynically. "Damn, Mike, I don't know what to suggest first, second, or third."

"The currency brokers I talked with didn't know of any major short seller of our dollar, yet there was considerable short traffic on the dollar prior to the bombing. It was spread out. Nobody saw anything abnormal, or so they say."

"No one smelled a rat?" Kaplan asked outraged.

"None they would admit to. What heavy shorting they saw was in foreign exchanges prior to the inauguration. Today's news must have been a joy to those who went short yesterday."

"Except when they bounced up a smidge after your speech. I haven't checked the exchanges the past couple of hours, but they probably covered. The shorts before Tuesday are sitting on billions of profits. Maybe we could float a loan from them and pay off our national debt."

Macdonald laughed. "The market has to know there's a bigger play going on. Traditionally our markets always bounce back, but if this one doesn't . . . well, we've got to plug the hole, fast."

Kaplan struggled to his feet. "We can freeze trading on all financial institutions and the commodity and currency markets. How 'bout I call Jacoby at the Federal Reserve."

"Good God, Kap, that'll set off a gigantic—"

"You're right," the SecTres replied, a glint in his eye.

Macdonald caught up with Kap's thinking. "I can put out a short statement about a major effort to drive down our financial companies, as well as the dollar. I could say it's a fraud, but most wouldn't believe me. Aha, how about this, Kap? We'll say it's in the best interests of the small investors. Go, cancel all trading, Kap."

The SecTres went to the phone and placed a call to Jacoby at the Federal Reserve to apprise him of the president's plan.

Macdonald buzzed Darlene, and then Cynthia, to come in. He wrote down the content of the message he had just verbally created. Kaplan reached the Fed chairman and explained the situation, and then returned to Macdonald, as Cynthia entered from one door and a moment later, Darlene from the other.

Macdonald explained the plan.

One of Cynthia's staff burst in and handed her a note.

"Sir," Cynthia said, "Harrison Fletcher, the president of—"

"I know, the New York Stock Exchange."

She nodded. "He's on line six."

Macdonald took two deep breaths and picked up the phone "Harrison," he said cheerily, and then abruptly held the phone out from his ear as Fletcher's bombast boomed.

Kap, hearing the venom being spewed at his president, went to Macdonald and reached out. "Here, let me handle this."

Macdonald gladly gave up the phone and moved to the women. "Cover your ears."

Darlene took his scribbled note and began to rework it for the press.

Kap's tirade was short, but the flags on the White House were still standing straight out. Then he sucked in a breath and quietly said into the phone, "If one trade is honored under this embargo, the SEC will come calling. Is that clear?"

Fletcher was still shouting.

"Will you be quiet?! The statement from the president is going out in one minute. Remember, it's because the Fed discovered severe irregularities, which must be analyzed. This is about a potential nuclear war, Harrison, so don't fuck this up." He gently hung up.

Macdonald had witnessed some of the famous Kaplan rages a dozen years earlier, but frankly didn't expect the old boy to still have it in him.

"I believe, sir, we can expect full compliance from the NYSE. Everyone else will grudgingly fall in line, I am sure."

"Thank you, Mr. Secretary."

"I've sent your message to A.J., sir," Darlene said.

"Mr. Kaplan," Cynthia asked. "Can I get you anything?"

The flushed-looking SecTres turned to the very proper, middle-aged lady and smiled. "A bottle of bourbon—hold the ice and the glass. I'm not fussy about the brand."

31

The news of the stock market's closing by order of the president was crushing to a country whose fingernails had been worn down to the quick, trying to dig out from under the rubble of a nuclear bomb. The media was screaming in the White House briefing room and all over radio and television. Social media exploded.

Calls came in from each political party's Capitol Hill leader asking why. Regularly scheduled programs were interrupted, some with scathing reports against the president's action.

The multimillion-dollar talking heads on cable news and financial networks were hysterical. They complained vigorously that the market was in recovery, and that given another day or two, it would have rebounded. Word came that the NYSE president had been hospitalized. NASDAQ was in turmoil, and the commodity exchanges were catatonic.

Accusations against the president flooded all media. The hero of the physical recovery was now a Satan: "There had been no advance warning to the press. Why was Macdonald being so obstreperously arrogant?" The press screamed that the engines of commerce would grind to a halt. The best comments Macdonald's supporters could come up with were ameliorating at best, such as suggesting that Macdonald was known as a financial guru and his plan would eventually become clear. Sane heads on Wall Street suggested caution.

While the haranguing continued, the president and a dozen of his closest advisors and cabinet officers were observing several TV screens in the Cabinet Room, giving it a sports-bar atmosphere: each screen was on a different channel.

Kaplan had called veteran financial experts to the White House, post haste. Some analysts' accusations were scary, even to the hardened veterans of political wars. The reactions to aired comments ebbed and flowed emotionally.

Unknown to outsiders, the public turmoil was, of course, exactly what Macdonald had hoped for. He wanted Americans to become fighting mad—even at the cost of his becoming the target for that anger. It was a gamble, but he had very few cards left to play.

Darlene, Cynthia, Kap, and he were the only ones who knew what had ignited this firestorm. Some in the crowded Cabinet Room thought they knew. Others didn't have a clue and said so. But for the most part, everyone present supported their president—except for a former NYSE member, who was vociferously expressing his opposition to the president's move. Macdonald listened patiently.

Cynthia waited for a pause and jumped in. "Sir," she said firmly enough to get her boss's attention. "May I have a word with you?"

He immediately recognized her expression of urgency.

"May we go into your office, please?" she asked.

"You'll have to excuse me," Macdonald said to the red-faced man. "I've got another problem brewing."

He didn't wait for a reply, but walked briskly out of the Cabinet Room and into the Oval Office. Kap was there with two men and a woman, all with very stern looks on their faces.

"Mr. President," Kap said. "The Asian exchanges have refused to go along with our request; they will not honor our situation and plan to trade American companies as usual, beginning about seven hours from now."

"Damn," Macdonald burst. "This shorting thing may be more widespread than I first thought, Kap. Could it be a multi-country conspiracy to drain us dry?" He was pacing now. "Okay. There has to be something we're not seeing. What strategies might they be employing? Let's play the elimination game."

"Right," Kaplan said. "We know now there's been a plethora of shorting coming from Europe and Asia. I'm told there may be as many as three dozen major players, almost like mutual funds, who have shorted over three trillion euros of shares in up to sixty major corporations and financial companies. I'm getting an update from the currency exchanges."

Macdonald continued his pacing. "There has to be shorting of the dollar too. Do you remember when one trader virtually brought down the Bank of England by shorting the pound?"

"That was a lesson for the ages," Kap sneered. "But the perpetrators' real target here is the driving down of the dollar as it relates to the euro. However, these actions don't seem to be coming from the usual suspects. And so far, nobody has spotted the Russians' hand in any of the deals."

"Unless," Macdonald said, a look of discovery on his face. "Unless they're into the shell game, insulating their participation under multiple layers to avoid detection."

"Of course. Shit, I should have seen that," Kap bemoaned.

"If you'd been sitting at home, looking at this thing play out, I bet you would have caught it right off. We're too damn close to see all of the ramifications."

"It's smooth as silk."

"Alexandra told me the Russian FSB wanted the Central Bank to deposit over a trillion euros into twelve corporations. Her brother heads that bank and said he could not do it. It would be like the government giving the private sector money, and I don't mean bailouts."

Kaplan was fully engaged. "Sounds like you're saying the Russians knew of our impending disaster and were positioning themselves to cash in when our dollar fell against the euro. The only way that kind of a commitment could be made is if they knew it was a sure thing."

Macdonald was nodding and pacing.

"We've been knocked down, Kap, but not out. We're badly injured, but we've got enough in the tank to—" he stopped. "Oh my God, that's it."

"What?"

"The killing blow. I know what it is!"

32

Oval Office
Thursday, January 24
1445 hours

For the first time in Mike Macdonald's short political career, he kept his own counsel and did not share his thoughts, not even with Darlene.

It had been an hour since his edict had created a firestorm of e-mails, texts, and phone calls: all heavily against his action. He had ordered Kaplan and his team to be insulated from any outside news. He wanted freewheeling, unconstrained, creative ideas that were not affected by him or anyone else.

He wanted pure brainstorming at the highest level. Kaplan and his experts were busy analyzing the effects of the market freeze. They were in the Cabinet Room. He wanted them to think outside the box.

He had told Kap, "Challenge them, even if you think they're right. A lot of those folks haven't been bogged down in government speak. Make them look at this as though they were home, watching the tube, and muttering to themselves about what should be done."

"You got it," Kap grinned.

Macdonald now sat alone at his desk and swiveled to look out over the South Lawn, his mind probing for ideas. He was calculating a strategy, but wondered if he were still on Wall Street, would he agree with the freeze? He wasn't sure. Of course, he wouldn't know the Russians were behind the bombing and the weakening of the dollar. And more audaciously, they weren't alone.

Then it hit him. He pressed the intercom button.

"Yes, Mr. President?" Cynthia asked.

"Get me the British Prime Minister. Seeing the hour, try his residence. I have a private number for him, if you need it. I will need to go on scramble. One more thing: this is just between you and me. Period."

"Yes sir."

He smiled, knowing how Cynthia loved being the only one "in the know." He took an address book from his bottom drawer and began making notes.

Darlene entered. "Kap has everyone scrambling and emphasized he wanted their ideas and not what they thought you might want to hear." She eyed his activity. "What are you up to?"

He rose and walked around his desk to her, saying softly. "Look, if what I am about to do backfires, I don't want you to have had any foreknowledge. I'm sorry, friend, but I have to go this alone."

She held her composure. "I saw your personal address book. Who are you calling?"

"Me? Did I say I was calling anybody?"

"All right, I'll leave you to your clandestine activities. Just be careful please. You know I don't give a damn about deniability. We came in here together—"

"Yes, we did, but I'm going out on a limb. If it all blows up, I want you to be as clean as possible, to help Bryanna—"

Her voice pitched up. "To help Bryanna? What are you going to do?" Her voice was uncharacteristically tight, her face flushed. "Please, Mike, be cautious. We're not dealing with idealistic college kids here. These are killers."

"Ms. Sweetwater, would you please leave my office," he said seriously, but without rancor. "Meet with Gus as soon as he arrives and fill him in on everything except—"

"Yes sir," she said, walking slowly out of the Oval Office.

Macdonald watched possibly the best friend he had in the world leave and close the door behind her. He returned to his desk and began writing down names and numbers, one to a page, after which he lay back in his executive chair and pondered. After a few minutes, he had a scenario worked out.

He reached for his secure phone and punched in the first number on his list.

33

London, England
Thursday, January 24
2030 hours GMT
1530 hours EST

Later that evening, following a dinner party in London, Prime Minister Reginald Howard let it slip that the American dollar was in more trouble than even he had thought possible. He was concerned it could reach such bad proportions that the Americans might default on their obligations, namely their T-Notes. He had it on good authority that the US President was in need of ten trillion dollars.

Not said was that Howard was that authority—a tactic agreed upon with Macdonald.

Actually, it wasn't too far from the truth. Macdonald was gambling on relationships he had developed over his years in finance, calling global trillionaires for help, counting on the strong financial alliances he had built with them.

Privately, Macdonald's bet was that the Russian Bear, having tasted America's financial blood, would thirst for more and fall for Reggie's rumor.

"I'm going out on a limb, Reg." Macdonald had told him. "Remember in my thesis, I had proffered how when a country fell on hard times economically, and given the right set of circumstances such as a gigantic catastrophe, it could be pushed over the edge."

"Good God, man," Reggie had said, "you may have written your own—"

"But who would have known that back in 1993?"

"True. Well I like the trap you're setting for your, as yet, unknown suspect, old boy, and will assist as I best I can. Maybe this will flush the buggers out."

34

It was 1745 hours in Washington, DC, and Macdonald had been tirelessly working the phones from the Oval Office. In shirt sleeves and no tie, he was now pacing the room with Cynthia standing off to the side, waiting for him to say something.

She was not too sure of his mood. The man she knew as always being composed and on top of his game looked ragged and out of sorts. She couldn't stand the silence anymore.

"Sir, you called me in and have said nothing. What is it you need of me?"

"I'm thinking of pulling a General Eisenhower on the eve of the Normandy invasion."

At first, she was puzzled, and then it dawned on her, with shock. "What are you talking about? You can't be blamed for the economic conditions of—"

"I've taken a very bold step, Cynthia, one I believe will strengthen our financial position in the global economy and regain confidence in the dollar. But it's a two-edge sword."

"All right, so you know the good and the bad; what else is new?" she said, her hands on her hips, looking dauntingly at him

He stopped pacing and broke into a wide grin.

She said emphatically, "Well, I know you wouldn't have done . . . whatever . . . if you thought it would fail, which, of course, it won't, because it can't! The world outside this room is in chaos. We can't handle the calls. Your own staff is frightened. I've asked Darlene about it. She only shook her head and wouldn't speculate.

"When have you ever shut out your closest advisors? I can answer that in one word: never. Mr. Kaplan, with Mr. Vaughn's help, is pushing those people in the

Cabinet Room to come up with something. They are having a hard time of it. If you hadn't called me in, I was going to soon break down your door."

He loved her angst. "It's part of my strategy. I want people to think that we're in terrible shape. Human nature being what it is, when our folks in the other room leave today, some will be intercepted by the press. And no matter how hard my loyal staff will try not to say what they have been doing, they will give away something, no matter how innocuous their words: *It sure was chaotic in there. I hope it's not nerve-racking like this all the time. The president has been in his office all afternoon, alone. Nobody seems to know why.* And so on. Get my drift?"

"Sounds like you want people to think you're losing it."

"You're a genius, but then I've told you that before. How's Darlene doing?"

She scrutinized him before answering.

"Darlene won't talk to anybody, outside of doing her job and seeing that others do theirs. Come to think of it, she hasn't been her in-command self, not that outsiders would—"

The door to Cynthia's office opened, and she whirled, but stopped short seeing Darlene.

"Come in," Mike said quickly.

Darlene quietly closed the door. She appeared tentative, reticent. He walked over to her. "I apologize for excluding you, but it was necessary." He then explained what he had told Cynthia about loose lips sinking ships.

"Well, your plan gets a four point oh, but right now your popularity wouldn't earn you a pass/fail," the former dean said ruefully.

"It's a gamble I had to take. Tell Kap and Gus I can't meet with them now, but we'll catch up at supper. You, Kap, Gus, the Ambassador, the DCIA, Alexandra and I will meet over supper. Make it for nine people in the residence dining room. The DCIA will be bringing one of his Russian experts. Maybe we should add Nadine."

"I can call," Darlene said, "but it may be a little premature to involve her. Besides, she's been calling on the embassies as a 'get to know each other' sort of thing."

"Great. Get her on the phone for me as fast as you can."

Cynthia left the room. Darlene stood on the nation's seal in the center of the Oval Office. "Are you going to tell me what this is all about?"

"As you know, I closed the markets this afternoon. I want the world to think we're in trouble, which frankly, we are. However, I may have found a way out, but that's all I will say right now. I want a message leaked to the White House press corps about the financial crisis overtaking events and that the US government may default."

"You're crazy." She stopped, realizing her words. "I'm sorry, sir, I didn't mean—"

"That's perfect, that's another thing I want leaked out, that frustration is extremely high over our inability to come up with a plan. I'm going up to change. Buzz me when you get Nadine."

Darlene was shocked to her core as she watched him burst through the French doors. She wanted to call out, but her vocal cords were frozen.

35

White House
Private Quarters
Same Day
1755 hours

The phone in the residence rang, and the president's valet answered. "President's residence. Ah, yes, Ms. Sweetwater. Yes. Certainly." He put the call on hold. "Sir, Ms. Sweetwater says that Ms. Mednorov is in her office. She also said they are setting up the dinner as you requested."

"Good. Ask to have Ms. Mednorov escorted up here to the sitting room." Ten minutes later, Macdonald entered the living room dressed in slacks, a striped dress shirt, and a pale-blue tie. Agent Hines was standing inside the room at the door. His guest was seated, reading. She looked up as he entered and rose, extending her hand, which he took gently.

"I'm glad you're here," he said, gesturing that they sit.

"From what I heard, I thought you would be more . . . what is it you say? . . . messed up."

He grinned. "I took a long shower and put on fresh clothes. I wanted to look good for my date tonight."

She raised her eyebrows. "Date?"

"Technically, no; but seeing you, I made it a date in my mind," he said with affection.

She smiled. "I think I am here to be questioned, not for . . ."

He wanted to hold her, make love to her. It was also the worst time to be thinking that way. She was right; she was here to be questioned. They were no longer in their early twenties with high ideals and no worldly responsibilities.

"Your mind wanders," she said winsomely, smiling warmly. "You were always such a deep thinker."

"Yeah, I was having a wisp of the past."

"Yes. The past haunts you because I let Raisa see your original thesis. I never thought she would copy it. Who of us had the money for such an extravagance back then? We were adult children, some days living like one and some days like the other."

Wow, had she struck a chord. His heart pounded.

"I will be very professional when I am with your very important people. I want to help, because I believe in what you want for your country. Please do not worry about me and do not defend me if someone accuses me of—?"

He stopped her, reassuring, "No. No one will be doing any of that. My people want to hear what you know or suspect. This is no inquisition."

He reached out took her hand. He felt flushed, giving in to his deepest emotions. Her eyes were studying him. He admired her poise. She massaged the back of his hand with her thumb. He felt his eyes water.

"Come," she said softly, "walk me to the window so that I may see the view."

He agreed. What he really wanted to do, though, was to embrace her as he had in his condo three weeks earlier. He wanted to taste her and caress her. He wished it was Bath and the hostel.

They stopped at the window. He heard her breathing change as she looked out at the Washington Monument and the Jefferson Memorial. She appeared enthralled with the view, as was he. Night had fallen, and all the ceremonial lights were on.

"When this is over, Michael, when you get your country . . . what is it you like to say? . . . in ship shape?"

"Right. Navy, Marine guys use that term."

"What do you wish for, Michael?"

He squeezed her hand.

She leaned her head on his shoulder. "I, too, with all my heart."

I am going crazy inside. He glimpsed back across the room. No agent was in sight. He turned her gently to him. She put her free arm around his neck, and they softly kissed.

He knew then that no matter what shape the world was in, they had to be together.

When he pulled back to see her eyes again, tears were running down her cheeks. She bowed her head and emitted an uneasy laugh, while he gently wiped under one of her eyes with his thumb. She laid her head on his chest.

He held her close and ran one hand over her hair, not wanting this moment to end, but knowing it had to. "It's time to join the others," he whispered, rubbing his cheek on the top of her head. He felt her release.

"Come, use my *loo*," he chuckled.

When she rejoined him, she had regained her poise and smiled adoringly at him. He made a call.

"Hi. We're ready. Would you have Nadine and Kap come—Oh? Anybody else? You're way ahead of me, as usual. We're on our way."

He pocketed his cell phone and smiled, shaking his head.

"What, Michael?" she asked softly and caringly, which always touched his heart.

"I want you to meet two of tonight's participants before we go in to dine. Darlene had anticipated me; they await us in my office, the next room over."

He paused, his hands on her shoulders, then bent and kissed her lightly on the lips. They shared a nervous laugh and went to join the others. As they entered the office, Darlene, Cynthia, Nadine, and Kap rose and greeted them. Macdonald stopped just inside the room, allowing everyone a moment to make their impression of the Russian visitor. He then escorted her to the tightly knit group and did the honors, introducing her as Dr. Alexandra Petraovna Mednorov. The SecState and SecTres, meeting her for the first time, formally extended their hands in greeting. Darlene and Cynthia nodded to her, which she returned with a smile.

"This is a very special time. I am honored to be in your presence," the president's guest said.

Nadine responded. "It is our pleasure as well. May I call you Alexandra?"

"Oh, please do," she said engagingly.

"And around here, I'm Kap, or Professor."

"Professor. Where did you teach, sir?"

Macdonald smiled. She had just made an instant friend. Kap's demeanor showed that he liked the extra attention.

"I taught our friend here," he replied, nodding his head at Macdonald. "At Wharton School of Business, University of Pennsylvania, where he earned his PhD in Finance."

"So," she said, looking at her Michael. "You have two former teachers working with you. You must feel greatly honored."

Macdonald thought he detected a blush on Kap's already ruddy complexion. The old goat had been taken in by Alexandra's charm.

"I am more than honored, I am blessed," he replied sincerely. "I have strong personal connections with several who are helping me do this job: these are four of them."

Nadine was quite taken by the president's former classmate. "Alexandra, I know you studied at Oxford, but where did you receive your doctorate?"

While Nadine and Alexandra talked, Cynthia interjected, "I'd better see to our other guests, Mr. President." She turned and left.

Macdonald leaned in closer to Kap and said, "I apologize for being so secretive. I can assure you my plan is very solid and very workable, with a minimum chance of failure."

"I'm with you whatever you've done," Kap said.

"Well, shall we? We have a lot on our plates tonight," Darlene added, laughing at her little pun.

36

Supper was meant for casual talk and banter. It appeared to Macdonald that Alex was feeling comfortable, unthreatened.

Kap regaled all in a couple of his cleaner stories and got some healthy dialog from Gus. It was a welcome break from the horrendous afternoon and impending meeting on the well-being of the country.

When everyone was finished eating, the table was cleared and coffee was poured. Darlene started off the more formal portion of the meeting.

"We have a lot to do this evening, and it promises to be a long night for some. Dr. Mednorov, I wish to officially thank you on behalf of President Macdonald and all of us for coming forward with your amazing revelation. As I am sure you can understand, we took the names and titles of those you had mentioned at lunchtime and did a thorough vetting of them.

"We confirmed the people you described to us as being who you said they were. Ms. Raisa Illyanavich appears to be an important cog in strategic planning; coordinating the nine services that comprise the FSB, which in turn studies the impact of information that affects the Russian Federation. Mr. President."

"Thank you, Darlene. I apologize for shutting myself off from everyone this afternoon. I understand that after I put a freeze on trading all financials, all hell broke loose. We'll discuss the reopening of the exchanges later this evening; however, it was necessary to protect the small investors who don't have in-depth access to the markets and who, according to the number of communications we were receiving, had begun to panic over their losses.

"The year 2008 still has everyone feeling skittish and negative when the financial institutions are threatened, because Americans know how bad things can become when that happens. The markets may have recovered eighty percent since then, with a lot of ups and downs in between, but by the time we closed the markets, they were down seventeen and a half percent."

Macdonald looked at his guest and their eyes met. "As Darlene mentioned, Alexandra brought us startling news earlier today. We thought you needed to hear it from her."

He related Alexandra's professional background up to the present, but left out Oxford until the end. "Why she is here at this very apocalyptic time is because she called to see me. Twenty years ago, we were at Oxford the same two years as Rhodes Scholars. She and her twin brother, Vasiliy, and I became good friends. There was a third Russian, Raisa Illyanavich, but she wasn't chummy."

Alexandra stifled a giggle. He took a drink of water, enjoying the moment.

"Oxford was also where I struck up a friendship with a dart-throwing whiz by the name of Reginald Howard, and we have remained good friends ever since. Alex and Vasiliy and I corresponded for a short time. Maybe it would have been longer if we'd had e-mail back then.

"Following my wife Sandi's death in June 2007, Vasiliy wrote me a condolence. After my book came out in 2009, I received letters from both Vasiliy and Alexandra. You can see who the less faithful letter-writer was in our group. Me.

"In October 2010, I was in Geneva at a conference on global currency and discovered Vasiliy was also attending. We had dinner, and he wanted me to visit Moscow. But I was becoming embroiled in politics and returned to the States."

"We know what happened after that, Mr. President." Vaughn chimed in.

There were various reactions and chuckles of agreement from the group.

"I've asked her here tonight to relate some strange financial maneuverings her brother Vasiliy had confided to her while she was back in Moscow over the Christmas and New Year's holidays. This needs to be looked at in the context of no bombing, because Vasiliy told her this back in December. Alex?"

"Thank you, Mr. President. I am honored to be here with you and your fellow dignitaries. My brother, a very level-headed person and director of the Central Bank of Russia, was deeply concerned about a situation that he shared with me during our visit together for the holidays."

She went on to carefully spell out the sequence of events that had alarmed Vasiliy. Since he had related that it involved Iran and China, she did not see that it had anything to do with the United States. She explained she knew little of the derivative and commodity markets and that her field of expertise was in finance, not in investments.

"My brother had been requested to prepare a transfer of the equivalent of three trillion dollars into a dozen corporate accounts, in eight separate countries. These were companies for which he had no information. He had googled them and found a listing of their officers, but could not find any product or staff.

"I don't know what happened after that, because he asked me not to call him once I left Moscow. At first, I thought that to be a strange request; when I worked in London we talked every week or two. I worried it might concern my coming to the United States and that he may be put under more scrutiny. Why, I do not know. I have not spoken to him since I left Moscow.

"Now you have the bomb, and I heard on all the news reports of how desperate your country was, that you were near collapse. I remembered Michael's—uh, the president's—paper at Oxford, and all the debates he would have with whomever would listen, that debt was a cancer and a major disaster could spell doom for . . ."

She coughed lightly and dabbed her napkin on her lips. *She is getting too personal,* Macdonald thought.

Alexandra continued. "He was not political then, but very outspoken about finance, currency, and debt. He was building his thesis based on a 'what-if' premise that the US dollar could become entangled in a series of events that would create a subtle decline, which would accelerate the dénouement of the Current Account Balance, especially if your Balances of Payments was continually negative.

"Back at Oxford, Vasiliy and I were very curious about this because we had not been exposed to his type of thinking: free enterprise, he called it. But he was always very worried that his country might fall prey to too much personal debt, as well as government debt.

"One day, he showed us a title for his paper, "The Theoretical Framework for the Collapse of the US Dollar." Vasiliy and I, and to some degree, Raisa, were surprised at this. Raisa's interests were in the books and not in theory, which I found fascinating the more Michael talked about it.

"Vasiliy and I could not understand how such a rich and powerful country could be thought of in the same breath with 'collapse.' Michael said it was only theoretical, hypothetical. It was something for people to study, realizing that even his great country could—"

"Kick themselves in the butt enough times to drop that far," Kap blustered. "I'm afraid it not only could, it has. As powerful as we have become militarily, we have become weak economically. People in this country accept debt as unthinkingly as they do air. It has become a way of life."

Anxious, Gus said, "Catch me up. How does this have anything to do with the bombing? Or are we talking about two different subjects: the bomb and the frosting the Ruskies—beg your pardon, ma'am—are giving us financially?"

Macdonald smiled. "I wanted Alexandra to give you the Oxford background. Though my thesis and book, which came about fourteen years later, were different in some ways, the overriding premise remained the same: *We could be ripe for a fall if we don't tend to our house.* We didn't in 2008 or in the financial decisions after that, which might have looked good then, but only made things worse later."

He nodded to Alex to continue.

"Raisa Illyanavich is the first woman to ever head a major department in the history of the KGB, now the FSB. She had a copy of Michael's original draft and must have compared it to his book back in 2007. She rose from directorate K, to directorate of Counterintelligence Support to the Financial System. She was a serious, pragmatic student, always wanting to make sure she studied every detail."

Macdonald said to Eubanks. "Pragmatic. Is that a criterion for advancement in all intelligence services, Jim?"

Eubanks smiled. "That all depends on what you're pragmatic about, sir."

Alexandra, sitting next to the DCIA, said, "I would, please, like to go back to the summer of 2012. Raisa had asked Vasiliy for a study on the United States debt history, who held significant notes. She was particularly interested in China, Japan, UK, and Middle Eastern countries. She gave no reason, her request was sufficient.

"After that request was fulfilled, Raisa asked Vasiliy to determine what it would take to create *untraceable entities* that could be used as a trading platform. Vasiliy assumed it was the euro, but asked to be sure. She surprisingly said, 'The US dollar.'

"He thought FSB was concerned for security reasons and noted that there were no anomalies in their tracking system, which someone could use to illegally move or trade any two currencies.

"Vasiliy thought the request specious, but fulfilled it dutifully. There are political pitfalls if one does not do what is expected of them, especially when the request comes from the FSB. He turned his results in on the eve of his family's vacation to the Black Sea in August.

"I was in both Geneva and London in September and October 2012, preparing for my next assignment, which I suspected would be Geneva. I had been promoted to vice president and made chief economist of the IFC. It turned out my transfer was to here. Life makes strange shifts."

Kap grunted. "I remember a former student, Mike Macdonald, who felt something was not right about how the US spent its money. Those western roots of his made him question how the piper was someday going to be repaid. He'd heard when he served in the Middle East that if the US kept buying foreign oil at the steady increase they had been showing, it would be harder to get our Balance of Payments in order."

"In Oxford," Macdonald said, "I was exposed to world views on finance, which heightened my concern. When I got to Kap at Wharton, I was one confused guy. I knew how to make money, but wondered if my country knew how to grow its economy and protect its financial security."

Darlene interjected, seeing the discussion getting a little off track. "You've heard the salient background. The president and SecTres have been digging into the markets to discover who the major shorts were on Friday, January 18, and again on Monday, January 21. Our exchanges were closed because of the Martin Luther King Jr. holiday. Inauguration was that day because they are not held on Sundays."

Kap explained. "However, the Asian and European markets were open on Monday, January 21. Over two trillion euros shorted the dollar that day on those exchanges. In the hours following the bombing, the dollar dropped precipitously against all currencies.

"We estimated," Kap continued, "the shorts on the dollar made billions and that some may have stayed in the markets as longs. We speculate a large majority of shorts had more than a premonition about the sudden fall in the dollar."

Macdonald picked up. "We think it was the Russians. Alexandra thinks that way too. That is why she called me. I have asked for a complete investigation on currency maneuvers in all of January. We hope to learn more about those twelve corporations Vasiliy mentioned." He sat back.

"Thank you, Mr. President. Most of us will move to the Cabinet Room, where others await. The president will rejoin us shortly," Darlene announced.

There was a short crisscross of conversation as the coterie prepared to leave the dining room. Cynthia went to where Alexandra, the DCIA, and Hester were talking.

"Mr. Director, the president asked if you and Mr. Hester would wait for him in the sitting room, directly across the hall from here, where the agent is standing."

Cynthia whispered to Alexandra that the president would be with her momentarily.

"Thank you, Mrs. Bolden," Alexandra said appreciatively.

Macdonald spoke to Nadine, Gus, and Kap. When he finished, he joined Alexandra and his secretary.

"Cynthia, please call Secretary Garrett and General Gibbons. I want them here at 0700 tomorrow morning. DCIA Eubanks and I will meet as usual along with Ambassador Hendrickson at 0630."

"Yes, Mr. President."

37

Left alone in the dining room, Macdonald said to Alex, "You revealed a great deal, for which I am very grateful, Lexi, but with that comes major concerns, which we are going to have to investigate. I need you to tell Eubanks and Hester everything about Raisa and Vasiliy, and anyone else for that matter.

"I have reached the same conclusion as you. Raisa's superiors shorted the US dollar, taking advantage of our devastated economy and crippled financial position."

Her brows knit with a sincere frown. "I do not see Vasiliy involved in any of this."

"I don't either," he assured her. "We will enlist all our resources inside Russia to track down who did this. You can help by talking with Eubanks and Hester. One thing you should know: at one time Eubanks and I did the same type of work in the Middle East, although we never were on a mission together. I trust him thoroughly."

"If you are secure with him, I will be also," she said.

He squeezed her hand. "They'll check out everything you tell them. This could very well go into the weekend."

"Whatever you need, I will do it."

"Okay, let's go." He released her hand, and they walked side by side to the sitting room.

The two CIA men were standing at the south window.

"That's a view and a half, isn't it," Macdonald said, entering. "Please, let's sit."

He indicated the sofa for them, and he quickly arranged two armchairs facing them where she and he sat, followed by the men.

"Jim, we are faced with an apocalyptic situation if the Russian government is behind the bombing. It could create a maelstrom I don't want."

Alexandra spoke first. "Mr. President, I do not believe this is our government, but rather a group within the FSB who are the architects," she said calmly and directly. "Raisa Illyanavich is a disciple of former KGB hardliners, something Vasiliy and I learned soon after we met her.

She went her own way, not wanting to assimilate any of the English culture. Even when she went with us to a pub or for sightseeing, she would not let down her hair."

"Jim?"

"Thank you, Mr. President. Dr. Mednorov, are you familiar with the inner workings of the FSB or Central Bank?"

"I worked in FSB after my return from Oxford, but had no interest to stay; they were too political. Some two years later, my fiancé Sergey introduced me to a banker who was in need of western-educated financial people to help him enter into the new world of banking. Our bank grew rapidly once we began working internationally.

"And because I spoke English, Spanish, and later, French, I traveled for the bank, networking. Sergey, then my husband, was an entrepreneur, always on the go. He did well also." She stopped, her gaze dropping slightly.

Macdonald understood her pause. "Look, I need to go down to the Cabinet Room." He took out a card Darlene had provided him that contained a list of White House locations and their extension numbers. He read two off to the DCIA. He then stood, as did the others.

He looked at Alex, "You okay?"

She smiled at his concern. "I want to help."

He wanted to hug her.

"Believe me, you are. I'll see you in a little while."

38

When Macdonald walked into the Cabinet Room, he sensed a dour atmosphere. It was very much the opposite of the atmosphere upstairs and his own jubilant mood. Yet he knew he was the source of the doom and gloom. Even Darlene was bland in her greeting to him.

"Okay," clapping and rubbing his hands together like a coach at halftime trailing by three touchdowns. He needed to get their heads turned around. He was very confident his game plan was a good one, and if properly run, they could wipe out their losing position in grand fashion.

"Okay, why did I shut down our financial world today and throw everybody into a panic? Because we have to fake our opponents into thinking they've got us beat. But I don't want anyone in this room thinking that's true.

"We came into office to turn this nation around. The bombing could not have been predicted. We woke up to positive vibes coming from last night's State of the Union address. We have our financial plan out there, but as will happen in this job, we got bushwhacked by midday by that rogue group from Iraq proclaiming its lie.

"That presented us with propaganda that could ignite many of our own 'patriots' to take things into their own hands and cause untold grief piled on top of what we were already dealing with. Kap, lay out what we're facing financially."

Kap cleared his throat as he loosened his perfect tie knot. "They know the background of what we've learned from Dr. Mednorov—that we are faced with a diabolical scheme to steal our country right out from under us."

"Excuse me," Vaughn said, like he had just been challenged. "With our technology and superior firepower, how is any country going to rub our faces in our own excrement? Look at what's going on in Detroit. We got the shit kicked out of us, and millions are determined—I mean bloody determined—to get things on the right track."

Insistently, Kap followed with, "We are diabolically being attacked with a crafty plan designed to undermine what little fiscal credibility we have left. Our unbacked fiat currency is continuing to sink into third-world status, which will tear us apart worse than the bomb."

Macdonald saw the fear in many eyes and said, "It's that serious. Drastic situations call for drastic measures. We have outspent our worth and are at an economic nadir."

"And we didn't seek this job to fail, regardless of the cards we are dealt," Kap said, his ruddiness becoming redder.

"Exactly," Macdonald said firmly. "That's why I was working the phones attempting to raise seven trillion dollars."

That elicited gasps.

"I have great faith in our potential benefactors," he went on, "and in you. This stays in this room. You all have to become actors; you must project fear and even bewilderment when you leave here. My game plan calls for a lot more than a Hail Mary pass or a gimmicky triple reverse.

"I need all the negativity we can muster projected to the outside world, so that our dollar will continue to lose value against the euro."

The puzzled looks were rapidly darkening into grave concern.

"That's asking a lot, boss," Vaughn piped up.

"It's only until late morning tomorrow," Kap said.

Darlene had been studying the faces and said, "This is asking a lot, and many of you may not be feeling very secure with what has been proposed, but stay strong inside."

"I know that seven trillion is an unfathomable number," Macdonald said in a less intense tone, "but we have a seventeen-trillion-dollar debt, which is even more unfathomable. I have friends with extremely deep pockets, and fortunately, I didn't break their bank in my run for the White House."

He gave a wry smile. His audience was not laughing.

"I have made deals and had help in making others. It's all legal. A friend informed me a rumor is circulating through the world's exchanges that we are about to default—that our debt, the weakening dollar, and the destruction of Detroit has dampened America's spirit. Even our vaunted treasury notes are suspect."

Kap said, "We aren't actually facing default, yet, but the *rumor* on the street says we are. We discovered the scam to push our dollar down further and are deliberately playing the patsy. And the media financial experts are unwittingly helping us by saying that we are artificially trying to stem financial collapse, delaying the inevitable.

"Shorting is an extremely daring position," Kap added, "unless you have four aces up your sleeve."

"Like a major catastrophe," Nadine Rankin blurted out.

"The bombing!" Gus exclaimed.

"Oh my god," Nadine said shocked.

"This is very tightly held information," Macdonald said sternly.

"You're saying the SOBs who killed and maimed millions of Americans and Canadians are also making trillions of dollars in the process?" Vaughn growled, his face red and the muscles on his neck bulging, as he leapt to his feet steaming.

"If this helps a little, Gus, we have a covert team on the ground close to where intelligence says the bomb was stored and may soon be standing on the very spot from whence it came."

"Hot damn!" exclaimed Vaughn.

"Okay, here's where we stand as of 1800 hours this evening. Nineteen separate financial sources have each made two different pledges to us. Collectively, we have the promise of an interest-free loan of five and a half trillion dollars, monies to be deposited—"

Everyone's various utterance of shock interrupted the president. He paused and couldn't resist a smile.

Kap said, "The word *default* has and is loosely being thrown around. We will continue fanning the flames of discontent, and financial bloggers and social media channels have gone for it big time."

Some of the group shifted uncomfortably in their seats.

"You're right," Kap said grinning, "we are playing dirty, and it's working. Our currency-exchange watchers are reporting an extremely high level of short activity on the dollar.

"Investors don't like uncertainty, so the exchanges will flutter, but the dollar will fall because of the overall downward pressure it has been getting."

"So what's going on?" Gus insisted. "I've known you too long, sir, not to know you've got something cooking."

Macdonald grinned. "Some of us will be up all night, analyzing. We'll watch every exchange in the world and expect significant shorting. The negative rumors about us and the uncertainty about when or if our markets will open will see to that. I am expecting our enemy to be a big part of the short volume.

"Timing is everything. When our newfound money is deposited, I expect the dollar to bounce up, and I'm hoping the shorts will be late covering. The European and Asian markets will be closed, which could slow down quick transactions. It's a very small window, but it could cost the shorts—our enemy—hundreds of billions of dollars, because they will be expecting the dollar to continue to fall.

"Our lenders who may go short will cover the moment our exchanges open, which will be one or two minutes before I speak to the nation. That should earn them a healthy profit, but their main goal is for us to succeed. A robust American economy is to their advantage."

Kap was pumped up. "All of the sudden, Uncle Sam's hat will be on a little straighter."

Macdonald nodded. "My halting trading for the last hour and a half today was not a bad thing. Yet the Wall Street crowd went apoplectic. TV pontificators picked up on them. I'm sure you all remember the vilification that was thrown our way during the campaign. Well, it's payback time.

"I want the enemy to feel safe. Friends will make sure rumors of us defaulting will send them to their beds as happy people. I am sure the reports of my abhorrent behavior and the White House's inability to cope helped erase their concerns."

He checked his watch. "I promised Director Eubanks I would rejoin his meeting." He stood and others followed suit. He felt comfortable they would dissect the ramifications of what he had presented to them, and if they had any problems understanding it, Kap could straighten them out.

Darlene walked to the door with him.

He whispered, "Please arrange with the Service for Alexandra to be driven home in about an hour. She will be in my study here in the West Wing."

Darlene nodded. "I was very impressed with Alexandra. Her call to you is the best thing that could have happened."

He smiled, thinking that was true in more ways than one. "It'll save us from running up a lot of blind alleys. Putting what Vasiliy told her in December together with the bombing demonstrates her brilliance."

39

"Keep your seats," Macdonald said, rejoining Alexandra, Eubanks, and Stephen Hester, CIA Russian expert, who were all in deep conversation.

"We've been learning things we didn't know about the FSB, sir," Eubanks reported.

Alexandra smiled, "I have been talking and talking, maybe too much."

"Oh no, not at all," Eubanks exclaimed. "Everything you said was informative and very helpful, and I thank you for your candor."

"Well," Macdonald said approvingly, eyebrows raised, "tell me what you have learned."

His DCIA responded at a rapid clip. "The FSB is a complex organization: a combination of finance, security, investigation, business, and counterintelligence. It is an information analyzer and disseminator to specific directorates. It is not necessarily new information, but Dr. Mednorov has given us insights we didn't have. As I said to you a day or so ago, sir, our Russian bureau had been severely trimmed down over the past four years."

"Meaning?" Macdonald asked.

"We've suspected the old KGB was strongly entrenched in the FSB, the so-called new and open government reorganization, but we didn't have the assets to verify that speculation."

"Could they be running covert, black ops-type operations out of FSB?"

"It appears they run everything out of there, sir. Everything."

Macdonald looked at Alex for confirmation.

Her brow furrowed as she nodded assent. "That was why I did not like working there. They were more interested in the financial structures of other countries.

Raisa liked very much the strategic planning and focus on foreign financial activity."

Macdonald shook his head. "I'm not as up on the internal machinations of the Russians as I should be. I believe some tutoring is called for, Jim." He turned to Alex. "So, Raisa's title of being the head of current information and international relations is not only financial but also governmental, impactive on all aspects of the Russian Federation."

"True. She is still a communist, as are many of those high up in the FSB."

"Jim?"

"We know where a good number of the old guard is, but many of the young disciples, such as Raisa, are unknown to us. They keep their allegiances closely guarded. As Dr. Mednorov explained earlier, there is no overt communist activity amongst them. They are a very tightly kept secret."

"Could this be an incubator for a deep covert group working outside the government?"

Alex jumped in. "May I? The FSB is a gatherer of financial information from whatever country they target. I am sure that Raisa has been following you, Mr. President, maybe for many years. You became wealthy in trading currencies, attained higher education and status, and then you became active in politics.

"She will know a lot about how you think. I am sure she has presented you as a person who departs from the accepted course, because the message presented in your book has not been given credence by your political leaders."

"I can see her doing all of that, but is she capable of killing millions?"

Alex blinked at the harsh figure and said softly, "I believe there were two plans coordinated at a very high level. However, even those of us who know Raisa would not know what was in her heart. That is the most tightly held secret of all. She shares nothing."

Macdonald commented, "We never knew her heart the entire two years at Oxford. Her passion was stoked somewhere else within her."

"Yes," she agreed. "Vasiliy and I had only met her before our leaving for England. We were strongly advised to not mix with others." She paused, her eyes dropping ever so slightly, and then she continued. "She was very true to that. The rest of us did many things together, made good friends."

"Good friends are the gems of life. You and Reggie are giving your all to help us, for which I will be eternally grateful."

He smiled at her blush, then said, "Jim, do you have enough to get started?"

"We already have gotten started, sir. After Dr. Mednorov gave us a briefing on the FSB, Steve, using the scramble phone, called the information in to our specialists, who are already working on it. It'll be a 24/7 operation, sir."

"I wouldn't have thought otherwise. Can we wrap this up for now? Unless you have any questions."

"No questions, sir. This has been very helpful, more than helpful. Can Dr. Mednorov be available for a follow-up?"

"Alex?" Macdonald asked.

"Yes, of course."

After the CIA men left the room, Mike turned to Alex. "I would never have dreamt in a million years that you and I would be together in this setting. Thank you for coming to me. Thank you from my country. Thank you from me."

She put her index finger to his lips. "*Mon cher*, if people in my country are responsible for this egregious act, they should be found out and punished."

He slowly enfolded her in his arms and gently drew her into him. She tilted her head back and looked into his eyes, a tear escaping from one. He brought a hand up and wiped it away.

"Having you in this room tonight melted away all the years we had not been together. I love you, Lexi. My wish for us is that we will always be together."

She pulled him into him and kissed him passionately. When they eased off, she whispered, "I have hoped to hear you say that."

Their next embrace was even longer and more fervent, and when they looked at each other their faces gleamed from perspiration and tears. She placed her hands on either side of his head and looked adoringly into his eyes. "I love you, Mr. President."

She giggled and he laughed. "We need towels to wipe our faces," she said lovingly.

He took her hand, and they went to his bathroom.

After straightening up, he said, "We'll go down to my office, but first let's take a look at the Monument." They walked arm in arm to the window. She tilted her head against his shoulder.

"This view is made more beautiful because I am seeing it with you," she whispered.

They turned and held each other close. She snuggled against his chest.

"Lexi, Lexi, Lexi," he said. He lifted her chin and kissed her lightly, yet he was conflicted. *Was he right to want her? Was it fair to her?*

They entered Cross Hall, heading to the open elevator door attended by

Agent Hines. Alex smiled at the agent, who nodded back, "Dr. Mednorov. Mr. President."

"West Wing level, please."

As the elevator door opened, Macdonald said to the agent, "We'll go to my study. Dr. Mednorov will leave from there shortly." He and Alex strode side by side through the office area of the West Wing and went into his study for a few more minutes alone. He closed the door and took Alex in his arms, their bodies almost merging into one. They kissed deeply.

Taking a deep breath, he said teasingly, "I'll never get back to work at this rate."

"You are again making me very happy, Michael. I have some of the old feelings, yet I have newer ones that pull more deeply at my heart. Our last time together at Oxford, we were lovers. Since that time, you married Sandi and I Sergey. We were very lucky."

"Yes, we were. We knew and loved two extraordinary people, and they loved us back. When I saw Vasiliy in Geneva and he told me you were in London, I thought of Bath. I realized then I still had strong feelings for you, but I was too caught up in the winds of change in my country to take the side trip to see you."

"Oh, *mon cher,* when I was assigned here, I hoped I might see you. I wanted you to win, but knew for a life together, you would have to lose," she said, giggling.

He shook his head lightly. "I had shut down my passion after Sandi and replaced it with a fervent effort for what Sandi and I had been building. I wrote my book and supported the work of my now vice president when she was building the DOER program."

Alex giggled. "I was jealous of her maybe having you. I googled her name, read much about her. She had energy and passion to match yours."

"She and I are great friends. She and I are in love with a cause: to create a viable Centrist party that could challenge the Democrats and the Republicans. While I was in Geneva, on that same trip, Bryanna called me. She wanted to turn up the burners on the new party and needed me. The public was disconnecting from both major parties. The midyear elections saw the Republicans make gains while the Democrats lost Senate seats and many house seats to both the Republicans and the independents.

"The rest is history and you are here." He let that hang as he gave into his impulse to embrace and kiss her. She drank him in and wanted more. He wished there was no overnight watching the foreign markets or hours packed with meetings. His heart wanted her back upstairs behind locked bedroom doors.

They were both breathing heavily. He felt his sweat against his shirt. Then a plan came to him. "I'm flying to Detroit midday tomorrow, following the rigors of my morning activities. I'm meeting with the Canadians. Gus Vaughn and Vice President Dudley have planned a mini summit between our two nations, sharing details of our recovery programs.

"When I get back to Andrews Air Force Base tomorrow evening, I'm changing over to a helicopter that will take me to Camp David." When he mentioned the presidential retreat in the Maryland mountains, she frowned.

He understood her look. "It's in the mountains seventy miles west of here. It is for the sole use of the president and his guests." He stopped and looked her in the eyes. "Like you."

Her joy was instant. "Us?"

"Let me find a way to work this out. For this, you'll coordinate through my personal assistant, Jane."

"Not Darlene?" she asked quizzically.

"Jane handles my personal life, such as family, you . . . she coordinates through Cynthia. People here know Jane, especially the Secret Service. She coordinated your visits in New York. By the way, you have a big admirer in her."

"Really? She is so motherly. So, for us, I use Jane, for business I use Darlene?"

"Or Cynthia. We'll play that by ear. The Secret Service . . . again, this is all new to me."

"It sounds wonderful to me!" She smiled and gave him a light peck on the lips.

"Okay, I'll get all the details worked out and have Jane call you." He walked to his desk and pressed a button.

"Yes, Mr. President," came a male voice.

"Dr. Mednorov is ready to leave."

40

Oval Office
PDB Meeting
Friday, January 25
0625 hours

Eubanks greeted a very tired president, slouched in his desk chair.

"Good morning, Mr. President. That is, I *hope* it's a good morning."

Macdonald rocked forward coming out of his doze and rested his forearms on the desk. "I guess," he said sleepily. "At least the foreign markets showed a very bleak picture of the American economy. Rumors of our defaulting caused a heavy shorting and trumpeted a decline of confidence in our fiat currency."

Eubanks called up all of his aplomb not to look as shocked as he felt. He was dismayed with his boss's blasé attitude, but immediately chalked it up to the man's fatigue. "Yes, that is in the PDB," he said, crossing to the card table. He had thought the president would be upset over that news.

Macdonald slowly rose, then grunted and stretched.

Eubanks opened the PDB. "Your shutting down trading sent the Asian and European markets into a tailspin. The dollar declined sharply against the euro. There appears to be a distinct distrust in all American interests as a whole."

"I, Secretary Kaplan, and two of his new Treasury appointees spent the night watching those markets. At one point, the Asian markets were down as much as twelve percent. They perceived our plight to be the worst collapse in American history," Macdonald added blandly and picked up his copy of the PDB and scanned it. "They're all blaming me for my inability to present a more positive picture of the future of the United States. Humph." He smirked. "Some are saying I'm prepared to default the dollar and trash the entire American economy.

Ha, I saw this," and he pointed to a place on page two, "early this morning when the European markets opened: 'Few saw anything good ahead for the once great and powerful country.'"

Macdonald smiled, put down the PDB, and yawned.

Eubanks almost choked on a swallow of coffee.

"You all right, Jim?"

"I'm sorry, Mr. President," he said, wiping off his chin and a drop or two that had gotten on his tie. "It's just . . . well you seem, eh, pleased, if I may be so bold."

"You may, and you're right."

Eubanks was dumbfounded and placed his cup down. "Sir, eh, please explain?" he asked cautiously.

"Jim, while you were seeking out the bad Russians, I and Secretary Kaplan put forward a plan to serve a crushing blow to some unscrupulous Russians. I elicited some strong assistance from Prime Minister Howard and seventeen of the world's wealthiest global families, some being small nations unto themselves. I may pull off the biggest scam in history."

He explained the precise plan that would culminate in less than four and a half hours.

"Sir, how have you prevented a leak? How is this so far flung?" Eubanks puzzled.

"These good people keep their own counsel, Jim. Most have wealth greater than the GNP of all but a few countries. During my campaign, I had met with most, and a good number of them substantially supported my campaign.

"When I became the Centrist party's choice to run for president, with Bryanna Dudley as my running mate, they'd become interested in me. In June of 2011, I was invited to visit two of the families, spending three days with them. A few weeks later, Darlene and I met with six other families in Lisbon.

"They wanted to know where I planned to take the country and the world. Darlene's view of world politics was invaluable. We explained our positions, which at my first visit were not fully developed. They listened and they counseled. We learned more from them than they did from us, but maybe that's what it was all about. They have a world view. They are not trapped in a political structure dealing in pettiness.

"Most of their families have strong lineages, going back many centuries. Some were disrupted; some were invaded; and some, as in the case of one or two, had to physically relocate, leaving their ancestral homes. Two were within communist-controlled countries and suffered great losses, but all have maintained a peaceful perspective.

"Modern transportation and communications has created a tool to create a more effective joint neutrality to dissuade aggressive neighbors, who need their commerce.

"They desire a strong United States and wish for us to be a more honest government. I first became aware of how much faith they were putting in me when tens of thousands of donations and millions of dollars began flowing into my and Bryanna's campaign coffers and to the Centrist party.

"They were all small, within the law, totaling hundreds of millions. That's why we took no federal funding," he said grinning. "You may remember my opponents going crazy, accusing me of taking illegal donations. We offered to open our books right alongside of theirs. That story fizzled out."

Eubanks shook his head. "I've seen a lot in my twenty-four years at CIA, but this beats them all, combined. Would I know any . . . without knowing of their extreme wealth?"

Macdonald nodded. "It's possible. They live well, but don't make tabloid headlines. They have the bells and whistles of the wealthy. If one of them happens to get out of line, I am told, the guilty party is withdrawn from circulation. Not killed, just isolated."

Eubanks was having a hard time digesting what the president was telling him. He took a page out of the president's book and paced, his mind searching for anything that could identify any people as Macdonald had explained them. "My apologies, sir, I need to ask a few things."

"Shoot."

"Have your friends theorized about who bombed us?"

Macdonald was surprised at the question. *Does Eubanks think I am withholding . . . ? No. He used the word "theorized" as opposed to "know."*

Macdonald responded casually. "No. I started out telling them what I believed had transpired, mostly based on input from you and Alexandra. No names, of course. They all asked if I was planning to retaliate. I told them I did not want to retaliate militarily, that I saw this as an opportunity to gain more by doing less. But I assured them I wanted my pound of flesh."

"Yes sir. You know some fascinating and trustworthy people, to be that frank and not worry about repercussions."

"Life's a gamble, Jim, but I have two aces up and two in the hole, against a king high straight flush. I hold their ace. We need to let the negative opinions continue to flow until I pull the plug on it a little after 1100 hours this morning.

"Just before the European markets opened this morning, we put out an announcement that the US exchanges would not open until that time, which will coincide with my going on the air, using DEFCON 1 as one muscle and the closing of the European markets as the other.

"When the American markets open, my friends will all close out their shorts, making billions because of the dollar's continued fall overnight.

"The American media has been a positive force in my plan, because they have been and will be knocking me all over the place. It's Shotokan Karate, Jim. I'm going to use their energy to make us successful. I will be outrageously vilified.

"Our markets will open down; the Dow could drop twenty percent, on top of the eighteen percent it has already dropped. Our currency will take a huge fall against the euro. At one minute after eleven, our investors will have covered their shorts, but stay long, and will collectively make seventeen separate deposits totaling five and a half trillion dollars into our Federal government account at the New York Federal Reserve Bank."

Eubanks was stone stunned.

"There's more. I will go on the air one minute late, allowing the network broadcasters one final shot of tearing me down, voicing the dire straits I have created for the United States."

41

The President Addresses the Nation
Friday, January 25
1100 hours

Director Eubanks, along with the American public, now viewed President Macdonald on a television screen. It was two minutes after eleven Eastern Standard Time. The American stock markets and exchanges, as predicted, had opened crushingly down.

Macdonald was originating from the East Room in the White House and saying, "Our situation has been brought on by years of fiscal neglect and a catastrophic disaster—an attack by people still unknown, reducing an American city to rubble and ashes, killing millions."

President Macdonald shifted his position, scanned the jam-packed East Room of the White House. He allowed himself a moment to look out over the media, cabinet members, agency heads, senate and house members, senior staff, and guests.

He longed to yell "I gotcha!" Instead, he cleared his throat and somberly looked into the lens of the feed TV camera, as though he was about to pronounce the collapse everyone predicted.

Seconds later, he delivered these words: "Over the decades, our government has made many mistakes in the management of this country's affairs, and not just in the last few years. While we were rich and powerful, too many in our country were unconcerned about our rising debt, even after 2008. There were a few concerned parties, but not enough. Unfortunately, their voices did not have the power to reverse a divisive trend.

"John Kennedy wrote in a speech that went undelivered in Dallas on November 22, 1963, *'This is a time for courage and a time of challenge. Neither conformity nor complacency will do. Neither fanatics nor the faint-hearted are needed. And our duty as a Party is not to our Party alone, but to the Nation, and indeed to all mankind.'*"

He paused again for effect, then: "People around the world are painfully aware and extremely alarmed at our misguided and reckless actions and attitudes. We have heedlessly disregarded sound economics and sound fiscal budget management."

Darlene walked to his side and handed him a note, which read UP.

"Mid-afternoon Eastern time yesterday, we learned of rumors swirling around Europe that we were close to defaulting on the dollar and that I was desperately seeking trillions from somewhere. Some said I was prepared to print many trillions of uncovered dollars. Some likened us to a sinking ship with no life rafts. Rumors abounded. Some may have even been propagated by people sitting before me this morning."

There was a rustling amongst the press corps. Several in the room had indeed written that or a similar false accusation.

"There have also been reports of divisions within my young administration, disunity. I personally read some of these e-mails, blogs, and posts. These called for my resignation. Vacuous hate mail was piling up. The anonymous pillagers of irresponsibility were ultra vulgar.

"Have you all forgotten what we are arduously doing *right now* in this country? As I speak, millions of Americans are selflessly volunteering, assisting, and searching for millions of people they never knew. Vice President Dudley has been tirelessly leading a fantastic group of governors, mayors, police, National Guard, US military units, and volunteers under the guidelines of DOER.

"Within hours on Tuesday morning, literally a quarter of a million people were leaving their homes and going to predesignated volunteer locations, setting into motion the wheels of recovery, not having to wait on any federal government agency or the Congress. The caregivers were assisting people rendered homeless, badly injured, and grief-stricken . . . a massive venture never before seen, and I hope never needing to be duplicated."

Holding a microphone, he moved to the side of the podium in front of where the media sat, his eyes blazing down at them. "Yet you said and wrote that I . . ." his voice rose, as he gestured at the media, ". . . had turned my back on them, on the American people?

"After all we've been through these past four days, do you honestly believe that?" He stared them down, while taking out his handkerchief to wipe the sweat from his face. He returned to the podium.

Cynthia had walked up onto the platform. Macdonald took a drink of water. He needed to curb his anger, while maintaining his intensity. She handed him a note and went back to her seat.

He looked down at the information on the piece of paper. It read: *T-Notes 11:02:30 a.m.* That meant that $1.3 trillion worth of US treasury had been purchased.

He looked up from the paper and said, "If any of you thought that . . ." he paused and then bellowed, "You. Were. Wrong!"

He took another drink of water and looked at the riled faces of the news media. "A half hour ago, I was given a capsulized account of what you in this room were saying. Oh, ye of such little faith."

He shook his head and shrugged, both gestures saying essentially the same thing: *how sad is that?* He paused; the berating was now over. It was almost five minutes after eleven. He held Cynthia's note in front of his face so the cameras couldn't miss it. He lowered the paper revealing a small smile. "At 11:01:30 a.m., barely three minutes ago, $5.38 trillion, that's with a 't,' was deposited into the United States' account with the Federal Reserve Bank of New York." He had to stop, because the noise in the room overwhelmed his voice.

Nobody in the media knew in advance. They didn't have an inkling and neither did the Russians.

Some news people were shouting questions, others were on their phones. The room became chaotic. Secret Service agents moved to the sides of the podium. The president stood calmly. A.J. and Darlene came up on the platform and called for order.

The shouting slowly quieted, but smartphone traffic did not. The phones were buzzing and binging. Macdonald waited and when it had quieted sufficiently for him to speak, he said, "And, at 11:02:30 a.m., $1.35 trillion worth of US Treasury notes were purchased by friends of the United States of America."

The noise swelled. He stepped back from the podium and six-foot-two A.J. Delarosa replaced him.

"You will have to quiet down," A.J. implored. They didn't. He turned to the president standing behind him, who nodded. A.J. turned back to the microphone. "Thank you, Mr. President."

The news people, realizing what was happening, quieted rapidly. The protective service agents relaxed. Macdonald moved to A.J., who stepped aside, but remained next to him.

Macdonald said evenly, "We have been the recipient of some much-needed cash from some very gracious and concerned people who do not want to see our country's economy collapse. This is not money Congress can touch.

"We will not have a repeat of the bailout fiascos. There will be no earmarks. This money will be allocated to the survivors, recovery, and the rebuilding of our nation's economy and infrastructure. You'll have specifics later today.

"You can search every law. Rest assured, we have. This money was not earned by the federal government. It didn't come from our citizens' income, but it is intended for their use! The Congress—with most of its members having never run a business—has weakened America's large and small businesses. By Congress's indiscriminate and profligate spending, which was nothing more than a monetary giveaway, it has weakened incentive and resolve. I campaigned against this irresponsibility, as you may recall."

Darlene handed a note to A.J., who read it, and then passed it on to Macdonald, who glanced at it and smiled.

"Today is a new day for the United States of America economically and fiscally," he said idly, putting the paper in his pocket. "The US dollar is rapidly rising against the euro, and we all know what good news that is."

The press corps reacted with muttering of approval while others acted as though they were not interested in *good news*.

"We seek parity with the euro and intend to reduce the two to one ratio of dollars to euros that we have been living with for too long. This infusion of money is our first huge step toward that goal. I'm not going to take your questions, because I am not obliged at this time to do so.

"We have it on very good authority that the people who bombed Detroit had invested hundreds of billions of euros, shorting the dollar on January 18 and 21 throughout worldwide exchanges. Nobody would do that unless they were one hundred percent certain something was going to force the dollar down . . . like a nuclear bomb."

The audience exploded in noise. Macdonald put up his arms asking for quiet, but it was slow to diminish. "They made hundreds of billions of dollars on American and Canadian blood," he shouted, and then stepped back to let that all sink in.

He focused on the networks' TV camera. "Millions of Americans have been on their knees, not because they are defeated, but to pray. This president prays with them and stands with them. We've taken heavy losses, but we as a nation *are still standing*. Today was our first step in retaliating against our attackers."

He paused for effect. "Today will become a historic day against tyranny." He broke his concentration on the TV feed camera, as everyone but the media in the room stood and cheered. He nodded his appreciation and waved them down.

"We are already on the road to recovery, which you will soon learn more about. Hold your head up America. Regardless of the prophets of gloom and doom, you have a president who cares about you and who is not afraid to take action on your behalf. I was hung in effigy, but I had to do what I did in order for all of us to get back on track.

"Wednesday night I presented you and the Congress with a five-point program designed to gain fiscal responsibility. Some of the cuts in spending will hurt. In sports parlance, it's called 'no pain, no gain.' However, with the help of the investments this morning, we will begin rebuilding programs that will be productive and not just maintenance. Hope is wonderful, but positive results are better."

There were more cheers. He knew it was time to wind things down.

"I'm going to visit Detroit right after I leave here. Vice President Dudley and I are having a conference with Canadian Prime Minister McEwen. We are each bringing teams of specialists who will meet and begin a lasting relationship, as we develop plans for restoration.

"If you don't know already what a fantastic vice president you have, you better pay attention. She is being assisted by outstanding people who understand that America comes first, not petty, partisan politics. Stop being Democrats. Stop being Republicans. Start being Americans."

He stood back, as more cheering rang out. It was good for the people at home and at work to hear. A.J. moved to the podium, and Macdonald strode from the platform and out of the East Room. The wails from the media were drowned out by the shouts of support coming from the rest.

42

A little before noon, President Macdonald, accompanied by Darlene, entered the dining room in the residence. He was going on thirty-one and a half hours hours without sleep, but he was reenergized by the jubilant success of the morning. Somehow in the blur of the morning's events, he had managed to talk with the Secret Service about Alex going with him to Camp David. The supervisor had been more than accommodating and would coordinate with Cynthia.

The president also made a point to tell Darlene about taking Alex to Camp David that weekend. "I saw it more from her than I did you." She did not comment further about his personal relationship, but did add, "She'll be a welcome addition to the team."

That, Mike thought, *covered a lot of ground.*

The lunch had to be brief, even though the list of things to do increased exponentially. Part of the coterie—A.J., Kap, Gus, Hendrickson, and Russell—were already eating, as Darlene had requested they not wait on the president, who was served the moment he sat.

"I like the service," he quipped. "Who's first?" he asked, his spoon poised over a bowl of beef stew.

"I'll take it," Kap said. "As you and I discussed late last night, sir, there would be a need to put the pedal to the metal when the inevitable dip in the upward progress of the dollar occurred. That happened about twenty-five minutes ago and my office shot out a news alert.

"We announced that one trillion dollars of our newfound money had been transferred into a new DOER account at the Federal Reserve, which the Treasury Department would oversee. Five minutes later, the anti-bloggers were complaining that it was illegal, unethical, or not enough."

"What could they say?" Russell asked. "I'm sure they are totally bamboozled and will lamely strike out when and where they can."

"I understand; however, I sent out a reply," Kap said. He cleared his throat: *"We thank each and every one of you for your sage humanitarian suggestions."*

"I'd have told them to fuck off," Gus Vaughn said, then gently blew on his steaming soup.

Macdonald chuckled. "Don't be shy on my account."

"That's what I said!" Kap chortled.

They all laughed and then fell to eating. Macdonald broke the silence. "Okay, that'll be our plan from now on, professor. We'll detach from their vileness and vulgarities and reply with faint praise. I wouldn't be surprised if a good many of the blogs weren't coming from a congressman's or senator's office."

"If they are, I'm sure they're heavily filtered as to origination," Russell said disgustedly.

"Darlene, check with the NSA and the FBI, see if they have been tracking bloggers. Ask for IPs. Once they have something definitive, ask Director Thornton about what to do. I'd like to see the Bureau go public with their names. If they're using government computers, we could consider prosecution."

"I don't think that is legal, sir," Hendrickson said.

"Maybe *Anonymous* shouldn't have First Amendment protection. Those cowards tie up law enforcement. Ask IRS if Anonymous pays taxes. I'm serious, it's a plague."

"It would set off a firestorm," Darlene added, "but I'd love it!"

"Maybe we could call the offending parties in for a little chat and scare the living crap out of them," Gus said.

"Okay. What's the next release, Finance or Auto?"

A.J. spoke up. "I'd vote Auto."

"Any objections?" There were none. "Okay, but first send your release to Bryanna. Let her schmooze it. Also, ask her to put out a separate announcement following ours by an hour, saying what DOER will be doing with its new largess."

"Will do," A.J. said enthusiastically.

Kap was smiling. "We're setting aside three hundred billion for Auto in a New York Federal Reserve account."

Macdonald nodded. "A.J., advise Bryanna about that too. Also, ask her to start thinking about appointing a working task force for the new Auto Industry Reclamation program, which I'd like to call AIR, and ask her from me to include Michigan Governor Carlton and a finance guru of his choosing as part of it.

"Kap, you assign somebody from Treasury. Have that person be our ears and report directly to you on their financial needs. Keep Bryanna informed, but relieve her of that day-to-day responsibility. Okay, Mr. Transportation Secretary, you're up."

"Yes sir!" J.T. Russell answered. "The plan is to have an official ceremony next Tuesday in New York opening the account for AIR. As soon as we break the news this afternoon, staff will be on the phones rounding up as many high-level union and management people as they can find.

"As for all the foreign automakers, let's set them up on a conference call with you on Monday. This will assure them they won't be left out. Plus, we can find out from them what properties they lost and then take it from there."

"That's another great idea," Macdonald enthused.

"It's brilliant," Hendrickson echoed. "They could have easily been overlooked. When I think of Detroit auto, I think American."

"Me too, Ambassador," Vaughn agreed. "We actually have staff looking into that, but I'll push them."

"Okay," Macdonald said. "Maybe we could get their home countries to help out, like a partnership. We need to find how many of their working plants exist in our country. If so, could those manufacturers increase that plant's output? We could finance the transfer of workers. This is also a perfect time for retooling."

"I'll get people on that," Russell said.

Macdonald nodded. "Kap, what time today are you announcing the AIR fund?"

"Two p.m., and Secretary Vaughn will do the honors."

"It fits. I like it. Spreading the joy around. America needs to know that this is a team event. What's with Finance, Kap? Are we prepared to put something out on that today?"

"It's not fully formulated for your approval, sir. But that's not all bad, because if we get a push from the Auto announcement like we did from DOER, we won't need Finance out there today. Having the weekend would make a big difference for us. The quiet time would also be very beneficial to the stomach. Besides, I want for our bankers to work over the weekend," the SecTres said. "I've alerted a dozen of them so far that if they balk and don't get off their dead asses, we'll set up our own lending institution and put them out of business."

Russell jumped in. "They have nothing to lose, since the money they'll be lending will come from our new funds and not their pockets."

"Okay, Monday for Financial, it is. Should I be at the New York presentation on Tuesday?"

"You can be anyplace you want to be, sir," Darlene injected, "but using your 'sharing the wealth' theme, maybe this would be a wonderful time and place for the vice president to get out of her bunker, euphemistically speaking, and let her light shine. With what she's accomplished throughout the Midwest these past few years, I'm sure she'll know many of those folks personally."

"Perfect. AIR and DOER will be serving many of the same people," Macdonald claimed.

"After what I heard at our meeting this morning with DOD and CIA, sir," she added, "you could be quite busy with the Russian front."

"Darlene is correct, sir." Hendrickson said. "It will be Commander-in-Chief time. You have appointed able friends, who will dutifully handle their assignments. I was impressed this morning with how far CIA has progressed in its investigation using Dr. Mednorov's information."

The mention of Alex spiked Macdonald's adrenaline.

"With the exception of your conference call on Monday, which I agree rightfully falls to you. Vice President Dudley is running with the domestic ball. You are well served, Mr. President."

"Right on, Ambassador," Kap laughingly said.

Macdonald appreciated his mentor's remarks and said humbly. "Thank you. I will see you tomorrow at Camp David. Darlene? Anything else?"

Darlene smiled. "I'm sure there is, or will be, but right now you have a helicopter waiting on you, sir."

43

Air Force One
Destination: Detroit
Friday, January 25
1250 hours

Once aboard Air Force One on the way to Detroit, President Macdonald was on the phone to Canadian Prime Minister Brewster McEwen, discussing the agenda for their meeting. The two leaders had met before, but this would be their first official gathering since Macdonald's election. They'd had several conversations, but McEwen mostly communicated with Vice President Dudley regarding their joint operations.

A cold front had pushed through overnight Thursday, as advertised, and the airport ground temperature was twenty-two degrees. The severe drop created an urgent need for more bedding, clothing, and towels at the recovery camps hastily going up throughout Michigan, Indiana, Illinois, and Ohio.

Following calls to Senate and House leaders from his airborne office, Macdonald acquiesced to the urgings of A.J. and Gus that he take a half-hour nap. He promptly dozed off.

Detroit was a no-fly zone. While President Macdonald and Prime Minister McEwen would be on the ground, fighter jets would patrol a two-hundred-mile radius, while NORAD and NRO had their satellites focused on a wider area.

The airport was heavily guarded by a company of combat-ready troops along with a company of MPs. The Secret Service had its early contingent already on the ground. Local police lined the roads feeding the airport.

On the tarmac, Vice President Dudley eagerly awaited the president's arrival.

She had not seen him in person since the final inaugural ball Monday night. A band was playing patriotic pieces as AF1 landed and taxied close to a hangar. When Macdonald appeared at the top of the stairway, the band flowed right into "Ruffles and Flourishes."

He raced down the long set of steps and into his dear friend's arms. They hugged as great friends, not perfunctorily. Their height difference being over one foot, he unceremoniously elevated her right off her feet and then gently let her down. Their powerful bond was evident.

They then moved into the hangar to await Prime Minister McEwen, acknowledging the people alongside the crowd-control line, but now was not the time for handshakes.

AF1 taxied away, making room for the Canadian plane, which had landed. When it pulled up to the hangar, Dudley and A.J. went to collect the American attendees. The president waited with Secretary Vaughn to greet their guests.

There was an abbreviated ceremony with an Honor Guard displaying the colors of both nations. There were no speeches. The group quickly headed for the hangar and once inside, the partially open, immense doors slowly closed. Simultaneously, the MP company, with armored vehicles, took up its outside position in front of the closed doors. The Army troops broke into platoons and moved to set up a perimeter defense.

Dudley and her team were experienced in conducting large meetings. The one hundred attendees sat two rows deep in a semicircle. A pair of eight-foot folding tables with a dozen chairs faced the inside of the arc. They were dwarfed inside the cavernous hangar.

Dudley opened with a series of comments, and then turned Phase I over to Michigan Governor Carlton. He was followed by reports detailing the well-being of the survivors and the support teams. Lt. General Leon Dominic, the overall military field commander for the Americans, gave a glowing report on how well the US military and the National Guard conjoined.

Once cleared to enter the affected areas, squad-sized groups had begun the daunting task of going house by house or rubble pile by rubble pile. Mortuary teams had been overwhelmed by the sheer volume of dead. Collecting DNA was a daunting task.

Map teams were working back in Washington, studying photos from before the bomb and then overlaying the after pictures. A few city workers had been located and blended in with analyzing teams as they moved toward the banks of the crater lake.

When Dudley's team finished their reports, she introduced Prime Minister McEwen. He thanked the president and the vice president profusely. "Our two countries are better off because of the coordinated rescue operations."

The top Canadian military and civilian leaders then gave their reports, which, too, tragically dealt with an immolated population. Wrapping up the Canadian portion of Phase I reports, McEwen said, "No tsunami or series of category five tornadoes could have been more devastating."

Dudley followed. "We will not know for months the numbers of souls who were taken from us, but we do know we will do everything possible to find out. In the meantime, we will continue to assist our brothers and sisters who have lost their material goods, their jobs, and their loved ones. We'll take a ten-minute break and then reconvene with phase two."

44

Phase two of the meeting began with small discussion groups on where to place the displaced. This included what to do about the people who did not want to return at all. The conversation was lively and constructive; however, after determining the two countries had greatly differing approaches, Dudley interceded and suggested that each nation handle those concerns separately. The meeting concluded with good feelings all around. The task was unfathomable, but everyone was determined to face it head-on. Rehabilitation of the survivors would come long before restoration or reconstruction. The final resolve came from Gus Vaughn: "The survivors' well-being is our foremost obligation."

During a short social time, McEwen said, "I understand Prime Minister Howard was planning a visit with you in early February, when he planned a visit with us. However, we were informed this morning that his trip has been moved up to this Thursday. Maybe we could plan a Saturday get-together here."

Dudley liked the idea. "Why not do a tour of the DTO?"

Macdonald and McEwen agreed. "We can ask for progress reports from today's efforts and give Mr. Howard a firsthand scenario of how we're jointly handling the recovery," the president added.

"Governor Carlton wants to have a dedication ceremony, affirming the state's and the nation's commitment to rebuilding the city," Dudley said. "We could coordinate that into our planning."

"Good," McEwen slapped his knees in satisfaction, rising from his chair. "Well, I best be off. Thank you both for your hospitality. With your joint leadership, I can see your country quickly reestablishing its position in the world. I don't know how you were able to do what you did to right your ship of state this morning,

Mr. President, but I believe it may go down in the annals of history as one of the world's finest acts of statesmanship."

"You're very kind, Prime Minister. I'm most gratified that you see us . . ." he indicated Dudley, ". . . as a partnership, because we are. Our Constitution won't allow co-presidents; otherwise, that is what we would be."

McEwen nodded. "Well, until next weekend."

Dudley and Macdonald watched the Prime Minister mount the stairway, turn, and wave, which they returned in kind. He then disappeared inside his plane.

"Mike," Bryanna said, "I want to thank you for those kind words, but make no mistake, you are Mr. President. We do things right the next eight years, my time will come."

"You better believe it will, my friend. You know I wouldn't have taken this on if you weren't at my side."

She eyed him with her usual knowing, confident gaze and said, "I understand I am going to New York to ceremonially preside over the establishment of a three-hundred-billion-dollar Auto Industry Reclamation project."

"Who else? AIR fits in perfectly with DOER. Gus and J.T. are supervising the search for old auto plants that are closed down but still standing and, hopefully, still operational. We might get the industry up and running faster going that route, along with upgrading and expanding existing plants situated elsewhere in the country."

He thought of another idea and added, "Look, when you're in New York Tuesday, ask the management and union folks for some time together and find out what parts of the manufacturing process could be up and running the quickest. See what they think about going to Kentucky or wherever."

"I believe there are several locations. I'll get Gus on that right now, maybe set aside two billion . . ."

He interrupted with a gesture and a smile. "You won't have to worry about set asides. You've got three hundred billion, just draw down on that. Kap's setting it up. I've been amazed at how fast his mind works and the functional ideas he comes up with. Our SecTres is a firebrand."

"Who'd've thought," she said wryly. "By the way, we're moving home plate to here in the terminal building. We've also taken over a motel just south of the airport as our residence and got three Marine One–type helicopters coming in here this afternoon. After you leave, my team and I are heading for ground zero and will begin the task of moving rubble into the crater."

"Anything you need, just call."

"I know that, Mike. But we want to keep this off your desk, so you can concentrate on getting the bad guys."

"I'm going to Camp David tonight. Bill Hendrickson has been a wonderful mentor for me. So much so that I've made him an official member of the administration. After his wife died early last year, he began going downhill. Working on our campaign revived him some, and now . . . well, he's like the man I knew twenty years ago in Kuwait."

"And to think, without him, you would be a Marine officer about to retire."

"That thought has crossed my mind a couple of times."

The president's military aide approached. "Excuse me, sir, ma'am. Air Force One is ready, sir."

"Thank you, Commander, I'll be a few more minutes."

"Yes sir. I'll inform the pilot."

Macdonald turned back to Dudley. "Division of responsibility is necessary. Your taking over this massive recovery has been a blessing to me and, more importantly, to the country. How are you and Gus getting along?"

She raised her eyebrows. "He takes a little getting used to, but he's bright and very determined."

"Oh, he is that, and you'll never find anyone more loyal. I like that he stirs people up. He's not mean-spirited. He thinks your DOER program is a perfect balance to Homeland Security and FEMA, which he believes should not be responsible for the rebuilding. They should specialize in disaster relief and how best to coordinate with DOER."

"FEMA never seemed to have enough people where they were needed. DOER has shown that volunteers can be mustered rapidly, and suppliers are responding more quickly because we pay them right away."

"Let's work on getting FEMA honed into an A-one rapid responder," he said.

She nodded. "I'm with you. They've done well here, worked well with the National Guard and DOER. FEMA hasn't received any funds from Congress yet for payroll and supplies, which is not a surprise. I'm taking over the payments. We'll bill Congress later."

"We've done that before. You've got the money. You might want to think about slowly downsizing FEMA's involvement in this situation now and have them begin restocking for the next disaster. Last year proved that's the right course to take. Let DOER and the National Guard take over. I know DOER's designed to be all volunteers, but it might not be a bad idea to pay for supervisory staff. We're going to be in here a long time, and there are a ton of folks looking for a job."

Dudley agreed. "DOER was your beginning in politics. I used Congress's apathy to drag you into helping me. You turned DOER into a well-funded reality. Donations come in every day."

He smiled. "We can make a difference, Bryanna. We've attracted fabulous people to our administration who have not been dragged down by Washington-speak." He checked the time.

She laughed. "We did go off a little, didn't we?"

He laughed. "Don't we always?"

"It's good; it's healthy. Don't worry, I can work with Augustus Vaughn. Is he married?"

Mike laughed. "Twice divorced, early on. He dates, I guess. He's pretty tight on that."

"I've only been divorced once."

They both laughed. "I'm staying out of this one. I won't be able to commit him here too much longer, though. He has a huge department to run and is yet to see his office."

"That makes two of us," she pointed out. "However, I'm well on my way to sorting out who can do what."

"It's all yours. My concentration is moving over to the investigation. Rather than give you what we're working on right now, I'll just say we have some leads, which will be difficult to corroborate. I'm meeting with CIA and DOD at Camp David tomorrow."

She looked at him questioningly. "Any hints?"

"Yesterday we learned some startling things. Of course, you have every right to know, but I'd like to keep you focused on what you are doing here. We won't move without your input, I promise you."

"You're right about not setting my fertile brain off on something I can do nothing about . . . well, not right now anyway."

They both cracked up.

"We are in an enviable position," he said. "However, we have to be mindful that our benefactors are scrutinizing our every move. They are counting on us to set things right."

45

Aboard AF1, Macdonald was on the phone. "Everything ran long, Jane," he said to his personal assistant. He sat alone in his airborne office, somewhere over southern Ohio.

"Oh dear. I hope that hasn't made you change your plans."

"We got started late and the second half ran long, but for good reasons: lots of great ideas. People were constructive. I met amazing folks, giving it their all."

"I seem to remember a young couple who sounded very much like that," she said fondly.

"I don't want Alex to worry anything has gone wrong."

"I'll call her. I always like talking to her."

AF1 picked up a little tailwind and landed in Andrews at 1916 hours. He deplaned, shook some hands, and gathered with his fellow attendees to thank them for their participation. The temperature was a mild thirty-eight degrees, compared to Detroit's sub-freezing weather.

A Navy lieutenant approached and saluted. "Mr. President."

"Lieutenant."

"I accompanied Dr. Mednorov on the drive here at Mrs. Bolton's request."

"I appreciate both Mrs. Bolton's concern and your assistance." *Cynthia*, he thought, *the stern lady with a soft heart.* "Where is Dr. Mednorov now?"

"Aboard Marine One, sir."

"Thank you, Lieutenant. Enjoy the weekend. You're dismissed."

He snapped to attention. "Thank you, sir." He saluted, did an about face, and marched off to his ride back to DC.

Macdonald bade everyone goodnight and boarded the helicopter. He handed his briefcase to a crew member, stripped off his outer jacket, and moved into the cabin.

Alex stood and threw her arms around him. They hugged with a hard squeeze, and then each rubbed their hands up and down each other's back. He kissed her lightly on the forehead.

"We have to sit before they will take off. You take the window; it's a great view."

"I only want to look at you," she said, sliding in first.

Macdonald had been told the Service preferred him to be on the aisle, in the event of an emergency.

Alex looked adoringly into his eyes. "We are beginning a new adventure, *mon cher.*"

And where will it lead? he wondered.

46

Camp David
Friday, January 25
1830 hours

At eighteen hundred feet above sea level, the lighted landing pad in the Catoctin Mountain Park appeared as a small football field, looming up out of the darkness to consume Marine One as it deliberately lowered onto the pad.

He explained to Alex that protocol called for him to go down the steps first and, once down, she could join him. He liked that she was with him for his first landing at Camp David. At the foot of the steps, he was met by the base commanding officer, Cdr. Stewart Fredericks.

Alex joined them, and he introduced her as Dr. Alexandra Mednorov, and then they were in the SUV for the short drive to Aspen Lodge, the president's residence in the hundred-twenty-seven-acre compound. As they rolled along the narrow road, they held hands.

I hope the staff doesn't feel compelled to give me a tour of the whole place, he wished.

At the front door, the commander introduced the cook and two petty officers who were there to meet the president and his guest, and then led them into the living room. There, they were greeted by a robust fire in the large inviting fireplace.

"Oh, how lovely," Alex exclaimed happily.

"It certainly is," Macdonald enthused.

"Sir," the commander said. "I will leave you in the staff's capable hands."

"Thank you, Commander."

Commander Fredericks gave the president a slight nod and left. Chief Stankowski, the cook, addressed Macdonald.

"Mrs. Bolden called me to say you were operating without any sleep these past two days and might like some hot tea and small cakes They are on the coffee table, sir."

"Yes, she sees to my every need," he said, cracking a large grin.

The Chief nodded and took a few steps toward a hallway. "This leads to the kitchen and dining room, and the hallway there," she pointed to the opposite side of the room, "is where the bedrooms are located," and then to another door, "and your office is in there. There will be somebody in the kitchen until after you retire, Mr. President. You will be holding your meetings in Laurel Cabin, which is a short walk from here. It has a conference room, small meeting rooms, and an office for you."

"Thank you, Chief."

"If there is nothing else for this evening, sir . . . ?"

"No, I don't believe so, but just so that you know . . ." he paused for effect. "I enjoy snacks, but I love the richest vanilla ice cream you can find loaded up with chocolate syrup. And I do like raiding the icebox."

He caught a stifled smile from Alex, who quickly looked down.

"Aye sir. Will there be anything more?"

He shook his head, no.

"Goodnight, Mr. President."

The cook and her people left for the kitchen. Once alone, he took Alex's hand and walked her to the fireplace. "Remind you of a little inn in Bath?"

As she snuggled up against him, he put his arm around her, pressing her close to him.

She smiled up at him. "I like your *dacha*, Mr. President."

"I am told that every former president has said this place is what they missed most after they left office."

"How long will we stay, Michael?"

"I hope until Sunday evening."

"And will others be staying here that long as well?"

"Most or all will leave by tomorrow night. I'm not going to encourage anyone to stay longer, although there are guest cabins. Hopefully, we will accomplish enough to keep them busy elsewhere."

"It would be nice if we could have Sunday for us," she said softly.

"My sentiments, my sweet. Shall we?" He gestured to the small, square table holding the tray, but first took her in his arms and kissed her gently, followed by a hug. "I love that we are sharing this place together for the first time. It makes it more special."

They sat on the sofa quietly, saying little, as they looked into the fire, idly nibbling and sipping their tea. He refreshed their cups and placed two cakes on each saucer, then placed them on the tray. "Shall we?"

She nodded and smiled. They moved into the softly lit master bedroom. Along the way, Alex had released the top two buttons on her pale-blue blouse, giving her an alluring look, which he noticed immediately.

Once in the bedroom, he placed the tray on one of the two dressers and gently took her into his arms and kissed her. Leaning his head back he said, "If we're living in a dream, don't wake me."

She giggled. "No, my sweet, we are living *the* dream."

His hands were on her blouse, undoing the rest of the buttons. He opened it slowly and brought his hands up to her sumptuous breasts, lightly pressing his thumbs on her nipples. She shivered ever so lightly and slid her arms around his waist, pulling him to her. He moved his hands onto her bare shoulders, and the blouse slid down her arms and to the floor.

At an increasing pace, their clothing was shed, and they embraced. She felt his hardness and giggled softly. He swooped an arm under her and carried her to the turned-down bed. Amidst fervent kisses, she squirmed toward the middle of the bed to make room for him, and he slid onto his side. She reached for his full erection and rolled to be over him on her knees. She eased him into her and bent over him, studying the emotion of his eyes. As he played with her nipples, she shuddered helplessly. Her hips gyrated as he moved more deeply into her. Kissing him wildly, she held his head in her hands as she slid up and down upon him.

Their motions quickened, and she rose up, sitting into him, his hands playing all over her. He pulled her to him, sending thrilling sensations of pleasure through her. She gave a heave of ecstasy and climaxed with a suppressed shout of glee as he followed her, thrusting up as hard as he could.

After their second round of lovemaking, Mike's two days of nearly no sleep and his waning supply of adrenaline caught up to him. Alex snuggled close, and he quickly drifted off.

47

It was 5:54, according to the digital clock on the nightstand, when she awoke. Mike was breathing easily and didn't look like he'd moved all night. She rolled out of bed and stretched, feeling wonderfully refreshed. After showering, she rummaged the closet nearest the bath, found two fluffy bathrobes, and took the smaller of the two. A pair of size-seven slippers fit perfectly.

She turned out the dressing room light and waited for her eyes to adjust to the darkness. There was no light leaking in from outside, just a dull, green baseboard nightlight near the bathroom door. Alex gently covered Mike. He stirred lightly.

Her robe secure, she eased out of the bedroom, quietly closing the door. The same dim green lights lit the hallway baseboard as she headed for the kitchen. Arriving, she saw the cook and a uniformed male sitting with their backs to her, having a quiet conversation.

She stood at the entrance twenty feet or so away from them. The smell of fresh coffee prompted her to speak. "Good morning," she said lightly.

They both jumped to their feet, turning to her.

"I'm so sorry to startle you," she said, with a smile.

They responded with tentative smiles. "Ma'am," the cook said. The guard just nodded.

"The president is still asleep. May I have a cup of that wonderful-smelling coffee?"

"Yes ma'am," the cook said moving to a double coffeemaker.

"What time are the first guests to arrive?" Alex asked.

"The first will come in at 0830 hours and the next about 0915 hours, ma'am."

Alex frowned at the strange way the time was given. "Is that this morning?"

"Yes ma'am. Camp David is run by the Navy. We use military time," the cook responded with a quick head-to-toe appraisal.

"Will the arrivals all come to this house?"

"No ma'am, most all will be taken to Laurel, up the road, unless President Macdonald says otherwise. As for who is coming, we have a list of names, titles, or rank."

"Which helicopter will Ms. Sweetwater be on?"

The cook went back to the table and picked up a clipboard that held several sheets of paper. "She's on the first one, ma'am."

Alexandra was sure Michael would want Darlene to come to Aspen.

Realizing she hadn't gotten the coffee, the cook went back to the urns. "How do you like it? Regular or—"

"How may I call you?" Alex asked softly.

"Chief or Millie."

"I like a little milk and sweetener," she said smiling.

"We have cream."

"No thank you, milk will be fine."

"I can make you some toast, a bagel . . . "

"A piece of toast, thank you."

Millie went about fixing the toast.

"Is there a view?" Alex asked.

"Be about a half hour before you can see anything. Weather bureau says it's going to be about twenty above and clear. In the winter, you can see south and east a good ways."

After Alex had her slice of toast and mug of coffee, she thanked Millie. "May I tell you something about the president, Chief?"

"Yes ma'am," the CPO replied.

"He likes his coffee black and hot all the time. Do you have some hot plates for cups? It will save you running-around time." She smiled and headed to the bedroom.

Mike had stirred and was on his right side. She sat in a chair by the shaded window and sipped her coffee. It was nearly 6:30 a.m., no, 0630 hours.

What happened when it got to after 12? she wondered.

She finished her toast and coffee and walked over to her half-covered lover. She walked around the bed, undid her robe, draped it on the foot of the bed, and crawled in alongside him.

She liked being naked with him, but she liked it more when he was awake. She decided to be naughty and traced her fingers along the side of his face. His nose twitched, and his lips pursed slightly.

"Good morning, Michael," she said in her low, soft voice.

He stirred. Her desire was to make love before he had to become *presidential* when they would have to revert to their formal relationship. She reached down to play with him and felt his instant response. He turned toward her, and she welcomed him into her arms, smiling as she did so. He would belong to the others soon enough—for now he was hers.

They shared a shower and continued their romancing there. They were silly together, knowing the daunting tasks the day held. They became more pensive as they dried each other off. The fifth day of his presidency was going to be immensely important, and it was about to begin.

48

Macdonald went directly to his Aspen Lodge desk, made two calls, and took one call from Darlene at 0725 hours. He took out his Blackberry; there was a message from Eubanks. Coming on the 0830 with PDB plus Phoenix info. Can we meet prior to others arrival?

He sent a reply. *Yes. All come to Aspen with Darlene.*

Alex entered as he was tapping in his message. She'd suspected correctly: he had rejoined the world. "You told me you would eat in the kitchen. Millie is all ready for us."

"Millie? Okay, let's do it," he said, getting up from his desk and stealing a kiss from her before she led him to the kitchen.

"Good morning, Chief. Sure smells good in here," he said in his personable way as he poked his head through the kitchen door.

The cook smiled and nodded.

"I hope you don't mind, sir; I have already made up two omelets, which just need a couple of minutes. I make a mean omelet, if I do say so myself."

"Then there is no question in my mind that I am going to like it. And tell me, what title do you go by?"

"My military rank is Chief Petty Officer. My name is Mildred Stankowski. The Navy and Marines call me Chief. My friends, Millie. We have a head steward, Lieutenant Commander Frank Malone. He'll handle everything at Laurel Cabin. I best get that omelet to you before the others come."

Within a minute, the steaming omelets were served. "Enjoy, sir," the Chief said, also setting down a linen-lined basket of homemade muffins.

He took a bite. "Excellent omelet, Chief."

He spoke softly to Alex. "I'm going to the office. The first meeting is classified.

When it's over, I'll call you. We'll be going to another building for the meeting you will be attending."

When he finished eating, he pantomimed a kiss to Alex.

"Take a hot cup of coffee," she said.

"I'll get that for you, sir," Millie said, taking the mug and refilling it. Alex smiled as he took the mug and gave her a wink.

Alex warmed her coffee and engaged Chief Millie, who was roughly her age, in conversation. After she'd turned thirty-five, Alex found herself inclined to engage others to find out what they had done with their lives. She wanted to know about Millie's life ventures. Millie proved to be an impressive peer who seemingly had not wasted a moment of her life.

Millie, too, was curious about this woman with an east European accent. She was obviously romantically involved with the president, but she would also be attending a meeting with generals and security people.

Alex expressed an interest in learning more about Camp David, so Millie ran down some of its history and what the duty was like. Millie had a husband and two grown boys. One was a Marine sergeant stationed at Camp Lejeune, North Carolina, and the other was in college. Their home was in Frederick, only a few miles from the camp.

The communications squawk box went off announcing the arrival of a helicopter. ETA: three minutes.

"I look forward to more times with you, Millie," Alex said, as she headed out of the room. She found Mike at his desk, reading. She knocked lightly, and he looked up.

"Your first group is coming in."

"Thanks. It's Darlene and Director Eubanks."

"They take good care of you here. I like your Aspen *dacha*," she said with a light air, going to him.

He swiveled to meet her extended hands, which he took and pulled her down onto his lap.

"I love you, Michael, more than I thought possible."

"I love you. In some ways, I may have never stopped."

49

Aspen Lodge, Camp David
Saturday, January 26
0830 hours

Two SUVs pulled up to Aspen Lodge's front door and Macdonald greeted them, feeling a sense of normalcy when he saw Darlene. He greeted her warmly and felt her intuitive eyes all over him. Steve Hester was with Eubanks, who introduced Dr. Archibald Montgomery and two other members of the NNSA.

"A driver will be taking Nancy and Jeri on to Laurel Cabin," Macdonald told Darlene, "where the meetings will take place. The head steward, Lieutenant Commander Malone, is there and will help them with the setup."

He escorted her through the living room to his office where they reviewed the morning's agenda, and then they joined the others in the living room. Chief Millie's team was doling out light snacks and beverages. Eubanks greeted Macdonald and handed him the PDB.

"There's nothing startling, sir, but I think you may want to review it before we move to other matters."

Macdonald read quickly. There had been a bombing in Pakistan, a country in constant chaos, including another border skirmish to the east with India. The Afghans had pretty much rendered the Taliban ineffective, and American troops and advisors were now down to under ten thousand trainers and medical personnel, with yesterday's return home of twenty-seven hundred troops.

He glanced at two other items and closed the folder. "It's nice to see some good news, except for Pakistan, of course. I like that our markets were up across the boards yesterday."

"Your actions brought about positive results, Mr. President," Darlene said.

The house staff finished serving and retreated to the kitchen. Darlene then started the meeting.

"Kap wanted you to know that based on uncorroborated yet reliable reports, our new benefactors made nearly a trillion and a half euros from their investments in us. And as a thank you, late Friday a little over six hundred billion dollars of additional T-Notes were purchased."

"I'll follow up with them on Monday. Now, if Congress would reduce spending . . ." He shrugged.

"Kap's unsure about the Russians' losses. He estimates they were in the hundreds of billions of euros. He was told two corporations failed to cover and lost a combined 150 billion euros."

"That's not chump change, anywhere," Macdonald said gleefully. "That was a pretty good day. After closing out their shorts, those who stayed long made some nice money, including the Russians if they stayed in. We couldn't control that."

Darlene nodded. "That's all I have, sir. Director Eubanks has some breaking news."

"One more thing before you start, Jim," Macdonald interrupted. "I want you all to know that the New York Federal Reserve Bank was not involved in any of these currency dealings. I know naysayers will be looking for something wrong, but the record will show the US government did not go short and then cover. Our friends did, but then that was their decision. Okay?"

"Understood, Mr. President," Darlene said.

Macdonald nodded. "Also, none of this is to be discussed outside of this meeting. What we do with our newfound treasure is how we will be measured. Recovery, restoration, and retribution are the new *three Rs*. Okay, Jim."

"Thank you, Mr. President. When I arrived at Langley at 0545 hours, I was greeted by some interesting news from Phoenix team, which will cause a major shift in our thinking. There was no break-in at the Gravastock storage facility. There were no missing bombs."

"What?" Macdonald exclaimed, rocking forward in his seat. "Are they sure?"

"They took a bold but calculated step, sir. Utilizing the team's two Russian assets, who knew the storage facility's commanding general, the team leader went to the facility and literally knocked on his door. They were escorted to General Orlovski's office.

"It's a different world over there from what you and I experienced twenty years ago, sir. They were served cognac and treated cordially. Our findings in Detroit as to the type of bomb used were relayed to the General and two of his general staff.

"Using the Russian 12th Main Directorate of the Ministry of Defense's manifest of all items stored in the CO's facility, they found that the exact type of nuclear device could only have been stored in his stockpile of weapons, of which there were over two thousand."

"Enough to annihilate the world," Macdonald muttered.

"Oh, that's not all, sir. There are thousands in storage facilities throughout the countries that once composed the Eastern Bloc, behind the Iron Curtain. After much discussion, our people were granted access and our Phoenix inspectors arrived shortly afterward to inspect the stockpile, abetted by the guardians of their trove. Our folks were in agreement; nothing was missing.

"One of our assets was a former colonel in the Ministry of Defense. The other one was a scientist who had once worked for the Ministry of Atomic Energy, known as Minatom."

"You cultivate some quality people, Jim."

The DCIA smiled.

"Okay, so no one stole a nuclear weapon. Where does that put us now?" Macdonald asked, looking around the room.

"We received some amazing cooperation," Eubanks iterated. "My team leader assured the Russian CO that Phoenix's visit would remain a non-event. The general opened up more and offered to have every storage facility, regardless of the vintage or payload, make a thorough investigation, even though the General insisted that nothing could have been removed, even by an insider."

"Do Secretary Garrett and the Joint Chiefs know?"

"Yes. They received the same message," Eubanks replied.

"I guess this refocuses our efforts," Macdonald said, a rock-hard seriousness to his tone. "If it's not Russian . . ."

"Oh, it's Russian, sir," said NNSA PhD Archibald Montgomery abruptly. "Excuse my interruption, sir, but if it didn't come from storage, then it was manufactured from stolen parts."

"But wouldn't they have come from the same place, Doctor?" Macdonald asked.

"The only conclusion I can draw right now, sir, is that a rogue group inside Russia is strong and deep enough in scientific expertise to make such a device."

"With what you uncovered in the financial conspiracy, sir," Eubanks said, "and from what Dr. Mednorov told us, I think it's a good bet it came from Russia, but not from the sitting government. There are theorists in Russia who feel Russia has a secret government that runs everything.

"I'm aware that we have people in our country who believe the same thing about our government. But I've been on the inside for nearly twenty-five years and don't agree with the likelihood of that here; however, I believe it's true in Russia, with the old KGBers and their disciples, like Dr. Mednorov's school friend at Oxford, and the recent money manipulations she told us about."

"Okay," Macdonald nodded thoughtfully, seeing a new plot evolving.

"Sir?" Montgomery asked. "With plutonium and highly enriched uranium being the essential ingredients for nuclear weapons, it is beyond the capabilities of rogue terrorists to produce the ingredients for a device like the one used in Detroit.

"However, some far-thinking planners could have siphoned off enough material from the many transfers of nuclear warheads between storage facilities, Minatom manufacturing plants, and Russian nuclear force units to stockpile the ingredients needed to produce the bomb used in the DTO."

"Good God, Doctor. Right under their own government's nose," Macdonald said with amazement.

"That's not an unlikely scenario, sir," said Eubanks. "Going from being the USSR to being Russia in the late '90s, the technical capabilities for verification accountability had not been fully developed. This would have given the hardliners plenty of opportunities to pluck out whatever they needed."

Montgomery eagerly added, "In our work with them over the years, we—and I believe, the CIA—have identified many former KGB who maintained a hard-line attitude."

"Overthrowing?" Macdonald asked incredulously.

Eubanks jumped in. "No, sir. Working from within, regaining power politically, and voting out the reformers."

"Then why bomb us?" Macdonald asked inflamed. "Did they need money that badly to injure or kill millions of Americans and Canadians just so they could short the dollar and walk away with mega tons of cash?"

Macdonald felt his pulse pounding and stood, waving them to stay seated, and paced the room. Quiet fell over the small group, each in their own thoughts.

Darlene checked her watch. "The others should be arriving soon, Mr. President."

"Okay, we'll reconvene in Laurel. Darlene."

He motioned for her to join him in the kitchen.

Alex was sitting with Millie at the dining table. "Hey," he said, making Millie jump to her feet. "What're you two up to?" he asked trying to sound casual. Alex smiled.

"Chief, I'd like you to meet Darlene Sweetwater, my Chief of Staff. Darlene, Chief Petty Officer Mildred 'Millie' Stankowski."

Darlene offered her hand to the chief. "Nice to meet you."

"Welcome to Aspen Lodge, ma'am."

Alex stood and smiled. "Chief Sweetwater, good morning."

"Dr. Mednorov," she replied neutrally.

"Okay. Please, get on a first-name basis when we're not in a formal situation. I'd feel more like I was among friends and you two are my dearest. Darlene, this is Alexandra or Alex, and Alex, this is Darlene. Please," he implored.

He realized Darlene preferred things formal, which didn't necessarily mean she was stiff-necked. He also realized she would do this for him. She smiled good-naturedly and said, "Alex."

"Thank you . . . Darlene," Alex looked at the president, brow furrowed. "This is so hard, Michael. She is such an important person."

"I understand, but she doesn't bite. She is true to her family name and is one of the *sweetest* people you will ever know."

Darlene moved to Alex. "I, too, have difficulty being informal with people of stature. If I appear stiff, it is not personal; it is my training. But I do want to get to know you and look forward to doing so. I know what you mean to Mike. Now, if you will both excuse me, I need to find a place to freshen up."

"Let me show you," Alex said, and the two went out.

Left alone, he pondered, *careful what you ask for.*

50

The second helicopter landed on the Camp David helipad at 0910 hours carrying Alisa Padget, the president's National Security Advisor; former Ambassador Bill Hendrickson; Secretary of Defense Ogden Garrett; and JCS Chief General Carla Gibbons, with Major General Salvatore Romano and Colonel Shawn Washington, both from Special Operations. Darlene left for Laurel Cabin along with Hester, Montgomery, and the two NNSA men. Ambassador Hendrickson and Eubanks remained at Aspen Lodge. While this all took place, Macdonald briefed Alex on Dr. Montgomery's theory, and then joined Hendrickson and Eubanks in the intelligence meeting.

"What I thought would be a preliminary meeting on military strategy has now turned into an intelligence operation. Director?"

Eubanks spoke directly to Alex. "We suspect now that the bombing is part of a covert plan buried deep within the Russian government, but not representing the government. Hardliners, old KGBers, brewing a plot to undermine their sitting government."

Alexandra's demeanor was bland, her face almost frozen. "I have held out hope, Mr. President," her voice steady, but quiet, "that my country was not involved in the bombing, even when I brought you the financial information."

"We're not saying it is the Russian government," Macdonald said softly. "Jim, Phoenix told you their meeting with Orlovski started out cordially, right?"

"It did, sir," the DCIA replied. He recapped what took place when the team arrived at the storage facility.

Mike studied Alex. She seemed to relax a little.

Eubanks finished by saying, "Alex, we don't know what to think. It would take powerful people, maybe dating back to the USSR, to pull off such a maneuver."

"Yes," she said her voice controlled. "Vasiliy said there were those like

Raisa who do not want capitalism. They want a centrally controlled socialist government. Vasiliy believed they were planning a financial scheme, involving many companies in several countries. They wanted him to transfer huge sums into each.

"This was something Vasiliy could not do. He is like your Federal Reserve, I think, but FSB does not allow deposits of government money into foreign companies. Days later, Raisa introduced a man, Nicolai—I never heard a last name—who was unknown to Vasiliy, who showed him papers that authorized him to tell Vasiliy to forget the corporations and, instead, place over a trillion euros in a special account for Iran and China infrastructure development.

"I have not talked with him since the New Year. I do not know if he did that, but I would think so. I worry that the China and Iran money was used for other purposes. I worry they will claim Vasiliy was responsible. But he wouldn't . . ." tears welled in her eyes. "Excuse me." She bolted from the room.

Macdonald felt her pain as he watched her leave.

Eubanks waited for a reaction from the president, but there was none. "Mr. President, Alexandra stated what I believe has been going on. The Russian economy has been in a tailspin for over two years. The hardliners needed their newly acquired wealth to face down their sitting government."

"Blackmail, Jim? Accuse their sitting government of bombing us to gain global power and capital over a weakened US government, which is the exact same thing this secret cabal wanted?"

Ambassador Hendrickson said. "On this past Thursday, our country was on its knees, Mr. President. Yet there was nothing coming from the Russian government."

"And we picked up no static from them," Eubanks added.

"So, they only made one bomb and felt confident our dollar would rapidly lose value in the global market, causing us to default."

"Yes sir. You certainly gave them great hope that we were on the precipice of default, if not already falling into that abyss. And the mood in our country only fortified that belief," Hendrickson said.

"And your tactic of making us look much worse off than we were fed their greed to maybe even short the dollar more heavily than they had originally planned," Eubanks added.

A stroke of luck for us, Macdonald thought.

"You put everything you had on the line, Michael," Hendrickson said. "I doubt anyone else would have had your courage."

"I had a lot of help, starting with Reggie Howard. He and I called in all our personal chips from folks all around the world. He put his credibility on the line for us."

"Your selfless tactic made it all the more effective."

"Now I understand why you closed the markets," Eubanks said.

"A successful scam is all in the setup, Jim. By the time they saw what was happening, they were three, maybe five minutes behind and got hit with calls to cover. Kap told me late yesterday that three of the shell companies were extremely late in covering and cost them up to twenty-five billion euros. Two others never did cover; they probably didn't have a big enough cash back up. He suspects they lost 150 billion euros. He has an army of CPAs going through all global financial transactions to determine how much they first gained and then lost."

"That is positively amazing," Hendrickson said awestruck.

"Okay, mull that over. I'll be right back."

Macdonald went to Alex's bedroom and knocked. No answer. He knocked again. Nothing. He called out, "Lexi." No answer. He opened the door. She was face down cattycorner on the double bed, a pillow pulled over her head, her body shaking.

He went around the bed and sat, placing his hands on her shoulders, lightly massaging them. "I'm sorry, Lexi. We'll find out quickly, but I'm sure Vasiliy's all right."

She convulsed in a quick burst of heavy sobs. He attempted to loosen her grip on the pillow, and after a few seconds, she let him.

"Come on," he implored quietly, his hands rubbing her back.

Her convulsions quieted to heavy breathing. He gently coaxed her to roll over on her back. She rubbed her eyes. He fetched a box of tissues and pulled out a handful. "Here. I'll get a cold cloth."

He returned with a cool, damp washcloth and placed it on her forehead. She reached up to hold it. He pulled a few tissues from the box, dabbed her nose, and wiped her cheeks. She was slowly relaxing, her sobs waning.

When her breathing had normalized, he eased her up and helped swing her legs off the bed. He sat alongside her, took the cloth from her, and handed her more tissues. She blew her nose, and then took two long, deep breaths. The first exhale wobbled, but the second exhale was steadier.

He hugged her lightly, and she let her head rest on his shoulder. He blotted her face softly with the cold cloth.

"Oh, Michael, I am so sorry. In front of—"

"Hey," he interrupted. "You have nothing to be ashamed about."

"I do fear for Vasiliy, Michael. He would not do well under people like Raisa."

"Then we have to figure out a way for that not to happen."

"But what? How can you . . . ?" Her eyes flared, fear clear in her expression. "Oh, Michael, you wouldn't—"

"Whoa, don't get ahead of things. I have no plans to make people suffer."

"Your people are demanding—"

"That's mob mentality. They were screaming for us to bomb anybody. No, that's not going to happen. Now, come on. I'm going back to the meeting. Freshen up and join us. I love you even more, if that's possible."

She quivered, then turned her face to his and kissed him. "Thank you, Michael."

"Okay. You are a valued partner. We're meeting with the others in ten minutes."

"I will only need five."

51

Laurel Cabin
Military and Intelligence
Saturday, January 26
1000 hours

Macdonald had called ahead to Darlene to update her on the new revelations. When he and his group arrived from Aspen, she took him aside.

"General Gibbons is concerned about Alexandra being in a meeting where secret military ops will be discussed."

"Tell the general she isn't going to be in the DOD group, but Ambassador Hendrickson, Dr. Montgomery, and the NNSA men will be. Alisa and Alex will be in with Eubanks."

"I'll tell her."

"Oh, then get with Jim. I only touched the surface with you about Phoenix, he can fill you in. That'll give me time with Ogden and the military before we start."

Darlene hesitated. "Was there a problem in . . .?"

"I think we gained some valuable focus."

"Good news is always welcome," she said.

Macdonald looked around for Alex and saw her talking with Nancy Armstrong and Steve Hester. He went over to them. "Hey. I need to steal Alexandra away from you two," he said, smiling. "There are some people I want her to meet."

"I enjoyed our talk," Alex said as he gently took her arm, guiding her to General Gibbons, SecDef Garrett, and two Army officers. "General, Mr. Secretary, gentlemen: I would like you to meet Dr. Alexandra Mednorov, executive financial officer and chief economist with the World Bank in Washington."

They all greeted her warmly, and she, them. Macdonald happily noted she appeared at ease, and hoped she really was. "Darlene and I will be joining you, Ogden. Dr. Mednorov is meeting with the intelligence team on the Russian involvement." He knew that would demonstrate her importance to the overall gathering.

"My pleasure to meet all of you," Alex said graciously. "Mr. President." She then left to join the intelligence group.

General Gibbons addressed Macdonald. "Sir, I don't believe Dr. Montgomery and the NNSA people have proper clearances to sit in on our—"

He interrupted, nodding that he understood. "It'll be on my say-so, General. Montgomery has far-flung experience with the Russian nuclear program and may have solid technical knowledge to contribute to an armed excursion."

"Yes sir," Gibbons acquiesced.

Darlene called the full meeting together and laid out the agenda. She closed her remarks with, "There have been changes and new disclosures. Director Eubanks."

Eubanks went through the whole report again. Macdonald admired how succinct the DCIA could be, without leaving out the salient details. Following Eubank's briefing, Darlene explained that the president wanted ideas and for no one to be shy with their suggestions.

Macdonald followed Darlene by saying, "I realize I may be coming at this more from a marketing approach, but let's give it a try. When I led a Force Recon team, I thought a certain way, which is much different from how I have to think today."

Darlene nodded to the president, and he stood, as did everyone else. They split up and moved to their respective next meetings. Secretary Garrett opened the DOD session.

"We came here this morning thinking we'd be planning a special operation into Russia. The Phoenix team's revelation that no bombs were missing from the Gravastock storage facility was shocking, to say the least.

"This questions the validity of a military operation at this time. We still don't know our enemy or anything about the bomb." He looked to the chair of the JCS. "General."

"Thank you, Mr. Secretary," General Gibbons said. "First, the Phoenix team has done an amazing job. It appears the CIA assets had some strong credentials in order to get General Orlovski to listen. I gather, from what Director Eubanks said, the general had been in the process of having the stockpile scrutinized before our team arrived there."

Macdonald, sitting at the foot of the table, leaned in. "General, if I may. That is only what we have been told; we don't know that for sure."

"Yes sir, I understand. My point being that if no bomb is missing from Gravastock, then where did the one come from? We were certain that when we identified the device, we would be able to locate the storage facility, which the Phoenix team obviously felt they had done."

SecDef Garrett interjected. "Now we are faced with the genuine possibility that a previously manufactured WMD may not have been used on Detroit, that it could have been put together from scratch."

"Which," the general added, "opens up a myriad of scenarios that have not yet been fully explored by DOD or CIA. What if it is not Russia?"

The president looked at each person. No suggestions were forthcoming.

"That scares the hell out me, General," Macdonald said. "I'm not saying I want it to be Russia, but I am saying that I don't see anything that says it is not them."

There were some questioning looks exchanged between the military officers.

Nobody appeared to offer anything, so Macdonald did. "There has been no military follow-up to the bomb. We were at our weakest right after the blast. Except for that bogus claim, nothing else has happened. All the attacks on us have been through the financial markets. Our currency value dropped, and our financial structure destabilized. I liken it to a coward who makes a sucker punch. If it doesn't work, they'd better run. This time, greed made them stick around, and we got 'em good."

"That's astounding," Garrett said. "I read about what happened this morning while traveling up here and, frankly, understood little of it, except that you went from hero to demon to hero again."

"I'm no hero, Ogden. I know greed, currency fluctuations, and the power of a rumor. Let me add one more thing, and then I'll sit back. One of our scenarios is that the old USSR hardliners are behind this.

"The downfall of the Russian economy after their windfall profits from oil and natural gas has created a lot of unrest. All the satellite countries who adopted a democratic form of government are doing better than their former mother country. Russia has known only czars and dictators. Their culture may not be able to cope with capitalism. A powerful faction wants a central power in a socialized state."

Darlene added, "It is the complication the intelligence team is struggling with."

Major General Romano spoke up. "If you are correct in your thinking, sir, where do you see Special Ops being employed?"

"Excellent question, General. Somebody is making bombs, or at least made one, someplace. If what we hear from Phoenix is accurate and the WMD stockpile is not the source we thought it to be, then we may have to go find it."

"Do you have any starting points, sir?" Romano asked.

"Not now," Macdonald answered soberly.

"Mr. President?" Garrett asked. "Is there anything from Phoenix regarding discussions with Orlovski about where a bomb-making facility could be located?"

"Not that they've reported. I'll ask Director Eubanks to have Phoenix bring that up. We were so sure we had the WMD—. That does not mean I am criticizing anyone. I am clearly not.

"However, once we received the bad news about no stolen WMD, the idea of another strategy was posed in a conversation between Eubanks, Dr. Montgomery, and Dr. Mednorov, which directed our attention to the Russian insiders working to destroy our economy.

"By the way, Dr. Mednorov and I first met when we were students together at Oxford as Rhodes Scholars. We provided you a short bio of her credentials. Believe me when I say she is one brilliant person. We are now dealing with abstracts and few facts. Please consider all *what ifs.*"

"All right," the SecDef said. "What if the Russians are behind the bombing, or what if your financial scenario and the bombing are two separate things?"

"Right," Macdonald responded smiling. "And everything in between."

"I hear you. We'll get to work on it," Garrett said.

Macdonald stood. "Please, don't get up. Thinking hypothetically, if it were us secretly making a nuclear bomb, where would we do it to be safe from satellite surveillance? I'm intrigued at where we might hide something as complex as a bomb-making and testing facility in this country. Maybe understanding that might help us with the Russians. Thank you everyone."

"Thank you, Mr. President," came the usual chorus.

Hendrickson and Darlene remained in the DOD meeting.

Macdonald hoped he had planted a seed.

52

Macdonald's entrance into the intelligence meeting immediately disrupted it. He had paused before entering because he heard a spirited dialogue between Dr. Montgomery and Steve Hester.

"Keep going," he insisted as he walked through the door. "I'm feeling some good energy in here. Don't lose it because of me."

"We're into the psychology of an enemy's covert operation and how using a bomb helped their cause. Forgetting for the moment what it did to us, we are trying to understand what positives were in it for them," Eubanks explained.

Macdonald took a seat next to Nancy Armstrong and pushed his chair back a little from the table to emphasize he was an observer. *I hope it works better in here than it did with the DOD folks.* He caught Alex's eye and flashed a smile. She shyly returned it.

"Let me back up a little," Dr. Montgomery said. "In Detroit, we determined the type of bomb it was, and NNSA knew where it was manufactured and later stored. Phoenix discovered no missing bombs. However, no one has inspected the ordnances themselves. Are they the real thing, or are they hollow shells?"

Macdonald came up out of his slouch and leaned forward, listening.

"We don't know," Eubanks said. "Steve, call ops and have them ask Phoenix."

The Russian specialist left the room.

Eubanks looked at Montgomery. "Arch, did you just develop this theory, or—"

"Yes," he interrupted. "It came to me when Steve and I were debating. I was wondering why the Russian general, whom I have met twice, was so uncharacteristically friendly.

"On my first visit, several years ago, he had put us through the hoops, split every infinitive when we didn't identify something just right. He had been more pleasant on our second visit eight months later, but that was because it was after the fact."

That caught Eubanks's interest. "You have an interesting history with Orlovski. I'll get you the names of our two Russian assets; you may know them."

Alexandra spoke up. "I, too, could not believe the cordiality that your team described had come from General Orlovski. It was a strong reversal from the general's public persona of years ago. He was a war hero putting down rebellions when the USSR dissolved. What you call a *tough guy*."

Eubanks reflectively glanced at Macdonald, who was smiling, but made no sign of joining in, so he turned to Montgomery. "Arch? Might there be a storage facility we don't know about?"

"Anything is possible, Director. I think it more likely, though, that elements were produced for a bomb and smuggled away many years ago. As Dr. Mednorov mentioned at our earlier meeting, many Russians did not see eye to eye with the reformers. Who knows what they might have done."

Eubanks looked pensive. "We need to dig deeper into the Russian system. We started out thinking a bomb was stolen, now we are told it wasn't. Could a bomb or bombs have been stashed away before the inspections? Was one actually made from smuggled ingredients? Could the ingredients have been siphoned from a casing that sits in Gravastock?"

Montgomery looked aghast. "They would have to have been magicians to replace the insides, maintain the same weight. No. Security was always extremely tight."

"Unless it was an inside job," Macdonald said.

The magnitude of that weighed heavily on everyone. Alexandra broke the silence.

"I could go to Moscow, talk with Vasiliy. He met a man new to him in the FSB, when Raisa wanted Vasiliy to fund those shell companies. The only name he mentioned was Nicolai. Raisa is very high up in the FSB—the head of the analysis, forecasting, and strategic planning service, called the International Relations Service."

"Alexandra," Eubanks said, "we believe there may be many hidden levels of authority; no clear corporate ladder."

"I, too, believe so, Director. They were to be gatherers of internal information, but they have moved their focus to gatherers of foreign financial information.

Vasiliy is high up in government finances for the Bank of Russia, as director of the Central Bank. He suspects former KGB would like a return to the old ways, even if they would not be actively involved in a new government."

Nancy said, "Something like a key bureaucrat or high-level staff in this country."

"Yes," Alexandra replied, "exactly. The chiefs need the skilled technicians to run things."

"How deeply do you think this might go?" Eubanks asked.

"I believe there are many, especially those my age and older, not too young. I believe Raisa wishes to enlist bank cooperation, because her position would be crossing too many boundaries, some of which might raise suspicion from non-Russian regulatory watchdogs around the world."

At that moment, Hester returned and whispered a long message to Eubanks who, at its conclusion, let out a long sigh. His body sagged into the chair.

53

Director Eubanks was visibly upset by Hester's message. "Excuse me a moment," he said, going back into a huddle with his Russian case officer. Both men wore glum expressions and displayed concern as they broke the huddle. Hester went to his seat.

Macdonald awaited an explanation.

Eubanks' eyes swept the room. "Mr. President, everyone, we've had a setback in Gravastock. About an hour ago, the Phoenix team was ordered out of the storage facility, denied further access to the WMDs. They were told they would not be allowed back in until they secured proper authorization.

"One of our team's Russian assets attempted to arbitrate with the junior officer bearing the message. A brief debate ensued, during which our asset determined that Orlovski was not only unavailable, he had departed the facility, most likely called to Moscow."

"Did he learn why?" Dr. Montgomery asked. "Phoenix may be many things to us, but it is a duly-authorized inspection team to others, allowed access to stockpiles. By agreement, they cannot arbitrarily be refused admission."

"True, Arch, but the Russians have the key," Eubanks said flatly, hoping to open the scientist's eyes to the reality of the situation.

President Macdonald interceded. "Where does this leave us, Jim?"

"On the outside and not even able to look in, sir."

"So, it's a stymie," Macdonald stated, his tone dark.

"We're temporarily blocked, sir, being that it is the weekend. Everybody can hide until Monday. Orlovski's aberrant behavior says to me that he knows more than he may be willing to admit. Alexandra, I am going to make some calls, after which I may want to sound you out on the answers I get."

"Certainly, Director."

Eubanks turned to the NNSA scientist. "Dr. Montgomery, can you reach your director? We need a whole new approach to these storage facilities, we may need to broaden our investigation."

"I can reach him," Montgomery replied, standing.

Eubanks stood. "We're in recess, unless, Mr. President, you—"

"Nope. Go do what you have to do."

Eubanks and Hester left the room, immediately followed by Montgomery.

"Nancy," Macdonald asked, "your boss is in with SecDef Garrett. Tell her what just went on here."

"Yes sir."

He went to Alex. "Want a cup of coffee?"

She laughed. "Is that the old Oxford code? Or have you forgotten?"

"An old fox never forgets. Alas, but no, I meant the real thing."

He took her arm and began walking. "Camp David is and will be the perfect place for us, even with an occasional Saturday meeting. We will be freer here than in the White House."

They laughed, and she squeezed his arm.

"Let's go for a walk," he said as they entered a common area adjacent to the conference room where there were coffee urns and light refreshments. He spotted a Petty Officer who had already snapped to attention.

"At ease, Petty Officer. Would you get each of us a Camp David windbreaker?"

"Yes sir." He disappeared down a hall.

Nancy caught up to them and reported that the DOD meeting was still in session and that the Darlene preferred to stay, unless needed otherwise.

"No. How you doing? Is Seth still in town?"

"He's apartment hunting."

"Tell him hi."

The Petty Officer returned with two jackets. "The Head Steward says these should fit, sir." He handed the president his and held Alexandra's out for her to slip into.

"Have a nice walk, sir," Nancy said coyly.

He grinned. "Thanks." He took Alex's arm and headed for the outside door.

"She is a nice lady. Have you known her long?"

"Sandi had hired her to be the chief operating officer under her at CAPABLE. Remind me to tell you all about that. She and her husband became great friends with us and remained so with me after Sandi died. They were tireless workers on the campaign. She and Darlene became close then and Darlene asked her if she would continue on and become her deputy. Seth is a lawyer and wanted to remain in private practice, otherwise . . . well, I'm lucky they are both in Washington."

He took her arm, and they went outside, ambling side by side, followed at a discreet distance by two members of his protective service. "It feels good out here," he said, squeezing her arm.

They took in the surroundings with abstract interest, content just being together. "My plan for us, if you agree," he said, "is to spend as many weekends as we can up here."

"It is already a special place for me. More so because we saw it for the first time together," she said lovingly.

They continued walking arm in arm, in the silence of their own thoughts, which he broke when they neared an ice-covered, ornamental pool. "I wonder if they keep fish in here all winter."

"They can, if they are the right kind," she offered.

"It seems," he said, looking over the land, "that every time we get close to a solution, it gets derailed."

"I can help, Michael. I can go to Moscow, see Vasiliy. We can call him today; it is only evening there."

"I'm sure there are security concerns. We don't want your call traced back to me."

"I understand. Someone must know—"

"I also don't like you going back there. We don't know if you are being watched. We've taken careful steps to disguise your movements to the White House, but . . . "

"Michael, please, I will be all right."

"Knowing Raisa and what you've told me she is like these days, you would not be safe. Millions have been killed to satisfy greed and ambition. The bad guys have a huge stake in this. They'll do anything to attain their goal."

"Michael, you are speaking from your heart, not as president, when you think of me. I called you, remember? Please, at least let me call Vasiliy." She took his arm and hugged it. "I want to help."

"Okay. We'll ask Jim. I'm not saying yes, but I'll keep an open mind."

She smiled and looked up, searching his eyes. "I would not go against your wishes, but you do know I could call him Monday from work."

He felt a pang of adrenaline. He knew she could. He broke into a broad grin. "You've got me. Let's see what Jim has to say. We'll do it his way; I'll back off."

She went up on her tiptoes and kissed him softly. "Thank you for caring and wanting to keep me safe."

He embraced her. "We need to get back," he said, reversing their course. As they reached the pair of agents, he smiled and asked, "Would one of you like to take the lead back to Laurel?"

"Follow me, sir," one said. The other fell in behind.

54

Darlene called out "at ease" as the president entered the conference room, and she went right to him. "Sir, General Gibbons and her team are ready to leave, unless you wish otherwise."

"Makes sense. But first, tell General Gibbons I have a few questions for them."

"Ogden's staying to sit in on the intelligence session."

"Glad to have him. Throw out the old agenda, and tell Director Eubanks it'll be his show. I'm sure he and Hester have been burning the wires seeking an answer about Gravastock."

"The Director wants to include Alexandra."

He suppressed a grin. "She'll be a willing partner. She also wants to call Vasiliy. They haven't talked since New Year's, and she's worried about his welfare."

SecDef Garrett approached. "Seems DOD has no mission to plan, sir."

"I understand; however, I have some things to discuss with the Special Ops officers."

"Let me get everyone's attention," Darlene interjected. "Ladies and gentlemen, we are ready to eat. The president will meet with DOD during lunch and would like Ambassador Hendrickson to join them. Director Eubanks, you and your team please have lunch and set your own agenda for when we reconvene at 1400 hours."

"Let's eat," Macdonald said to the group. He turned to Darlene. "After you."

"I'm not hungry."

"No, no. You're not doing what you did on the campaign." He took her arm. "After you, please." She reluctantly moved unenthusiastically along the buffet, picking lightly, while he filled his plate and kept an eye on her selections.

They ate with little chatter. Nobody even brought up the Washington Redskins's impending Super Bowl game against the San Diego Chargers on February 3.

He leaned his head toward his COS. "Darlene, the Canadian Prime Minister and I tentatively agreed to meet again next weekend in Detroit, when Reggie visits. The Super Bowl is next Sunday in Arizona."

"Yes. It was one of those many *little* things we talked about after you had dinner with your family Tuesday evening. The NFL Commissioner had called—"

"Oh right. Am I going to the game?"

She nodded, and whispered, "We're planning for you to go, but the Secret Service is not happy about it."

Some fragments of their conversation leaked out to General Gibbons sitting on the president's immediate left. "Excuse me, sir. I couldn't help overhear . . . the British Prime Minister will be here next weekend?"

"He is arriving in Ottawa this coming Thursday. I'd forgotten the Super Bowl was Sunday."

"The Redskins are a very big deal in this town, sir. This is their first Super Bowl in twenty-one years. When you get away from the White House, it is the major topic of discussion, even in the Pentagon, where burgundy and gold is sprouting up everywhere."

"I was growing up in Fort Collins when Doug Williams and the Redskins destroyed my Broncos with five touchdowns in the second period. I don't look too favorably on your team, General."

There was a smattering of chuckles around the table.

"I wouldn't broadcast that, sir; your Washington-area approval rating would drop below the unknown bomber."

The chuckles grew to laughter, even from the New Jersey-born, but long-time Pennsylvanian, Darlene Sweetwater . . . a diehard Steelers fan.

"So, are you saying 'Hail to the Chief' may be replaced by 'Hail to the Redskins'?"

Gibbons laughed. "No sir, but you get the idea."

The frivolity broke whatever tension existed. Once the tables were bussed, the president began the meeting.

"This morning hasn't turned out as we'd hoped. Without a target, we can't plan a mission; we're in limbo. I remember in my Force Recon days when something like this happened, it left us feeling very empty. However, I'm not a Marines captain; I'm the commander-in-chief and am no longer concerned with how the mission will be carried out, once I've approved it."

Macdonald felt it necessary to dispel any trepidation the military felt about his involvement. He then explained his philosophy and opened it up for questions.

Major General Romano looked at Gibbons, who nodded.

"Mr. President, we train every day, as I am sure you did in Force Recon. We study maps, read about local cultures, learn languages. In other words, sir, we work every day to be ready when we are needed. When our target is revealed and our mission clearly stated, we will assemble the resources needed to execute our orders.

"General Gibbons told us this past Tuesday that we could be called upon. All logistics and support backup are on the ready. Once we have been given our orders, we will select what we need and deploy."

Macdonald remembered how meticulous his Force Recon commander, Colonel Bingham, had been when explaining each of his missions. He was picturing that now as General Romano described his preparedness.

"Thank you, General Romano." He turned to Gibbons, but Romano wasn't finished.

"Sir, the only question remaining is under whose command we will operate. The coordination of our security, intelligence, satellite-mapping, and logistical support is very involved."

"It's yours to put together and operate, General. Since I don't have my director of National Intelligence in place, I want DOD's Defense Intelligence Agency, also leaderless, to be combined with CIA under DCIA Eubanks. You will find he has a wealth of knowledge in insertions and extractions and can very ably support your mission.

"However, if we don't have a military mission, the military Special Ops would stand down and Director Eubanks would run the show. I will discuss this in greater depth with Secretary Garrett, because military backup may be necessary. However, for now, we're looking at a search-and-destroy mission, and that's your baby."

General Gibbons replied. "Being in DEFCON 1, I can assure you that all of what you mentioned is at the ready to either launch an attack or defend our soil."

55

Darlene sat with the president in his Laurel Cabin office. It was almost 1400 hours, time to resume the meeting. They had tried to reach Canada's Prime Minister, but were only able to reach his Chief of Staff, who did confirm that Saturday was the right day to meet in Detroit and Windsor. Britain's Prime Minister Howard would arrive in Ottawa Thursday morning.

Darlene's attempt to reach Howard had failed; he and Mrs. Howard were dining with the Queen. Darlene left a message and phone number. She next called Secretary Rankin about where the State Department was with the Howard visit. The SecState was unavailable.

"Well, we're one for three, sort of. I thought the DOD meeting went extremely well. Ogden told me the Ops officers were relieved that the former Marine Force Recon leader had explained his position. It turns out there had been concerns in the ranks."

"They can thank General Bingham for not having to put up with that."

"I think you are handling your changed roles with Bingham and Hendrickson very well. Those who knew you before, like Kap, are settling in as well."

Nancy appeared in the office doorway. "Director Eubanks and Mr. Hester are now in the conference room, Mr. President," she said with lighthearted friendliness.

Darlene grinned, "Thank you, Mrs. Armstrong." Nancy left. "There's a good example of adjusting to new roles."

"I never thought she'd take your offer to be your deputy."

"She has skills I'll never have. We're still trying to find our way in this maelstrom, but she shows she can run with the ball."

"Darlene," he said, pensively.

His tone stopped her. "Yes?"

"I don't want to lose my friends because of this job."

That startled her.

"You won't, Mike. We wanted you to become president. Everybody has given up something to be here, because this is where they want to be. You are 'Mr. President.' We, I, will never forget *Mike*. We are proud to be here, working for *both* of you," she said, laughing at her little play on words.

He chuckled and said softly, "I'm just damn lucky to have all of you."

"The feeling is mutual, Mr. President," she said firmly.

He laughed. "Okay, Chief, let's go take on the world."

56

Arriving in the conference room, Mike sought out Alex and spotted her leaving a huddle that included Alisa and Steve Hester. Her eyes sparkled as she approached him.

"You have been busy, Mr. President," she said straightforwardly, her eyes gleaming.

"Seems my time has been taken over by events, all manageable, I'm happy to say. I put in a call to Reggie, but he was dining with the Queen."

"Reggie?"

"Yup, your pal, Reggie. He's crossing the pond to visit Canada and then to come see us. I didn't tell you?"

"There were other things on your mind, sir."

"Yes, you have that effect on me."

She seemed very upbeat. "Steve took me into a room filled with TV screens, computers, and telephones. A very busy place. I had a short lunch because I was with them. I have good news; I won't have to go to Moscow."

That was a blast of fresh air. "You . . . what happened?"

"We called Vasiliy from the communications center. It was wonderful to talk with him. I said I was planning a trip home, but he is leaving Tuesday to attend the Global Institute for Economics and Finance conference in Davos, Switzerland."

"And?"

"The director already had four assets going there. He has asked me to go with Steve on Tuesday or Wednesday until Saturday. What do you think?"

"Can you get away?"

"Yes. I have been to that forum two times. I attended last year, going from London. I forgot Vasiliy had been there a different year. Now, we can see each other there."

"When would you come back?"

"Saturday," she said with an inflection saying *I already told you that.*

"Sorry. This makes you an official part of Jim's team."

"I am an *asset*," she said, grinning.

"Which means your involvement is classified. We'll have to remind everyone here of that. I better talk with Jim before our meeting starts," he said, grinning. "You are an amazing woman."

She was startled by his statement, but he was on his way before she could respond. She watched him move easily past people, making a comment or two that elicited smiles. She felt giddy with joy.

Darlene approached her. "Alex, I have your seating assignment for the meeting."

"Thank you, Darlene," she said, using the COS's first name and not finding it difficult this time. She wanted to say something personal about the president, but thought better of it.

"We will be starting in a couple of minutes," Darlene said, already moving on to Macdonald and Eubanks, who were huddled in discussion. "It is a little after the hour, sir."

"Okay," he said cheerily.

Everyone took a seat, and Darlene turned the meeting over to Director Eubanks, who began with a summary of what had taken place at Gravastock and the sudden reversal when they were denied further access to the facility.

"There does not seem to be any official dictum regarding Phoenix. One of our Russian assets found that the general had indeed gone to Moscow. We don't know if that was his decision or if he was ordered to leave the facility. We don't have enough assets in place, and being the weekend, their access is curtailed."

"Excuse me, Jim. Do you mean you couldn't or didn't have enough assets?"

"Couldn't, sir. Lack of resources. There were too many political budget cuts. We are constantly adjusting our manpower arrangements."

"Consider that changed as of now, Director. You may have who or what you need. Along with seeing to our stricken countrymen, this has the highest priority. We need extensive intelligence, or we'll never keep up."

"Thank you, sir," Eubanks replied. "We have several retired Senior Intelligence Service officers and experienced analysts who were forced into taking early outs. I'm sure most, if not all, would be happy to return under your administration. They'll be easy to bring up to speed."

"Get them." He looked at Garrett. "Mr. Secretary, please get with Senator Woodward and have her convey our request to the Armed Services Committee."

"Absolutely, sir."

Macdonald nodded to Eubanks to continue.

"We believe our culprits reside in Russia and are part of an underground movement made up of old KGBers and their disciples. They are well assimilated into the current bureaucracy and hierarchy of the FSB.

"Dr. Mednorov had learned about huge amounts of money that were to be transferred into foreign corporations, which were only shell corporations set up by the Russians. These transactions were cleverly disguised as loans and investments in manufacturing equipment and infrastructure projects in China and Iran.

"President Macdonald's recent maneuvers in the currency market were done to make the dollar appear on its last leg. You can make a lot of money betting that something is going to go down in value, as long as you control the cause, as the bombers did on January 22.

"However, overnight this past Thursday, the president pulled the rug out from under those betting on our failure, primarily using the Russians' strategy against them. They got caught with their shorts down, possibly costing them billions of euros to cover their positions. Whatever the final amount, it had to put a big hurt on their ill-begotten gain in treasury.

"As you may know, I came up through the ranks and was director of National Clandestine Service for nine years. When the then-DCIA resigned, it caught the administration short, and I was named interim in August 2010, amid all the domestic natural disasters. After six weeks, I received a call saying I had been appointed director. No ceremony.

"After Mike Macdonald was elected president, my wife and I began collecting travel brochures, but he called me."

Macdonald interrupted. "May I, Jim?" Eubanks nodded.

"I had been impressed by Jim's record, but had concerns about CIA overall. Once he explained that he had steadily lost excellent agents over assets being compromised in Europe by the State Department and the Pentagon, I understood the problem, and that is why he is still the DCIA." Macdonald sat back, and Eubanks continued.

"Two assets had gone missing, and we presumed they'd been assassinated. We never made that public, but people in the global intelligence community knew our people were compromised.

"CIA is not what it should be, nor what it once was. Our foreign enemies saw our weaknesses and played them for all they were worth. We can rebuild our numbers; however, it will take some time to regain our lost prestige.

"Equally disturbing traitorous acts by Americans with foreign connections have been uncovered, all by the FBI and foreign intelligence agencies. A couple include American politicians who were associated with the previous administration and others who go back much farther. They are still active and intent on tearing down our economic structure."

The discomfort in the room was evident.

"There is a very tight lid on all of this. Right now, we have learned nothing that says those individuals were involved with the bombing. Only one of them has any known ties to Russia. FBI is watching all of them. Now, how does it relate to today? They are all involved in offshore activities and brokering out-of-the-country corporate manipulations, all of which could be abetting our financial collapse. One particular incident dates back to 1994."

Eubanks rearranged his notes. Macdonald sat back with a very pleased look on his face.

"FBI Director Thornton and I have worked together on several antiterrorist operations. We have developed a strong trust between us. I recently learned from him that there were certain activities he had not shared with me, involving Interpol, MI6, and Scotland Yard.

"Late yesterday, I had cause to call the director and ask for a face-to-face meeting. I told him that I would be coming here today. We met for two hours last night, and I was given his permission to share what I have known for almost a year, but President Macdonald just learned from me only a few hours ago.

"Minus the details, the FBI and international agencies have been working on a smuggling organization that includes Russians, Eastern Bloc countries, and some international billionaires. One of the smugglers' favorite ports of entry into the United States had been Detroit. We believe they are the conduit used by the bombers."

His small audience exhibited their surprise.

"Director Thornton believes the smugglers were only the unwitting conveyors. Distracted by all this country had to deal with, no one put the smugglers and the bomb together until my meeting with Director Thornton last night. It was only two days ago that we learned of a possible Russian connection."

"Excuse me, Jim." Macdonald said, as he leaned forward into the group. "We were working through a series of events totally separate from each other. Last night, Director Eubanks and Director Thornton tied the two activities together. Jim."

"Thank you, sir. Director Thornton made calls to Interpol and MI6 very early this morning. They found our connection imminently conceivable. A huge jigsaw puzzle of tiny parts is being constructed by hundreds of agents and assets. Our bombers are now in their equations.

"In my frustration with this morning's Gravastock situation, I called Director Thornton immediately after our break to fill him in on what we now know. And, as I just said to you, he had already been in conversation with Interpol, and at the time of my call, they had two Russian smugglers in their sights.

"Also, the FBI and Immigration began a search last night for highly skilled technicians and scientists with nuclear bomb experience who had immigrated or matriculated to the United States beginning with the end of the cold war. A few have gone missing. Some are teaching or working at universities on science-related projects."

"Mr. Director," Ambassador Hendrickson interrupted, "I recall that in the early 1990s, when the cold war was fizzling down, all ambassadors received a directive from the Secretary of State requesting we compile a list of non-Russian technicians, engineers, and scientists, so that when the Iron Curtain collapsed, we might tap that available talent pool."

"I am not aware of any such list, sir," Eubanks said. "However, we'll look into that."

"Possibly Secretary Rankin might know," Macdonald offered. "She was ambassador to Hungary around then."

"Yes, she was, sir. Would that be something I could help with?" Hendrickson asked.

"Absolutely."

"That's all I have, sir," Eubanks said, looking drawn.

"Do we need to know whether the ingredients for the bomb could have been siphoned from existing casements or whether they have been assembled from raw materials?" Macdonald asked.

"Dr. Montgomery?' Eubanks asked.

"Please, give me a moment," the NNSA scientist said, obviously searching his brain. Then his head began to nod. "Yes. One is like crude oil, and the other, a refined product. What is in the bomb casings is ready to go. The crude is like collecting all the elements and processing them in a large, environmentally clean, and extremely secure location, hidden away from the nosiest of spy satellites. Crude leaves large footprints, refined literally none."

"That's succinct. Thank you for the laymen's language, Doctor," the president said. "I gather this means I should be rooting for crude over refined?"

Montgomery answered carefully. "From what you want, sir, I would believe you'd favor crude. However, I believe, given what we know of the bomb, it was otherwise."

"So the answer is in the Gravastock stockpile."

"That would be a start, yes sir."

"Thank you, Doctor. Unfortunately, that is a daunting task given this morning's setback," Macdonald said grimly.

57

Laurel Cabin
Two and a half hours later

President Macdonald was drawing the meeting to a close with his grateful thanks. He had asked Eubanks, Hester, and Hendrickson to remain for dinner, where they could discuss Alexandra's trip to Davos.

Earlier, Darlene had expressed a desire to leave with the first chopper. This was the day she was to move out of Blair House and into her apartment. Cynthia would be helping her on Sunday, having moved into a Pentagon City condo herself already.

Many of Darlene's things had been moved to her Foggy Bottom rental, but she had much more to do. She also relished the idea of having some time to herself. So she joined Secretary Garrett, Jeri, Nancy, Alisa, Dr. Montgomery, and his two associates on the flight back home.

The remaining group bade them a fond farewell and then walked the short distance to Aspen Lodge. It was dusk and the air had a bite to it, but all agreed it felt good to get out and stretch their legs.

A Petty Officer greeted them at Aspen. The male guests were offered a room for their use and followed the PO to their respective quarters for a quick freshen-up. Alex had dressed in a business suit and wanted to change into something more casual. Macdonald also chose to dress down, changing into one of his favorite pullovers.

When he reached the living room, he was greeted only by the warm glow from the fireplace. Seeing no one, he went into his office with its clear desk, except for a writing pad and pen. Rather than entertain himself, he went to the kitchen, where he found Millie with a female and male Petty Officer seated at the dining table.

"At ease," he said, but they stood anyway, the POs at attention.

"Please, at ease," he repeated.

They relaxed. "May I get you something, Mr. President?" Chief Millie asked.

"The others weren't in the living room. I'm just roaming. I assume Ms. Sweetwater called you about dinner."

"Aye, she did, sir."

"Is there a bar?"

"Petty Officer Johnson will wheel it in, sir."

The PO snapped to and quickly left the kitchen, followed by his fellow PO.

The president sniffed. "Do I smell homemade bread, Chief?"

"You do indeed, sir."

"What else is on our menu?"

She described the variety of meats and vegetables.

"I like all of that," he said, obviously pleased with the selections. "I might take one of each," he chuckled.

Chef Millie smiled, "And of course, we have the wheat bread in the oven."

"I'm looking forward to it." He turned and went to the living room, where he found the rest of his meeting attendees standing around the bar, awaiting their drink of choice. "Ah, I see you've met Petty Officer Johnson. After you've filled their orders, I'll take a bourbon and branch."

"Yes sir," Johnson replied.

"I just got a rundown on tonight's menu, gentlemen. It will please any palate." He wondered where Alex was. Hendrickson approached him, drink in hand.

"Doctor Mednorov is very impressive."

Macdonald looked at his mentor and smiled. *If you only knew how much.* "I thought I knew a lot about her, Bill, but I, too, am impressed by the scope of her knowledge."

"You were Rhodes Scholars together, and she, like you, went on to earn a doctorate in finance. I was especially interested in the time she spent with the Royal Dutch/Shell Group as its chief economist."

"She never planned to go that direction, but when she graduated from Bonn and returned to Moscow with her doctorate, she found too many memories lingering there. Royal Dutch had shown an interest in her at graduation and asked her to stay in contact. So, she called them and two high-ranking executives flew to Moscow to meet with her.

"She worked some in London, but mostly in The Hague. I believe she did some traveling for them, as well."

"You mentioned 'memories,'" the ambassador said.

Mike told him about Sergey.

"How awful for her. It seems you and she share another parallel. Did she leave Royal Dutch for the World Bank?"

As he asked that question, Alex entered, stopping at the entrance. She almost took Mike's breath away. She was wearing a wispy, white cotton dress with a full skirt dotted with small, mixed-pastel flower blossoms. She wore no jewelry. Her look was frolicsome, ethereally lovely.

"I hope I am not late," she said beguilingly.

All the men were caught up by her specter, a far cry from the dark business suit she'd worn earlier.

"No, no," Mike mumbled, as he stepped to her, extending his arm to escort her. "What's your poison?" he asked, as they moved to the bar.

"What are you having, Michael?" she asked softly.

Hendrickson sidled up to the couple. "You look ravishing, my dear." He tipped his glass, and she smiled demurely.

"I'm, uh, I'm having bourbon and branch," he said, still a little flustered.

"How very American," she said, with a twinkle in her eyes. She addressed Johnson. "I'll have vodka on the rocks."

"How very Russian," Mike said, smirking.

58

Mike Macdonald and his guests enjoyed a relaxed and congenial supper. He was especially curious about the Global Institute, so, once they were all back in the living room, he asked Eubanks to elaborate for his and the group's benefit.

Eubanks happily obliged. "It's a membership of twelve hundred who each pay a half-million euros per year to sustain it."

"The World Bank pays a bigger fee," Alex interjected, "which allows me and other of its employees to attend gratis."

Eubanks noted that, "Governments are not members, but pay a modest attendance fee for their bureaucrats. Heads of State—or as in our case this year, Secretary Royce—are guests of the membership."

"The prestige factor," Mike stated flatly.

"They say they are nonpolitical," the DCIA said, "but that's hard to do these days, too many global interactions. Nothing sinister. It appears they attract people who are dominant in world financial and currency affairs, or want to be."

"They have noted speakers," Alex added, "run effective workshops, and offer many fellowships. People network and I am sure some alliances are born there."

Mike thought about that. If it was that benign and Eubanks was right about no sinister plots for James Bond to untangle, maybe some of his benefactors attended.

"Davos sounds like my kind of place. I grew up skiing, but have done little over the past decade."

"Oh, Mr. President," Alex said teasingly. "It is truly a beautiful place for that."

"You ski, Alex?" Eubanks asked.

"Vasiliy and I were taught by our parents. Unfortunately, under the communists, if you were not a competitive skier, you had little opportunity. Sergey and I could afford to ski and did many times. I have not skied since my accident . . ." She let that hang, her eyes dropping.

Mike picked up the slack. "After settling in New York in the '90s, I rarely skied, except on visits to see my Mom in Fort Collins. Jeanne Marie or James would drag me out to Winter Park or Breckenridge, usually over the Christmas holiday. I doubt I'll be taking it back up anytime soon."

"You never know," Alex said, smiling at him, which immediately made him smile in acknowledgment.

"We've had our people and assets attending long before I became director. It is a very comfortable place to meet and exchange ideas," Eubanks said.

"No espionage, Jim?" Macdonald asked grinning. "I was never into going to those types of events. My work was cerebral: analyzing, studying. My interactions were done mostly electronically."

"Many world leaders attend," Hendrickson put in, "although I don't believe an American president has gone." He looked to Eubanks for attribution.

"Correct, sir. I believe some Senate and House leaders have attended."

"If there's a resort in the offering, I'm sure our esteemed legislators . . ." Macdonald let that drop. "Okay, so we agree that Alex and Vasiliy can get together there for a family reunion."

"Probably be as safe as we could hope for, sir." Eubanks turned to Alex. "I'd like for Steve to become involved with Vasiliy."

"I think he will be comfortable with Steve," Alex said.

Hester nodded. "I will be Stanley Mortimer, an American entrepreneur. I will be the new guy on the block. It's not as easy to hide identities anymore, so we resort to real people who lead a double life."

"That must be tough on recruiting."

"It's a delicate process, sir," Eubanks commented.

"I took the liberty," Hendrickson said, "of looking into your background, Alexandra. I must say, you have established quite a fine reputation in the field of finance and economics, both from your days at Royal Dutch and since with the World Bank. I would imagine people will be hoping for a little of your time, some old friends?"

"Yes, I am sure you are right, sir," she said, smiling.

"You might want to consider following through with that." Mike said to her. "It would give a good sense of normalcy to your visit."

"My presence will mean I will be asked to attend side meetings on Africa. I have represented the Bank on several African programs. It has become my specialty, one could say."

Hendrickson smiled approvingly. "Mr. Director, will Mr. Mednorov be meeting with more of your people than just his sister?"

The director shook his head. "Except for Steve, no sir. Alexandra will naturally be with him, as brother and sister."

"I understand. It is an excellent plan."

Eubanks addressed Macdonald. "Sir, I will be putting this all into motion tomorrow. Steve will arrive in Zurich early Tuesday. Alexandra and I have discussed her plans, which she will solidify with me early Monday morning."

"Yes," she concurred. "I will arrange a meeting with my successor in London for Tuesday morning. I will fly to Zurich early Wednesday. Vasiliy will arrive there at noon. We will go to Davos together."

Macdonald nodded his approval. "A lot's been going on these past couple of hours. Who will be keeping me apprised of our progress with Vasiliy?"

"Me," Eubanks said. "I will have several sources sending progress reports to our communication center."

Alex smiled at Mike. "I will most assuredly be more protected than I have at any other time in my life."

Mike sheepishly laughed. "And that's not a bad thing!" he chided.

"This is very tightly held, sir. Our director of the National Clandestine Service and two of his deputies are the only ones who know about Alex. One will always be on duty. Our field agents and assets have contact with our watch office. Steve and two operatives are central control in Davos. Everybody has their own assignment."

"I guess that's as secure as it gets," Macdonald said.

"I agree, Mr. President," Hendrickson said reassuringly. "I believe everyone is in very good hands."

Macdonald knew in his brain, the logical part, that there would be no way anyone could suspect Alex of being anything other than who she was.

"We must also remember, Vasiliy is there to work," Alex said. "He has meetings he must attend. There will be several FSB there as well, which will mean an all-Russian party, which I will attend, because I have in the past. Since I will be making plans early Monday, may I call Vasiliy to let him know when I will arrive?"

"Sure." Eubanks said. "Not a problem."

"That will probably involve his asking about Michael and the United States. If you wish, I will not say that Michael and I have talked since he became president. There could be people at the conference who remember we were at Oxford together."

"That is all normal," Hendrickson said. "Everything before the inaugural is not a problem. You are old friends . . ."

"I agree," Macdonald interrupted. "Somebody might know about her past. Any denial would raise a red flag. Vasiliy knows, of course, and he may have mentioned that to others from the FSB. Raisa for sure knows."

Macdonald reminded himself that Alex was accustomed to dealing with international activities and global leaders. *She is a leader herself.* His love for her blinded him to her talents, ones she had been honing for twenty years, as he had his.

59

As the rising sun's rays found their way into the president's Aspen Lodge bedroom with two thin streaks of light playing across the bed, Mike and Alex snuggled close. They had loved and talked and loved some more, before begrudgingly giving into sleep, content to be in each other's arms. They discussed little of the coming week.

When they had crawled into bed the night before, they were less tired and less frantic in their lovemaking compared to Friday night. This time, they enjoyed the foreplay, teasing, and exploring. They were experiencing a satisfying blend of youthful romance and mature love.

They spoke of their new love, which they both found different from Oxford. Twenty-years different, in fact, during which time they had, apart, experienced a loving partner and two decades of living. Yet, as they cuddled together in a new world for both, everything else seemed but a wisp in time.

In the newness of day, Alex sensually caressed and aroused him, keeping him that way as she kissed him all over. "This is my morning," she whispered to him, letting her hands take over from her lips so she could kiss him long and deeply. He returned the playing without taking over.

She knew when it was time. Exhilaration levitated their bodies as they experienced the delicious nectar of love. They lay spent for some time before he unwound from her and swung his legs over the side of the bed. He stretched his arms in a big yawn, trying to feed some oxygen to his brain. She lightly scratched his back, and he moved in appreciation.

"I love you, Michael, more strongly than before."

He rolled back onto the bed and kissed her. "We had sex back then, this is something much deeper." He kissed her lightly on the lips and whispered, "I love you." He rolled back to the edge of the bed and put his feet on the floor.

"I think we should take separate showers," she said.

He laughed, stood up, and walked around to her as she stood to greet him. He embraced her. She then slipped on the comfy bath robe, and he went to take a shower.

Not one for lingering in a shower, he was the first to greet Chief Millie, as he entered her warm, aroma-filled kitchen. Inhaling the scent of freshly baked biscuits, he let out an audible sigh.

"Smells like biscuits to me," he said reflectively.

"My spies told me you were partial to cinnamon and walnuts," Millie said, pleased with his appreciation. She took down a mug and began filling it with coffee.

"The communications officer was in a little bit ago, sir, and put some papers on your desk."

"Oh?"

"He made no mention of anything special, but he stayed long enough to have a coffee and a biscuit with blueberry jam."

"Jam? Doing some midnight requisitioning, Chief?"

"Somebody's usually making a run to town."

"When things settle down in the country, I'm going to have my mother come east. I'd like for the two of you to get to know each other."

She was taken by his comment, "I look forward to that, Mr. President."

Alex appeared in the doorway wearing a cashmere, light-blue, V-neck sweater, denim pants, and a pair of pink "fluff ball" slippers.

Millie greeted her with "Good morning, ma'am."

Mike turned and felt his heart jump. "Hey, Tar Heel."

"Un unh," Millie chided. "This is Terrapin country, sir."

He laughed, shaking his head. "That's my nickname, along with Lexi, that I have for her. Light blue is her favorite color. I once promised I'd take her to Chapel Hill. She'd be like a kid in a candy store." He laughed.

"Maybe we will still get there, Mr. President."

"Absolutely, Doctor Mednorov," he teased.

"Doctor?" Millie asked.

"PhD in finance. The same as Mr. President."

"Oh my . . . I'm . . . If you don't mind, sir." Surprise was still etched on her face.

"Not at all. We were Rhodes Scholars together twenty years ago."

"I'm going to forget my place, sir, ma'am, but you both light up this room. And when together, as you are now, you brighten things up even more."

"Millie," Macdonald said, "I love the normalcy you bring to me, to us. You don't ever have to apologize."

As he and Millie continued to chat, Alex retrieved a presidential mug, fixed her coffee, and stood next to her man. Feeling her presence, he put an arm around her waist.

"Camp David has already become our very special place, Millie," he said, giving Alex a hug. "We each saw this place together for the first time Friday night. It affords us more privacy than we can have in the White House. So that you know, my Chief of Staff, Darlene Sweetwater, and my White House secretary, Mrs. Bolden, know about Lexi and me, other than the Secret Service and your folks here. But that's about it, and we'd prefer to keep it that way for now."

"I understand, sir. I'll make sure everyone here knows *not to know.*"

"Okay. So, what delectable morsels await our palates?"

Alex snuggled, resting her head on his shoulder.

60

Sunday was going to be a cold gray day, heavily overcast with a forecast of snow mixed with rain in the higher altitudes by mid-afternoon. The commanding officer at Camp David informed the president that the latest the chopper could leave was between noon and 1300 hours. After that, he'd have to be driven back.

Mike consulted Alex, and they both chose to stretch the day out in the camp for as long as they could. The seventy-mile drive back would give them more time to be together, riding in the back of the Beast, the nickname for the armored presidential limousine.

After their delicious breakfast of sausage, eggs, and Millie's homemade biscuits with blueberry jam, they prepared to take a walk. With the morning temperature in the upper 20s, they bundled up for what turned out to be a fifteen-minute trek.

Back in Aspen Lodge, they headed for the kitchen and a hot drink. To Alex's surprise, he chose hot chocolate. She selected an herbal tea with lemon. They sat in front of the living room fireplace for a while, before he had to break away and tend to business. As Mike went to his office, she wished to make some calls and went off with a Petty Officer to a place where she could have a table and phone. Near noon, Alex went to the kitchen for more tea and a mug of hot, black coffee and peeked in to Mike's office, as the door was open. He quickly finished up a call and turned his attention to her.

"It is a nice break we both deserve," she said softly. "I spoke to the president of the World Bank regarding my schedule change. We will meet in his office this evening."

Just then his phone rang, signaling the end of their break. She gave him a light kiss and went back to the living room.

By 1300 hours, when Mike emerged from his office, he found Alex curled up on the sofa in front of the fire reading a book. He came up to the back of the sofa, leaned over it, and planted a kiss on her upturned lips. *How wonderful it is to be this way with her.*

"I've stirred up enough bee hives to keep droves of people busy," he said.

After a sumptuous late lunch served up by Millie, Mike asked for a driving tour of the entire camp. It helped to have a tour guide to get a better feel of the place. By 1500 hours, they were on the road to Washington, starting out in a light snow fall that turned to rain as they descended the mountain.

At the White House, the Secret Service transferred Alex to a normal sedan and drove her to her apartment in Foggy Bottom. When he entered his office, Darlene was waiting for him. They transferred to his study and emerged two and a half hours later with an agenda of domestic issues.

In creating the agenda, they had consulted with Bryanna, Gus, the Ambassador, and DCIA Eubanks. The week was well arranged. Their public face would be firmly on recovery and investigation. Mike and Darlene dined in the small dining room in the West Wing. She heaped praise on Alexandra, amazed at her breadth of economic knowledge and the extent of her dealings with world leaders. Darlene suggested that Kap should meet with Alex and get her perspective on global finance.

Macdonald was more than pleased with Darlene's acceptance of Alex as a working partner.

"Kap should probably be in Davos too, but I can't afford to have him away."

Darlene left around 2000 hours to spend her first night in her new apartment. He went down to the kitchen for a bowl of his favorite vanilla ice cream with chocolate syrup. He hit the sack a half hour later, a content man.

61

Oval Office
Monday, January 28
0640 hours

President Macdonald put down the PDB folder and took a swallow of coffee. "The international markets and currency exchanges are in a tizzy, Jim."

Eubanks nodded his agreement. "As I've heard you say, sir, they don't like uncertainty, and they've been getting buckets of that. The mood of the chatter we and NSA are hearing is one of disbelief. Most were writing us off as an economic power. *'The fall of Rome,'* as one European blogger put it, *'has been put on hold only temporarily. There could be no truth to what the President of the United States announced, so glibly and so arrogantly.'*"

"That doesn't do much for my ego." Macdonald laughed. "I guess this guy wanted us destroyed. That makes it all the sweeter, Jim. Here's one with a western twang: *'They done themselves in and deserved what they got.'*"

They shared a hearty laugh.

"At your suggestion, sir, I met with Secretary Kaplan yesterday."

"And you survived?" Macdonald said, pretending amazement.

"He is certainly the character you warned me he was."

"He spent years pounding good financial fundamentals into starry-eyed, overly intelligent, but sometimes not very bright students. He developed a form of shock therapy to help get his points across. I was a former Marine and successful trader by the time he got me, and I didn't feed him the crap they did."

Eubanks laughed. "He's direct and defends his positions astutely. With him, you know where he stands. That's refreshing."

"I was sandblasted with objections to his nomination. I knew him pretty well at Wharton, but much better over the past half dozen years. I knew he had the backbone to pull this off. People talk about bringing change to Washington; he's the real deal. I trust him. I trust his instincts."

"The Secretary and I worked out an arrangement that he felt comfortable with—assigning one of my officers in Davos to communicate with him on what people were whispering about us. He had talked with Secretary Royce, and she, too, will communicate with him. She arrives in Davos on Wednesday morning."

"I'll give her a call and prepare her for Kap. She wasn't on our campaign team and has never seen him in action. Oh, I forgot. I will be able to introduce them at a working lunch here at noon on domestic issues."

"General Orlovski returned to Gravastock. Our team leader had left a standing request to meet with the general first thing this morning. That has not yet taken place, and it's nearly 1500 hours over there."

Macdonald sat back. "I've been giving this some thought. I'd like to make a suggestion."

The CIA director waited.

"Stay seated." Macdonald walked to the French doors and without turning said, "Have Phoenix ease off on the general about seeing the bombs." He turned back in and ambled around. "I'm thinking that if his instructions came from some cabal leader and not from President Novorken, they might worry Novorken could get wind of a problem. So, I'm thinking that we don't want to force Orlovski's hand. Meantime, we're in Davos with Vasiliy, hopefully learning some good stuff.

"Alex told me yesterday that Vasiliy may be the highest-ranking Russian bureaucrat in Davos. He also has knowledge of the 'money shifting.'" He moved back to the table and picked up his coffee mug. "Maybe we should stand down, take a different position."

"But sir, we need to observe. They may be planning a switch on the WMDs in the storage facility."

"I understand, but I'm thinking Orlovski is scared shitless. If thievery or tampering *did* take place, and they correct the situation, which our satellites can tell us, that's the place we are looking for. If not, we look elsewhere. I'm using Dr. Montgomery as the authority on that."

"I'll call them off, sir. I'll also pow-wow with my people here and get their reading."

"Jim, please understand, I'm not questioning the professionalism of you or your people. It's just an idea. I'm worried Orlovski's visit to Moscow could have changed the dynamics and not in our favor."

Eubanks sat back and pondered the president's words, as the chief executive went back to his breakfast. "You are counting heavily on the Mednorovs, aren't you, sir?"

Macdonald swallowed a morsel of bagel. "If we come across top people in the FSB hierarchy tied in with the military or with scientists, wouldn't that be a good first step? Alex has provided some grist for the mill: how the FSB is setup. That's where Vasiliy becomes so important. It only takes one name from him to lead us to a powerful enough person who could orchestrate a military plot. Your assets in Moscow might see a familiar name or two and put two and two together. Then you could arrange one of your infamous accidents."

A smile crept across Eubanks's face. "An extraction?"

"Why, Jim, I could never be a party to anything like that," Macdonald said firmly.

Eubanks grinned. Macdonald had planted a seed: be aggressive. What was out of his control, of course, was the speed at which the flower would bloom.

62

Alexandra called Darlene Sweetwater later that morning and gave the president's Chief of Staff her complete itinerary, beginning with a flight that evening out of Dulles at 7:30 p.m. She would land in London on Tuesday morning and leave for Geneva on an early morning flight Wednesday, going from there to Davos with Vasiliy.

Secretary Kaplan was sitting in the Oval Office, explaining to the president his take on the European equity and currency markets. "Shorts on the dollar are nonexistent, and American corporations are up, but only marginally.

"The questioning by financial gurus around the world has quieted. However, our government's mystery benefactors have them baffled. They're taking a 'wait and see' attitude."

"Anything on the Russian shell corporations?"

"They show no liquidity. What they had in those accounts is gone. I am as anxious as a horny teenager on his first date to learn how much Vasiliy Mednorov says they lost."

Macdonald wrapped up his meeting with Kaplan and rang up Cynthia for his messages.

"Mr. Vaughn would like to talk to you, sir. Also, Senator Woodward would like a few minutes of your time before the lunch. There are others, but staff can handle them."

"Ah, my *gatekeeper protectorate*."

There was a pause. He waited. Then came her retort. "Just call me *Olivia* Cromwell. I'll get Mr. Vaughn for you."

He chuckled over her use of the feminine derivative of "Oliver." Keeping a sense of humor these harried days was critical. He poured a half cup of coffee from the hot pot, sat at his desk, and reviewed the PDB, particularly the collection of quotes on his financial coup of Friday. His intercom buzzed.

"Mr. Vaughn is on line three, sir."

He picked up. "Gus, how're things going?"

"We've had a good weekend organization-wise, but the weather was brutal. The numbers of dead are mind boggling. We've relocated over a million of the living, of whom about a third had sustained injuries. The National Guard units are deep into the destroyed neighborhoods. There wasn't a miracle recovery all weekend.

"It's what you would expect to find after a blanket bombing run. The vice president is an amazing person, boss. You know me; I go, go, go, but I'm in this lady's dust."

"What are the radiation readings like?"

"Almost zilch, but we're operating with precaution. We've had five to eight inches of snow, depending on where you stand. The public works folks are out of business, and I'm like a larcenous supply sergeant begging, borrowing, or stealing any snowplow I can make a deal for.

"I don't hold out much hope for rescues, boss, but we're big into helping survivors. I think everyone who was able to get out, got out. As the heavy equipment rolls in, we're clearing out mall parking lots and putting up tents and parking FEMA trailers. Recovery villages are going up ten to twelve miles out. Sanitation's a huge problem. We also need to house fewer or none of the survivors close in. Use that billeting for the workers we're moving in."

"You've got an open checkbook. Get a bunch of somebodies tracking down what you need."

"Oh, the Veep's doing that. She's relentless."

"You and she set for our working lunch?"

"It's on our agenda. I'm moving into DTO with some Guard units. They'll patch me in on a conference call. Bryanna spent yesterday touring ground zero with infrastructure engineers. That money for DOER is already being spent," the Homeland Defense Secretary said.

"Go at it my friend."

"Oh, on Saturday, we're hoping to chopper you into downtown from the Detroit Metro Airport."

"The British Prime Minister will be coming in with Prime Minister McEwen, but don't put out any red carpets. I'll be wearing my old combat boots."

"The Secret Service has had talks with us. They're shipping in a bunch of combat Hummers. By the way, I've personally talked with the CEO or president of every foreign auto manufacturer who will be on your conference call this afternoon. For the most part, they've got their acts together. You'll see. I gather Secretary Russell's people will be the facilitators on this."

"Yes, I made an executive decision on Friday. You get it set up, and turn it over to J.T."

Darlene entered.

"Gotta go, my boss just arrived."

Gus chuckled. "Tell Darlene I said hi."

"Talk to you later," Macdonald said, hanging up.

Darlene was uncomfortable with his casual demeanor at times, this being one of them. "Who were you talking to?"

"Gus, reporting in from the DTO."

She shook her head. "I should have known. Margaret popped into my office, said she had asked for a few minutes of your time before the lunch. I took care of her concerns, which centered on the 'money.' I assured her it was all legal and completely aboveboard. I promised we would supply her some talking points she could present to the Senate."

"That shows we're not keeping our congressional caucuses up to speed. Don't we have a congressional liaison?"

"We do, but he's been sidetracked into helping us here, as others have. Maybe we could have a dinner with our congressional folks along with the cabinet. Thursday's our first available night."

"Why don't you float that idea at the lunch?"

63

At noon, President Macdonald and Darlene Sweetwater joined coterie members Kaplan, Russell, Hendrickson, and AG Jamison along with the secretaries of Commerce, HUD, HHS, and Labor. Rounding out the group were Centrist party Senate and House leadership, A.J. and his press staff, Nancy, and other senior White House and Treasury staff.

The primary subjects under discussion would be the DTO, the upcoming conference call with the foreign automakers, and Tuesday's ceremonial deposit of three hundred billion dollars for America's auto industry.

Macdonald was aware that the congressional leadership who had been around two or more terms were having conniptions at being passed over by the newfound money they could not touch. The money was already being allocated and spent, and there would be no earmarks attached to any of it.

He had a plan, not yet formulated, to appease Congress. He would work with his House and Senate caucuses to develop a new way of doing business on Capitol Hill.

Macdonald realized most people didn't understand what happened with the country's finances. They probably knew that the new money was going to mean new jobs as well as sustaining current jobs. They knew businesses unaffected by the bombing were gearing up to increase their manufacturing volume in the United States, a caveat he put on using the DOER money.

"Americans for Americans" was one of many slogans being bandied about. The sleight of hand with over a trillion dollars of taxpayers' money back in 2008 and 2009 taught him that lesson.

Darlene and Cynthia had arranged the seating so that each table had a Cabinet secretary, a congressional senior staff member.

Macdonald and Darlene greeted everyone as they arrived.

They then ate lunch and networked until the president stood, which called everyone to attention.

"Thanks for coming. We have Vice President Dudley and Homeland Secretary Vaughn on speaker phone. Bryanna, Gus?"

"I'm here, Mr. President," the vice president replied.

"I'm near ground zero, Mr. President, alongside the crater lake," Gus stated grimly. "It's all pretty ugly."

Macdonald smiled at Gus's dramatic air.

"Okay. We're about to break new ground in many ways and places my friends. I am asking all branches of the Executive to join together in this rebuilding cause. Our country was almost put out of business last week and could have had no money for our Cabinet Departments and Agencies. Education, Transportation … you name it.

"We are starting right now to develop a working partnership with domestic and foreign auto manufacturers. This is a concerted effort to bring management and labor together to plan a new way to rebuild businesses and lives.

"This is not exclusive to the auto industry, but it is today's focus. The auto industry is at the core of rebuilding Detroit. But we also know that other sectors are equally needy, which is why you are all here. Cabinet officers will play a big hand in this recovery. We need your input. Nothing is insignificant.

"At the outset, with auto, the coordinating branch will be the Department of Transportation. Secretary Russell is establishing a task force headed by an undersecretary. That person's responsibility will be manufacturing. Vice President Dudley is building three community centers, one each south, west, and north of the city that will work with auto employees and families. The Labor Department under Secretary Lewis will be responsible for placing these people in new or expanded auto plant operations in other parts of the country.

"Secretary Vaughn has been acquiring information on where old facilities might be upgraded or newly outfitted to manufacture parts for assembly. The former Big Three may have to form new partnerships. They'll talk about that tomorrow and Wednesday in New York.

"The premise is simple. Get people back to work. Get them into new housing, and get their children back into school, which is Education Secretary Baldwin's responsibility. We are building temporary medical facilities. HHS Secretary Dr. Sutton has been in the DTO since Friday working with Michigan Governor Carlton and the National Guard."

"If I may, Mr. President," Vice President Dudley interjected. "Dr. Sutton has presented us with a detailed list of what is needed, and we are already clearing land for more neighborhood centers. The National Guard has completed a five-hundred-cot tent city with medical teams at the fringe of where people can safely live away from ground zero.

"Secretary Royce has several 'bucket brigades' of food stuffs flowing into the area; we're parking refrigerator trucks, water tankers, and portable johns by the hundreds—everything people need. We must have a thousand generators by now. We've located a few of the city's engineers, and they're working hard to find ways to reconfigure an infrastructure. The outpouring has been phenomenal."

The president and vice president continued with a lively discourse as to what was working and what had to be done. Macdonald then opened the floor, and Darlene took over the facilitating. The energized group covered the gamut of *how to* and *what if* to *this is how* and *can we try this?*

64

Macdonald sat alone in his private study just off the Oval Office. The conference call had gone well. The foreign auto executives had supplied information on their losses to the Secretary of Transportation, along with locations where they were manufacturing in the United States.

Now with the brainstorming behind him, Macdonald wound down. He thought of Alex and wished she was coming over for dinner. Instead, she would be flying to London.

He thought of Reggie, and their swilling ale and throwing darts in an ancient Oxford pub twenty years ago. Number 10 Downing Street and the White House were a far cry from there.

Twice earlier in the day, he had called a benefactor and received glowing reports. He pulled out his pad from the bottom drawer; making sure it was working hours, he made another call. All his benefactors had private numbers that did not go through switchboards or an intermediary. This particular family had put up four hundred billion dollars. Realizing a thirty-eight percent gain from the shorts and staying long. The family purchased two hundred million dollars of T-Notes.

He called Darlene and brought her up-to-date on his foreign investors. She had Alexandra's itinerary, but couldn't have dinner with him unless it was a must. She had a pressing agenda on the home front.

It was 4:45 p.m., 1645 hours.

He called Cynthia and was greeted with a list of people who had called, but none that he had to call back. She had some papers for his signature and would put them on the Oval Office desk, asking that he sign them today.

"A.J. said the press was pleased with receiving the announcements about today's and tomorrow's automotive meetings and the summary sheets of the president's conference call with the foreign auto manufacturers."

"Yeah," Macdonald said, "we are trying to put on a happier face with the media. Turn over a new leaf."

"They're the ones who need a change in attitude," Cynthia said. "However, A.J. also told me the White House press corps is intrigued about the vice president being in New York tomorrow."

"As well they should be. Alex has a 7:30 p.m. flight. Please get her for me."

He tried to busy himself. It took about five minutes before Cynthia buzzed him.

"Dr. Mednorov only has a couple of minutes. She's on line two."

"Thanks, pal." He picked up. "How you doing? Everything working out as you planned?"

"I packed last night and have my things with me at the office. They have a car—"

He interrupted. "I miss you. I love you," he blurted.

"I love you too, you big—" she stopped and changed gears. "I talked to Vasiliy. He is excited I will actually be there. What will you do this week?"

"Lots of meetings. Saturday I'll be in Detroit with Reggie and the Canadian Prime Minister."

"I return to Dulles at 3:30 p.m. Saturday. I will be driven home."

His heart beat faster. "Okay. Call the Secret Service."

"The number I use when they pick me up?"

"The same. Call when you get to your apartment on Saturday. Dress casual and bring an overnight bag."

Her glee was palpable. "We will go to Camp David?"

"No. We're staying here."

"I will stay overnight at the White House?" She sounded as though she would burst.

"I hope you will," he said teasingly.

"You hope?"

He laughed.

"Oh, you tease."

"Look, I'm not telling Reggie in advance about us. We'll surprise him together. Hopefully, they'll also stay at the White House on Saturday."

"Oh. Michael, they call me; my car is here. Will I have to be searched at the White House, like in New York?"

"Only by me," he said, feeling like a kid. "I love you. Give my best to Vasiliy."

"I love you, *mon cher.*"

65

Tuesday morning when he reached the Oval Office a few minutes before 0600, DCIA Eubanks was waiting for him. Adrenaline shot through him. "A problem, Jim?"

"No sir. I'm just a little ahead of schedule."

Macdonald calmed. "I'm going to have to settle down. I'm acting like I expect a second bomb!"

Eubanks handed him the PDB. As the president began scanning the brief, Eubanks helped himself to scrambled eggs and picked out some bacon strips from the steam tray.

"The world markets seem to be holding steady," Macdonald commented.

"Many are intrigued at the speed with which we are getting things done."

Macdonald finished a bite of jam-layered toast and went back to reading and munching.

"Ha," the president chortled, but made no further comment. He finished reading and then grinned at the DCIA.

Eubanks looked at the president blankly, stifling a laugh as best he could.

"You son of a gun!" Macdonald exclaimed.

"Sir?" Eubanks replied innocently.

Macdonald picked up the PDB and read aloud. "*London. A senior executive with the World Bank flew in from the States for a day of meetings, before flying on to Davos where she . . .* ' Was I that obvious?"

"Obvious, sir?"

Macdonald grinned. "Thanks for letting me know she got there all right, Jim. I'm busting up . . . this is the real thing."

"Oh, no doubt in my mind. Actually, I see it more from her than I do you."

"Here I thought we were being so cool."

"I will say, sir, Alexandra's financial acumen and her ability to interact on a high plane has been her best cover. Only those closest to you—your inner circle—would know. Others would only see her as an advisor. I know Steve was quite taken by her."

"Oh," Mike said reflexively.

Eubanks laughed. "No. Not that way. He's happily married with two great kids. When she appeared on the scene last Thursday, we did some vetting. We learned that you two were in Oxford at the same time and that you and she were . . . *friends*. There was no mention of anything deeper than that. I also came across your early association with Prime Minister Howard."

Macdonald grinned. "Actually, I'm glad you vetted her. It had to happen sometime. Do you, or have you, shared this with Director Thornton?'

Eubanks looked squarely at the president. "Not yet."

"It's okay if you do. How tightly will he hold that?"

"I can stipulate it is for his eyes only."

"He'll do that?"

"I'm sure he will," Eubanks said, in a way that said more.

66

"It went beautifully, Mr. President," Vice President Dudley said on the phone from New York City. "There were two CEOs, twenty-five to thirty executives, a couple dozen union leaders, and many employees. We came together in a common bond. They know we will do whatever to keep them functioning. Most realize that relocating, which the AIR and DOER fund would cover, was their best bet for employment."

"Maybe use just DOER funds for that and save AIR for Detroit stuff."

"You're right," she said."We will need professional business and accounting people to get a permanent operation up and running that focuses on these folks."

"I'll talk to Kap, get his people on it."

"I'll get you a summary on all the logistics."

"Don't worry about me," he said. "You're in charge out there. Keep operating as you have been. Did Secretary Russell get there?"

"He was right up front with a half dozen people from Transportation, including two former undersecretaries who he brought back in. They're on board and will be great mentors for J.T.'s neophyte staff and the new undersecretaries."

"All this unity is getting a little scary," he joked.

"I think some are gaining a Centrist mentality."

They shared a good laugh. "It shows there is still hope. I hear there are no partisanships in a foxhole."

"I'll let you go. You're the best."

He called Darlene. "Yes sir?"

"Good news from New York. Management and union are of one mind: rebuild. I'll tell you more later."

"Will the vice president be putting out a release on today's progress?"

"I didn't ask. Have A.J. call her and offer press support, maybe send one of his deputies to Bryanna. Her press staff would normally be here, but they're all over the place."

"I'll see that it gets done."

"Okay, next case. I want a half hour of broadcast time Thursday evening at eight. I haven't mentioned this to Bryanna, but she and I will be doing this one together from here. She'll be getting great props out of New York. She's got the momentum. People are going to want to see and hear from her. The emphasis will be on recovery and rebuilding.

"She's staying over in New York tonight for more auto meetings tomorrow. Have her come here after they wrap things up."

"You haven't told her about coming to Washington."

"No, just thought of it."

"I have something for you from DOER, sir. The vice president's Chief of Staff called me about nonprofits who want to help, like Habitat for Humanity a la Katrina and the 2010 natural disasters. It could ease the normal attrition rate of DOER volunteers having to get back to their regular jobs."

"I'm all for it. Give that to Gus and tell him to hire some more people to help supervise it. I don't want him stretching his permanent staff to the breaking point."

67

Oval Office
Wednesday, January 30
0628 hours

The president had already started breakfast when the DCIA arrived. Eubanks sat and took out the Wednesday PDB. However, before giving it to Macdonald, he related his Phoenix team's response to the president's request.

"Our folks saw the sensitive nature of things and accepted your perspective to protect Davos. They recommended that Phoenix stand down."

The president smiled. *I'd like to know what they really said*, he thought.

"We sent a message to General Orlovski saying we had misunderstood our authority and were withdrawing the request for access to the storage facility. Almost shockingly, General Orlovski became congenial and assured us that reentry to the storage site would suffer only a short delay. He was quoted as saying, *'Let the bureaucrats earn their wages.'* We told him we'd not return until he invited us back. Though we pulled out this morning, we have maintained a close surveillance of the underground facility's lone entrance. Our satellites are in position."

"The ones that read license plates?" Macdonald asked.

Eubanks laughed. "Better than that, sir." He handed the president his PDB.

"I'm just glad we've got those birds in the sky."

They fell silent as the president ate and browsed the report. Eubanks fixed his plate and began eating.

After a couple of minutes, Macdonald put the PDB on the table. "I, ah, didn't see anything in this morning's brief about a certain World Bank executive."

"An oversight, sir," he said feigning shock. "Reports are that she arrived in Zurich this morning and met a gentleman coming in on a Moscow flight. They were then driven to Davos, where they have checked in."

"Was one of your people on her London flight?"

"Actually, two."

"Why am I not surprised?"

"Everyone's in place. One asset works for the World Bank and actually worked for Alexandra two years ago in London. We call him George.

"We are also introducing a female agent to the mix who will couple up with George. There is considerable socializing at this event," Eubanks concluded, as he placed his PDB into his briefcase.

"Sounds good. Keep me posted."

Eubanks left, and Macdonald asked Cynthia to get the British Prime Minister on the line. Then he called Darlene.

"We finished here early, and the world is still intact. Is the staff meeting still at eight?"

"It is."

He hung up and looked at an ominous stack of documents. He plucked off the top one and sat back in his large swivel chair. He was reading when Cynthia buzzed him.

"The Prime Minister will be on line four, sir."

He punched it. "Reggie?" No answer.

A pause and then, "Are you there, old boy?"

"Right here, my friend."

"I gather we have all been a bit busy."

"Oh? Is that what you call *dining with the Queen?*"

"Oh dear, was that when you called? My apologies, that message must have gotten lost in a croquet game."

"Not a problem. However, Prime Minister McEwen said you were arriving there Thursday and that you would be joining us in Detroit on Saturday."

"Quite so."

"McEwen and I are getting along well; we had a mini summit meeting on survivor recovery last Friday in Detroit. We're planning a tour for you in Detroit and Windsor, all in the name of international relations."

"Happy to see you are catching on to the important aspects of your job. We will be in your town through Tuesday before Louise and I escape to a warm sun on our way home with a four-day stop in Bermuda."

"I would like you both to fly back here with me after our get-together Saturday and be my guest at the White House Saturday night, before moving to the embassy."

"That would be delightful. We haven't done that. Sunday? Isn't that your championship football game? The super-duper cup or such."

"You nailed it," Mike said, laughing. "It's being played in our southwestern desert. I'll be leaving here around noon on game day, so I'll feed you twice. You two can even sleep in the Lincoln Bedroom, and we'll have breakfast in our sun room, which I have yet to see, in the south portico."

"Well, let me see . . . tell you what. I do need to talk to . . . there may be something scheduled, of which I am not aware. My plane will be in Ottawa, but they can fly it down. Yes, at the moment, I believe that is workable."

"Have your guy call my gal," Mike said jocularly.

"Ah, the American Indian. Her family probably fought with the French three hundred years ago," Howard said wryly.

"I have no idea, but she does have a scalping knife."

"How gruesome."

"It'll be great seeing you, Mr. Prime Minister."

"What? Oh yes, thank you, Mr. President. We'll chat Saturday."

"Cheerio," Mike managed to get in before he heard the line go dead. He checked the time—0740—and then went back to reading. It seemed in a blink that Cynthia was announcing the staff meeting.

There were many more people than he had expected, almost filling the Cabinet Room. He took a few minutes to say good morning personally to everyone. Two had to tell him their names; they had not been part of the campaign.

Darlene ran through a series of items in her very efficient manner and alerted everyone that Vice President Dudley would be in the offices on Thursday before returning to the DTO. She asked the president if he had anything to say.

He charmingly responded by thanking them for their hard work under very trying circumstances and apologized to them if he had thrown them into a panic last Thursday.

"You don't know this, but you played a very important part in my strategy to upset some very nasty people."

They looked dumbfounded, and Darlene jumped in to explain that the president was kidding. She looked at him sternly, and he stood, making everyone scramble to their feet.

He was enjoying this. "Have a very good day." He went through Cynthia's work area and told her he was meeting Secretary Kaplan at 1000 hours in his study and would prefer not to be disturbed.

"Yes sir. You are having lunch with the Education Secretary, some teachers, and members of the NEA."

"Are members of the Praetorian Guard joining me, to defend against spit balls?"

"Sir," she said forcefully. "A.J. and I will protect you."

"My worries are over." He proceeded into his study and closed the door.

Kap was calmer than Mike had seen him since before inauguration day. Maybe it was due to the two lovely female students from Wharton he was squiring around.

They would be joining Bryanna's team in the DTO, helping to establish the three family centers for auto workers and their families. The young ladies were engaging, and he regaled them with some stories about their professor.

They, in turn, told him a couple tales of their own. Kap had promised them a little time in Washington, so they wouldn't leave for the DTO until Monday. Nancy came and got them.

He and Kap then met for ninety minutes, ending a half hour before his lunch appointment. He returned to the Oval Office and addressed the growing pile of papers on his desk.

He had Nancy join him at the lunch with the education folks. She'd had experience in that field. Also, it would be like old times, them sitting in a meeting together.

The whole luncheon focused around the DTO, and he was pleased that Secretary Brooke B. Baldwin had a solid handle on what was needed. The NEA people were a little stiff, but to their credit, they got into the flow of dealing with a major startup program.

He returned to his office and dug into Cynthia's pile of dry documents, which really weren't as bad as those he'd had to deal with in the financial field. The government-ese was mind numbing. At 1640, his intercom buzzed.

"Sir? Dr. Mednorov is on line one."

He punched the line. "Hey."

"Mon cher!" She sounded excited.

"Wow. It's great hearing your voice. How's it going? How's Vasiliy?"

She laughed. "Vasiliy is wonderful. This is a place you will have to visit . . . with me."

"Yeah, like right now."

She giggled. They were pumped. She wanted to know about the automotive meetings. They went back and forth in rapid-fire fashion, like they couldn't get enough of each other. He told her about the vice president coming back to Washington on Thursday and the TV program they had planned.

"I am happy they are keeping you busy."

"Me too. Have you met up with old friends?"

"Yes. We had an all-Russian dinner tonight. There were seven of us. With two of them, I go back to childhood. It has all been social. Tomorrow after three, we have some down time. Vasiliy and I are going to ride the gondola up to the mid-level chalet for an early dinner and watch the sunset."

They chatted about Reggie and the Super Bowl, neither wanting to hang up, until she finally had to end it.

"It is getting late here. I am almost adjusted to the time change and want a good night's sleep. Good night, my love."

"Have a great day tomorrow, my sweet. I love you."

68

White House
Thursday, January 31

His morning ritual went off without a hitch, and after Eubanks left, he had a cup of coffee with Bryanna in his West Wing Study. They scoped out the evening's TV program. They would meet at 1500 to survey the setup.

Following her visit, he took out his writing pad and wrote down random thoughts about the bombing, people in general, and the Russians specifically.

Were we bombed for money?

People had always looked to this country for the opportunities and education it presented to build a better life. Now, many or most people come to this country for what they can get out of the government, which often makes them better off than the poorer American citizenry.

The people who achieved through their own talents and wits were able to pick themselves up by the proverbial boot straps, building self-esteem and solid families. Mike struggled to understand why politicians and radicals wanted to eliminate initiative.

He wrote: *What do Americans want to get from everyday life? Too many times people say "all I want is to be left alone," which can be translated into "I want to consume, but I don't want to contribute."*

He put down his pen. Writing helped him through difficult situations, sometimes taking one side, then the other. He also had good people around him who weren't afraid to voice differing opinions. One of those with whom he particularly enjoyed banging ideas around was Bryanna.

He went off to meet Darlene for lunch. After they were seated, she mentioned the vice president had caused quite a stir amongst the West Wingers. "She has rock star appeal."

"It's good having her here, but following our dinner meeting and the TV presentation tonight, she's flying back to Detroit. She'll be at ground zero all day tomorrow getting ready for our tour with the two prime ministers."

"She had great success with the auto people. That was a gigantic undertaking. I'm glad it was not on us."

Darlene reflected for a moment and then asked, "Does Prime Minister Howard know about Alexandra?"

The question caught him off guard, but then he smiled. "No. I'm going to spring her on him Saturday night. I've asked them to stay over in the Lincoln Bedroom on Saturday night, before moving to their embassy for the rest of their stay. If Alex's schedule holds, she'll be back in her apartment before six. I'm planning a dinner for four."

"I know."

"Of course you do."

They laughed and went back to eating.

"I'm taking Nancy and Seth to the Super Bowl. Do you know anyone real hot to go?"

"I have no idea," she said aloofly.

At 1500, Macdonald and Dudley visited the State Dining Room where the dinner and TV presentation was planned. She immediately suggested that the show be moved to the East Room where the attendees could sit auditorium-style. She didn't like the lack of ambiance created by a lot of empty dinner tables.

"That's fine with me; it's really your show anyway. I'm going to start it off with a five-minute 'state of the union' and then turn it over to you. DOER and AIR are your babies."

They started walking back toward the West Wing going through the Green, Blue, and Red rooms when they were approached by a member of the Uniformed Service Division.

"Excuse me, Mr. President, Madam Vice President. Chief Sweetwater says you are needed, sir."

"In Darlene's lexicon that means *immediately*," he said to Dudley.

"You go ahead," she said.

"The elevator is ready, sir."

"Catch you later," he said, already moving across the entrance hall. He went down to the ground floor and then trotted down the Center Hall to the Palm Room and out onto the Colonnade to the Oval Office.

Darlene, Cynthia, Alisa, Nancy, and Hendrickson obviously knew where he would be entering, because as he came through the French door, they were all facing him wearing grim or glum expressions. Darlene stepped to him.

"What?" he exclaimed.

"We have a problem," she said.

A shot of adrenaline coursed through him. He froze, thinking the worst.

Alisa moved to alongside Darlene, and Nancy a little closer to him. "We have been monitoring phone traffic from Davos."

He swallowed hard, his anxiety building.

"There was a call from Steve Hester. Alex and her brother were to meet with him when they returned from their visit up the mountain, and the last scheduled gondola has come down," Darlene added.

"Where were Eubanks' people?" he demanded, his voice shaky.

Hendrickson moved to his side. "We called CIA Operations. Two agents went up, one in the same lift with them, the other an hour later."

"And?"

"The director is on his way here, maybe ten minutes out," Alisa said.

His intensity was building. "Have we talked with Hester or tried to reach him?"

"No," Darlene said calmly. "Our waiting for the director will have no affect on what was or is going on."

"I suggest, Mr. President," Hendrickson said gently, "we might be better off in the Situation Room. Better communications."

Macdonald blankly looked at his mentor, and then focused. "Okay. I'd like to know if those agents are equipped with satellite phones." His throat was tight.

"We will ask the director when he gets here," Darlene said assuredly.

"There have been no accidents, no injuries reported?" he asked vacuously.

"We've scoured the Internet, sir," Nancy said. "There have been no incidents of any kind coming out of Davos."

Darlene kept a steady hand on things. "I put a call into Secretary Royce to see if there had been a power failure, which wouldn't make headlines. It's almost 2200 hours there."

"May we move to the Situation Room, Mr. President?" Hendrickson asked firmly, to grab his attention. "Sir, I'll walk with you."

Macdonald moved with the ambassador. Everyone followed.

A communications officer greeted the president. "Sir, we received a call from hotel security in Davos. There have been no problems with the lift; no mechanical problems. In fact, the final gondola has just come down."

"Those folks know their business, Mr. President," Hendrickson said, as he and

Darlene moved Macdonald along the conference table to his seat. "You know the Swiss," he said jauntily.

Macdonald cracked a small smile as he sat. The others found chairs and sat. The com officer announced, "Director Eubanks has just cleared the gate."

69

In his twenty-four years with the CIA, James Riley Eubanks had seen the gathering of information go from tedious to instantaneous. Today, news that his agency would formerly covet was now on the Internet, text, or Twitter as fast as his agents could transmit it. Here, though, it was Steve's private call involving Alexandra and Vasiliy Mednorov—*"I don't know where they are"*—had been heard by NSA, and they had erroneously passed it along immediately to the White House without checking with CIA's command center first. A mistake that will be addressed.

The Davos plan had looked to be foolproof: no slip-ups, no danger.

He and Steve had talked with Alexandra on Thursday evening a week earlier in the presidential sitting room and again on Saturday at Camp David. They both observed how quickly she absorbed very technical communications and computer system matrices. He had asked if she would talk with Vasiliy about the Russian banking system and how it did or didn't mesh with the FSB.

Even with all the electronic wizardry, he still believed in the power of the simple one-on-one, eyeball-to-eyeball. Based on her willingness and the president's permission, it was how he had planned to use her.

By the time he'd returned to Washington from Camp David that Saturday night, he was convinced Alexandra Mednorov was extremely gifted. Her memory was acute and accurate to the smallest detail. He imagined Vasiliy would have many of his twin's traits.

He bet she was the strategist, and he, the operator.

Alexandra could take the whole system and homogenize it, take it from the poet's ether and reduce it to common-day life. That unique ability had made him think deeply about the value of the Davos operation and was why he had called her three times on Monday.

He had tested a memory theory on her, asking what she thought of the Camp David computerized system to which she had only superficially been exposed. She didn't disappoint, coming back with a strong understanding of its capabilities. There had been no hint in her background of such an ability.

She had both fascinated and confused him; charming and self-effacing on one hand, with a scholarly savant-like intellect on the other. Was the president aware of this about her? The biggest complication involving her was that she was the president's mega-girlfriend. He had seen the electricity between them.

Both Macdonald and Mednorov had been widowed for several years and neither had had a serious relationship until they reunited. Seeing them now, it was as though they had been waiting for each other without knowing it.

He had purposely made time Saturday to ask Nancy Armstrong about Macdonald and his late wife, Sandi Robbins. She had chuckled at being asked to think back to that time. "He and Sandi were special. Seth and I have a wonderful life together, but those two . . . we loved them, and they us. They were an amazing couple."

Now Mike Macdonald was full-swing into a revival of an eighteen-year-old relationship, which sounded very much like what Mrs. Armstrong had described to him about the relationship he'd had with Sandi Robbins.

Admittedly, two days after the bombing, the agency had more loose ends than a frayed mop. They'd had to struggle through the bogus claim by the Iraqi group, which created tension and frustration. Then the president had talked with Alexandra about some strange financial maneuvers confounding Vasiliy.

After the bombing, Alexandra had put the weakened American economy together from a paper Macdonald had written almost twenty years earlier. It seemed fairy tale-ish, too good to be true. However, the more he learned about the Russian internal upheaval, the more he saw the validity in what Vasiliy had told her. But the situation was filled with intangibles; there was no proof.

When he saw her mind at work at Camp David, he became convinced that her knowledge of the Russian banking system was considerably greater than even she might have been aware. The more he asked her about Vasiliy and the FSB, the more he witnessed the breadth of her knowledge—and the plot thickened.

She *saw* things other people only *looked at*.

He needed that talent, that insight. He needed to get her brain wrapped around the FSB. The Mednorovs were a treasure trove of inside knowledge, ready for the tapping. He had quickly built a covert team that could farm the Mednorovs' fertile brains, and he'd convinced the president that she would be safe.

He carefully chose *George and Betty*, veteran clandestine officers. George had extensive banking knowledge, knew Russian and knew Alex, having worked for her in London. Betty had nine years of Russian studies and, for five years, had worked out of the US Embassy in Moscow. She knew of several in the FSB, including Raisa by job, not personally.

Betty was currently at Langley. She knew of Vasiliy. She and George would meet up in Davos and get close to Alex and Vasiliy.

Was there something he had missed?

Right now, however, he was about to face a president who had received troublesome news, which should never have gotten to him in the form he had received it.

70

Situation Room
Minutes later

Eubanks, accompanied by two men and a woman entered. "Mr. President," he said, gesturing to his associates. "These folks are from our Russian Desk. Bryce Wren, our communications specialist, went into the Com Room."

"Where is she, Director?" Macdonald asked harshly.

"Safe, sir," he said easily.

"Where?" Macdonald pursued, gruffly.

"Sir, Alexandra and Vasiliy are all right. Secure. Two Russian men intruded on them while they sat in the mid-level chalet enjoying some vodka and the view before going in for dinner.

It wasn't hairy, but it was disruptive. We are busy sorting things out as I speak. I understand you were told that they were missing."

"Yeah, they didn't meet up with Hester, and nobody knew where they were."

"Actually, that's not accurate, sir. It was only Steve who didn't know where they were, and he was justifiably concerned. His was an internal call, not meant for publication. He called it in as he should have, because something could have gone amiss with them. I was advised of Steve's call and rushed to the Clandestine Service desk and learned Ambassador Hendrickson had called.

"Because the White House received a message from NSA that was out of context, I immediately ordered a blackout on all interceptable communications. I especially did not want anybody hearing that CIA was involved with Russian Nationals."

Macdonald visibly blanched.

Darlene, concerned about her boss's mood, jumped in. "That's understandable. We've only known Alexandra a short time and forget she's a Russian citizen." She glanced at the president and saw the tension slowly dissipating.

Eubanks continued. "That's why I purposely phrased it the way outsiders would see it. Two operatives, George and Betty, were at the mid-level lodge in sight of Alex and Vasiliy. The space has high alpine ceilings and large windows exposing a startling view.

"George and Betty sat on stools at a high table on a platform behind the grill room tables. They had both the view and the Mednorovs in plain sight.

"A long bar sat at the back on the platform. George observed two men in business suits sitting on stools resting their backs against the bar, eyeing every woman who walked by. However, that scene changed as the two suddenly headed for Alex and Vasiliy's table."

Darlene sensed Macdonald's flinch.

"There was a short conversation, and then the men sat. It wasn't clear if they were invited or not. In a few minutes, Alex got up and left the table, returning about ten minutes later, but she did not sit. In fact, she was quite animated. Betty didn't know what had caused that, but Alex was pointing away from the table, as though she was telling the men to leave.

"Although my two could not hear Alex, George noticed people sitting near them turning their heads in the Mednorovs' direction, so they assumed that Alex's voice was raised. Finally, the men nonchalantly stood up. Alex stepped back defensively, it seemed.

"The men then lackadaisically strolled away, returning to the spot where they had previously been at the bar. George and Betty paid up and ambled to a step-down area between the tables and the large viewing windows. They played tourist, and then casually turned in the Mednorovs' direction and went up the short steps as though they were leaving when George acted like he had spotted an old friend.

"Alex, knowing George, made that an easy act. At that moment, she didn't know he was one of ours, so she was spontaneously surprised and happy, motioning to Vasiliy, who stood. George and Alex made the introductions, and then they all sat, George ordering a round of drinks."

Macdonald appeared restless. "That all sounds very warm and cozy. Is this going to be a long story, Director?"

Darlene was surprised at his impatience and put her hand on his arm to get his attention. She was shocked at the tension she felt in him.

"I don't intend it to be, sir. My agents are fluent in Russian. Betty thought

Vasiliy to be very relaxed. I had discussed with Alex that disruptions could occur and to adapt, go with the flow. Alex didn't mention the earlier intrusion, but did glance in the men's direction twice.

"Not knowing who the two Russian men were, Betty excused herself. She used her satellite phone and called in. Those calls go through a labyrinth and are scrambled. That's how I know what I just told you.

"We decided to treat the two Russians as Secret Police and informed our people accordingly. Steve was not on the link-up. We wanted to avoid raising concerns that Vasiliy was doing something more than enjoying his sister's company. If they were police, they would have very likely known Alex.

"We let George orchestrate, and he treated at dinner. He said Alex protested, but he had insisted for the sake of old friendships. George did see a change in her attitude, like questioning in her mind who he really was. He said the meal was cordial, and they enjoyed a gorgeous sunset. When all four boarded the gondola, so did the two Russians along with others.

"George concocted a plan to shake the two men. Alex told Vasiliy they were going to play a charade, for which she would explain the reason later. So it was arranged that when they debarked, Vasiliy would argue that he and Betty no longer wanted to party.

"George wanted to see what the two Russians would do. So after a faked animated discussion, Vasiliy waved George off, and he and Betty left. The Russian men didn't follow. Once out of sight, Betty sent a confused Vasiliy off to the hotel, and she circled back and took up a position where she could track the four, and then called us.

"Steve was waiting for them at the conference center."

Macdonald was disturbed. "Okay, let me get this straight, Director. Alex and this George were now alone with two possible Russian operatives in close proximity?"

"They were far from alone, sir. We had two armed undercover security agents in constant view of Alex from the moment she got off the gondola. We have that capability there. We don't take chances with anyone's life," he said firmly, hoping to diffuse the president's ire.

Darlene caught Eubanks's tone and jumped in. "I think what we need to know is where things stand right now, Director. We can get the backstory later. It is obvious you have taken many precautions and had people in positions to react to protect our mission in Davos."

Her preciseness brought Macdonald back to his senses. He drained his bottle of lemon-flavored water and held it up toward one of the uniformed guards, who had a new bottle to him in a flash. Everybody waited. Darlene sensed Macdonald wasn't going to say anything. "Director, where is Alexandra now?"

Eubanks appreciated her business-like demeanor. "Please understand that what I am about to tell you was camouflage—what we wanted the two Russians to think was happening. George and Alex made like a couple and went into the Tavern. Both Russians followed. One of our security agents followed, the other took up a position across the street, out of sight, but where he could observe the tavern, as Betty was also doing.

"George waited for some sort of move from the Russians, but that didn't happen. Without all the details, Alex and George had a drink and grabbed a taxi. The Russians surprisingly did not follow. Alex accompanied George to his room . . ."

Intensity gripped the Situation Room with everyone in the mode of *what now?*

". . . where she is now. Understand, there are cameras on every floor. Someone who was keeping a close eye on her movements could easily suspect a charade. Steve is currently debriefing Betty, who will depart Davos immediately afterwards."

Eubanks hoped he wouldn't have to ask his wife to break out the travel brochures again. He'd hate leaving before apprehending the guilty parties, but knew his people could carry the investigation out to a successful conclusion.

He knew his duty and did it, protecting a very valuable asset and, in doing so, had served his president well.

71

There were a few more details from Eubanks, and then Darlene abruptly ended the meeting. Hendrickson and Macdonald left for the president's study without a word. Darlene remained behind, while the DCIA huddled with his two Russian specialists. He was about to go into the com center when he realized the Chief of Staff was still in the room.

Darlene approached him. "What do we know now that we didn't know when we awoke this morning?"

He smiled inwardly, fully understanding her question.

"First, I want to clear the air," he said. "No one from CIA informed the president of a problem. A message was intercepted and taken out of context. That should not be laid at the feet of any of my operatives. We keep careful tabs on all our people. To Steve, one asset, two field officers, and a critically valuable informant were missing."

Darlene shifted her weight slightly at the director's mild rebuke.

Eubanks was calm, but direct. "When someone doesn't show at the appointed time, we become concerned. Alexandra Mednorov is a uniquely talented person and quickly becoming an invaluable asset."

Darlene raised a hand slightly as she interrupted. "What exactly are you saying?"

"Alex has a mental brilliance I have rarely seen. For example, I asked her about Russian banking and about the inner workings of the FSB. Understand, she's been away from both for a decade. I was amazed at the detailed explanations she gave on what was ostensibly her brother's job."

"When did all this take place, your questioning?"

"During three phone calls on Monday, while briefing her on what to expect in Davos. When she responded about what she understood, I was impressed.

A veteran operative could not have expressed her mission any more clearly. At Camp David, she constantly demonstrated a phenomenal depth of knowledge."

"Why didn't we see this? We've certainly talked . . ."

"Excuse me," he interrupted. "Actually, until Saturday, we only saw her as a source of information regarding the root cause of the bombing and as the president's very special friend.

"Tell me, weren't you skeptical of what she was bringing to the table? We all were. She quickly changed our minds, though, as we experienced her knowledge of Russian finance and how she detailed her thoughts on how Vasiliy could help us."

"Are you saying you deliberately put her on the line to see what fish you might attract?"

He half smiled as he shook his head. "Please. She was never used that way. We truly only wanted her to spend time with her brother, to glean names and his thoughts about those huge transfers of money. We know there was shorting on our currency, but we still don't know for sure that they funded their so-called shell corporations to do the shorting.

"As far as the two Russian men were concerned, we had several photos of them before they left the lodge. We learned who one was. "

"Oh?"

"FSB Secret Police. We assume the other is as well. We'll know soon. Let me explain how we are handling this. We don't want any outsiders perceiving that either Mednorov had any protective service around them. They were to be who they are: a brother and sister enjoying a rendezvous in the Swiss Alps, while attending an economic conference. If we had stepped in, we'd have blown everything and compromised Vasiliy.

"Any sign, any hint of protection would have been a total giveaway. They could have been keeping an eye on Vasiliy, but gave up after the ride down on the lift. By their attitude in the tavern, they weren't particularly interested in Alex, most likely because of George replacing Vasiliy. That's why George did the switch. We probably will never know their mission, but I can say it was one strange way to conduct a surveillance.

"Believe me, we would have liked nothing better than to have taken those two down and questioned them, but that would have sent a nuclear alert to Moscow."

Darlene nodded her understanding.

He calmed. "We stayed on them after Alex and George left. They had a drink and left the tavern, walked a short distance to a small hotel where they met up with a third man. We'll keep tabs on all three."

"I take it then, you don't expect any—?"

"I expect everything and plan accordingly. We have plenty of people around Alex, overtly and otherwise. It's a team event."

"That's reassuring," Darlene said.

He cleared his throat. "Do you think the president harbors any thoughts that I may have put Alex's life on the line or that I deliberately put her in danger?"

"I don't know, but beyond his superficial reactions earlier, I would doubt it."

Eubanks pursed his lips. "I hope you're right. I'd like to see this assignment to its conclusion, Chief Sweetwater. I am very caught up in what the president is all about and believe he is the right man in the right place. I've enjoyed the give and take he has afforded me with him. I believe we are closing in, and I'd hate to miss out on the end."

He began returning papers that he had used earlier to his briefcase.

Darlene's face showed shock. "What are you talking about, sir? There is no way the president is going to dismiss you. I am sure he is upstairs right now telling Ambassador Hendrickson how poorly he controlled his emotions. Because that's him, president or no.

She fretted over the thought of losing Eubanks. "Mr. Director, I know him better than anyone, including his family. He has confided his deepest feelings to me, including about Alex. I went from being skeptical about her to being a believer, the same as you, and not because she is the president's friend."

"She is a unique and valuable asset for all of us," he said, feeling a little uncomfortable with the COS's personal comments.

"Truthfully, I thought she'd be a distraction, but her effect was the opposite. He's more engaged. She fills an important place in his heart that has been empty for over six years."

She realized she was getting preachy and took a lighter approach. "Women have always flocked to him. He's had his choice of many outstanding ladies even before he began running for the presidency. He enjoyed a good laugh, but had no interest in a relationship, which dented some fairly healthy female egos.

"Then Alex showed up last November. I knew her only as a former classmate from Vasiliy's letter after Sandi's death, and also when he and Vasiliy met in Geneva in 2010. That was when he learned Alex was in London, and I'm sure he thought about stopping off there, but he was heavily involved in DOER and helping Bryanna form an official Centrist party. He wanted her to run for president, you know."

He acknowledged that he knew. He found it a little out of order; her running on like this. There were other things he needed to be doing.

"Alex visited him in New York on Thanksgiving weekend. He put her up at the Plaza. He later talked with her by phone twice, once when she was in London and the second time when she was staying with Vasiliy in Moscow over the holidays.

"I believe the romance was fully rekindled for both during her second visit to New York on January 5. He told me he wanted to see her again. I saw it in his eyes and heard it in his voice that he had strong feelings for her. I was concerned and suggested he put off seeing her until at least a week after the inauguration. He agreed.

"I was upset when she called last Wednesday, thinking the timing couldn't have been worse. Surprisingly, he told me he couldn't see or talk with her. But when she insisted through Jane in New York, he became concerned and asked me to arrange it. Little did we know or expect what she had for us. The rest is history."

Eubanks had studied her as she talked. He realized that Darlene saw everything with very clear eyes. He took a deep breath and looked over at his two analysts busy on their smartphones and computers.

He let out a sigh. "We have nine names."

"Nine . . . Russian?" she said amazed. "She made a list?"

He shook his head. "It was in her head. Vasiliy hadn't written it down either. These nine were political opponents of Novorken. Vasiliy knew of no plot. We're vetting and compiling information on the nine now and will be staying here for a while. We need this ready for Steve and George when they meet Alex and Vasiliy in the morning."

"Mr. Director, you amaze me."

"It's not me, ma'am. It's the dedicated folks who work their butts off for our organization. Oh, I expect the president will be receiving a call in a short while."

72

Macdonald needed to walk off his emotions, so instead of returning to his study with Hendrickson, he asked his mentor if he would walk with him. It had turned blustery outside, so he suggested they walk through the West Wing and go up to the State Floor of the White House for a walk there.

When they entered the hall that ran between the State Dining Room and the East Room, they ambled toward the room where the TV broadcast would emanate. Workers were busy setting up two eight-foot digital screens and arranging the room to Bryanna's specifications. Two of his protective agents had gone ahead to tell the workers that the president might enter the room, but to continue their work.

As they walked, Mike talked about the building. The ambassador commented about the presidential portraits adorning the walls. With the East Room busy, they went into the Green Room, and then into the Blue Room, which sat in the south portico.

They looked out at the roiling skies and agitated tree limbs buffeted about by the gusty winds. The outside seemed a metaphor for what had been going on in his gut earlier in the Situation Room.

"I'm not pleased by at my behavior," Macdonald said, continuing to look out the window. "I am concerned at what happened to me in the Situation Room. I can't . . . my body . . . I tried to suppress the anguish."

He took a deep breath and exhaled forcibly.

The ambassador spoke softly. "You have been under a tremendous strain, Michael, and you've handled it with amazing sensibility. Today, you were confronted with a different emotion, one of the heart.

"We are all falling in love with your 'Lexi.' I am infatuated with how you two are together. I only met your late wife once, but heard wonderful things about her."

"She was a volatile version of Lexi. Beautiful, bright, engaging, caring . . ." Macdonald choked on emotion, swallowed, and cleared his throat. "I have been in love with and been loved by two incredible women," he said respectfully to his mentor. "Lexi was my first love, but I didn't understand *love* then. I learned that with Sandi. Now Lexi has reentered my life. I've been given much. "

"And you give much. You inspire people. I am sure you are not quite comfortable with your new role. You have every right to act human and be emotional. Don't forget, most everyone in the Situation Room knows the carefree Mike who shares his wealth and his heart.

"I believe, in the moments before Director Eubanks arrived, everyone was crying inside at the hint of a possible tragedy. For as long as I am *compos mentis*, I will hold a memory of Alexandra standing in the living room doorway at Camp David. She was a vision.

"What I saw transmitting between the two of you was as spiritual as it was physical. Jim Eubanks saw it too. He talked about her on our way back to Washington and said he sensed a mental brilliance in her, of which he didn't think even she was cognitive."

Mike looked at the gentle man. "She's bright . . ."

"Jim thinks a savant genius."

"A what?"

"Think positive, Michael: a mind with almost total recall, which she does not display overtly in normal, everyday activities. Jim had planned to test his theory, and I believe he did this past Monday, when they were going over what she could expect in Davos, not having been around a lot of Secret Agents."

Mike became tense.

"It is not anything for you to worry about, my boy—unless, of course, you teach her chess," he said chuckling.

Mike grinned while shaking his head. "This is a day of learning for me. Thank you." He addressed an agent at the door. "Would you ask if CIA Director Eubanks is still in the building?"

"Yes sir," he responded, and quickly spoke into his radio. The answer came in seconds. "He is in the Situation Room, sir."

73

"I am fine, Michael. I am fine," Alex said imploringly.

"I'm just . . . it's good to hear your voice." he said softly.

"Vasiliy has been forthcoming. He wants to help."

"Jim told me. Nine names plus."

"Yes. He has more. Two he thinks had old contacts with the Ministry of Defense."

"You sound great."

"I love, love, love you," she burst out.

"I love, love, love you." He laughed, and she giggled.

"Everybody in the Situation Room certainly knows, after my emotions got the best of me, when we didn't know where you were."

"Oh, I am so sorry."

"No. You were doing fine. From what Jim said, doing great. I can't wait for you to get home," he said softly.

"I can't either, but it is wonderful being with Vasiliy."

"Sweetheart, I've got to go. Knowing you're okay has made my day. Bryanna, who is here for one day, and I are doing a TV show tonight with a report on domestic progress. Oh, Reggie said they'd be happy to stay at the White House Saturday night."

"That is wonderful. Good night, my love."

"Yes, good night to you my love."

74

Oval Office
Friday, February 1
0630 hours

Eubanks joined the president at their usual time. Macdonald greeted the CIA director with the same friendliness he had all week long. They'd had a frank discussion alone late Thursday afternoon after the scare the White House had created for itself.

He later told Darlene that he had cleared the air with Eubanks. She opted not to share her own conversation with the director.

Eubanks handed the president his PDB, and they both sat at the breakfast table. It had been a week since Macdonald turned the financial world upside down, arranging for over five trillion dollars in loans and receiving the purchase of $1.35 trillion in T-Notes.

Macdonald snickered. "I see the same media who were screaming that we were in default are still screaming, only now it's the slowness of our recovery work in the DTO. One look at the currency exchanges tells me the market is not affected by their hypercritical drivel. Fortunately, we're getting high grades on the recovery, thanks to Bryanna."

He chuckled and laid down the PDB. "Speaking of the VP, did she 'wow' them last night or what? I looked at a playback before going to bed; she's as three-dimensional on TV as she is in person. Even our senators and representatives at the dinner were riveted by her. It may have been their baptism to the Dudley Dance."

"Dance?" Eubanks asked curiously.

"My private nickname for the flair she demonstrates when doing her dog-and-pony show. I orate; she performs."

Eubanks laughed. "I was still at the Agency working with our analysts on the Davos intelligence, but we stopped to watch your program. I have to say, sir, I've never known a president to step back and let his number two take the limelight, as you do with her."

Macdonald laughed. "Ha. I'm not a politician. I was a volunteer raising money for DOER, since the Congress had abrogated any interest in funding it. She was running a state and trying to establish a new official political party.

"I had felt for a long time that the two-party system, especially in Congress, needed an overhaul, no matter who was in power. Too many of the senior legislators had lost it. My fundraising efforts for DOER introduced me to a lot of wealthy and powerful Americans, who, I found, were also disgusted with our government leaders in general.

"We drew them into our effort. Ms. Dudley was an independent governor and had been a Democrat lieutenant governor. Her leadership was awe-inspiring. I was her biggest supporter and still am. I figured if we got a presidential campaign going, she'd be our nominee."

Eubanks nodded and took a helping of scrambled eggs.

"You probably know all this, but I'll say it anyway. She had a strong and loyal following, which included me. In early 2011, we officially formed the Centrist party, and she was unanimously elected chairwoman. While we continued proselytizing for candidates to run for office in their state or for the US House or Senate, I was touting her to be our presidential nominee.

"I didn't know that, quietly, she was touting me to our leadership to be the nominee. I told her no, it was all hers. Besides, I had my irons in a lot of fires, and I was enjoying those challenges. She kept pushing me. I kept saying no.

"As you've observed, I'm short on tact, although Darlene is working hard on me to gain some polish. But Bryanna wouldn't let up and neither would our leadership, which numbered thousands of influential people, working hard to establish a viable third party.

"When I acquiesced, it was on the proviso that she would be my running mate. Now it was her turn to object. She said she could do more chairing the party, while remaining governor. She was extremely popular throughout the Midwest, and that meant a lot of electoral votes. We needed her charisma and dedication. She finally agreed."

Now it was time for Eubanks to chortle. "She's diminutive in size, but imposing in stature. Very impassioned."

"We knew we had a tough job in righting the financial debacle created over the past decades, and she was slated to take the lead in one aspect of that recovery—

little did we know how quickly. The bombing pushed her right into her element, working for the people at the grassroots level."

Eubanks pulled a plain manila folder from his briefcase as he said, "The vice president is a credit to your administration, Mr. President. You two make quite a team."

"Thanks." He nodded at what Eubanks was holding. "Is that something from the European front?"

Eubanks nodded. "Everything's been going smoothly in Davos, sir. Alex and Vasiliy are attending their seminars of choice this morning, after having had breakfast with George and then Steve, who just happened by."

The president chuckled as he ate.

"George gave him a *'Hi, how are you? Why don't you join us?'* greeting. He then introduced Steve, a.k.a. Mortimer Stanley, to Alex and Vasiliy."

Macdonald asked. "There's no chance he'll be found out helping us, is there? Your 'hands off' approach will spare him any—" He interrupted himself by taking a gulp of coffee.

Eubanks studied his boss and then opened the plain folder. "Mr. President, we currently have twenty-seven names."

Macdonald almost gagged on a swallow. "Twenty-seven?"

"Yes sir, and we've vetted about two-thirds of them. Vasiliy, through Alex, provided us with a few more names at the breakfast. In that group, we believe we have three 'high-ups.' One is in the Ministry of Defense; another in the 12th Main Directorate, which ensures nuclear weapons security; and the third is in the 6th Directorate, which tracks each warhead's location."

"That can't be a coincidence," Macdonald insisted.

"They're all valuable resources, but we believe they're penultimate in the chain."

"And?"

"Someplace in their labyrinth of conspirators is the wannabe dictator of a new Russia. Most over age fifty were KGB or military. At the beginning of the new Russia, we had access to a lot of old KGB records. A good example of what had been found was the unmasking of the traitorous FBI agent."

"Yeah, I remember that shocker."

"Our assets in Moscow have been burning the midnight oil; we're rotating officers on a twelve-on, twelve-off schedule." He handed him the folder. "Sir, there is a next step: a dangerous yet rewarding one, if we are to be successful."

Macdonald paused. "An extraction?"

The director nodded. "We'll need some 'eyeball-to-eyeball' with more than one," he said assertively.

"Not something you hadn't anticipated, right?"

A smile of understanding crossed the DCIA's face. "I had a quick conversation with SecDef Garrett on Saturday, before he left Camp David, and then a follow-up this past Tuesday."

"Thinking high-tech?"

Eubanks nodded. "Also, Phoenix viewed the satellite tapes of Gravastock and identified the crates that were removed as the ones they saw. Same markings. Our observers make thorough mental notes of what they see. The videos corroborated their recollections. Doctor Montgomery's folks are going over the tapes this morning."

"Nothing is sacred any more, is it?"

"Better not be," the CIA director said earnestly.

75

Following the 0800 staff meeting, Macdonald sensed a "TGIF" feeling throughout the room. All looked forward to the weekend and enjoying some home life. Walking back to the Oval Office, he remembered it had been a week since he had last talked to his personal assistant Jane. As he crossed through Cynthia's office, he asked her to call Jane for him.

A minute later, Cynthia buzzed. "Jane is on line two."

Picking up, he said jauntily, "Good morning."

"I like the tone of your voice. It sounds like it really is a good morning," she said wistfully.

He laughed. "You're right, and it's Friday: our day to talk. How are things going?"

"We need a large portrait picture of you to hang up in the CAPABLE reception room. An autographed one."

"How big?"

"Thirty vertical by twenty-four inches wide. We'll frame it."

He made a note. "Consider it done. What else?"

"We could use more paid staff at the school."

"Losing volunteers?"

"That's not the problem. We're short of certified instructors. Hopefully, nobody looks too closely; a lot of the evening classes are being taught by volunteers only."

That concerned him. Nancy used to take care of all of that. The new COO was more an administrator and a good one, but . . . "I'll talk to Nancy."

"That would be wonderful. How's Alexandra?"

He paused. How much should he say? "She's great, although she's been in London and Switzerland most of the week. She gets back tomorrow afternoon.

My old buddy Reggie Howard is in Ottawa, and we'll meet up tomorrow in Detroit."

"I heard on the news . . . you, him, and the Canadian Prime Minister, according to one newsperson I heard."

"That's right. Afterwards, he and Louise will fly back to Washington with me. Alex should be home from Europe by then, and the four of us are to have dinner together here."

His intercom buzzed.

"That'll be nice," Jane said softly.

"Cynthia's buzzing. I'm going up to Capitol Hill and twist some arms."

"Well, don't let them twist yours."

He laughed. The line went dead. Cynthia came on two seconds later.

"I have everybody in the Roosevelt Room, sir. You have forty minutes before going up to Capitol Hill."

He joined the group that included J.T. Russell, Darlene, Nancy, Kap with four people from Treasury, two congressional liaisons, and A.J. with three of his press aides. Gus Vaughn and Bryanna Dudley were present by teleconference. Darlene facilitated.

The dinner meeting the night before had demonstrated how chaotic the three-party system was on all the legislators, creating a tension that was thicker than the Senate's famous Navy bean soup. He and Bryanna took up most of the meeting to discuss new ways the Senate and the House could work things out.

The Centrists agreed that a Dem or a Rep should chair all committees, with a Centrist party member being the ranking member on each. Of course, the Dems with their plurality wanted all the chairmanships, but no one found that equitable. Macdonald agreed to arbitrate a meeting with the three party leaders and get them functioning.

In both the House and the Senate, when a bill was approved in committee, the chair and Centrist ranking member would present it to the Speaker or Senator pro tempore. It would then be scheduled for floor debate. In effect, the Centrists would be the power brokers, even though they chaired no committees.

The Democrats and the Republicans could try to upset that plan by voting together as a bloc, but most in attendance gave that little credence, because of the contention between the liberals and the conservatives. They'd thrown so many bricks at each other over the decades that there was too large a masonry wall between them.

Macdonald, Dudley, and Centrist senators and representatives promised to be unrelenting in getting the recovery act bills into committee. They were elected to turn things around, and bomb or no bomb, turn them around they would.

76

The day before, Macdonald had asked for four-by-four-foot, blow-up maps showing one hundred square miles centered on the middle of the flood-filled crater: ground zero. They were to be mounted on easels in the Oval Office, his private study, and his private office in the residence.

They were in place when he returned from Capitol Hill. A series of concentric circles had been drawn on the maps every half-mile out. The preparer had tinted the crater a medium blue. Places of interest were depicted by colorful stickies.

The boards would be updated every morning and early afternoon. Darlene arranged for the Canadians' input.

Cynthia buzzed. "Director Eubanks is on line four."

"Mr. Director," Macdonald said anxiously, hoping to hear about Alex and Vasiliy.

"Mr. President, I'd like to see you."

Macdonald rocked forward in his swivel chair. "I'll be here. What's up?"

"First, Alex and Vasiliy are on a train to Zurich, where they will stay overnight. He has a flight at 0830 Zurich time. Hers is at noon. I have four of my folks on that same train."

Macdonald exhaled. "Okay. What do you have?"

"What we have been looking for, sir."

77

Macdonald called Darlene, "Eubanks is on his way here. Have the ambassador and Alisa join us."

Within minutes, Hendrickson and Alisa were in his office, and Cynthia announced the Director was on the grounds.

"Bill, Alisa, it looks like Alex's trip to Davos has been fruitful. I've seen a plethora of names, but I gathered from Jim's tone we may have hit the mother lode."

There was a knock and Eubanks entered.

"Come in, director." Macdonald gestured to the facing sofas. "Sit here, I'll pull up a chair. Okay, Director, it's your dime."

"Thank you, sir. We have made considerable progress. We have linked several names to a single source outside the Russians' official chain of command."

"Not a political leader?" Macdonald asked curiously.

"He's a supposedly retired private citizen, who in the early 1990s headed Russia's largest black market ring, which almost destroyed their economy. Through his contacts and an accumulation of great wealth, estimated in the tens of billions of euros, he worked out a deal with the government some fifteen years ago to virtually help them close down all black marketing operations in exchange for trading credentials and cash.

"His arrangement would be like having control over our Department of Commerce and profiting from their trades. About an hour ago, FBI Director Thornton confirmed to me that this individual was still up to his old tricks: smuggling black marketed goods.

"His name is Vladimir Aleshkin."

Macdonald thought and then shook his head.

Eubanks smiled. "Another name, Oleg Balastov, is the current director of the Ministry of Defense. He and Aleshkin are old KGB comrades, going back to the early 1980s. Aleshkin is known to us as a communist with the heart of an entrepreneur. In my early years as an operative after Desert Storm, my team had infiltrated certain Russian operations.

"During the time you were working on your advanced degrees and working in the currency and derivative markets, Aleshkin was going to school too—learning about trading goods, both legally and illegally."

Macdonald leaned in. "Okay, but how does he fit in?"

Eubanks was enjoying this. "One of his 'fishing buddies' is the current director of the 6th Directorate, which tracks each warhead's location. Aleksandr Illyanavich, first cousin to Raisa Victorovna Illyanavich."

Macdonald's eyebrows shot up.

"Mr. Illyanavich's name had also cropped up in our background check of Aleshkin's black marketing. Prior to that, Illyanavich had been a military officer who became renowned as a specialist in tactical nuclear weaponry, the type that could be assembled in the field to be used with short-range rockets."

Everyone's gasp almost sucked the air out of the room.

Eubanks continued in an ominously low voice, "They are low yield, allowing ground troops quick access."

"Good grief," Hendrickson said. "That was something the Russians adamantly denied having developed, to which we held deep assertions to the contrary, but couldn't prove."

Eubanks nodded. "We've requested every one of our current and former analysts and operatives, dating back to those years, to come to Langley and go through the old files from that era. We've also contacted recently retired operatives familiar with the USSR military and KGB. They have a nuclear operation that escaped detection, sir."

"Incredible," Macdonald said.

"We believe Aleshkin's billions have sustained these arms. Dr. Montgomery and his NNSA specialists are examining their records and are also calling back those familiar with small, tactical nuclear weapons. When I spoke with Arch on my way here, he was dumbfounded, saying the Russians had adamantly asserted they had completely shut down that operation; it was never even tested."

Macdonald rose and began pacing. "Could Aleshkin have thought the bomb would only affect a small area?"

"I've asked that of Montgomery. He needs to question his people. Interestingly, it had been placed in a low-populated area. According to Montgomery, if it had been a tactical bomb, it would have created only a three- or four-hundred-yard-wide crater affecting less than—"

"Saving us half or more of the injuries and deaths we sustained," the president said, his tension spitting out the words.

"Its design allowed it to be moved about easily. I doubt they have another one, because in my estimation they would have used it by now, following our pattern against Japan in World War II. We dropped the second bomb three days after the first, and that one was the deal maker," Eubanks concluded.

Hendrickson was rapt. "Maybe they had no intention of destroying us militarily. As I believe you said once before, Mr. President, they may have wanted only to cripple us economically, allowing them a more neutral rise to the top as the dominant power in the world, not as a conqueror. Maybe even become our benefactor."

Macdonald nodded. "Diabolically creative." He studied the four-by-four-foot map a few feet from him. "If I was in Aleshkin's shoes, I would certainly have hidden away more than one, unless it was the only one, maybe the prototype."

"Sir," Hendrickson said, "Possibly Mr. Aleshkin was running low on money and needed that 'sure thing' to short the dollar?"

"Maybe," Macdonald said, "Aleksandr Illyanavich had earlier learned about such a strategy from cousin Raisa. Maybe she was encouraged to explain the tactic to Aleshkin, and he plotted the event, while Raisa built up a financial scenario to earn hundreds of billions of dollars."

The ambassador's eyes lit up. "And without Alexandra coming to you, they may never have been exposed."

78

Macdonald, Eubanks, Hendrickson, and Alisa Paget were joined at a working supper by Secretary of State Rankin, Secretary of Transportation Russell, Darlene, Nancy, AG Jamison, FBI Director Thornton, and Secretary of the Treasury Kaplan.

Information was streaming in from Langley, FBI field offices, and Interpol. Dr. Montgomery had been with his NNSA staff combing their files for anything relating to tactical nuclear weapons. The sense of the group during their meal was that there was a secret Russian cabal that dated back to before the end of the Cold War.

Hendrickson saw wisdom in that. "Of course, meaning that there were some very patient and determined individuals who wanted their 'ism' to someday become *the* world power."

Kaplan snorted. "That kind of belief breeds zealots."

"Unconscionable zealots," Macdonald stated firmly.

Eubanks agreed. "The most difficult to stomp out."

"'*Aye,*' as the Bard said, *'therein lies the rub,'*" Kap intoned.

"Maybe we don't *rub* them out—we neutralize them," Macdonald posed. "Maybe we don't fight fire with fire."

Following supper, all but the president, Darlene, and J.T. Russell adjourned to the Situation Room. The three went to the Oval Office for an arranged teleconference call with Dudley and Vaughn.

The subject up for discussion was the smuggling operation that the FBI, MI6, and Interpol had been tracking for over a year.

"The investigation is known to a very small group. Director Eubanks was only informed about it last Friday night. Gus, they'll get you up to speed, but I don't want you to shift your focus away from the DTO."

"But it's how the bad guys got the bomb into the States, right?" Gus asked.

"We suspect so. It gives credence to what my predecessor complained about: lack of cargo security. Okay, how's tomorrow shaping up?"

Gus laughed. "The vice president ordered up some good weather, and it looks like her command is being obeyed."

"If only it was that easy," Dudley said wryly. She then explained the rebuilding phase in southeastern Michigan. She and Vaughn had spent the day with engineers, state officials, the commanding generals of the Corps of Engineers, the National Guard, and Canadian officials.

"We did an extensive flyover beginning north of the DTO, flying in an east-to-west and west-to-east pattern, while working our way downriver to south of the afflicted area. We were also joined by members of the Michigan Department of Environmental Quality; Detroit Water and Sewage; the Ontario Ministry of Natural Resources; Ministry of Environment; US Fish and Wildlife Service, Great Lakes, Big Rivers Region; Friends of the Detroit River; Detroit River Remedial Action Plan; and other officials. We flew around in an armada of military helicopters at seven hundred fifty feet. Gus?"

"Thank you, ma'am. The clogged Detroit River is an immense threat to public health and safety. Combined sewer overflows and municipal and industrial discharges were once a major source of contaminants. The debris has created an immense coffer dam south of the crater, which needs to be breached. We can't blow it, because the surge could overflow the river banks and flood low-lying areas downstream of the crater which spans the river, creating a huge logistical problem.

"We've agreed with the Canadians that a hundred-foot-wide spillway needs to be dug on their side where the river bends left, and they have begun bringing in the heavy earth-moving equipment. It'll run like an elongated hypotenuse in a triangle and will be widened to roughly double its width as it reaches the river below the debris dam.

"We'll dig a half dozen twenty- to thirty-foot-wide, eight- to ten-foot-deep escape canals that will connect the lake to the spillway. We're worried about creating too great a force with the escaping water, so the canals will be ninety degrees to the river, decreasing the speed of the overflow. When number one canal gets clogged, they'll blow the entrance to number two canal, and so on," Gus said, wrapping it up.

Dudley added, "The hope is to keep the flow in the spillway from building up a head of steam and eroding the bank on the American side. Having said that, the Corps of Engineers plans to install at least a quarter mile of steel plates along our shoreline opposite the spillway."

"That's an awesome task," Macdonald commented.

J.T. Russell asked, "Gus, you using only military workers for the river project?"

"So far, Russ."

"Madam Vice President," Russell said, "could we utilize private contractors to work on building the mini villages in the suburban areas, relieving the Corps of that task?"

"Get me man-to-man replacements, and I'll release them. Those survivor support areas are crucial."

J.T. offered, "How 'bout I take that off your hands, ma'am? In doing my workup on the auto manufacturers, we came across several heavy equipment manufacturers within a three-hundred-mile radius of the DTO."

"Yeah," Gus jumped in, "maybe we can move the combat engineers to the river to work with the Corps."

"All right, we'll aim at using all military engineers on the river," Dudley said. "We can start with moving the combat engineer companies over to the Corps of Engineers first. We'll build up the number of National Guard and skilled civilian labor to operate the heavy equipment that comes from the manufacturers.

"I'd like to put a high-ranking general in charge of supervising the combined military and the private sector guys, get everyone marching to our music while integrating them into cohesive working crews. A general can separate the wheat from the chaff, so to speak, and slowly build a tremendous team."

"I'll get on those heavy equipment manufacturers right away, Madam Vice President," Russell said.

"Great, Russ," she responded. "I happen to know the chairmen and presidents of two of those companies." Dudley went on to explain her prior associations with them. "If you have problems with them or others, let me know."

"Maybe they have some drivers they'd be willing to shift over to our payroll," Gus said. "That could be huge."

Dudley picked up on that. "And those manufacturers will know farmers who during downtime might be willing to give us a week or maybe a month. We'll pay 'em. Russ, grab another phone and call me on my private line, so I can get that list from you."

"J.T., use my office," Darlene said.

The Transportation Secretary hustled out.

"I understand Secretary Baldwin is out there," the president said.

"I'm glad to have him. He's lifting the education load off our shoulders. We've got our good situations and our bad ones, but each day we're making progress somewhere."

"I'm sure more places than you think. I'll let you go."

"Thank you, Mr. President."

"How close into ground zero can you safely work?"

"Right down to the water's edge." Gus said. "We're putting the survivor camps at least five miles out now, like around Grosse Point, Highland Park, Dearborn, and Dearborn Heights. We have our biggest camp in Lincoln Park, south on I-75. That highway's open from there south to Toledo. I-75 and I-94 are our two most heavily used overland arteries."

"You're using these locations as hubs for survivor aid?" Macdonald asked.

"In the first week, they were all processing points for the injured, where they were triaged, and then moved on to hospitals or temporary housing, like the motels."

"What about looting?" the president asked.

"The State Police and National Guard are handling that. I'm told it's been minimal. You made it very clear that looters would be severely treated. Of course, some never get the word. We may face more as situations change, unless we've hired all of them."

Secretary Russell returned as the president asked, "How are we doing with families that were split up or who've lost a family member?"

"There's no single solution to that problem," Russell said. "We've logged in everyone who's gone through the camps, and that information is automatically entered into the master computer. We've had some heartrending cases with an instant matchup. Others—"

Gus interrupted. "The State's been picking up on them real good. Governor Carlton is doing a tremendous job with the family situations. We allocated ten billion dollars out of DOER to him for family assistance.

"The vice president wants us to concentrate on the heavy stuff like building the sites for survivors and workers: mini villages. We've got trailers for the human service centers, which are up and operating. The DOER volunteer coordinators and local and state officials are picking up on all of the personnel stuff.

"Governor Carlton likes what we're doing for the auto workers and employees and has asked if we could set up similar centers for the non-auto people. We do the physical part of that; he's ready to supply the manpower, using some of the ten billion dollars. That should put a lot of people back to work. We won't manage any of the human services except for what comes under AIR's jurisdiction."

"Gus, what about FEMA's modular homes?"

"They've been shipping them in since day one, sir. A farmer in northern Indiana turned a two hundred sixty-five acres of land he'd cleared over to FEMA a couple of days ago and FEMA's been in there setting up a waste water system plant and running in power lines. Gravel's down. About two hundred DOER volunteers were running backhoes, bobcats, you name it.

"As soon as a footer is approved, they're pouring concrete and setting cinder blocks. They're looking at putting up one hundred seventy-five units, plus an eighty-by-forty multiple-use structure. A retailer donated a dozen commercial grills. We're getting lots of stuff.

"We're also running in about five hundred house trailers right now, sir. They're fully-equipped, self-contained. We can park 'em and move 'em wherever. The US Army's doing a helluva job with portable sanitary equipment, like in bivouac camp."

"Secretary Baldwin was in the DTO last Friday and Saturday and met with the governor," Dudley said "He was back again the day before yesterday with representatives of the National Education Association. They're trying to find teachers and administrators, and get satellite schools up in two weeks."

And so it went. A massive rebuilding, not unlike after a huge natural disaster, but with a much greater loss of life. The half million initial volunteers were being lost to attrition, as many needed to get back to their jobs. Unemployment centers were instructed to get people working for pay.

Macdonald saw no reason to pay any able-bodied people for not working when so many new jobs were begging for applicants.

Dudley said. "Secretary Royce called me, she is flying in on Sunday to begin discussions on the flow of commerce or lack of same that normally uses the Detroit River."

Macdonald voiced concern about the health problems and couldn't remember if they'd heard or read of anything from the Centers for Disease Control and Prevention, commonly referred to as the CDC, being on-site. He buzzed Cynthia.

"Get me the director of the CDC."

It turned out that the CDC had just finished testing in Detroit and determined there were major health risks. Saturday's tour would be all airborne.

79

Detroit
Saturday, February 2
0830 hours

Air Force One landed in Detroit at 0830 hours Saturday, a half hour before the Canadians would land with the Howards on board. Vice President Dudley had arranged for a reception area inside one of the hangars. She and Vaughn, dressed in military field gear, greeted a casually dressed president, dignitaries, and guests as they deplaned from Air Force One.

The University of Michigan Marching Band played as Macdonald walked across the tarmac to greet Governor Carlton and other officials. The temperature was a mild fifty-one degrees with only a slight breeze. It was anticipated that the greeting between Howard and Macdonald would be a raucous, joyful one; therefore, it was arranged that Macdonald would greet Canadian Prime Minister Brewster McEwen first to prevent him from getting lost between the two former dart-playing competitors.

Upon their arrival, Macdonald took a few moments to introduce the Howards to Darlene and Cynthia, and then to Nancy and Seth Armstrong, making a point to emphasize that they were very close friends to him and Sandi.

Following an hour-and-a-half flight tour of Detroit, all returned to the airport and were feted to a catered lunch followed by an informal gathering with assembled survivors from America and Canada. Vice President Dudley followed with a fifteen-minute summary of the rebuilding, and a representative of the Canadian Prime Minister did the same.

It was all very casual. The press wanted more of the president, but he modestly declined. "Vice President Dudley is running the operation here, and I am happy to say that no president has ever been better served by a vice president than I am by Bryanna Dudley."

Shortly after 1500 hours, Air Force One took off with Reggie and Louise Howard in tow. Macdonald and Howard spent most of the flight to Washington regaling their cohorts with stories of their earlier years together.

After about a half hour in the sky, the guests were given a tour of the magnificently refitted Air Force One. Macdonald stayed back, and once alone, he called Eubanks.

"The plane from Zurich landed twenty-three minutes early," the DCIA said. "She is in her apartment."

80

"You may have your choice of the Queen's Room or the Lincoln Bedroom," Macdonald said to the Howards, as he and Darlene walked them across the south lawn after departing Marine One. "I haven't slept in either and make no recommendations," he said lightly.

A cold wind whipped at them. "You have fireplaces in here, old boy?" Howard asked, hunkering against the wind.

"They're all sealed up. When the Head Usher heard that a Brit would be staying in the White House, he removed all temptations for having a fire," Mike said jocularly.

"You Yanks are just sore losers," Howard shot back.

"Whaddaya mean?" Macdonald said colloquially and laughed. "We won that war."

"So you did, so you did," the British Prime Mister said ruefully.

As they reached the Rose Garden, Macdonald stopped and pointed to the right side of the White House. "The Lincoln Bedroom is in that upper corner and has a better view than from the Queen's Room, which is across the hall from it."

The Howards looked up at the window and then turned one hundred eighty degrees to inspect its view. Teasingly Howard said, "That's a bit of a choice. What say, Lou, we check out the mattress first?"

"Yes, we must. They may be a bit bumpy after all these years," she replied straight-faced.

Macdonald let out a hoot. "Okay. Let's go in and somebody will fetch you up to the residence's second floor for that inspection."

Darlene walked ahead and called the head usher asking him to meet the president in the Oval Office, to which Macdonald was leading the Howards.

"Lou's not been in the White House," Howard said as the three stepped up onto the Colonnade and turned toward the Oval Office. "I was, once, about three years ago, for a short visit with your predecessor in April 2010. But you know that. You were but a mere civilian then and flew down from New York for dinner with us at the Embassy."

The head usher was standing with Darlene when the president and Howards walked into the Oval Office. She introduced the Howards to him.

"Okay," Macdonald said. "After you make your bed selection, you will be returned here, and I'll show you around the West Wing."

"My, how domesticated you've become," Howard chortled.

"You'd be surprised how much," Macdonald chided as the Howards followed the head usher out of the office.

Darlene closed the door. "Alex called the Secret Service about twenty minutes ago to say she was ready to be picked up. They told her you were on your way in from Andrews and that they'd wait to talk with you."

Mike felt his pulse jump and his face flush. "Okay. Give the order. I want to stage a little surprise on Reggie . . . like, have them walk into a room with me, and there she will be."

Darlene went to a phone. "Does it matter where?" she asked curiously, picking up the phone

"Make your call first."

She did, asking an agent to pick up Dr. Mednorov, as quickly as possible.

Having a moment to think about his surprise, he said, "How about we have the Service bring her to my study and you meet her there and explain what's going on. When Reg and Lou come back here, take Alex to the Roosevelt Room. I'll take care of the rest."

"This is a completely new side of you I'm seeing, and frankly . . ." she deliberately faltered as he looked at her curiously, ". . . and frankly, I like it. I'll call you when she is in the Roosevelt Room, and then you can run your caper. Does Mrs. Howard know Alexandra?"

"I don't know what she knows about the Oxford days."

"Oh, about tomorrow," Darlene added quickly, "Nancy asked where you want her and Seth to meet up with you to go to the Super Bowl."

"Have them meet me in here, and we'll chopper out to Andrews together."

Darlene left to await Alex's arrival. Mike picked the Saturday morning report from his desk and browsed through it. He was reading the sports section when Reggie and Louise entered. "I'm catching up on tomorrow's Super Bowl Game," he said, putting the paper down.

Howard snorted. "You mean that funny-looking, oblong, pigskin thing that you *throw* around?"

"Don't be so harsh on the colonists, dear," Louise said, grinning. "They're slow learners."

Mike mocked surprise. "Whoa, you've been giving her lessons, my dart-throwing chum."

"Who me? Most surely not. She writes her own material."

They shared a good laugh.

"I'm flying out to Arizona for the game, which starts at 6:30 p.m. Eastern Standard Time. However, I won't be leaving here until around noon, so we can have the morning together. Have you made a selection of beds?" he asked, gesturing upstairs with his head.

"We found the Lincoln bed very comfortable and will stay there. You are right about the view."

Macdonald's phone buzzed. It was coming from Cynthia's desk. *Lexi must be in place,* he thought. He picked up, listened, said thank you, and hung up. "Come on, I'll show you around down here. Several of the staff are putting in extra time; we're still trying to catch up."

"A damnable thing," Howard groused.

Mike escorted them out through Cynthia's office and into the Cabinet Room, where they paused to look around.

"Okay," he said, trying to control his excitement. "We'll go through here to the Roosevelt Room named for the first Roosevelt, Teddy, who had this West Wing constructed, allowing all of the offices to be removed from the mansion area itself."

He arrived at the door ahead of them, and Alex spotted him and stood. He ushered the Howards in ahead of him. Louise stopped upon seeing a woman standing. Reggie stopped alongside his wife, staring. "Hello," he said, in the surprised tone of the Brits. Alex was wearing the beautiful, white, gauzy dress from last Saturday at Camp David.

Macdonald's heart was pounding.

Howard turned to him questioningly. "Alexandra?" he asked, not quite certain looking back at Alex, who grinned and spoke with calm formality. "Mr. President. Mr. Prime Minister. Mrs. Howard."

Her accented voice sealed it for Howard.

"Alexandra Mednorov, you are indeed a most pleasant surprise," Reggie said.

Mike went to her, and they embraced and exchanged a quick kiss. *That set the relationship.* Mike put an arm around her waist and said, "Louise, this is Alex. We were at Oxford together, the same time I met that lout of a husband of yours." His grin was electric as Howard advanced on them.

"Out of my way, you sneaky cad."

Mike stepped aside as Reggie embraced Alex, and then held her back for inspection. Louise trailed her husband, and Reggie turned to her. "Lou, I thought this lug had completely lost his mind some twenty years ago, giving this lady up when they'd graduated and he'd returned to the States. Alexandra, this is Louise, the lady who has tolerated me these past sixteen years."

The women clasped hands in greeting, and Alex said, "I have heard much about you from Michael, when he and Sandi visited with you."

Mike was in awe. Alex had answered a question he was sure would be on Louise's mind.

"I, too, was married, but lost my husband in an accident many years ago."

She is amazing, Mike thought before regaining his equilibrium. "Alex is a World Bank vice president, stationed here in Washington."

"You sly, old bastard. Eh, can one surmise a rekindling . . . ?" he let that hang, studying them both.

Alex answered by giving Mike a one-armed hug and tilting her head on his shoulder.

Howard appeared flustered. "I must admit, this . . . you two together would not have been something I would have predicted. Is one allowed to ask . . . ?"

"Reggie," Louise Howard said nudging her husband.

"I beg your pardon," Howard said gallantly.

"Hey, no problem. We're unofficially engaged and that's only because I haven't introduced her to my mom, yet."

Howard chuckled. "I am relieved to see there is at least a bit of chivalry in you."

"This is wonderful." Louise waved her husband off with a small flip of her wrist and said to Alex, "We are very fond of Michael. He is like family to us. I look forward to our getting to know each other, as difficult as that may be, knowing our men's worldly positions."

Alex blushed and smiled shyly. "I hope we will become good friends."

81

The four dined in the residence and adjourned to the oval Yellow Room in the south portico of the residence. It was a spacious, informal room. Mike and Alex allowed Reggie to take the lead, unsure of what Louise knew of her husband's earlier years. However, Louise squelched their concern, saying, "Reggie told me how the four of you would troop off for the day or weekend. I can't remember with which one of his girlfriends . . ."

"You most certainly know," her husband dismissed her. "It was mostly Lori, whom, by the way Louise has met. She is married to a barrister and has five children."

"Five?" Mike and Alex chorused.

Alex was relieved she could speak freely. "Your husband played matchmaker, giving us his car and a weekend in Bath. While I worked in London, I drove there and stayed in the inn where Michael and I had dinner that first night. We," she said shyly, "found another 'inn' last weekend."

"I think it's brilliant," Louise said.

"We're keeping it a secret. My tight-knit group knows. What gives us a good cover is Alex's work with CIA Director Eubanks, which was what her just-concluded trip to Davos was all about."

"At the Economic Conference?" Reggie asked her.

"Yes. Vasiliy was there. We spent much time together. He is very sad over the bombing, but happy that Michael is president and will fix everything."

"I always thought there was something screwy about him," Reggie muttered, and then chuckled. "What's he up to?"

Alex told them about his job and family. "I will bring pictures to our next visit."

Mike turned serious. "Vasiliy and Alex may have broken the back of the Russian conspiracy. We needed to know who in the FSB belongs to a secret cabal, which we believe wants Russia to return to its old communist ways. We've connected the dots and come up with a scenario."

Reggie nodded approvingly. "You have made progress since last Wednesday."

"We're in the process of seeking interviews with a couple of them." Mike decided not to mention Raisa or her cousin. He would tell Alex privately, but not right away.

"Your money scheme worked well?" Howard asked.

"We believe they lost hundreds of billions. Why don't we walk, and I'll fill you in on the rest."

"I have clearance, Michael," Alex complained lightly.

"Probably higher than mine," he rejoined.

"Well, Louise does not. I keep her completely in the dark about everything."

"Reggie! Don't believe him, Alex. I just don't care for the vulgar. Come along, have you seen the Lincoln Bedroom?"

Alex stood, as did the men. "I have seen no bedrooms in the White House, but I believe that is about to change," she said, giggling.

"Oh?" Reggie exclaimed, and then quickly added. "But we shan't go there."

They all shared a gentle laugh. "Let me make arrangements," Mike said. He went to a phone and in a moment was back and said to the women, "An agent will accompany you and act as a tour guide." He checked the time. "How about we meet back here in forty-five minutes for a nightcap?"

Mike took Reggie, and they walked out into Cross Hall, and then took the stairs down. Lights, which had been at low level, suddenly brightened as they walked down the grand staircase. He indicated to Reggie they'd walk toward the East Room.

"It appears you have learned a lot in the past few days," Howard said, referring back to their telephone conversations regarding the currency scam.

"Thanks to Alex, who is more of a genius than you and I ever suspected. Eubanks was really the first to observe that at Camp David last weekend. We had a working meeting on Saturday with DOD and CIA. She was on Eubanks' intelligence team, which included his top Russian analyst.

"It was then she called Vasiliy and found he was going to the conference. That made involving her a lot easier. She'd been to two previous conferences. The CIA director followed up with three briefing conversations with her on Monday. She just got back from there this afternoon.

"Eubanks told me yesterday how tremendously impressed he was with her analytical thinking. He didn't think she was aware of the depth of her rare talents."

Reggie took Mike's arm. "I don't have to ask if you love her—that's spread all over your big mug," he said, giving Mike a nudge in his side.

"Yeah, so I'm told. It's an amazing circumstance, for which I am very grateful."

"I'm sure you are." Howard stopped their amble at the entrance to the Blue Room. "Tell me about these upcoming interviews you mentioned."

"Raisa's involved, Reg. She has a cousin." He went on to explain the intra-connections that led to Vladimir Aleshkin and the smuggling operation—leads his MI6, Interpol, and FBI had been tracking for over a year.

"You'll never get anything out of Raisa," Howard said firmly.

"I agree, but at last count Eubanks had twenty-seven names. We may need your James Bond for a fortnight to get this thing wrapped up."

Howard grunted. "You think this Aleshkin is like Bond's *Dr. No* or *Goldfinger?*"

"All signs say he's interested in world domination. He's only in his late fifties."

"How are you going to combat this would-be dictator? How tied to the Russian government is he?" Howard asked.

"I don't want to nuke anybody, Reg. You saw our devastation. Canada and the US have suffered greatly. That bomb was intended to drive us into the mud, destroy our wobbling economy," he paused. "But I can't do that to somebody else's innocent population. I can't do eye-for-an-eye on this one.

"I'd rather see the guilty strung up across Red Square in Moscow, alive, and let their people throw rocks at them 'til they were no more. When the hell is this crap ever going to end?" he exclaimed in a snap of anger. "We've received hundreds of thousands of e-mails demanding retribution—many want us to nuke somebody, and some don't care who."

"I've seen some of the same over the years, as had my predecessors."

"Can a humanitarian response work? I don't know," Mike said, answering his own question. "We're looking at the possibility of my having a clandestine midnight meeting somewhere in Europe with Russian President Novorken."

"You've not met him?"

Mike shook his head.

"No, of course not, no time," answered the Prime Minister. "I have on several occasions. We've traded state visits. He's a pragmatist. He's not former KGB like his prime minister, Mashnikov. Novorken's fifteen years younger, nearer your age. Novorken's popular like Gorbachev was. If you need a go between . . . ?"

The six-foot prime minister looked up at his friend. "Maybe we might fashion a plan while I'm still here. Louise and I don't leave 'til Wednesday for our holiday in Bermuda."

82

The White House
Super Bowl Sunday
February 3

The day began with a relaxing breakfast and visit with the Howards. They would be spending the rest of Sunday and a good part of Monday at their Embassy on Massachusetts Avenue NW. Alex planned to meet with her secretary at the office, while Michael was "off playing games."

Macdonald consulted with Darlene by phone while flying to Arizona. The Prime Minister would be able to keep late Monday afternoon open for the 4 p.m. critical planning session at the White House.

He arrived at the Super Bowl an hour before kickoff. When it was announced he was present, the half-filled stadium became a bedlam of cheers. After a consultation between the NFL commissioner and the Secret Service, it was agreed that President Macdonald would make a brief on-the-field appearance.

Both teams were notified and the respective head coaches readily agreed to meet him midfield immediately following the pregame entertainment. For an impromptu gathering, it went well. He was given an official NFL Super Bowl game ball, which the two head coaches had autographed.

President Macdonald was whisked back up to the commissioner's box, where he rejoined Nancy and Seth, and the Secret Service breathed a sigh of relief.

At halftime, the Redskins led 17-6 on the strength of their stifling defense and two long offensive drives that ate up a total of 18:32 minutes. During the usual halftime spectacle, Macdonald received guests, mostly as a courtesy to the commissioner and Arizona politicians. Meanwhile, the Secret Service prepared for the president's quiet departure from the box about five minutes before the end of the third quarter.

Each team had traded touchdowns in the third quarter, and Washington was methodically driving into field-goal range when the presidential party quietly departed on board Air Force One. They were in the air with six minutes and twelve seconds to go in the game and Washington still comfortably ahead. They watched the rest of the game during the flight; Washington won 30-13.

"Well, maybe the White House will be a little happier place than it's been," Macdonald commented. He was sincerely happy for the team, knowing its lengthy absence from the limelight. He offered the sleeping suite to his good friends and then called Alex.

83

Oval Office
Monday, February 4
0630 hours

CIA Director Eubanks arrived with the PDB promptly at 0630. Opinion polls showed the president's overall approval rating was high, especially on the rebuilding progress in Detroit. On Sunday afternoon, the British Prime Minister had sat for an interview with the British and Canadian press. The reporters had a great deal of concern for the Detroit River and the joint efforts to divert its flow and lower the water levels, so horribly dammed-up with debris.

Macdonald did not want to take up the CIA director's time on domestic issues. However, he briefly referred to Dudley's international call for earth-moving equipment and that the response had been overwhelming. Rosters of manpower were being sent to US Immigration for expeditious clearances.

They finished with the PDB and then reviewed each aspect of the investigation's progress. When all was covered, Eubanks handed him a Russian news report.

Macdonald read: *"Ivan Strylotov, head of the Russian nuclear weapons security in the 12th Main Directorate, along with his wife, died Saturday night outside Moscow in a fiery crash; their bodies were burned beyond recognition."*

"Reuters had a short mention of it in the overnight." Eubanks paused. Macdonald made no reaction. He was waiting for the explanation.

"In actuality, sir, Mr. and Mrs. Strylotov were kidnapped Saturday afternoon, driven about three hundred kilometers to an unused airstrip southeast of Moscow and extracted three hours after dark in a converted stealth fighter jet designed specifically for this purpose. He has been undergoing interrogation at our old airbase from which we fly observation flights. Strylotov has ties to Vladimir Aleshkin. Reports are that he is cooperating," Eubanks said flatly.

"My God, man, you put that together overnight?" Macdonald asked amazed.

"Extracting the Strylotovs, yes, but the plan for an extraction such as this has been in place for years."

"And his wife?" Macdonald asked, concerned.

"Insurance. She's being well attended to. No harm will come to either. Hopefully, though, Strylotov will be thinking otherwise. He's neither former KGB nor military. He's more an intellectual, an analyst. Our Russian assets are investigating others, including Raisa Illyanavich and her cousin."

Macdonald squirmed uncomfortably in his chair at the breakfast table. "There's definitely a connection between Raisa and Aleshkin?"

"Maybe a step below, like between Nicolai Trevenkov, their corporation maven. She and Trevenkov had meetings with Aleksandr Illyanavich and Strylotov, whose job it was to verify that what Raisa and Trevenkov proposed was feasible. Even though the cabal borrowed a trillion euros from the Russian treasury for their scheme, it appears others added about one hundred fifty billion euros of wealth into the pot. We don't know if they stayed in for the second go 'round."

"Let's hope so," Macdonald said with an edge.

"FBI Director Thornton's people have heavily scrutinized the names. There are definitely ties between the smugglers and Aleshkin.

"The Davos intelligence has changed our thinking. You can be assured, sir, Alex and Vasiliy came through for us, big time."

Macdonald told Eubanks that Prime Minister Howard has offered assistance with the Russian President.

"His perspective will be very helpful, sir. However, even when faced with our mounting evidence, I'm not sure where President Novorken fits in all of this. We've studied him and still don't know what makes him tick."

"Just like you did with me, right?"

Eubanks quipped. "Maybe a little more with you, sir." He then became serious. "Novorken has shown a reticence in corralling and closing down black marketers even though it was thought Aleshkin had accomplished that feat for them some ten, twelve years ago.

"A stab in the dark is the FSB. They may have a hand in that, holding something over their president's head."

"A little like a former FBI director?" Macdonald asked rhetorically. "What about Prime Minister Mashkinov?"

"He goes back forty years, deep into the Cold War days. He's a hardliner, but we don't see anything linking him to a cabal. We doubt he would get in the way of a coup, if or when one was made."

Macdonald stood, waving Eubanks to remain seated and wandered over to his map of the DTO. He was truly troubled. In talking with Reggie, it had all seemed a slam dunk—put the information and names together and then meet with Novorken. Lay it all out to the Russian president and say that to avoid a nuclear holocaust, the Russian government needed to announce what had happened and who was behind the bomb, and then prosecute the guilty. All of them.

Reggie was convinced that such a speech by Novorken would show the rest of the world that no country had attacked the United States, but instead was a crazed group of power-seeking Russian communists, who wanted to regain their former prominence as a dominant world power, while extinguishing America's economic and financial dominance.

Macdonald stewed a bit longer on these thoughts.

"Jim," he said abruptly without breaking his stare into the distance. "Vice President Dudley and Secretary Vaughn are flying in for our meeting at 1600 this afternoon. Prime Minister Howard will also be joining us."

Macdonald's face was somber, when he turned back to Eubanks. "I am thinking this might be where we lay out our strategy.

"However, it won't work without a strong Russian president to execute the arrest orders. Without his leadership and his coming forward about the conspirators, I will be left with no alternative but to respond in the most crushing way possible and that would be the ruin of us all."

84

As much as Macdonald wanted to focus on the international investigations, he was often interrupted with progress reports from Detroit. In one instance, Cynthia brought in the results of interviews the FBI had conducted on the Detroit River smuggling operation and no sooner had she left than an aide to the vice president delivered an update on the latest acquisition of equipment and material.

He didn't need to know about every ton of debris pulled from the river and subsequently deposited in the crater designated for clean landfill. Yet he read each one. After the better part of the morning, he'd lost his ability to concentrate on the Russian investigations and called Darlene and Cynthia to his office.

"There's got to be a better way to do this," he complained. "I'm deluged in paper, and I am finding it extremely difficult to wrap my head around the things I need to be thinking about."

I'm probably overplaying it, but I really do need some sort of a plan.

"Darlene. How'd you do it during the campaign? Stuff was flying all around, yet it didn't all end up on my desk."

"Nor should it," she replied quickly. "I wasn't aware this was happening."

He nodded. "I should have addressed this sooner. Vice President Dudley is in charge of the DTO. She and Gus are the only ones who should have direct access to me, everything else needs to go to a central location or something."

"The same is true with Intelligence and DOD. I see Director Eubanks every morning. Enough is enough."

Darlene asked Cynthia, "Do we have any space?"

Cynthia referred to a large notebook. "The Situation Room is not assigned to anyone at the moment."

Macdonald brightened. "Okay. Let's set up a 'war room' down there. We'll need high-level CIA and FBI manning it at all times. Didn't Director Thornton promise us an assistant director?"

Darlene nodded. "The AD came every day, but after a week there wasn't . . ."

"Okay, get me the director. I'll tell him what we need and ask that he work it out with Eubanks."

"Right away, sir," Cynthia said, rising to leave.

"And tell Ambassador Hendrickson I'd like to see him."

"Yes, Mr. President."

85

By noon, two new operations were up and running and staff assigned. The domestic operation was turned over to the vice president's staff in the Executive Office Building, next door to the White House. Dudley knew exactly who she wanted supervising it.

Darlene and the VP had become fast friends during the campaign and quickly came up with the idea of providing the president with a *DTO Morning Report*, which would be delivered to Darlene each morning Monday through Friday. She would present it to the president following his PDB with Director Eubanks, unless circumstances dictated otherwise.

With Eubanks's agreement, Director Thornton assigned Special Agents in Charge to cover the war room on a twelve-on/twelve-off basis, along with field agents who would rotate two at a time every eight hours. A half dozen CIA analysts from the Russian desk would rotate with overlapping shifts, but with a minimum of two there at all times. A CIA/NCS deputy director would supervise the agency personnel.

Darlene assigned Nancy Armstrong as her liaison to the Situation Room because Nancy had participated in the Camp David intelligence meetings. Ambassador Hendrickson, now special assistant to the president, would coordinate with Nancy and be the president's liaison.

After lunch, President Macdonald and Chief of Staff Sweetwater toured the new operations and thanked everyone for transitioning so seamlessly, answering any questions they had. He and Darlene then returned to the Oval Office.

As much as he had wanted to shut out the rest of the world, he couldn't. This would be the first day of fulfilling a prior promise to Darlene that he would devote two afternoon hours Tuesday through Thursdays to receiving those who were instrumental in keeping the government functioning and who needed his blessing or thanks for their worthwhile projects.

His last visit this day ended at 1520. He then went into his private study and called Alex. The communications gurus had devised a way for him to be able to make an untraceable call to her at the World Bank. He punched a button for the dedicated line, and upon receiving a dial tone, he punched in Alex's special number.

Over the weekend, a single-line, voice-recognition phone receiver had been installed at Dr. Mednorov's World Bank desk. Only her voice would activate the call. Once she answered, he was to take a one-second pause and then begin their conversation.

If someone other than Alex answered, the call would automatically disconnect. Of course, she could always call Cynthia on the president's White House number, but he liked the idea that they had their own encrypted line.

It worked perfectly on his maiden attempt. The phone line clicked, signaling that his call was answered. After a second, he heard her hesitantly say, *"Mon cher?"*

"Hey," he said softly. "How's your day going?"

He heard her sigh. "I've had too many people in my office and calling my other phone," she complained. "The economic conference is all people wish to know about."

He laughed. "I'm sure. Have you talked with Louise today?" he asked.

"Last night. I had given her my cell phone number. I am to meet her 5 p.m. at the British Embassy. She is going to give me a tour, and then we will ride together to the White House by 7 p.m. and wait for you and Reggie in the residence."

"You're bringing an overnight bag, right?"

He heard her giggle. "Will you provide me with a drawer so I do not have to carry so much each time?"

"All the drawers you want," he said, feeling a shudder run through him. "It's great seeing Reggie, isn't it?"

"Like all of us, he is different from twenty years ago, but also is much the same. I like Louise. She is so proper. I feel I will learn many useful things from her."

"You do fine. Gotta go. I love you."

There was a slight pause before she replied. "Ah, you made me shiver. I love you with all my heart. I never thought I could be so happy again."

"Me too. See you later. Cheerio."

She laughed. "Yes, cheerio."

Mike rocked back in his large leather swivel chair. *How did I ever get so lucky?*

His repose was only momentary; he was interrupted by Cynthia. "Prime Minister Howard is in the Oval Office, sir."

86

In the intervening years between Oxford and now, Mike Macdonald had visited England several times. He had hung out with Reggie, before either was married; he'd been in Reggie and Louise's wedding; and he'd visited again when Reggie became a Member of Parliament.

After Mike's campaign kickoff, he and Reggie would talk every couple of weeks. His British best friend and prime minister tutored him on foreign policy.

And now Reggie was in Washington. Being together Saturday evening and again on Sunday morning helped bring the two couples closer together.

In the few minutes they would have alone before the meeting, he and Reggie shared their personal thoughts about what was eventually going to be the biggest decision Mike Macdonald would probably ever have to make.

"Look, old boy, this is your show to run, but I am curious about your intentions toward the Russians. I mean, you are quite certain that it is not their government, but rather a rogue group within their country. Am I right?"

Macdonald nodded and said firmly, "Director Eubanks went fishing over the weekend and came up with a big catch: Ivan Strylotov, the Russians' nuclear weapons security chief and number two in the cabal to Vladimir Aleshkin."

Howard smirked. "Strylotov? He was mentioned in my intelligence brief yesterday as having been killed along with his wife in an auto crash Saturday last."

"It's a miracle," Mike spoofed. "They are warm and cozy at our former airbase in eastern Turkey, which we covertly use with the permission of the Turkish prime minister."

"An obliging fellow. How much is it costing you?"

Mike laughed. "I don't want to know, but it's under an old arrangement from a few presidents ago. Maybe a warehouse full of whatever he needs today. I gather that changes."

"You're catching on; that's jolly good. Would I have an interest in Strylotov? Would MI6 thirst for a go at him?"

"I'm short on details, chum, but FBI Director Andrew Thornton will be here this afternoon. Maybe you, he, and Eubanks could squirrel off someplace after we go over our main topic. A word though . . . outside of the two directors, you, me, and Darlene, nobody at our meeting will have any knowledge about our midnight snatch."

"What is it you Yanks say? . . . *No problemo*. I appreciate the opportunity."

"We will discuss the smuggling ring, since it has ties to Aleshkin, who appears to be the ultimate prize fish. Eubanks will handle the sensitivities of that. You'll probably notice that I rely heavily on him."

"He was a good keep. Have you made any decisions about your form of retribution? Nobody would fault you . . . well, the usual suspects, but . . . do you know?"

"There's a segment of my population that insists I nuke somebody."

"I can imagine. That will be a rough go."

"I don't want to retaliate in kind and slaughter innocent people. I've had DOD looking into alternative non-nuclear responses. I'm going to stay open to suggestions."

87

Cabinet Room, White House
"Operation Retribution"
Monday, February 4
1600 hours

P resident Macdonald was two weeks and four hours into his presidency. In attendance at this epic meeting were Vice President Bryanna Dudley; British Prime Minister Reginald Howard; Secretary of State Nadine Rankin; Secretary of the Treasury Millard Kaplan; Secretary of Defense Ogden Garrett; Secretary of Commerce Francis Royce; Secretary of Transportation J.T. Russell; Secretary of Homeland Security Gus Vaughn; Attorney General Martin Jamison; CIA Director James Eubanks; CIA Director of National Clandestine Service Ansell Watkins; CIA Russian Specialist Steve Hester; CIA Special Assistant to the Director, Major General Barry Bingham; Director of NSA Lowell Kuhn; National Security Advisor Alisa Padget; FBI Director Andrew Thornton, with Special Agents Fleet and Snider; Director of Counterterrorism Edna Cole; Joint Chiefs of Staff Chair, General Carla Gibbons; Joint Special Operations Commander, Lieutenant General Eric Donner; Special Assistant to the President William Hendrickson; and from the presidential staff, Chief of Staff Darlene Sweetwater, Deputy Chief Nancy Armstrong, Special Assistant to the President Cynthia Bolden, and two secretaries.

"Ladies and gentlemen, the President, the Vice President, and the British Prime Minister."

There was a momentary scramble of people rising and adjusting to face the trio as they entered. The three leaders waved warmly to their fellow comrades along the way to their seats.

The president introduced the prime minister to Cabinet members. Dudley said hello to as many staff, most former campaign workers, as she could. There was an air of team atmosphere for this considerably disparate group.

Darlene gave it a couple of minutes before requesting, "Ladies and gentlemen, please be seated." Dudley sat to Macdonald's right with Darlene next to her. Howard sat to Macdonald's left with the Secretary of State next to him. The two generals sat directly across from the president bracketed by the SecDef and CIA director.

The photographers were ushered out.

Macdonald opened. "Thank you for being here. I know it's your job, as it is mine, but I thank you all the same." He paused for effect. "Mr. Prime Minister, Madam Vice President, it is nice to have you both with us again in Washington."

There was a roll of laughter due to Dudley's extended absence. He smiled and continued. "It's been a busy two weeks. We were slammed up against a wall before we had a first cup of coffee in our new offices, but we've caught up and are at the top of our game.

"On that horrific morning, we had no idea . . . We were shaken, and we were scared, but we knew our duty and performed it at the highest level."

He scanned the table. He had everyone's attention.

"Most of the Cabinet members were hard at work long before they saw their new offices. I think the vice president has only been in hers once."

Warm laughter in admiration of Dudley spread through the room.

"Okay. Through considerable diligence, highly skilled investigating, and some good fortune, we have determined the genesis of the attack, if not exactly all the players. We have many names, most of them members from a cabal within Russia, who are intent on overthrowing their government. We firmly believe this cabal used the bombing as a catalyst to affect that."

Macdonald paused, understanding the unsettling that permeated the room.

"We are focusing on eight Russian individuals, although we know of over fifty. We started out searching for a country that had the capability. We had quickly dismissed that Iraqi group's false claim. Within an hour of the attack, General Gibbons and I discussed defense and reprisal. We were at DEFCON 1.

"DCIA Eubanks, Deputy DIR/NSA Nolan Stroud, FBI Director Thornton, and counterterrorism agents pressed their technology and assets for leads. I quickly became a student of military warfare twenty-first-century style. General Gibbons faced not only an attack on her country and being at DEFCON 1, Code Red, she also had to deal with a rookie president."

Howard made a soft guffaw. A few chuckled. Most were still.

"My thinking and experience was that of a Marine Force Recon commander. An individual in this room set me straight a couple of hours later that morning. I was not that captain taking orders anymore; I was the guy giving them. I had to refocus and realize that truth, along with the fact that I had extremely capable people to execute the orders."

He addressed Gibbons directly. "General, you are a soldier in the true sense of the word. You have been patient with me and guided our military efficiently in the DTO recovery areas, while gearing up to take on an unknown enemy. Without a SecDef in place, you stepped up.

"Tuesday, January 22 was Day One. On Day Three, we were faced with the bogus claim of responsibility for the attack. General Gibbons and DCIA Eubanks immediately debunked that group. Meanwhile, I had concerns that a certain segment of our own population would jump to conclusions and cause great harm to innocent people and to our overall recovery.

"Also on Day Three, I was visited by a fellow Rhodes Scholar and former Oxford classmate, Dr. Alexandra Mednorov, who many of you have since met. It's too detailed to go into here, but suffice it to say, what Dr. Mednorov told us changed our thinking on who had attacked us. And please, that information is just between us," he said emphatically.

"Secretary of the Treasury Kaplan and I, with some sage advice from the gentleman on my left, spent long hours strategizing on how we could strengthen the dollar against the euro. We came to believe the bombing and the attack on our currency came from the same people."

Macdonald turned to Howard, and they had a whispered exchange, after which he turned back to the group. "Before we turn to General Gibbons, I've invited Prime Minister Howard to say a few words. Mr. Prime Minister."

"Thank you, Mr. President. Madam Vice President. It was mid-morning for us when your bomb went off. Our whole nation mourned with you and immediately stood ready to assist in any way we could.

"Our Intel, Interpol, and your director of Central Intelligence were at it within minutes. We immediately brought up the usual suspects; but because of good intelligence, most were eliminated. They simply did not have the resources."

Howard looked at Macdonald. "When I talked with your president—also my old dart-throwing chum—during that time, he had the situation in good hands. When he called with the startling news that it could be the Russians or a cabal within Russia, I was, quite frankly, taken aback, but the president convinced me. We then spent hours devising a plan to thwart an imminent attack on your currency—the rumors were legion.

"As your president had, I, too, trusted the source of his Day Three information. We all had laid witness to Dr. Mednorov's brilliant mind on many occasions. My Intel along with your CIA and FBI has since gathered an incredible amount of data, which substantiated and went beyond what we'd suspected."

He looked at Macdonald. "We are prepared to back you all the way, Mr. President."

Macdonald nodded to his friend. "Thank you, sir." He looked across the table at the chair of the Joint Chiefs of Staff. "General Gibbons."

"Thank you, Mr. President. I would like to officially introduce Lt. Gen. Eric Donner, chief of our Joint Special Operations Command. The general is heading up Operation Retribution." She said the words emphatically and with pride.

Macdonald smiled. "Welcome, General."

"Thank you, sir," Donner said formally.

Gibbons was looking at an open notebook before her on the table. She addressed President Macdonald. "When you and I met in the Oval Office on Day One with Ambassador Hendrickson, you expressed your personal philosophy on a response, given certain sets of circumstances. I found your perspective to be extremely useful, as it allowed us to look at our capabilities, while waiting for an enemy to confront.

"On the evening of Day Three, that picture began to take shape. On Day Five at Camp David, we received your data regarding Russian oil and natural gas, and it became clearer. We have taken that precise information and drawn up a variety of attack plans.

"Due to our decades-long surveillance of North Korea, we have held war games in the Sea of Japan, some in the Sea of Okhotsk north and west of Japan's northernmost island—Hokkaido—and east of Sakhalin Island.

"As you pointed out, sir, Sakhalin contains vast hydrocarbon resources. Oil reserves are now estimated to be near thirteen billion barrels and natural gas reserves are at ninety trillion cubic feet."

That information created a stir with low-voiced comments. Some may never even have heard of Sakhalin Island or its hydrocarbon reserves.

Howard muttered to Macdonald. "I say, that would keep one toasty a few fortnights, now wouldn't it?"

His overheard comment elicited chuckles, including one from General Gibbons.

Howard looked at the general. "My apologies, General," he said politely.

"Not necessary, sir," she said smiling, and then returned to her notebook.

"Due to the international consortium on the island, it would not be a bombing target. We have chosen an old export terminal in Dekastri on the Russian mainland, which feeds the Asian Continent, while other lines from the island feed a steady flow of tankers.

"Two Marine brigades have already departed Camp Pendleton aboard troop transports for northern Hokkaido to supposedly join in the 'war games.' Two battalions, one each, will be on separate American tankers steaming for Sakhalin, arriving this Saturday. Two Army brigades are off the shore of Alaska's most southerly island for the war games. Twelve hundred Special Ops troops are currently on Hokkaido.

"B-52 stealth bombers are to be used only under extreme conditions. We have one nuclear cruise missile submarine in Okhotsk and one in the Sea of Japan.

"There are very few if any Russian ground troops on the island. Security is supplied by private organizations, of which two are American."

The president showed concern. "And we've made provisions to advise them?"

"Yes sir. It will all come from the Pentagon, followed by Special Ops making prearranged coded contact. That is the overview of Sakhalin, Mr. President."

"Sounds like a plan, General."

Gibbons turned the page in her notebook.

"On the European/western front, we have two targets. The first will be twin refineries that have been reduced in importance due to newer facilities at nearby Samara, whose many manufacturing plants are our second target. It is also a major nexus for their northern European pipelines.

"The older refineries will be taken out by Special Ops on the ground. We've selected this approach due to the sensitive timing, based on your negotiations with the Russian president, sir. The Sakhalin invasion will follow only on your command, Mr. President, and a B-52 attack on Samara will be forty minutes out, waiting for a direct order. If none is given within thirty minutes of the attack on the refineries, the planes will return to base.

"We have two other targets we are developing, which we need to discuss, sir, but can have ready in forty-eight to seventy-two hours from your request to activate," the General concluded, sitting back ever so slightly.

"Okay. Thank you, general," the president said.

"Sir," SecDef Garrett spoke up. "Is there any chance that President Novorken will acquiesce and that we won't have to do any of this?"

Macdonald took a thoughtful pose. "That is my greatest hope, Mr. Secretary, but I am not going to be patient. It will all be up to him."

"Right. What options does he have?" Gus Vaughn asked, which turned heads. Not everyone was familiar with the brash-talking retired Marine colonel. "I mean, we're telling him there's a plot to oust him, and I'm sure he doesn't want us to nuke him. We're doing the guy a huge favor even confiding in him."

Typical Gus Vaughn, thought Macdonald.

Vaughn leaned forward in his chair looking down the table at the president. "How much damage are we going to do to them even if he promises to go along with you?"

Macdonald held up his reply until reaction to Gus's seemingly brash question quieted.

"You know me too well, my friend."

Howard chuckled as did Kaplan.

Macdonald continued. "We'll take over Sakhalin Island and temporarily appropriate its oil and natural gas and the Russians' profits. We and the Canadians are working on compensation. The multinational consortiums will be allowed to continue their operations undisturbed."

"Do you expect President Novorken to be okay with losing a significant percentage of his income from oil and natural gas that easily?" SecState Rankin asked.

Right on cue. Macdonald had suggested the planted question. Rankin had been in on those talks. "He will need to produce more oil on his western side and stop blackmailing the Europeans with it. He's going to need them to become happy customers.

"Plus, he's going to need friends as he rebuilds his government. I would think he might even consider being our friend; he's going to be obligated to us for a very long time."

That elicited some quiet chatter.

Prime Minister Howard spoke up. "This plan would have certain benefits for us as well. We've been having a deuce of a time getting those blokes to deal honestly and consistently with us. We have been promised a new North Sea pipeline for petrol and natural gas, but that keeps getting waylaid in their bureaucracy."

Thank you, Reggie.

"Well, we'll have to make that a priority. General, how much advance is needed for Special Ops to be in position at the twin refineries?"

"Sir," Donner replied. "They are at their jumping off point. Depending on weather, twenty-four to thirty-six hours."

Macdonald smiled, remembering some of his missions' standbys. "Okay. Let's get into our smaller groups. We have work to do, and we don't have a cooperative Russian president—yet."

88

The one-hour-and-ten-minute meeting in the Oval Office concluded, and Generals Gibbons and Donner along with SecDef Garrett departed for the Pentagon. Kap and Howard fell into a jocular spin about Russian finances, with Kap giving the PM some insight as to what he estimated their losses were after the final scam on their shorting the dollar.

Cynthia had some coffee, tea, and nosh brought in. Macdonald was busy reviewing the Russian cabal list with SecState Rankin. Bill Hendrickson was chatting with Hester and Director of the National Clandestine Service Watkins.

Kaplan soon left for the Treasury, freeing up Howard. Eubanks was explaining the Davos conference, including the distraction the two Russian Secret Police had created. "Vasiliy was the key that made it all work. Alex saw to his comfort zone, and the twins carried it off like pros."

"The morning after the incident," Hester said, "I deliberately sat adjacent to three of the Russians with whom Alexandra and Vasiliy had eaten dinner on their first night. Alexandra's name was very prominent in one conversation, but it was all about how well she had recovered from her accident and then very bravely gone out on her own. One attributed that to her schooling at Oxford."

Eubanks philosophized on various approaches Macdonald might consider when meeting with the Russian president. Howard joined in. "We've profiled him extensively. He's more pliable than your usual Russian politician. He's a progressive thinker and not a friend of the hardliners."

Macdonald liked the route this was going. "Steve, you know their culture. Prime Minister Howard has dealt with the man one-on-one."

Howard chortled. "I have one more day here, although I am sure these gentlemen are extremely capable. So, as long as you promise not to upset my five days in the sun, on which Louise has set her heart . . ."

Macdonald laughed. "Jim? How much time will you need to have everything's ready?"

"Three days. We have the basics in place now; however, we will need to give President Novorken time to adjust to the information we feed him."

Macdonald smiled at that. "Can we tell him we have corroborated intelligence about an attempt to dislodge him from office, without saying who?"

Howard groaned. "That's your sticky wicket, old boy; but I do think it possible, because you have the big stick—that being you uncovered it while investigating who bombed you. Maybe drop the implication that the people behind the attack are planning to assign blame on him."

"That may work, Reg."

"Maybe your envoys can imply that. Make him worry," Howard added quickly.

"I don't remember you being so cagey twenty years ago."

"The political wars in the UK are a tough training ground, old chap. We learn to coat our cyanide with sugar."

"It's called diplomacy, sir," Hendrickson said genially.

89

White House
Tuesday, February 5
0500 hours

Mike Macdonald was expecting to roll out of bed at his normal 0525 and go for his thirty-minute workout. However, Alex was with him and she had, unknown to him, reset his alarm for 0500. He wished more workouts were like the one she put him through that morning.

After he left her a half hour later for his workout in the gym, she showered and was dressed for work when he came back up and did the same.

She had read the capsulized versions of the morning papers and the more informative Internet. Two articles speculating on possible Detroit attackers weren't even close to being right.

He flicked on a TV weather channel. It was slushy out. He donned dark-gray slacks and a thinly striped, white dress shirt and walked into the sitting room.

"Ah, anything earth-shattering?"

She looked up at him and smiled. "Too much speculation. As I have heard you say, 'They have no clue.'"

He laughed and leaned over to kiss her forehead. "I'd be making bad speculations, too, if it hadn't been for you. We're having breakfast with Director Eubanks in the Oval Office in eleven minutes." He went back to the bedroom to finish dressing.

Due to the inclement weather, they took the elevator to the main level and walked through the gallery to the West Wing and the Oval Office. He draped his coat and tie over a chair and informed Cynthia he'd arrived with Alex. She came in to greet Dr. Mednorov personally.

He and Alex were sitting at the breakfast table when Eubanks arrived. To his credit, the director showed no signs of surprise at her presence. They greeted all around.

"Alex says the morning news is replete with erroneous speculations on the bombers."

"It's nice to see that no leaks have occurred." Eubanks handed the PDB to the president. "For us, this is a fairly bland day. No upheavals anyplace."

Eubanks pulled out separate folders, handing them to his boss. "We are building an excellent dossier on the cabal conspirators, sir."

Macdonald indicated he'd like Alex to have a look.

Eubanks handed her the folder and she smiled at being included. "May I encapsulate, sir?"

"Sure."

"None of those we've interviewed admits to knowing about the bombing; however, they were aware of the effort to raise money to use in their effort to unseat Novorken. No one owned up to the black marketing, smuggling, or bombing."

"Sounds like a layered operation. It appears Mr. Aleshkin runs a tight ship."

"Now that we have Illyanavich, who is supposed to be on a skiing trip in, of all places, Switzerland, we may learn more of the intricacies to the whole operation."

Alex looked up from her reading. "Raisa's cousin?"

Macdonald nodded. "It appears he is the new director of the 6th Directorate and tracks warhead locations. He's also tied to Aleshkin's black marketing and smuggling operations. According to Strylotov, Raisa and cousin Alek have a close relationship. He probably introduced her to the boss man."

"Illyanavich provided the bomb, Raisa the shorting, and Aleshkin the smuggling."

She looked sad. "It is a terrible thing, Michael, that someone we knew, even if not so closely, could be an architect of such a despicable act."

90

If the day had not been so inclement, Alexandra could have easily walked the half dozen blocks to the World Bank building. Instead, Darlene made arrangements for a taxi to meet her at the southwest gate, and Nancy escorted Alex to it.

People crucial to the preparation of evidence—to support the premise that a Russian cabal carried out the attack on Detroit—assembled in the Cabinet Room. President Macdonald strode in, brisk in manner, and went straight to his seat.

He gave a brief summary of what needed to be accomplished before his special envoy met with Russian President Boris Novorken. Eubanks then took over.

He and Hester laid out the background and Ansell Watkins, director of National Clandestine Service, explained the extraction of a key cabal member.

"Ivan Strylotov is the number-two man in the cabal and serves in the government as the director of Nuclear Weapons Security, 12th Main Directorate. He is in our hands on an airbase we control in eastern Turkey.

"He has corroborated most of the names that Vasiliy Mednorov gave to us and has added several more. Two were involved in the handling the nuclear device turned over to Aleksandr Illyanavich, director of the 6th Directorate, who was specifically in charge of tracking warhead locations."

"Thanks, Ansell," Eubanks said. "We are also tracking other highly ranked persons in FSB and the military. Illyanavich is our key link between the bomb and the currency scheme the cabal had engineered.

"His first cousin, Raisa Victorovna Illyanavich, is the first woman in the history of the KGB/FSB to ever head a major department. She rose from Directorate K to Directorate of Counterintelligence Support to the Financial System."

Eubanks turned to Hester. "Steve."

"We've learned so far that many cabal members were aware that its leadership was planning a major event that would help them raise the billions of euros it would need to successfully oppose Novorken.

"We don't believe, outside of Strylotov, that any members knew the cabal was planning an attack on us. The planners needed a perfect storm of occurrences. The 2008 and 2009 financial crisis showed our weaknesses, which were highlighted in the 2011 recession. They knew what they needed based on Raisa Illyanavich's currency plan."

Hester paused, but seeing the president wasn't going to add anything, he explained the course of events that led to Dr. Mednorov contacting the president, who then presented that revelation to CIA Director Eubanks.

"This is why their plan would have worked to perfection if it had happened during the previous administration, when—"

Kaplan interrupted. "May I, Mr. Hester?"

Hester took a beat to realize he was being interrupted. "Eh, certainly sir."

"Thank you. Actually the late spring and early summer of 2011 would have been their best time due to the discontent growing across our country. The people were suffering from an insurmountable national debt that was on the verge of breeding out-of-control inflation.

"At the president's request, we put together economic numbers for 2010, '11, and '12—because those numbers were the foundation of the attack on us." Kap nodded to Hester. "I just felt that needed to be said, Mr. Hester. Otherwise, I agree with your position."

"Thank you, Mr. Secretary," Hester said. Poised, he continued. "The information to which the Secretary referred was extremely helpful as we progressed in our investigations. Of course, the previous administration did not have the 'Oxford' connection.

"Dr. Mednorov was in the nexus of information when her brother Vasiliy told her that he thought the FSB was planning a major investment scheme that he could not approve. He essentially is like our director of the Federal Reserve, but not as independent.

"Vasiliy Mednorov, whom I've met and spoken with, could not, by Russian law, approve the use of a trillion euros to be dispersed into a dozen or so shell corporations. He told his sister this less than two months ago when she was in Moscow, before she moved to Washington from London in early January.

"In the long run, Raisa Illyanavich got what she wanted by setting up an account that was labeled *China and Iran Infrastructure*. Vasiliy knew of this, but it was out of his control; it had the authority of the Russian president.

"Nicolai Trevenkov, a financial whiz in Russia's corporate world and an assistant to Raisa, supervised those funds. He is currently in Bonn, Germany, and last night Interpol took him into custody to question him about a smuggling operation. He has not been cooperative, but at least he is where we can get at him."

Eubanks nodded. "Thank you, Steve."

"Mr. Director," Kaplan injected. "May I, again?"

"Mr. Secretary," Eubanks said approvingly.

"I wanted to point out that Trevenkov and Raisa Illyanavich, in supervising the shorting of our dollar, had to know about the bomb in order to know when to short and when to cover. We are certain that they stayed in the game for the second go 'round back on Day Three when it looked like we were losing our socks.

"They lost big time on Day Four when President Macdonald announced the multitrillion-dollar investment and loans made to us." Kaplan sat, a contented look on his face.

Eubanks had a difficult time not cheering, but a smile did escape his controlled demeanor. "The key man, the wannabe dictator of a new Russia, is most likely Vladimir Aleshkin, a well-known black marketer from the late 1980s thru the '90s, who turned entrepreneur in the import/export business. Strylotov has corroborated our earlier intelligence on the man.

"Another underground activity of his is smuggling. He appears to be extremely wealthy, having turned his former KGB experiences into an immense web of subversive contacts all over the world."

Eubanks turned to Thornton. "Mr. Director."

Thornton laid out the thirteen-month investigation, in which the FBI, MI6, RCMP (Canada), and Interpol had been engaged. "It started with Interpol and MI6, then expanded into Canada and the US, as they tracked a smuggling operation.

"Port cargo containers were coming under heightened security as the technology for identifying every container improved. Aleshkin and his cohorts seemed to stay one step ahead of the newest security, with an occasional slipup. Those became our openings.

"With the help of MI6 and Interpol, along with several smaller countries' clandestine operatives, patterns of routing became clearer. Occasionally, the smugglers would zap an Interpol operative, and they'd pull in their horns. However, the combined investigations were making headway, primarily in backtracking seized contraband." He looked at Eubanks.

The CIA director picked up the narrative.

"Their biggest obstacle to overcome was the United States, and they actually began thinking of creating a nuclear disaster that would be blamed on somebody like Iran or Pakistan, two nuclear nations. But when the oil and natural gas boom hit Russia, the government became immensely wealthy and more powerful. Aleshkin and his buddies went back underground.

"Russia was becoming a hydrocarbon dynasty. Countries went bidding for their oil and natural gas, and pipelines began crisscrossing Eastern Europe and western Asia. The new, reformed government in Moscow had promised, if elected, they would establish a consistent relationship with their buyers and not play games with costs, shipments, and taxing.

"Aleshkin and company saw this as a weakness, and with the American government in turmoil, the cabal saw their opportunity to form an opposition party.

"Their plan was to put pressure on the Novorken government. They campaigned that Russia could have a much larger slice of the world's economic power, not just what came from their own natural resources.

"I'll wrap up our portion with this. According to Strylotov, that was when Raisa was brought into the inner circle by her cousin Aleksandr. Her knowledge of how the western stock markets and currency exchanges worked became the lynchpin to take down the US economy, feigning friendship to the distraught foreign power that had been a lifelong enemy."

Eubanks nodded to Thornton, who took over again.

"A big break occurred in our smuggling investigation when Interpol intercepted an undocumented shipment and traced it to Russia. One lead led to another and eventually to Aleshkin, who had supposedly become a legitimate exporter, through Mikhail Pronichek, another so-called exporter.

"That was last July. The thing to understand here is that the FBI and Interpol were concentrating on breaking up a worldwide smuggling operation. We had no knowledge of the internal political upheavals being conjured up within Russia.

"Director Eubanks told me ten days ago, when I told him about our smuggling investigations, that CIA had been so weakened by our politicians that they had too few assets to look deeply into what appeared to be a rather benign political atmosphere.

"Back to Aleshkin. Along with learning about Pronichek, we uncovered a so-called businessman named Yuri Brotsken, who traveled extensively between Russia and ports in Canada and the United States. He quickly became a person of interest, and we began tracking his every move.

"He had bona fides and a legitimate passport. He was listed as representing a Romanian textile company, who exported the finest rugs, draperies, curtains, and bolts of exquisite materials used for clothing. We checked it out; they were bigger than we expected and very authentic.

"Being Russian and having some contacts with Pronichek, we remained convinced he was tied into the larger smuggling picture, although it seemed his legitimate business kept him occupied and wealthy.

"Pronichek's main ports of call in the Western Hemisphere were Montreal, Cleveland, and Detroit. He'd meet the ship, take possession of his property, and see that it was sent on its way. We didn't track him beyond that because we never came across any contraband.

"When Detroit happened, and then three days later, when we learned the Russians might be involved, we agreed to open up our investigation. When Director Eubanks called me on another matter on Day Four, I opened up to him. That moment of discussion is showing fruitful results." Thornton sat back.

There was a slight pause. The president picked it up.

"In the past two weeks, we have learned much more. After Davos, we shared what we'd learned with Director Thornton and the smuggling investigators. Pronichek turned out to be prominent in Russian internal affairs. In subsequent interviews conducted in Russia by Interpol, moles inside the Russian Secret Police discovered he'd met with Aleksandr Illyanavich several times in early 2012.

"We know from Ivan Strylotov that on at least two occasions, he met alone with Illyanavich, and on one occasion, with him and General Orlovski, the guardian of the storage facility that Phoenix visited on January 25 and were locked out of on January 26.

"Darlene, we will need to move our request for a meeting with President Novorken back one day to Thursday evening to give Bill and Steve time to review everything. Director Thornton, please talk with Interpol, MI6, and RCMP. I'd like somebody, outside of us, to be a part of that meeting with Novorken."

"That person will most likely be from Interpol. I have a preplanned noon conference call with the heads of each service. As a side note, sir, they all have been fascinated with our speedy ability to put the bombing part together."

"Sometimes it's better to be lucky than good, Director."

91

President Macdonald was living in a whirlwind of meetings. The variety of subjects was staggering. His next meeting was all military strategies and tactics. He couldn't remember ever looking at so many topographical maps, terrain analyses, weather patterns, tide tables, and satellite photos.

He realized that, if he had kept up with it over the years, he wouldn't bat an eye at the massive technological changes that had occurred. He was glad he had Barry Bingham sitting alongside him as General Donner talked about the new warfare tactics they'd be using.

Macdonald listened attentively, and Bingham whispered translations to him. The one thing the former Marine did understand was the concept and the strategy. By lunchtime, he was getting the hang of things and enjoying it. He also thought that his questioning was a little more mature than two hours earlier.

He had lunch with Darlene, Nancy, and his now senior advisor, Bill Hendrickson. They were joined halfway through by Bryanna, who had gone from her military meeting to the meeting on smuggling. A few minutes later, Gus plopped down at the dining table.

"Mr. President," the vice president said exhausted. "Those generals numbed my brain. I needed to get back on my own turf with Gus and Director Thornton."

Gus jumped in. "The FBI guys are onto something bigger than they thought and are close to nailing down how the Ruskies got that nuclear device into Detroit. They must have had help stateside opening doors and knowing when the border security was looking the other way. We had to scrutinize our own people. I felt right back in my element."

After lunch, Macdonald did his promised two hours of community service for Darlene, having short sessions and photo ops with government bureaucrats and nonprofits. An occasional senator or representative accompanied a constituent hoping to present their cause, setting up an earmark to slide into some bill down the line.

Cynthia pinned him down for fifteen minutes with papers to sign and memos to read. They whittled down the list, dashing off personal notes to five and asking her to put in a return call to three.

After those calls, he called both Cynthia and Darlene into his office before he buried his head into homework given to him by General Gibbons, Director Eubanks, and Bryanna. The VP had decided to remain in Washington the next few days, while Gus returned to the DTO.

"That last call, Cynthia, that you placed for me a few minutes ago turned out to be the brightest spot in my dragged-down, war-mentality day. Our ranking member on the House Appropriations Committee and the chairman have come to an agreement with the chairman of the Senate Committee on Finance on our balanced budget legislation. The Republicans have promised a unanimous 'aye' vote when the committee votes this afternoon. The Speaker of the House has promised to bring our Balanced Budget Bill to the floor immediately."

Darlene was elated. "That is fantastic."

"Tell the kitchen I'll eat in the West Wing dining room around 1830. If you or any others want to join me, let the kitchen know. I don't want a working meal. I want to relax, maybe have a few laughs."

Cynthia let out a "Ha!"

Macdonald looked at her quizzically.

"I'd better invite Mr. Kaplan."

Macdonald squeezed in a twenty-minute telephone conversation with Alex after supper. She was an oasis in the swirl of politics, military strategies, and intelligence reports. He missed not seeing her, but she was joining him Wednesday for supper, although she would not be staying over.

That would happen Friday when they returned to Camp David and would remain there until he flew out to meet with the Russian president in Reykjavik Sunday night. He went back to studying up on the three potential military targets.

Darlene had found a book on the history of Sakhalin Island, a one-time penal colony off the east coast of Russia. *I guess not everyone was sent to Siberia*, he mused. He barely made it to the end of the first chapter, when he conked out around nine.

Wednesday promised to be a series of sit-downs, so he had set his alarm for 0500, giving him a longer workout to help build up his endorphins.

92

Oval Office
Wednesday, February 6
0630 hours

At the PDB meeting, Director Eubanks had brought some ripe intelligence from his Russian assets. They had found it curious why *Pravda* hadn't gotten wind that Russian bureaucrats were coming up missing. They would be tracking that more closely.

As Eubanks was packing up, Macdonald said, "I'd like for General Bingham to attend Saturday's meeting at Camp David."

Eubanks chuckled. "I noticed yesterday that he was 'advising you' during the DOD presentation. I'm sure he would be pleased to assist you."

At 0830 hours, General Donner arrived to brief Macdonald on the details of his and General Gibbons' presentation two days previously. It was compact, specific, clear, and logistically understandable. He found Donner to be a "no frills" officer, although Gibbons had told him the general was a creative thinker. *You have to be in that job*, Macdonald remembered from his time in Force Recon.

On the heels of Donner's forty-five-minute briefing, Cynthia informed her boss that Secretary Rankin was on her way. The Secretary of State arrived shortly thereafter with the good news that President Novorken would gladly receive our special envoy.

"We replied that we were sending three members and that the subject was too sensitive, even on a scramble-phone."

"That ought to spike his interest."

Later that morning, Macdonald met with several key House Centrists, who would be the whips and thrashers on getting the Balanced Budget Bill through all the drudgery and platitudes that House members were wont to indulge in. They knew the Democrats would launch a battery of objections. However, the Centrist goal was to not lose any Republican support.

Macdonald later told Darlene and Kap, "We Centrists are in a fun position, and I like that our caucus is following our five point program and open to the Republican's more conservative concerns. It makes for good theater."

His afternoon was brightened by a group of Girl Scouts who had earned a few days in the Nation's Capital. They proudly displayed their emblems of rank and sashes replete with merit badges. They were escorted by a Democrat and Centrist Senator and a Centrist Representative, from whose district they came. He took the opportunity to privately prod his Centrist congressman to push hard on the Balanced Budget Bill.

Once he finished dealing with Darlene's two-hour agenda for him, he met with Bill Hendrickson, who was packed and waiting on Steve Hester to arrive from Langley. They would chopper to Andrews for their nonstop flight to Moscow and meet up with the US ambassador to Russia.

Macdonald felt the same excitement of anticipation as he had before a big football game or when waiting to see Alex. All the preparation and planning was done, now the game was about to begin.

Darkness was descending as he walked his two envoys out onto the colonnade and bade them farewell. He watched them cross the South Lawn and go aboard Marine Two.

He went back in the Oval Office and watched the chopper slowly lift off, the gleaming white Washington Monument in the backdrop of what would be a monumental trip.

He signed the papers Cynthia had left for him and went over her day's notes and a list of what had been assigned to others for a response, and then he buzzed her. "I've done my duty and am going up to the residence."

He was relaxing in his favorite lounger, reading, when Alex arrived. They greeted with strong hugs and gentle kisses.

"*Mon cher,* I have missed you. I know it has been only two days. We are so near, yet so far, *n'est pa?*"

She cupped her hands behind his neck and pulled him to her. He willingly responded. The evening was theirs.

93

The White House
Thursday, February 7
0615 hours

From the moment he awoke—even after a workout, shower, and fresh change of clothes—Macdonald felt sluggish. He didn't know why after such an exhilarating night with Alex. She had lifted his spirits somewhat, joining him in the Oval Office at 0615 for a quick breakfast, but would be gone before Eubanks arrived.

"*Linebacker*, you have been preoccupied. Do you worry about your envoys? They will do well, such talented men."

"I know and I'm fine, really. It is more the enormity of their mission than—"

"It is so with me; I think of Vasiliy."

Cynthia poked her head in. "Dr. Mednorov's car is at the gate."

Mike walked Alex to the stairs and then returned to the office to await Director Eubanks's arrival.

After they had discussed the rather benign PDB, both admitted their minds were more on the mission to Moscow. They shared their thoughts of the tremendous burden each was feeling and about the consequences they might face.

Following Eubank's departure, he talked to Darlene about the Centrists party's first negotiation with Congress. Their first cosponsored bill was working through committee and would soon hit the floor for debate. To bolster Republican support for the bill, Darlene had selected some of their key legislators for him to call and thank for their support.

Talking with seven of the eleven committee members took nearly an hour and covered domestic conditions and the progress of the DTO recovery, as well as the bill. Darlene felt exhilarated, talking positively about the party's future and the headway the legislators were making.

Two of those she had him call were moderate Republicans, elected in 2008 and twice reelected. She had them pegged as being moderate enough to switch to the Centrist party in their 2014 reelection bids.

Macdonald was buoyed by Reggie Howard's call from his fun in the sun on Bermuda. Since he'd made the call from the British Consulate using the Hotline, it was automatically scrambled. Macdonald filled him in on the military progress, emphasizing that he really didn't want to use it, but felt he must prepare.

"I would say you are at the starting line, chum. All you need is Novorken."

"It's nearly 7:30 p.m. in Moscow. They should be through the vodka and into the first or second course. I would imagine that having a high-ranking member of Interpol in our party had to spark some questions in the Russian president's mind."

"Knowing Boris, I would expect he took it with the savoir faire for which he is known. Rather un-Bolshevik."

"Give me your number, and I'll call once I know something. Don't forget to use plenty of sunscreen."

"Ha, Louise bought a barrel of the stuff. Cheerio."

He hadn't been off the phone but a breath when Cynthia buzzed. "Mr. President, Secretary Rankin needs to speak with you on the secure line."

He picked up the phone.

"What's up, Nadine?"

"The Norwegian and Icelandic ambassadors visited me this morning. They were concerned over our having a clandestine meeting on their soil."

"Trouble?"

"No. It quickly boiled down to money. They would have to keep the airport facility open after their last flight. They were also fishing to learn whom we were meeting. But actually, it was all about money."

Macdonald laughed. "How much?"

Rankin exhaled in weariness, "I've been around diplomats my whole adult life and clearly understand 'diplo-speak,' but these two were overdoing it. They mocked an extreme concern about our security requirements. Rather than go around in circles, I undiplomatically flat out asked them if five million dollars would ameliorate their concerns."

Macdonald laughed. "Did they stay stone-faced?"

"Not one blink for about three seconds before the Norwegian smiled and looked at his colleague, allowing a wisp of a nod. The Icelander then smiled. 'We will be happy to cooperate.'

"I explained negotiations were ongoing, but that I should be back to them before the end of the day."

"The important thing is that we can do it. Thanks."

"Yes sir. I'll get a message to our Moscow ambassador. His political attaché is in the Kremlin to facilitate anything regarding our envoys. Oh, who will be our security honcho? I've got a couple of names and numbers in Reykjavik."

"I imagine Secret Service, as it is with all presidential trips. Hold on, I'll have Cynthia pick up. Again, thanks."

"Thank you, Mr. President."

He passed Rankin over to Cynthia. His mind went to his men in Moscow. The sensitive nature of telling the leader of another country about a plot to depose him was not something one practiced every day or once in a lifetime.

He was pleased he had Reggie as a backup in the event the Russian president balks. The prime minister was prepared to call Novorken either way to let him know he would be accompanying the American president.

It was 1345 hours, and he realized he hadn't eaten. He buzzed Cynthia. "Ask the vice president if she is available to meet me upstairs in the living quarters for a late lunch, even if she's already had hers. Ask the chef to put together a tray of cold cuts and a couple of bottles of cold water." He remembered from the campaign that she rarely ate lunch. "I'm going for a walk. Text me."

He took his smartphone from a desk drawer, checked the charge, and turned the volume up. He was barely out of the West Wing when he received a text. Bryanna was available in about ten minutes.

He returned with an "okay" and continued his walk through the gallery and into the mansion where he eschewed the elevator and took to the grand staircase two steps at a time. It was like going up two flights.

He found the exercise rejuvenating. He told the agent who greeted him on the second floor, "I'm going to visit the Lincoln Bedroom, let me know when the vice president is on her way."

"Yes sir."

Macdonald browsed the historically refurbished room. He sat in a chair and read the Gettysburg Address and paused to think of Lincoln's meaning, which got him ruminating about the country now and how war after war did nothing to actually end the wars.

He thought, *Everybody is always in the moment. If we just do this one thing, life will be better. I'm faced with that now.* As he worked for a more a peaceful, humanitarian solution, he questioned if that would make things better. America was in the process of rebuilding its infrastructures, rebuilding the nation, putting families back together, finding places for people to live, and getting the kids in schools.

Creating a new beginning for millions.

He considered the irony that the Israelis and Muslims stem from the same religious book as Christianity, and yet their focuses are more about eliminating the other, conquering by war and terrorism, instead of joining together in love.

Not analogous to the Congress, Michael thought, *but if we can't get along at home, in our own country, what does that project to the rest of the world?* Maybe as a major third party, the Centrists can get the Congress to refocus, to concentrate on what's best for the country.

Maybe that's doable. If we can't do that at home, we will never be able to do it in the world.

He looked around the room that memorialized the assassinated president, a man reviled and revered, who had sought renewal. His thoughts were interrupted by a Secret Service agent.

"Mr. President, the vice president is the elevator."

He nodded. As he stood, he looked around the room and said a wistful *thank you* to the spirit of Lincoln. He didn't know why he had spontaneously visited the sixteenth president or what it all meant, but he was glad he did.

He was halfway down the Cross Hall when Bryanna came into the hall from the elevator.

"Out strolling?" she blurted before seeing his solemn demeanor. "What's wrong?"

That surprised him. "Wrong? Eh, nothing's wrong."

"You look down."

"Oh, ha, I just paid old Abe a visit. It got me thinking."

She smiled. "Like why are we doing what we're doing? And if we did or didn't, would it make any difference?"

94

At 1445, Cynthia buzzed the president, who was busy visiting with a group from North Carolina. *She wouldn't interrupt unless . . .* he thought, as he excused himself from the seating arrangement in front of the Oval Office's fireplace and picked up his desk phone.

"Sir, Secretary Rankin is on line two."

"I'll take it in my study." He hung up. "I have to take this call, but don't go anywhere, I shouldn't be long."

They all thanked him, as he rushed to his study and the phone.

"Nadine?"

"We're on, sir."

He exhaled in relief. "Just like that?"

"I know—a big buildup deserves a big reply. Bill said Novorken was humbled by their visit and excessively appreciative of our efforts to keep it secret. Of course, he had a lot of questions. Bill said he explained, without specifics, that the intelligence had come from separate sources, which unexpectedly overlapped and resulted in an entirely different investigation: we discovered that there appeared to be people high up in his government involved in bombing us. Novorken found this hard to believe. Bill then held out our list of Russian names and said, 'We would like to know those who you most trust. To compare with the suspected bad guys that are on our list. To see if we've uncovered people you have been trusting.'

"That created tension in Novorken, because he wasn't prepared for what Bill asked. However, Bill successfully debated, with Steve's help, how important it was that the upcoming presidential meeting be kept secret.

"Bill then told him your thoughts and where to meet."

"Novorken complained it would be a problem to keep his flight to Reykjavik a secret. However, he was effusive in thanking you for the magnanimous gesture of sending envoys to inform him in such a personal manner."

"He sounds very un-Russian," Macdonald said.

"Bill said that having Steve as his interpreter made the flow of dialogue very smooth. Steve said Novorken traded ad libs with him.

"That emboldened Bill to press President Novorken about writing out a list of names, people who he could confide in to keep his trip secret. Novorken bristled, but Steve took it upon himself to discuss the reasons. It seems that Steve's bedside manner was impeccable."

"So, Novorken agreed?" he asked anxiously.

"Yes sir. He wrote out fourteen names, which Steve compared to our list and came up with only three that matched, which he shared with Novorken, who appeared relieved and said he felt more comfortable and was now certain he could put together a tight-knit group to handle all the arrangements for the trip.

"Steve and Bill discussed all the names we suspected might have been involved in our bombing with the president, who showed sadness over ones he personally knew, especially those in the FSB. He made no comments about anyone. Novorken now very much liked the idea of a late Sunday night meeting in Reykjavik."

"Okay."

"Novorken's final question was, 'How much will this cost me?'"

95

White House
Preparation for Upcoming Presidential Summit Meeting
Friday, February 8

Macdonald squeezed in separate conversations with Prime Ministers Howard and McEwen that afternoon about Sunday's covert meeting in Reykjavik. Darlene worked out the logistics. On Sunday, Reggie and Louise would fly into Andrews from Bermuda, landing at 1730 hours. McEwen, with an entourage of five, would land there fifteen minutes later. The Secret Service would bring them all to the White House.

In between meetings, Macdonald tried to follow the progress of his Balanced Budget Bill in Congress. True to his word, the Speaker scheduled a floor debate to begin Friday morning.

Everyone worked late Thursday and were back at it bright and early Friday morning.

At 1330 hours Friday, Marine One lifted off from the White House lawn for the seventy-mile trip to Camp David. With Macdonald were Darlene, Nancy, Alisa, a tired Bill Hendrickson, Hester, and Alex. They would have a conference call from Camp David at 1600 hours with the Pentagon, CIA, DIA, NSA, FBI, and the Secret Service.

It was Alex's and Michael's first trip back to Camp David, which they had eagerly looked forward to. Alex would participate in all the meetings, not only because her input was invaluable, but also because of the respect she had garnered on her work in Davos. She would call Vasiliy from Camp David to inform him about Sunday.

She confided to Michael that Vasiliy was enthralled at being of such value to him.

Although it was mid-February, the weather forecast called for daytime temperatures in the low 50s with no rain. That would mean some walking time.

"It will be fun to see Millie," Alex said, snuggling up to him in their helicopter seats.

"Yeah. That reminds me about my saying how much Mom would enjoy her and being at Camp David."

"I so look forward to meeting your mother. I hope we will become good friends."

"Friends?" he asked surprised. "She'll probably adopt you and take you back to Colorado with her."

"You tease."

"I have no doubt about how well you two will get along," he said, squeezing her hand.

"If we can come to terms with President Novorken, and that looks promising, I can follow his announcement to the Russian people about the Russian traitors and the bombing. They will probably have been arrested by that time. Others are or will be in Interpol's and our hands. He will also explain the equitable compensation package we are hoping will be resolved in Iceland. With that resolved, I'll meet with the Congress . . ."

"You are feeling good about Novorken?"

"He was extremely thankful for what we had done and gave every impression he would cooperate. The biggest concern he voiced was that the world must know it was not the Russian government that bombed us, but a renegade group bent on hurting Russia as well as America."

Alex was pensive. "He was very popular with the people when elected, but he has been less than honest about some of his economic programs. Maybe that is why Raisa and her crowd . . . is that the right word?"

"Perfect."

"Why they and the hardliners planned a revolt."

By the time they were in Aspen Lodge, it was 1425 hours. Alex and Mike changed clothes and visited Millie in the kitchen. Before taking their walk, they had received the promise of hot coffee and tea upon their return. The others who arrived in the two helicopters were shown to their cabins. Mike wanted Aspen Lodge for just them. However, they would all eat dinner in the Lodge and retire around 2000 hours.

They convened in Laurel Cabin for the 1600 hours conference call and reconvened at 1700 hours for cocktails followed by supper.

Chef Millie and her crew put on an outstanding meal. It was a little after 2000 hours when everyone retired and Mike released the kitchen crew. He and Alex cuddled on the sofa facing the fire, enjoying a little brandy and the quiet time that was so reminiscent of the little inn in Bath.

96

Aspen Lodge
Camp David
Saturday, February 9

Alex awoke first at 5:47 a.m., according to the bedroom clock. She was wide awake and thought about waking her bed partner, but instead chose to wash her face, run a brush through her short hair, and don her bathrobe. She tiptoed out of the room.

There is something about Camp David that makes our lovemaking rapacious, she thought.

She found the kitchen empty and was trying to remember where everything was when Chief Millie arrived.

"You're an early riser, ma'am," she greeted in her folksy tone.

"There is something about this mountain air."

Millie smiled knowingly. "I better get the coffee and teapot going."

Alex hugged in her robe and sat at the dinette table watching Millie go about her business. "The president is thinking of inviting his mother to come visit him at the White House and here, maybe in two weeks."

"That must mean things are looking up."

"That is what today is all about. Many important people have been working very hard for a special meeting that could happen very soon. We will see."

Millie smiled and shook her head in amusement. She had been specifically thinking more of the relationship between the president and Alex, not the world.

The chef took two bagels from the refrigerator and sliced them open. "Would you like something to munch on now?"

"I think later."

When the teapot began to sing, Alex plucked a tea bag from the selection Millie had laid out. She chose raspberry and placed it in a Camp David mug, into which Millie poured the steaming water.

"Coffee will be ready in a couple of minutes."

"You make things so homey here," Alex said, tying her thick, fluffy robe a little tighter. *I just want to scream out my happiness.*

She tried a thin sip of the tea that was very hot. She blew into her mug.

Millie sat across from her. "With the chopper arriving at 0830 hours, when will you and the president want breakfast? Everyone else will be going directly to Laurel Cabin for a buffet, unless he says otherwise." Millie eyed the coffee urn. "It's almost ready."

"I think maybe your 0730 hours," Alex said, overemphasizing the number, which made Millie laugh. "I will call if Mr. President says otherwise." She giggled.

"Seems the coffee's ready. There's a hot plate on the dresser; the switch is on the cord."

Alex smiled, took the two mugs, and went off to the bedroom.

They'd have about an hour.

97

Camp David
Retribution Task Force
Saturday, February 9
0830 hours

The rest of the Retribution team had arrived—Eubanks, Thornton, and Generals Gibbons and Donner, plus two Signal Corps NCOs—and all went to Laurel Cabin where they were joined by Darlene, Nancy, Alisa, Bill Hendrickson, and Hester for breakfast. Mike and Alex had theirs in the Aspen kitchen and then walked to Laurel together. Once there, he and Darlene conferred while General Donner's NCOs taped an eight-by-six-foot map of Sakhalin Island onto a side wall.

Macdonald officially greeted everyone and turned things over to Donner, who promptly gave the details of the troop buildup and then addressed Special Ops strategies.

"Our reconnaissance teams are already on the island and confirm no Russian military presence. The considerable security is all private contractors.

"Each team matches up to one of the larger combat teams coming ashore from the two nuclear subs. The tricky part is timing. All private security companies will be notified at their home headquarters and asked to immediately inform their Sakhalin Island people to stand down. They will be given a series of codes to verify each American team.

"Fifteen minutes later, each reconnaissance team will move to its rendezvous point and await its corresponding combat team. Once together, they will contact the security forces using the codes. The companies will know that no resistance will be tolerated. The consequences would be significant, obliterating their protectee and be a horrendous waste of human life and property."

"General?" Macdonald asked. "You've done this before. Would you walk us through the process?"

"Yes sir." Donner went on to describe a previous covert operation. The question had been suggested by General Gibbons to break up a monologue.

Macdonald didn't know if it had really taken place or it was a hypothetical, but it was a good tactic and everyone sat more upright, anxious for an "inside look." The questions that followed pertained to saving lives, which was ably handled.

The generals and aides flew out an hour and a half later. They had a live operation in the field.

The discussion next turned to President Boris Novorken. He was fifty-two and had been in office almost four years. He was never a part of the old guard. He held a master's degree in history from Moscow State University. Alexandra remembered him from when she had returned from Oxford in 1994. Sergey once had business dealings with him.

She had been working in The Hague about two and a half years when he became president. Vasiliy said Novorken had proffered good ideas to move the nation in a new direction. The people believed in him.

Directors Eubanks and Thornton followed with a report on the people of interest in the smuggling operation and those who appeared to have a connection with the bomb plot. Eubanks said that assets in Moscow reported Novorken had been in long meetings Friday with his Secret Police.

"As Interpol had not been contacted by the Russians regarding names the envoys had given him, Thornton believed that would appear Novorken was only concerned with internal matters. We've had no reports of anyone on that list being arrested."

Macdonald cleared his throat, which got everyone's attention. "Excuse me, Jim. Doesn't it seem strange that he would risk the possibility of tipping his hand, that one of the insiders we identified as a cabal member would get wind that something was up?"

"We've not picked up any noise indicating those concerns, sir."

Hendrickson added. "Sir, he constantly referred to those names we gave him as traitors. However, we have no knowledge any are involved in anything traitorous, other than maybe being unhappy with his regime and joining a rising new party to oppose him."

Hester, sitting next to Hendrickson said, "I agree. Intangibles are floating all over, making me wonder if we're missing something. One thought Bill and I banged around was whether Novorken is fully cognizant of why we gave him the names. Meaning, does he understand we want to interview them? What we got back from him was that they were some sort of gift from us to him, so that he could put down a revolt before it happens."

Hendrickson took that a step further. "In my separate discussions with Director Eubanks and Secretary Rankin, since our . . ." he indicated Hester, ". . . trip, I related my observations of President Novorken's conduct. There was no 'what can I do for you' coming from him. He became obsessed with wanting to tag all of the names as being traitors."

"Thank you, Bill, Steve, for your superb contribution toward bringing this ugly business to a conclusion." Macdonald turned to FBI Director Thornton. "How's the smuggling business, Andy?"

"I have to say, sir, that my dealings with the smugglers was more straightforward than yours with Novorken, who sounds very self-absorbed."

"Good point, Director," Bill Hendrickson said.

Thornton opened a folder. "I believe Chief Sweetwater supplied you all with copies." He held his up. There was a shuffling of papers, and then everyone had theirs in front of them.

"It is in considerable detail, which you don't need to absorb right now. The keys to our investigation came together expeditiously, ever since we had the opportunity to interview Director Eubanks's detainee, Mr. Strylotov.

"We shared his information with our Interpol contacts working on the smuggling. That information led them to take Illyanavich and Trevenkov into custody. Interpol is now tracking Aleshkin, which has been mundane, at best.

"Director Eubanks has gleaned considerable information from Strylotov. From Illyanavich, they have learned of a lynchpin in the smuggling operation: Mikhail Pronichek. He is a close associate of Aleshkin, which the other two are not. Pronichek's movements have been traced across Europe and into Canada and the United States.

"Pronichek is mostly a legitimate import/export dealer, but takes on side jobs for big cash. Although he is Russian, we have not pegged him to the bombing itself. We believe he was the unwitting delivery boy. It was his habit to meet his shipments in the city of call, and we placed him as being in Detroit on January 4, 5, and 6 of this year.

"He signed for three shipments. Two containers were textiles, and their destinations were to two American wholesalers, all very legitimate. The third container was addressed to a location that no longer exists. It was to a warehouse near the Detroit River. The shipping manifest listed machine parts for looms and various household items that were supposed to be assembled at the warehouse and then shipped.

"We uncovered the name of the individual and the company. However, neither exists. Unfortunately, the warehouse address was replaced by the bomb-created Crater Lake. Right now, although it might not hold up in a court of law, what we've learned serves our investigative purposes and ties us to the mastermind, Vladimir Aleshkin."

98

Keflavik Air Base
Reykjavik, Iceland
Sunday, February 10

The C-130 military cargo plane, carrying armored vehicles and forty heavily armed troops, sat on the runway, shielding Air Force One on its right side. Both faced outward in case of the need for a hasty getaway. Slightly to its rear sat an Airbus with Russian markings. Each country also had a wing of jet fighters; two from each nation were always in the air. An American fuel tanker sat about three hundred yards to the rear of the presidential planes, adjacent to the fighters.

The troops from both countries were positioned around a hangar in which the two presidents and two prime ministers were about to meet. A contingent of Secret Service, Russian Secret Police, and personal bodyguards were arrayed throughout the inside of the hangar used by private and corporate jets. The structure was smaller than the mammoth hangar they had used the previous weekend in Detroit.

It was 12:30 a.m. Monday in Washington, DC, and 8:30 a.m. in Moscow.

The tables were setup in a "U" shape, but not connected at the corners. Macdonald and members of his team sat along one leg of the U, their backs to the closed hangar doors. Novorken, who appeared edgy, anxious to get on with things, sat with his people along the leg opposite Macdonald. Prime Ministers Howard and McEwen with two interpreters between them sat at the bottom of the U. There was a row of chairs behind each section for members of their respective entourages.

Eight feet separated the two presidents' tables. There were duplicate translators for each language at each of the three stations in the event there was an interpretation problem. Wearing a headset and microphone, Steve Hester sat to Macdonald's right with Eubanks to his right. Rankin and Padget sat to Macdonald's left. Hendrickson and Darlene sat immediately behind Macdonald, with other staff.

Sitting with Novorken were his interpreters; General Rostov Rodenko; Director Ministry of Defense Oleg Kalastov; and Nicolas Bortnikov, director of the Financial Monitoring and Foreign Exchange Control Department. Two colonels with an aide each sat off to Novorken's left along with three civilians.

None of the Russians wore headsets except Novorken and his interpreter. All of the Americans, the two Prime Ministers, and their staffs wore them.

It was a raw setup, no frills; the dull lighting gave it a grayish look.

President Macdonald began by thanking President Novorken for meeting with his envoys. He hoped for a long and productive relationship with Novorken and the Russian people, "with better accommodations," he jokingly said, emitting chuckles from his side. The Russian sat impassively.

"Mr. President," Macdonald said, "I find this to be a very ticklish situation, finding ourselves involved in your internal affairs as we attempt to unravel the mystery of who bombed Detroit and Windsor nearly three weeks ago."

Keeping steady eye contact with Novorken, Macdonald discerned smugness in the man, unlike the attitude he had shown Bill and Steve, where he had seemed unsure. Macdonald decided to adjust his normal flow of speaking to allow for the translations, a new experience for him. Steve kept up very well.

After the preamble, Macdonald got to the matter of the Russian traitors and the United States's desire to interrogate them. "There are some who, we believe, have intimate knowledge of our bombing and others who conducted certain financial transactions connected to that disaster."

"President Macdonald, we do not understand your insistence that Russians were involved in your terrible disaster," the Russian president said condescendingly,

Concern was evident from the Americans. *What was going on?*

"We thank you for coming to us and informing about plans against my government, but to tie them—"

Macdonald got the gist of where he was going and didn't wait for the catch-up, interrupting the Russian firmly. "Sir, we have discovered certain individuals in your country who prosecuted the bombing of my country."

Novorken waited for the translation. "So you say, but where is your proof? Your envoys told me a very intricate story about some cabal within my government. Yes, I know there are dissenters to our program and certainly some minor illegal activities, but then who does not have that. Not so?"

Macdonald grimaced. *It's a good thing Gus isn't here; he'd have jumped this guy by now.* He replied tersely. "Sir, you forged an understanding with my envoys that Russian cabal members were behind the bombing and nefarious financial activities, along with other illegal activities that we have not yet divulged to you."

Novorken waited, and then smiled, saying grandiosely, "I have not seen any proof of this. You say you do not want to interfere with our internal operations, but here you are. I was in the process of conducting a mass arrest when you contacted me, as these gentlemen will attest."

He indicated men sitting with him with a gesture, and they all nodded.

Marionettes, Macdonald mused.

"However, I could not believe my good fortune. Your information fit very well into my plans. Your envoys were most helpful, and this also presented an opportunity for you and me to meet. I did not think you were going to be making these outrageous accusations."

Macdonald turned and whispered to Darlene during Novorken's last spiel.

Novorken continued. "We can ask these traitors if your allegation is true. If it is, I will apologize and make arrangements, come to some consideration—"

Macdonald interrupted sternly. "Mr. President. Canada and the United States were viciously attacked; millions were killed and millions more were injured. I have received hundreds of thousands of communications from my countrymen asking, pleading for retribution. They want me to nuke somebody, and they don't care who."

Novorken was visibly taken aback. "You are not seriously considering—"

"I don't want to kill innocent people, I've seen too much of that, but we do want retribution, and I was led by you to believe we were going to begin that here."

"Then you thought wrong. We have done nothing to you. I will arrest my traitors, and they will all be tried and executed. You will have no one to question," the Russian said, with a shrug: *so what are you going to do about that.*

Macdonald wondered: *Why did he say "no one to question"? What does that tell us?* He held on to his emotions and nodded to Eubanks, who then left the hangar. Novorken idly observed the activity, but continued his denials, his hubris driving him. He had taken a lot of air out of the hangar.

"You have made an error in judgment, President Macdonald," he said wryly. "I believe we have concluded our business."

That said, however, he didn't make a move to get up. He was enjoying the moment. "You have given everything without ensuring even one euro in return."

That's a strange thing to say, Macdonald thought. *Novorken is too cocky.* Still silent, Macdonald continued to consider the implications of what was evolving in front of him. Then he smiled, startling the Russian, whose eyes questioned the American. Macdonald spoke in a friendly tone, "Mr. President, I would like you to do me a favor."

Novorken snapped. "What foolishness is this?"

Macdonald nodded to his military aide, who held a smartphone. The aide walked around the table toward the Russian president, and a Russian military aide briskly moved to intercept him. The American put up his hand in an assuring gesture, while extending the device to the officer, who looked at it and then to handed it to his president.

"What game are you playing, Mr. President?" Novorken asked puzzled. "What is this picture?"

"No game. I am deadly serious, sir. I'd like you to make a call."

Novorken snorted a laugh and shook his head hard, handing back the device. The Russian officer handed it back to the American officer.

Macdonald smiled. "All right, we'll call the number for you."

The American officer slowly tapped in a number, as Steve said it aloud in Russian. Novorken seemed stunned at the undertaking. "What trickery . . . ?"

"No trickery on our part, sir. You have just blown up two of your oil refineries. Take a look," and he gestured for his officer to hand the device back to the Russian officer. He looked at it himself, showing shock, and quickly handed it to his president.

Novorken went pale. The Russian spoke, paused, and then exclaimed something in stammering words. All the Russians were startled and questioned each other. Steve interpreted what Novorken had said: "Two refineries southeast of St. Petersburg have blown up!"

"What have you done?" Novorken screamed, jumping to his feet.

Macdonald smiled. "Me? Nothing. You did it. You made an agreement with my envoys that you now deny. If you continue your deceit, the next event will cost you tens of billions of euros and the next one after that hundreds of billions."

Novorken dropped the device and slammed the palms of both hands onto the table, startling the armed personnel in the room. "You have created an international incident." He was livid.

"We have more than ample proof of Russian complicity," Macdonald said calmly.

Novorken waved his arms wildly. "I already knew of many hardliners in FSB. We were watching those traitors."

Macdonald remained cool. "Of course, we all have to do that, even in a democracy. Let me ask you, were the three names you gave us as loyal members of your regime, were you watching them?"

Novorken paused, unsure of what he was asked.

Macdonald continued. "You say they were plotting against you, yet you also said they were among your closest advisors."

"We have our own ways of operating."

"I'm sure we all do." Macdonald turned to a transfixed Darlene. "The proposal please."

The two Prime Ministers already had their copies and had read them. An aide delivered a copy in Russian to Novorken.

Macdonald spoke. "We want to see the guilty punished, preferably by you, after we have questioned them. We need to know how they did it; something I would think could be beneficial for both of us to know. You said you are or will be arresting those people who we named and gave to you."

"At this hour, many are already in custody," Novorken snorted, "but you will not be allowed to question them because they are traitors and would say anything to discredit me and my government."

Macdonald was enjoying this. "I have no doubt about that, but we are not interested in their politics. Besides, we only want to talk to the ones who were in on the planning and carrying out of the bombing, while earning blood money shorting the dollar."

Novorken looked at Macdonald quizzically. "Why do you persist in saying Russians were behind the bombing?"

"Because we know they were."

"I, too, believe that, Mr. President," Prime Minister Howard said.

"Ah, you British, so naïve. You two are long-time friends. You are blindly helping him now."

Howard nodded. "Blindly, no. Assisting, yes. Yes, I am, Boris, because he happens to be right."

Macdonald quickly asked. "Mr. President, did you experience a sizeable drop in your treasury about two weeks ago?"

Novorken looked at Bortnikov questioningly.

Macdonald forged ahead. "The plotters against you made a fortune by shorting our currency immediately before the nuclear device destroyed Detroit and Windsor, Canada."

Bortnikov was shaking his head. Novorken looked confused and sputtered, "This is all ridiculous." Bortnikov had just given away that he knew English.

Macdonald picked up the pace. "Your FSB recently set up a trillion-euro account dedicated to a joint Iran/China infrastructure construction project."

Worry flickered in Novorken's eyes. Macdonald overlapped the translation. "You signed off on it. President Novorken, do you review your government's finances?"

Novorken snapped. "What are you trying to accomplish with these lies?"

"That was a question. Are you not concerned? Who could authorize that? Somebody withdrew the money from your treasury to finance twelve shell companies, registered corporations in eight to ten different countries, all with phony officers, but with a bank account and a signatory."

Novorken was spellbound.

"Imagine this. A trillion euros shorted the US dollar on the Foreign Exchange in mid-January. They made hundreds of billions of euros in profits when our dollar crashed."

Novorken laughed derisively. "You tell a fairy tale. No one makes money like that so easily. It is a farce."

"You'd be surprised. Of course, the smart move would have been to then go long as the dollar bounced back, making money both ways, and then get out. However, they got greedy and shorted one more time, when it looked like the United States was going down for the final count."

Novorken look stunned, his hubris long since dissolved.

"Unfortunately," Macdonald added solicitously, "this time they were not in control of world events like when they bombed us. This time they were on the wrong side, and by the time they covered, they'd lost billions."

"You tell stories, but show no proof."

"Okay, check with your Central Bank."

"You could call now, Boris, it is 0930 hours in Moscow," Howard said solicitously.

"I do not need to; it did not happen."

"As I said, they were greedy, and they got burned."

The Russian translator had a problem with "burned." Steve Hester gave them the gist of what "burned" meant.

"You have seven minutes. Do nothing and—"

"We will shoot you down," Novorken threatened.

"There's nothing to shoot down."

Novorken stammered unintelligibly. He gestured to his aide that he wanted the phone.

"We will call the bank," he said arrogantly.

99

Macdonald watched Novorken squirrel off to a far corner of the hangar. His financial proposal to the Russian president was a product of conversations he had had with Prime Minister McEwen during two phone conversations earlier in the day.

Prime Minister McEwen had suggested that in recognition of the Americans shouldering the military operations, they should receive the first quarter billion barrels of oil that would have been fed to the Russian mainland. The next three-quarter billion barrels would be shared sixty/forty in the Americans' favor. The income from the natural gas would be split one-third each with the Russians for twenty years.

Macdonald's advisors had agreed to McEwen's generous offer.

In conversation with the two Prime Ministers, Macdonald mentioned, "Since Novorken doesn't know that *we know* he's been running a scam and had put on a charade for Bill and Steve, we're one up on him."

"It's a good show all the way around," Howard offered.

McEwen said. "I've been watching Novorken across the hangar. He's certainly been on the phone a lot. Maybe he ordered a search, calling in fighters, sending in troops."

Macdonald grunted. "Oh, I am sure he is doing more than just talking to his banking people."

"Quite so," Howard said. "I believe one call may be his giving orders to implement his so-called roundup of traitors, which might not have begun, contrary to what he wanted us to believe."

Macdonald looked at Howard admiringly. "Good point. He is showing us one plan, but is going to flip it at the last second. Maybe that is something we should get to Interpol?"

"He appeared distracted with the arrests," McEwen said.

"I think we can't trust him and that we should take Sakhalin Island, Reggie, as insurance. Let me get things going on that." He sent Darlene to get DCIA Eubanks.

McEwen showed concern. "I know you told me about taking Sakhalin, but now that it seems a reality, I must say I am concerned, Mr. President. What about the multinational firms? There are at least six countries, one being us, involved there with as many as ten thousand citizens from all over the globe. Besides, won't that take weeks to develop?"

"From scratch, it might, but this was an early contingency from Day Five at Camp David over three weeks ago. We currently have in theater four brigades of Marines and Army troops, a wing of B-52s, two wings of fighters, and four nuclear submarines with eight twelve-man Special Ops combat teams, some already on the island."

McEwen was incredulous. "Good grief. What about the civilian workers?"

"We have a plan in place. Our reconnaissance teams have been on the Sakhalin for three days, and our satellites are giving us a good window on the island. Each team is within minutes of their target facility. When our Special Ops troops offload from the subs, each company's CEO will be contacted at their headquarters by the Pentagon.

"The FBI has been tracking each company's top officer and knows exactly where they are at all times. Director Thornton and SecDef Garrett established a 24/7 communication operation joining them at the hip. When Director Eubanks gives the go to Special Ops, the FBI simultaneously gets the word.

"I recorded a message that SecDef Garrett has at the Pentagon, explaining why troops will be showing up at their Sakhalin doorstep. I gave those companies my personal assurance none of their people will be harmed, unless they foolishly move against us. We are not there to interfere with oil operations, only to keep their product out of Russian hands.

"All our troops and equipment were deployed over ten days ago under the guise of participating in our war games conducted in the Sea of Japan and off the coast of Hokkaido. We've been doing them for years. Even the North Koreans ignore us. No one will be expecting our move on Sakhalin."

McEwen sat back in amazement. "You've been in office how long?" he asked in awe.

"He game-plans well, Brewster," Howard said. "It must have something to do with that game he used to play."

"I understand now. Thank you, Mr. President," McEwen said positively.

Eubanks and Darlene joined the group and Macdonald asked, "Jim? Give us your reading on Novorken."

Eubanks smiled knowingly. "Yes, I have noticed some anomalous behavior."

Of course, Eubanks knew substantially more, but would keep his own counsel.

"I believe he should be worried, but he's not. The trick he tried earlier? I think it's still in his mind, and as soon as he knows his 'traitors' have been rounded up, he'll look us in the eye, agree to what we've been discussing, and once airborne . . ." Eubanks made the Italian gesture, thumb flicking out from under his chin.

Howard enjoyed the demonstration. "Well, Mr. President?"

"Jim, give General Donner a fast 'go' on Sakhalin."

"Yes sir. What about . . . the other, sir." Eubanks asked before heading back to Air Force One.

"We'll do Sakhalin, but nothing else. Let's get Novorken back to the table."

Eubanks nodded. "Will you need me?"

"Absolutely, I'm getting ahead of myself again. Get things rolling and then come back. Darlene, go on board and be my eyes and ears. Use the military aides and courier them to me as necessary. Start when Donner confirms all units are moving."

"Yes, Mr. President." She went to both aides and then took one with her to Air Force One. Eubanks had already scooted on board.

McEwen excused himself to huddle with his foreign minister and security specialist.

With a few minutes of wait time ahead of them, Macdonald nudged his old friend. "Well, Reg, Operation Retribution is about to make or break my presidency."

"I take it you haven't told Brewster about Novorken."

"No. Tell me, am I being too cautious with Brewster? He is a partner, after all."

"But not quite an equal one," Howard replied. "You are doing the Canadians a large favor, making them a lot of money. It is best you get your mind off Brewster's feelings for now and get back to that two-faced bastard from across the table. Oh, will he be able to track your lads?"

"I don't know what Donner's escape plans were, but he assured me the technique had been successful every time it was used."

"Right. We don't always need to know the 'how,' just revel in their success."

"Gotcha. I see Novorken is off the phone and moving our way. Shall we re-engage?"

"It would be my distinct pleasure."

Macdonald did some more quick thinking. Novorken had no way of knowing that CIA and Interpol had seven members of the so-called cabal either under wraps or under surveillance. Director Thornton had assured him of that. The three names that the Russian president had identified to Hendrickson and Hester had been immediately put under surveillance. One was in St. Petersburg; the other two were in Moscow.

Interpol also had Aleshkin under tight surveillance, and they had Nicolai Trevenkov and Aleksandr Illyanavich in custody, as did Eubanks with Ivan Strylotov. Macdonald had purposely left Raisa Illyanavich off the list given to Novorken. He didn't want to take the chance that Vasiliy could become implicated. Eubanks planned to turn the surprisingly cooperative Strylotov over to Interpol. Macdonald thought the entire investigation was bearing very ripe fruit.

Macdonald asked SecState Rankin to reconvene the meeting. Without niceties, Novorken abruptly announced, "This meeting is over. We are leaving."

Macdonald pretended concern. Novorken plowed ahead.

"We are not guilty of anything, Mr. Macdonald," Novorken said rudely. "We acknowledge your assistance in helping us find some traitors, but your claims of Russian involvement in your tragedy are outrageous."

Macdonald feigned his protest. "But Mr. President, we know some were behind the bombing, and we must interview them," he said.

Novorken smirked. "I repeat; there were no Russians involved in your unfortunate bombing. The pressure you have been under has made you delusional."

"President Novorken," Howard protested, "there is no need—"

Macdonald interrupted. "What about your finance people misusing funds from your treasury and the billions of euros they lost?"

"You have a vivid imagination, sir. No such thing ever took place. You have acted rashly and will pay for destroying Russian property. You will lose in the eyes of the world. You are finished!"

Keep it going, Macdonald thought. "Property? Were those refineries deliberately blown up? I thought that was an accident, Mr. President. Who could do such a thing?"

Novorken's expression was priceless.

Macdonald loved it. *The Russian is caught short. He thought he was going to waltz all over us.*

"Of course you did it. You admitted it."

"You must have me confused with someone else, sir. We came here as friends sharing a severe problem with people in your country who want to destroy both our governments. I thought you and I had forged a trusting, working association to right the wrongs done to both our countries."

"You have perpetrated the only wrong." Novorken's anger was viral.

Macdonald smiled and took on a conciliatory tone. "Are you sure it wasn't your revolutionaries who bombed Detroit and . . . no, wait, that wouldn't work."

"What are you babbling about?" Novorken charged, trying to regain the lead.

Macdonald waved his blunder off. "You're right, forget that. We wanted to help you out of your problem and at the same time find who bombed us. We were about to suggest to you that instead of it being *us* who came to *you* with names, it would be *you* who came to *us*, seeing our distress and wanting to help."

Novorken's eyes widened, he looked unnerved, but continued his assault. "You are wasting my time with your pathetic accusations. I feel sorry for you."

As the pace increased, the interpreters were struggling to stay up, which afforded both presidents a few more seconds of precious thinking time.

"Well, I sometimes feel sorry for me too, Mr. President," Macdonald said wryly.

Novorken was stymied by Macdonald's self-deprecating comment.

Macdonald jumped on that. "Look, we felt we could help your image by saying assistance came from you, not the other way around. That you told us that you indeed had factions in your country plotting against both of us, but that you didn't want to admit to that second part.

"Then we could say you came to us in good faith, because your ongoing investigations into illegal activity in the FSB had uncovered evidence that some of your troublemakers were also plotting against America."

Novorken was bewildered. Macdonald laid it on.

"The secret cabal was intent on destroying our economy and along the way pick up a few hundred billion euros for their troubles. They smuggled a nuclear bomb into Detroit and heavily shorted the US dollar on the Foreign Exchange.

"You were saddened that you hadn't discovered this sooner and saved us from such a great loss of life. We, of course, were extremely grateful to you for bringing this to us, and together we would prosecute the perpetrators."

Howard and McEwen were studying the Russian president intently.

"That's an oversimplification, but I believe you can understand my tactics."

Novorken's wind had been taken away from him. "I . . ."

Macdonald was on a roll. "We can't understand how this could have happened any other way. I mean, we know that you didn't do it, yet all signs lead to Russians being behind it. We, of course, will be in your debt for unraveling the mystery, and together we will both come out of this the best of friends."

Howard stifled a cough. "Excuse me," he protested. "It must be the air."

This break gave Novorken a moment to collect his wits. "My finance director . . ."

he indicated Nicolas Bortnikov, his director of the Financial Monitoring and Foreign Exchange Control Department. " . . . Nicolas has conferred with Vasiliy Mednorov, his director of the Central Bank, who checked the accounts of the Russian Federation and found everything to be in good order. There are no shortages in any of the accounts as you so claimed."

"Well, I guess I was wrong," Macdonald said abashedly. "Somebody, though, painted a scurrilous picture of your involvement to make me think that."

Howard was a good actor, but he daren't make eye contact with Macdonald.

"Yes, well, you are wrong," Novorken replied quietly.

"We see that," Macdonald ventured.

"I am happy you realize it."

"Yes; however, we would still like to interview—"

Novorken became intense. "Why do you keep playing this game? I would turn the guilty parties over to you, if there were any. But there are not. Can you prove even one person's culpability? Just one!"

Macdonald wanted to end this. Sakhalin was about to be occupied. "Okay. Enough of this foolishness, as you like to call it, Mr. President," Macdonald said earnestly.

Novorken thought he had regained the upper hand, but his expression showed his realization that the tables had turned, again.

Macdonald shook his head, sadly. "This is your last opportunity to cooperate with us."

Novorken stormed, "YOU ARE THE—"

"NO," Macdonald spat. "No sir," his spittle flying, "we are the aggrieved. We have the proof."

Novorken began to protest.

"DON'T interrupt me!"

Novorken recoiled from Macdonald's ferociousness.

"We know all about the smuggling operation and the way one of your undeclared nuclear devices came into my country. We know the two leaders of the coup, who I *accidently* left off the list we gave to you. Those two are in Interpol's custody. They told us about your banking arrangements and about your game of playing one side against the other to get rid of your political opponents."

Novorken was frozen in place.

Macdonald did not actually know that last part, but it fit. He bore in, playing on the ideologies involved and rattling off Novorken's surrogates who had convinced the *top person* that bombing the US was the perfect way to cause the US dollar to collapse and for him to make some big money.

He stared the Russian down. "That 'top person' was you trying to fatally injure an old enemy, us, and you attempted to destroy our economy, while all along blaming it on so-called revolutionaries in your own country."

Howard and McEwen were solidly with Macdonald; they stared at the Russian sternly. Novorken looked at the members in his party. They were expressionless, except for his finance director, whose face reflected fear.

Macdonald laid down the hammer. "This subterfuge created a very delicate situation, Mr. President. You have now refused our offer of a peaceful pact that would help us and Canada to rebuild and that would save millions of Russian lives.

"We understand from a person in your phony cabal that you wanted certain people eliminated, which is why you set up this very elaborate and deadly scheme."

Novorken spat. "Your country is weak and without purpose. Your brave talk, your lies about me are a poor attempt at trying to save your own face. YOU HAVE FAILED."

"Fine," Macdonald said, throwing off the word. "We will let the world know of your duplicity. We will take your oil and natural gas and break you like a dried twig."

Novorken jumped to his feet. "DO NOT—"

Macdonald topped him. "AND we will bring you to justice."

Novorken screamed. "I HAVE—"

"WE gave you the chance to gracefully—"

"NO! IT IS YOU—"

Macdonald stood, cutting him off again. "OKAY. ENOUGH." His arms waved Novorken off. "We are through here. You will see how serious we are about this. We are prepared to stand in front of the world court. We have evidence. We have the people."

"Not anymore," Novorken said haughtily. "Every person on your list has already been arrested."

Macdonald smiled. "Yes, we expected you to say that, which only proves your duplicity. You are the rogue in your government, and you have ruined lives of those in your country who had put great faith in you."

Novorken was blistering hot. "You LIE!"

Macdonald froze him in place. "Enough of this, Mr. President. We are through here."

With that, twenty armored SWAT-dressed Secret Service came through the hangar door and positioned themselves on three sides of the dozen Americans and friends.

Before the team of armed guards was halfway in, Novorken stormed, "WHAT IS THIS?"

Macdonald put up both hands, waving Novorken down.

"Have no fear of us. My security people just want to ensure my safe departure. We bear you no harm." Prearranged, all of Macdonald's party were being ushered out by the Secret Service as he spoke, leaving only the twenty-man SWAT team, Macdonald, the two prime ministers, and Steve Hester facing the Russian, whose bravado had vanished.

"President Novorken, you have until midnight Monday—tonight, Moscow time—to accept my offer of a peaceful resolve. I plan to speak to the American people from Washington, DC, five hours later at 2100 hours Eastern Standard Time.

"At that time, I will accept your generosity and willingness to allow the United States to prosecute the guilty or for you to announce that you have arrested and will name the traitors responsible for bombing us.

"In the meantime, to ensure your cooperation, the next financial penalty I promised you is already underway. I did not want to end things this way. The future is in your hands, only this time we are ready."

Macdonald nodded to the SWAT commander, and Howard, McEwen, Hester, and he walked out within the halo of protection that engulfed them.

As Air Force One ascended into the sky, reaching for forty thousand feet, the horizon to the east showed the breaking of a new day.

100

Aboard Air Force One
Retrospect

It had been back on Friday morning when Eubanks brought the conundrum that was Novorken to Macdonald's attention.

Strylotov had given Novorken up as the plotter. According to Strylotov, Novorken had created a secret cabal, a so-called underground opposition party, to protest his governance. This slowly attracted real players, hardliners who wanted to get Novorken out of power.

CIA operatives had informed Strylotov of the upcoming meeting of the presidents to discuss those cabal members who were in on the plot against the Russian president and who might have been involved in the American bombing.

Unexpectedly, Strylotov gave in to save himself. He'd been worried he might be implicated in the bombing, he said later on.

After meeting with Novorken in Moscow, Hester and Hendrickson flew back to Washington to join Macdonald and Eubanks at the 0900 meeting on Friday. Macdonald decided not to tell his two envoys about Eubanks's revelation regarding Novorken until after they had briefed the president and CIA director on their trip.

Hendrickson said the Russian president had made a mistake when he complied with their request to write out a list of people he could trust. Novorken's list of fourteen names had included three already identified by Vasiliy Mednorov and Interpol moles. One was known to have associations with Aleshkin. The other two were like Senate and House whips, pushing their party's agenda and the agenda of the cabal simultaneously. What Strylotov told the CIA had corroborated the three as important insiders.

Macdonald and Eubanks decided to wait until Saturday's small session meeting at Camp David to reveal their findings. This gave the DCIA time for further investigation into Novorken as the man behind the cabal.

By Saturday morning, it had become unequivocally clear that Novorken was the architect of the bombing and the shorting of the dollar.

It was then that Macdonald, Eubanks, Hendrickson, and Hester understood that Novorken's covert operatives, acting under his direction as secret members of the opposition, had fostered ideas of rebellion, which drew many hapless zealots to the phony program.

When the time came for developing a relationship with black marketers and smugglers, one of the Novorken insiders, who was living the double life as a member of the cabal, contacted Aleshkin in early 2011.

It took time to develop a trusting relationship with Aleshkin and that job eventually fell to Aleksandr Illyanavich, a former black market operator and army officer who had helped to elect Novorken and had been rewarded with a high-ranking post in the 6th Directorate, where he was recently promoted to director.

Aleshkin filled the bill in more ways than smuggling. He was rich and wanted to become wealthier. Illyanavich played on the man's greed with promises of operating freely, without fear of the Secret Police breathing down his neck. To test and secretly track Aleshkin's operation, Illyanavich provided illegal products to be smuggled to European and American destinations. They were all delivered without detection.

In the summer of 2012, Novorken's plotters were ready to make their move.

Individual pieces of a stripped-down nuclear tactical device and other hardware were included in crates of legitimate products. Just as in the previous test runs, all went without a hitch. The explosive materials were shipped intact using the crate FBI Director Thornton had told the Camp David group about.

As best the FBI and the few remaining Detroit city employees could determine, a 130,000-square-foot warehouse had been purchased by a Polish wholesaler in the summer of 2011 that assembled looms, sewing machines, and clothes presses, and wholesaled expensive fabrics.

They worked a legitimate operation, according to Strylotov. They had planned to set off the nuclear device in mid-October 2012, but were suffering setbacks on the financial end.

Strylotov had never met Raisa Illyanavich, but Novorken had told him that Aleksandr Illyanavich had brought her plan to him, not to Aleshkin as Eubanks had originally presumed. Strylotov then met with the two Illyanaviches, and Raisa presented her currency-shorting scheme to him.

Bortnikov's first attempt at moving the trillion euros was thwarted by Vasiliy

Mednorov, because what they wanted to do with the money was outside the parlance of the Central Bank. Mednorov could not move the money into private corporations on his own. The FSB had created systems and double-checks to prevent that.

That was basically what Vasiliy had told Alexandra over New Year's. However, Nicolas Bortnikov explained to Novorken that, under the president's plan, the money would have to be transferred into an authorized government account. They created the Iran/Chinese Infrastructure Aid Program for that purpose.

Then, following Raisa's detailed instructions, Bortnikov arranged the deposit of one trillion euros into that account in the Russian Central Bank. It was similar to what Macdonald had arranged in establishing the AIR and DOER accounts in the Federal Reserve Bank of New York.

Bortnikov began the transfers on January 3, 2013, in deposits of a billion to nine billion euros over a ten-day period into the accounts of the twelve phony shell companies.

According to Strylotov, Trevenkov, under Raisa Illyanavich's direction, began shorting the dollar on January 15, 16, and 17, 2013. Everything was in place for the bombing on January 22.

When Eubanks satisfied everyone that it was Novorken and not Aleshkin, the whole cabal scheme became much clearer. Through Aleksandr Illyanavich, Novorken had set Aleshkin up to be the "wannabe" dictator of Eubanks's earlier scenario, when it turned out he was the man.

Macdonald was now more convinced there would be no nuclear war. The Russians had patiently established bogus political subgroups that stirred up the cabal. The secrecy worked two ways; people joining the cabal did so secretly for practical purposes, and Novorken and his henchmen were, in actuality, double agents. They ran the government and the cabal. Ingenious.

According to Strylotov, the operatives in Detroit decided to use the celebration of the American inaugural as their cover. On that Monday afternoon, two work trucks drove to the rear of an empty high-rise about to be demolished and transferred the fully assembled bomb concealed in a crate to its roof.

The workmen had first run tests on the freight elevator using a powerful electric generator powered by lithium batteries. Once at roof level, the elevator with its cargo was locked in place and the timer set. The men then walked down the dozen or so flights and left the city, their handiwork soon to become history.

When Air Force One set down at Andrews Air Force Base early Monday morning, the refinery explosion was all over the Internet. There were no reports of injuries or loss of life. A history of those refineries was included in most blogs, but there had been no statements forthcoming from the Russian government as to the cause.

Macdonald was also told that there were no reports regarding Sakhalin Island. It appeared that the Special Ops teams had done their job, and the private security companies contacted by the Pentagon had gone along with the plan.

101

White House
Monday, February 11
0600 hours

Everyone from the flight had dispersed by 0600. Macdonald and Howard then showered, dressed, and quickly joined Louise and Alex for breakfast in the private dining room. Soon after, the Howards were winging their way back to London. McEwen's plane had been awaiting him when Air Force One landed at Andrews. He'd boarded it immediately for Ottawa.

Early that afternoon, Cynthia buzzed. "Mr. President, a representative of President Novorken's is on the line."

"Have Steve Hester take it; he's in the Cabinet Room. Round up everyone on the list I gave you and have them go to the Situation Room ASAP. I'll call Darlene." He hung up and punched in Darlene's line.

"Yes sir?"

"It's time. I'm heading to the Cabinet Room, where Steve is on the phone with a representative of Novorken's."

"I'll be right there."

Please, he thought, *of the two choices, make this the most peaceful one.*

Darlene approached him in the Cabinet Room, as he was listening to Steve on the phone. She said, "Is his calling this early a good sign?"

"Let's hope."

Steve hung up the phone and stood to face Macdonald, and then grinned. "Novorken will teleconference with us in few minutes."

The three went down the stairs to the Situation Room.

CIA Director Eubanks awaited them at the door to the Situation Room. "Sir, may I have a moment? Steve, you stay."

"I'll go on in," Darlene said, leaving him.

"What's up, Jim?"

"According to one of my top operatives, Aleksandr Illyanavich was murdered in his apartment, but we'll hear it was suicide. Interpol had released him. Hoping he might lead us to others, they and we had a surveillance team on-site when he arrived home by 6 p.m. their time. Fifteen minutes later, two men entered Illyanavich's apartment building. They came back out twenty minutes later.

"My operative and his Russian asset used the rear fire escape to check on Illyanavich. They found him in his bathtub, both wrists slit, a kitchen knife lying next to him. They went out the way they went in."

"Novorken's cleaning house," Macdonald said unemotionally.

Eubanks nodded. "Illyanavich was one of only two, and we're fairly certain that's all, who'd had direct communication with Novorken on the scam; Strylotov being the other.

"We don't think anyone else had the bad luck of having direct contact with Novorken on the cabal side. We hadn't been tracking Raisa Illyanavich, but I asked the two operatives who lost their mark tonight to check on her."

"Good," Macdonald replied, tight-lipped.

"Novorken is a master of deceit, sir. He insulated his involvement in the scam beautifully. Illyanavich's responsibilities were the smuggling and the bomb. Strylotov had the political and financial side."

"And to Novorken, both are now dead," Macdonald said grimly.

"We have not developed much on Nicolas Bortnikov, but suspect he was involved in the transfer of funds. Interpol will be watching him."

"What about the others we met in Reykjavik?"

"Steve, you want to answer that."

"I noticed an interesting circumstance there. None except Bortnikov made any reactions during the normal flow of conversation. They only reacted when their president got emotional and when our Secret Service SWAT arrived. Our guess is that none except Bortnikov knew English and had no idea what we were saying."

"That's fascinating. Novorken is a crafty guy. Let's be triple sure about what he's agreeing to."

Eubanks nodded. "Our people in Moscow say most, if not all of his ministers and senior staffers are very supportive of him."

"Are there others who could come up missing, Jim?"

Eubanks shrugged. "You never know how deep his neurosis runs. Once Illyanavich moved the bomb into Aleshkin's hands, the chain between Novorken and the bomb was broken."

Nancy Armstrong approached Macdonald. "Mr. President, everything is ready."

"Thanks, Nancy." He smiled. "This is going to be very interesting."

102

Situation Room
Moments later

Macdonald entered the Situation Room and Darlene called, "At ease." He scanned the room then nodded to Darlene who said, "General Gibbons?"

The image of the general suddenly appeared on a small screen that faced Macdonald. "I'm here, sir."

He smiled shaking his head. "Good afternoon, Chief."

A second screen came up displaying Vice President Dudley. The two screens bracketed a blank, sixty-inch screen.

"Madam Vice President," he said, "welcome."

"Mr. President."

He put on ear phones, as had others. The center screen came on, revealing President Novorken sitting on an opulent throne in front of an ornate wall.

"Good day, Mr. President," Macdonald said.

A camera was centered in each screen, so that Macdonald could look at the screen and it would seem that he was directly addressing that person as if they were in the room. "Good day to you, President Macdonald." Novorken said cordially. He appeared calm and poised. Style points were very important. "You and I have embarked on a very important voyage."

Macdonald sensed a touch of tenseness beneath his calm veneer. *This has to go well for him or he could lose everything,* Macdonald realized. "I agree, sir."

Novorken continued. "We have been and continue to be very sad over the horrendous tragedy that has befallen your great country. We are very pleased to have been of assistance in your investigations."

That's a good beginning for our side, Macdonald noted.

"The unimaginable revelation that Russian citizens were involved in your bombing was beyond belief. That was why we eagerly joined your investigation and discovered, to our disgust, that it was true. You and I have discussed this through your envoys last Thursday night and our secret face-to-face meeting last night."

Macdonald jumped in. "Yes, Mr. President, we deeply appreciate your immediate willingness to hunt out the perpetrators and bring them to justice."

A slight smile cracked Novorken's stoniness.

Macdonald continued. "What additional information do you have for us today?"

Novorken appeared pleased and leaned slightly forward.

"As you told me, you plan to speak to your countrymen tonight. We have been busy rounding up suspects and have found that some had more deadly intentions than just running a political opposition against me.

"With the great help of Interpol and your CIA, who have been investigating a smuggling ring, we have determined who some of the cutthroats are. Maybe not all. That investigation continues."

"Yes. CIA Director Eubanks told me those arrests have proven a valuable link to how a bomb came into my country."

"This is true," Novorken said quickly. "We have identified those persons."

Macdonald's adrenaline was pumping. "Have you identified the supplier who smuggled it in?"

That appeared to catch Novorken off guard, making him go off script or at least rearrange it. "Oh, yes, I was coming to that," he added rapidly.

"Excuse me for interrupting. Please continue," Macdonald said, fighting back the urge to cheer.

There was a pause, as Novorken was handed a slip of paper, which he read quickly. Macdonald wondered if that was a prop, as his own "note" had been ten days earlier.

The Russian president looked into the camera. "We have good news and not so good news," he said seriously. "Unfortunately, one of my highest ranking ministers turned out to be a key person in your disaster. He was discovered dead in his residence. He committed suicide."

That created murmurs. Novorken had set the table. As their conversation continued, Novorken offered promises of reciprocity and plans of compensation. It all came from what Macdonald had spelled out in his written proposal during their meeting in Reykjavik.

Novorken made no mention of the US military occupying Sakhalin Island.

Novorken agreed to meet with Secretary of State Rankin and a US delegation to work out all the details of bringing the perpetrators to justice and to put some faces on the disaster. He also agreed to making the guilty available to Interpol and the combined investigating team.

He promised the immediate payment of one trillion euros to be equally shared between the United States and Canada. Russia would need to raise more capital and would start by healing bad feelings in Europe. He would no longer tolerate game-playing with their oil and natural gas deliveries.

"I promise you that Russia will assist you in your recovery, and although we cannot undo the deaths and injuries, we will take on a major responsibility in your restoration as a small recompense for the ills that were perpetrated upon you by some ruthless Russian citizens and military.

"I understand how easily you could have retaliated with a nuclear bombing of us. We know many people would want that. Some misguided people in my own country even went so far as to blow up two of our old refineries in hopes we would think it was you and thus cause more hardship. They have been captured and will be dealt with."

Now there is one neat resolution, Macdonald thought.

103

White House
Situation Room
An hour and a half later

At 2200 hours Moscow time—1400 hours or 2:00 p.m. in Washington—President Boris Novorken went on Russian television. His speech was heard around the world.

"I come before you to explain activities taking place this day. A ring of black marketers and smugglers, including those in our government abetting their illegal operations, have been taken into custody by Interpol and Russian Security Forces."

He went on to explain about the investigation.

"So you see this was a combined effort," he concluded. "We have been conducting a unilateral investigation of traitorous activities and uncovered a cabal, which was intent on overthrowing our duly-elected officials.

"Interpol made it known to me that certain Russians were behind the smuggling, an outgrowth of the diabolical black marketers who have plagued our economy."

He explained the involvement of the CIA and British Intelligence. Then he put the stamp on his speech.

"I want to assure the entire world that I and the Russian government had no prior knowledge of this despicable act. I spoke with President Macdonald an hour or so ago to assure him of our complete cooperation and our desire to make reparations to him and Canada, as a goodwill gesture, because the same Russian provocateurs intent on replacing our government were those who set off the nuclear device, killing and injuring millions.

"Talks between Russia and the United States and Canada will begin tomorrow on how we can best assist them."

Novorken continued for a few more minutes, more or less going over the same ground, wanting to make very clear to the world that rogue Russians were involved in the nuclear disaster, but that it was in no way the Russian government.

"Well," the Macdonald said after Novorken had signed off. "We have a country waiting to hear from me. I don't think we should wait until 2100 hours. Novorken's speech will be instantly interpreted and spread across all the communication media, we need to follow up as quickly as possible.

"Darlene and I have worked on various outlines for statements I might make. We definitely have one for this scenario."

The intense atmosphere that had prevailed during Novorken's speech exploded into hilarious laughter. It was a venting built up over three weeks of uncertainty, grief, and pain.

"Let's get this show on the road," Gus Vaughn called out.

Macdonald participated in the revelry and let it run its course. When the jollification subsided, he spoke.

"There were many tedious moments, but President Novorken came through better than I thought he would. Now, I want to hear from you," and he swept his eyes over the room.

"I want to go before the country right away, and yes," he looked at A.J., "I will even take questions. To be really dramatic, A.J., tell TV I want to break into programs using the Emergency Broadcast Alert, *'we interrupt this program'* announcement."

Spontaneous cheering erupted.

"You may also brief the press that we did have envoys, no names, in Moscow last Thursday and that I did have a secret meeting with the Russian President in Reykjavik early this morning, accompanied by the Canadian and British Prime Ministers."

A.J. raced out.

"Madam Secretary," Macdonald said, to SecState Rankin. "Please call Prime Minister McEwen and advise him of my announcement and news conference, and that I plan to say this was a joint effort between us, aided by Prime Minister Howard. I won't be giving details of any of the meetings. Ask if he and I can spend some time tomorrow morning on a joint release on the reparations."

"Yes sir," Rankin replied.

"Please use my private study."

"Thank you, sir," she said, leaving with an aide.

The assembled were slow to pick up on Macdonald's request for comments, a rather daunting task for most.

"Okay, I'm going to step out for a few minutes, I understand the dilemma." He turned to Darlene. "How'd you do it when you wanted a class to participate, professor?"

"Mr. President, I could only flunk them." He laughed. Everyone caught on.

"Okay, I'll be back."

He hustled up the stairs and then he realized he had to use his study, where he had sent the Secretary of State. As he entered, she was about to place a call. "Nadine, sorry, let me move you to the Oval Office. I need to use a special phone that is only in here."

"Certainly, Mr. President."

"Tell Cynthia you're using that office, and tell her I'm in here and don't want to be disturbed." He was trying hard to contain his excitement. "I just . . . thank you."

Secretary Rankin smiled. "Yes sir."

As soon Nadine and her aide had gone, he called Alex.

She answered. "*Mon cher*, I have not left my office, hoping for your call. I have not been near a TV."

"Everything's great. Novorken promised cooperation and delivered the goods in a speech to the world. I'm going on TV within the hour. How soon can you get here?"

"My mind has been with you ever since breakfast. I will now bring my body and join the two," she said, giggling.

He laughed. "I love both of your you's." He was pumped.

"And both of me love you. I will come now and watch you on TV there."

"Yeah, that's probably best, I'll need to focus. Come to my private study. I'll tell Cynthia. I'm heading back down to the Situation Room. I'll see you later."

"It is a wonderful day, *mon cher*," she said softly.

When he arrived in the Situation Room, it was abuzz in several conversations and Darlene and Nancy were busily writing. The room silenced as he entered.

"Don't stop on my account," he said, as he sat next to Darlene. Nancy joined them, and they huddled, sharing ideas from staff that they had collected.

"SecDef Garrett and the generals were curious about Sakhalin Island," Darlene said.

"Novorken will handle our presence, saying he requested assistance there after the refineries were blown up, that he knew we had war-game forces in the area and felt our presence on the island would deter any rogue group from trying to blow it up."

"You two covered a lot of ground in your conversation this morning," Darlene said.

"Yeah, he was a different person. You heard how he handled the refineries. He doesn't want anybody thinking that he was behind the bombing. We're going to get everything we asked of him, probably more."

In the excitement of the moment, he wanted to talk more, but Darlene and Nancy had work to do, readying him for his TV speech.

"Nancy, as soon as Darlene and I leave for the briefing room, call Vice President Dudley. Tell her I'm going on the air and that she and I need some phone time, say a half hour after I've finished. I want us to put out a joint statement about the progress in Detroit."

He was hit with another idea. "Better yet, we'll tell the nation together, tomorrow. I still want to talk to her, though."

"Darlene, inform the Secret Service I'm going to Detroit tomorrow morning. We'll set the time with Bryanna. We'll originate our joint speech from there. Tell her to pick the location."

"Yes sir. Give us fifteen minutes on your speech."

He wandered around in the Situation Room. *This moment is our victory*. He then parked in front of a TV screen watching C-SPAN and the balanced budget debate, or rather, speeches.

Twelve minutes later, Darlene had the cheat sheets ready for his review.

As he took her notes, he said. "I was watching the House floor debate on the Balanced Budget Bill."

"It seems to be going well," Nancy said, "but I'll find our liaison and have him ready to give you a full report."

Darlene pointed to his cheat sheets. "Is everything in order, sir?"

He laughed. He'd barely looked at them. "Yeah, they look great."

She frowned. He laughed some more.

"Okay," he said, holding up the cheat sheets. "I've got people to talk to."

"Go get 'em, Mr. President," Nancy said. "I'll call A.J. and tell him you're on the way."

He gave her a wide grin. "Yeah," He looked at Darlene. "Ready, Chief?"

She nodded. With that, Mike Macdonald and Darlene Sweetwater walked together down the corridor to the press briefing room.